The suppressed memoirs of
Edgar Allan Poe

Black Plume

David Madsen

SIMON AND SCHUSTER

NEW YORK

Designed by Eve Kirch
Manufactured in the United States of America

1   2   3   4   5   6   7   8   9   10

Library of Congress Cataloging in Publication Data

Madsen, David.
Black plume.

1.   Poe, Edgar Allan, 1809–1849, in fiction, drama,
poetry, etc.   I.   Title.
PZ4.M1838Bl   [PS3563.A344]   813'.54   80-13596
ISBN 0-671-25599-1

For Christine and for my parents

Black Plume

October 6, 1852

Mr. George Putnam
155 Broadway
New York

Dear Sir,

Tomorrow marks the third anniversary of the death of my beloved nephew and son-in-law, Edgar Allan Poe. The intervening years have seen no decline in the popularity of my dearest Eddie's writings—writings which his admirers and detractors alike have interpreted as pure fiction—the morbid speculations of his macabre imagination. Until now I'm sure his readers were correct in this collective assumption.

I say "until now," because you hold in your hands Eddie's only work of autobiography. Every word of the shockingly candid manuscript you are about to read is the Lord's truth, as sworn to me by Eddie himself!

As my son-in-law's last publisher you are of course aware that Eddie wrote little that was of interest or merit following the death of my daughter (his wife), Virginia. Indeed, it was the death of the unfortunate child that hastened his insanity and eventual destruction from the ravages of alcohol. In the three unhappy years since Eddie's demise, I have often contemplated presenting you with this manuscript, but the painful nature of many of the revelations contained herein constrained me to keep the knowledge of this final work of Eddie's to myself.

You may well be wondering by what curious circumstances this manuscript fell into my hands, and what now prompts me to submit it to your able perusal.

To the first question, I must respond at length. Edgar Allan

Poe treated me not only as his aunt by blood and mother by marriage, but as his nurse, servant and confidante. While he wrote, his mind was not his own—it resided in whatever fantastic, misty region his imagination carried him. It was therefore I who shopped for him, bought him his clothing, cared for him when he was infirm and saw to it that a fresh cup of coffee lay on his desk every hour. It was I who handled the money matters for which he demonstrated so little aptitude. It was I who delivered completed manuscripts to his publishers, *and* it was I who just as often retrieved them with the accompanying notice of rejection. Virginia was his angel, his life's love and desire, but in the matters of day-to-day survival, I'm afraid the dear girl was as unskilled as Eddie.

The death of my dearest Virginia did not cause him to strike me from the place of honor I had won in his heart—if anything, his gratitude and generosity towards me grew greater, though we were often apart. He seldom wrote to me during the last two and a half years of his life, but his charity and concern for my well-being were still considerable. On one occasion which I immediately recall, Eddie found himself alone in a strange city with no prospects and down to his last two dollars. Rather than squander his remaining funds on drink, he sent a dollar to me.

Yet he returned periodically to our cottage at Fordham, delirious, hungry and pale with grief. It was during these periods of recuperation spent under my roof that Eddie first told me of the lengthy confessional he was writing during his all-too-infrequent periods of sobriety. It was obviously of great importance for him to set down these facts, and I would often look in on him following one of his devastating bouts with his illness, to find he had written until his strength was gone. He would collapse into the tormented delirium that had become for him a hideous substitute for sleep, and upon awakening, continue his narrative. The enclosed manuscript was completed two days before he left my house for the last time—his condition was such that the final sixty pages were written from his dictation in my own hand—his being too weak to grasp a pen. Entrusting the manuscript to my care to do with as I saw fit, he left New York and plunged into the final downward spiral of his life, which ended in a Baltimore hospital less than three years after the death of Virginia.

It was thus that this astounding confessional came into my possession. As to why I am now coming forward with the manuscript, the answer is concise and painful. I have no money. I can no longer be sure of the continued charity of my friends and acquaintances, and whatever arrangements Eddie made with the many small firms who published his work, I have not been privy to them. This manuscript is my only possession of value left unsold.

I know I am no writer, Mr. Putnam, and I find it difficult to convey to you the urgency of my situation and the literary importance of this work. Perhaps it is best that I let Eddie speak for himself by quoting from the foreword he had written.

She is not yet twenty-five today as she is laid to her grave by the soiled, indifferent hands of the cemetery workers. The black, oppressive cloak of Death envelops me again, threatening to forever expunge from my memory the life I passed in the graces of my sweet and delicate wife, Virginia Poe.

I am not destined to produce an heir, but it is not a diagnosis leveled by a medical man which nurtures this hideous conclusion within me. It is an assumption, both logical and charitable, that the world, once burdened by my presence, would not wish to be endowed with a replica. I therefore preclude the possibility of a successor from the meager supply of hopes and aspirations Virginia's death has left me. Thus, the chronicling of our life together is left solely in my trembling, anguished hands.

Fate is an inequitable and ungrateful governor. Were she a fair-minded mistress, she would make happiness the most pervasive and easily obtainable of all human conditions. Yet men murder and are murdered in the name of bliss. I myself have been driven to the threshold of death (and very nearly beyond), so that the happiness and enlightenment I knew with my beloved Virginia might be preserved. And therein lies a tale of fantastic proportion!

In its unflinching examination of the terrors that can possess a human soul and press it to the brink of disaster, this homely narrative I begin today may well prove the equal to any fiction

I have yet penned. But in its portrayal of elegance and serenity, in its careful and truthful homage to the angel that was my Virginia, it should prove a welcome departure from the grotesque and perverse tales for which I am known. Yet more than the tenor of this untold tale distinguishes it from my published work. Every word of it is true!

And now that the awful consumption that plagued my wife during our marriage has seen fit to finally take her from me, I feel the most insistent need to finally make the truth known. May God grant me the strength and sanity to see this tale to its fateful conclusion!

On that mournful note I must close. I pray for your favorable response in this unique matter, and hoping this finds you in good health, I am

Sincerely yours,
Maria Poe Clemm

One

As she steppcd from the hack that September day in 1835, Virginia's cloudy countenance well matched the overcast dreariness of the Baltimore afternoon; had a passerby observed her gloomy demeanor as she entered St. Paul's Episcopal Church in the company of myself and her mother, Maria Poe Clemm, he would scarcely have guessed that this dear girl was to be married within the hour!

Yet neither I, her husband-to-be, nor her doting mother earned the slightest word of reproof from Virginia, for the circumstances of the impending marriage were well known to the three of us. So vehement in his opposition to our nuptials was my cousin Neilson Poe, at that time also a resident of Baltimore, that we were forced to conduct the service in the utmost secrecy. Even the slightest hint of our marriage would bring the angry objections of the Poe clan crashing down upon us. Neilson's objections to the match centered chiefly on Virginia's age, for she was barely thirteen. But what did he know of my passion, my respect, my reverence, my untarnished love for my cousin?

My love for Virginia was not unrequited—indeed her feelings

for me were every bit as strong and true as mine for her. Her mother, Maria, with whom I have enjoyed the most intimate and sharing relationship for years, was equally devoted to the match. It was therefore not the marriage itself, but the regrettable lack of flowers and lace, congratulatory friends and relatives, food and festivities—the delightful trappings of the wedding ceremony for which a young girl's heart yearns—that caused Virginia's happiness to be less than complete as we entered the church, feeling more like co-conspirators in an act of sabotage than a couple about to be joined in matrimony.

The ceremony was brief and simple, but it was a time of extreme nervousness for me, as I half expected my relatives to burst through the church doors and spirit Virginia away. My fears were, of course, groundless; and with Maria Clemm as our only witness, Virginia and I became husband and wife.

We offered our heartfelt thanks to the minister, and, true to our agreement, he promised not to record the nuptials in the parish registry. Our romantic deception thus completed, we three returned through the late-afternoon carriage traffic to our modest, though comfortable, lodgings.

Upon reaching our little house on Amity Street, mother busied herself with the preparation of a marriage dinner; and after I was assured that my new wife was comfortably ensconced in the parlor where she could recover from the rigors of the day, I turned to the important correspondence my precarious financial position necessitated.

An explanation is in order here, for you are undoubtedly wondering what manner of husband it is who devotes his wedding night to letter writing and monetary worries rather than to his wife. The truth of the matter is, Virginia, Mrs. Clemm and I had lived under the same roof before, not as husband, wife and mother-in-law as we now found ourselves, but as nephew, aunt and cousin. This arrangement was sound enough economically, but following the death of my stepfather, John Allan, and the appearance of his will which made no mention of me, we fell into serious straits. It was Mrs. Clemm's firm contention that through the fortuitous combination of her talents as a seamstress, cook and landlady, with mine for literature, we should find it within our means to provide for the three of us. Deathly afraid as I was to ask for Virginia's hand, Mrs. Clemm's suggestion that our happy relationship be cemented with marriage vows came as a welcome and ecstatic surprise.

Mrs. Clemm upheld her end of our economic bargain with efforts which, although admirable, unfortunately met with poor financial success. It therefore fell upon me to garner the lion's share of the income necessary to maintain our small household, a task which demanded my immediate attention following the wedding. Our pitiful savings rendered the usual honeymoon an impossibility, and it was with a heart filled with sympathy for the drabness of dear Virginia's wedding day that I threw myself into the correspondence that lay before me.

I longed to return to Richmond, Virginia, the city of my youth. But I was in the unenviable position of a beggar—though it was not alms I sought, by my reinstatement as an editor of the *Southern Literary Messenger*, a Richmond publication from which I had recently been dismissed—dismissed under a cloud of shame and scandal occasioned by my drinking.

It is my unfortunate plight to be a slave—but not in the sense one usually imagines. I am a slave to a master whose cruelty and capriciousness even the lowliest plantationer could not hope to equal—my master is alcohol, but unlike the slaves of our South, I can never buy my freedom.

My writing was interrupted by a cheerful call from the kitchen that dinner was ready, and I gratefully put aside my work and joined my wife and mother at the table. It was a scene I shall find difficult to forget. Despite our financial difficulties, mother had prepared a dinner worthy of the sumptuous wedding that the need for secrecy had unhappily confined to our imaginations.

Ready to appease our hunger were home-baked bread, sweet potatoes, roast goose festooned with fresh currants, corn, peas and carrots in melted butter and a bottle of wine, which, judging by its rather dusty label, mother had been hoarding for some time. We drank a toast to the success of our married life, and as we ate I considered the two women with whom fortune had blessed me.

In her stark black-and-white apparel, starched collar and white cap, and the almost pious manner in which she clasped her hands during the infrequent moments when they were not busy, mother resembled a devout, yet worldly nun. Her flat, broad smile which seldom displayed teeth conveyed to the observer a sense of unshakability. Her piercing, heavily hooded eyes demanded attentiveness on the part of a listener, yet promised to repay such attentiveness with wisdom. Her strength never wavered—my brother, Henry, had died of consumption under her roof—yet the horror of the disease and its attendant symptoms never caused her to falter in her ministrations.

Virginia was every man's female ideal. Beautiful, yes, but there was a transcendent, unstained quality to her which defied traditional description. She was pure white in complexion; had she been a regular visitor to the salons of wealthy society she would have been the envy of every woman there. Her deep black hair, pulled back from her forehead and gathered in a knot behind her head, gave full rein to her rounded, madonnalike face. So pale and so clear was her visage, that her features—the long, delicately arched eyebrows, the large, hazel eyes semiconcealed by flowery, drooping lashes, her classic, perfectly formed nose, and her demure, yet fleshy mouth—stood out in sharply etched, unforgettable detail. She smiled as often with her eyes as with her mouth, and I hoped that the step she had taken today into adulthood would eventually serve to increase her cheerfulness rather than burden it with uncharacteristic sobriety. I determined that the wedding that lived in her imagination would have a counterpart in reality as soon as finances permitted.

Virginia defined young womanhood in all its languishing, ethereal, wistful unapproachability. I had grown up with her and had watched the years work their magic. Whatever flirtations I had undertaken during my earlier years faded into oblivion whenever I was in her presence. And now I had succeeded in making this woman my wife.

Following the marvelous dinner I have described, mother and I turned our attentions to the prodigious assembly of dishes and pots that awaited scouring, while Virginia went to the parlor and took out one of the many games with which it was her habit to pass the evenings.

Once our business in the kitchen was concluded, mother led me to her bedroom door where our conversation could not be overheard by Virginia.

"Eddie," mother began hesitantly, "she's so very young, such a weak constitution."

It was true. Virginia was frailty personified; she could be taken ill from a breath of cold wind no one but she could sense.

"By law you are man and wife, but I hope that my opinions still carry weight. You and Virginia have the rest of your lives together . . ." The tense uncertainty of the situation prevented her from finishing the sentence. I grew extremely uncomfortable.

"We'll maintain separate rooms—today's marriage shall be in mind only."

"Just for a while, Eddie, to let her grow up."

I kissed her cheek reassuringly, and taking a novel from the bookshelf, she disappeared into her bedchamber.

I joined Virginia in the parlor, pulling up a chair next to the spot on the floor where she played. Involved in her game as she was, she seemed peaceful enough, but when she looked up at me her face appeared blemished by restlessness and fear.

"Would you like a friend over or someone?" I asked, attempting to alleviate the confusion and pain I sensed she was feeling.

She shook her head.

"No, Buddie, I'm afraid I shouldn't be able to keep our secret. I'm dying to tell the world as it is."

"It's only for a little longer. Once my business affairs are settled, everyone shall know. But in the meantime . . ."

"Oh . . . in the meantime, I'm sworn to silence. I'm not going to let you down."

I drew my darling to her feet and she pressed against me, dissolving into my arms. I could feel her trembling with indecision:

whether to retreat back into childhood, or advance headlong into womanhood.

She stiffened suddenly, and drew away.

"I'm exhausted," she declared. "I'm going to bed." She threw the game pieces onto the floor with surprising contempt. "This is a ridiculous game. It's merely for children."

She paused. Her fear had vanished and was replaced by sincerity.

"I love you, Buddie. I'm suddenly so awfully important."

She kissed me with a curious mixture of passion and adoration (how strange to feel physical passion emanating from someone you have long considered a disembodied dream), and she strutted off to her bedroom with an uncharacteristic haughtiness which I knew she had affected to mask her childlike fragility.

Torn with emotion, I entered my darkened study and collapsed into my habitual late-night chair.

Outside, the street lanterns dimly illuminated the labyrinth of narrow alleys and thoroughfares which formed a confluence near our home. The solitary intoxicants who weaved and wobbled past my window at that hour were a pitiful but familiar sight. Baltimore was a thriving commercial and port city, and the poverty which we shared had necessitated our living not far removed from the docks. Thus, within easy walking distance of our cottage could be found several of the vilest and most dangerous public houses imaginable. The clientele such caverns attracted were scrupulously avoided by mother and Virginia, and it was a rare night that found them on the streets after dark.

Would that the same could be said for me!

I had been tempted by and had penetrated that sordid underworld as a young man, and it was to be my continued involvement in that odious milieu that unleashed the deadly series of events that overtook me soon after our marriage.

Rather than burn a light, I preferred to drift there in the undemanding darkness, free from the intrusions of illumination.

But where I drifted, let no man follow!

David Madsen   *18*

The kingdom of nightmares, the realm of fear and obsession, the scarred and ashen landscapes barren of human feeling and forgiveness opened their pallid gates and welcomed me.

If I were to faithfully fulfill my duties as a husband, what chance did Virginia's youth and innocence stand against the nameless, unspeakable presence that lived within me? How I feared the consummation of our union, how I railed against the passion my beautiful wife caused to soar in my heart! There was no choice but to forever hold at bay the voracious evil which I knew in these dark moments of revelation that I personified, and which I knew would destroy my sweet wife were it ever released. But how to keep it from rearing its hideous head, how to keep it caged, tied, pinned down? To this end I knew my thoughts must be directed.

Perhaps a sip from the bottle which, despite the darkness, I knew lay just to my right. Not a full measure of the stuff, God, no! But a sip. The tumbler rested barely two inches from the bottle. What an insignificant series of moves it would require to pour myself a sip. Just one sip . . . one sip . . . or two.

Two

Alcohol was maid- and manservant to me throughout those first nights of our marriage.

Alcohol had seen me fired, but curiously enough it proved to be the agent which lobbied most vigorously for my reinstatement. Following an admittedly intoxicated round-table discussion with his colleagues in journalism, T.W. White had decided to offer me my old position (with the *Literary Messenger*), under the condition that my personal habits should not interfere with my work. Accordingly, in the winter of 1836, leaving instructions with mother and my bride of four months to close our house on Amity Street and follow me as soon as possible, I boarded the steam packet for Richmond.

Baltimore's Chesapeake Bay was as congested a commercial thoroughfare as there was to be found in the United States—surely the naval equivalent of the hectic boulevard traffic of Paris which French visitors to our shore seemed to delight in maligning. Packets, dories, barges, schooners, skiffs and ships of every description jostled and jousted with one another as they competed for the insufficient berth space provided by the city. Fortunately, the coastal steamer was a regularly scheduled run, and I was spared the lengthy and often unpredictable wait that passengers bound for more distant destinations often endured.

Mother and Virginia bore the strains of our dockside farewell stoically. Intimate conversation was difficult, shoved about as we were by sailors and passengers alike, including two particularly rude, veiled Gypsy women who attempted to embroil us in an argument they were having with a ship's officer concerning seating arrangements.

I nevertheless managed to clasp Virginia to my breast and breathe to her a few words of encouragement: "I'll write as though possessed. I'll have an encyclopaedia awaiting publication by the time you arrive. And see to it that that efficient mother of yours hurries along."

"But, Buddie, why can't you wait for us to go with you? It's not too late. You can sell your ticket," protested Virginia while mother watched our scene with concerned amusement.

"It must be now—Mr. White's an impatient sort. Besides, with my connections in Richmond—I'll have a life ready for you to step into when you arrive."

She accepted my logic reluctantly and, dejectedly proffering me a kiss, withdrew to allow her mother to embrace me. I took from her my two bags and, waving continuously, made my way onto the teeming deck of the packet. Evidently our good-byes had lasted longer than I had imagined, for I was scarcely aboard before there came a hellish blast from the vessel's horn, and dock personnel rushed to release the ship from her moorings.

With a sickly shudder, like that of an expiring consumptive, the sea-weary vessel lumbered from the docks and into the crowded channel.

I waved to my loved ones, until I could no longer distinguish them from the mass of well-wishers gathered on the docks. Then, grasping my two valises, I made my way into the ship's lobby as the sun, blood red and smoke-filled from bayside industry, sank into the horizon.

My stateroom was functional and cramped, and once I had un-packed my nightshirt and razor, I grasped the smaller of my bags and gratefully evacuated the confining chamber for the compara-tive freedom on deck.

The receding lights of Baltimore had assumed an eerie and unearthly cast as the thick Atlantic fog swept in and settled on the bay. Soon, the city vanished entirely from view, and we were surrounded by a muffled darkness which accentuated the creaks and groans the aging vessel periodically emitted.

Lost as I was in my anxious thoughts concerning my future and that of my family, I had scarcely noticed the rapid chilling of the air, and I soon found myself alone on deck. The gloomy expanse of the ship swayed around me, broken only by the dull glow from lights in the dining room, where people moved, drank, laughed and ate, now mere phantoms obscured by mist and the window's translucence.

Separated from my dear Virginia, I once again fell prey to the incorporeal sense of dread that I knew marked me. I would never share those diners' gaiety, never revel in the frivolous activities which in their eyes comprised life. I opened the leather valise which lay between my feet and extracted one of the ten bottles of bourbon I had purchased to soothe the weariness of the voyage and my solitary life in Richmond.

I raised the bottle to my lips, yet suddenly found I could not bring myself to drink from it. It symbolized all too clearly that torturous existence I had sworn was behind me! Twenty-four ounces of depravity, corruption, *faiblesse* of the spirit and the soul. And as I peered into the valise, I saw twenty-four ounces more, twenty-four ounces after that and still twenty-four ounces! I was seized by a fit of fury and shame, and in one glorious, brutal motion, I picked up the valise, swung it over my head in a gentle arc, and shook its ghastly contents into the dark waters of Chesa-peake Bay. In the silent, fog-enshrouded gloom, I heard ten crisp and distinct splashes as my tormentors went to their appropriately watery graves. Drained of emotion, I felt also somewhat purged of my sins—as though I had disposed of the last of the world's whis-key, the last of the world's temptation.

"Now, shall you instruct the bar to ignore your requests for a drink as well?"

An accented female voice interrupted my musings, and I turned, half in shock and half in indignation at having so personal a moment observed, to face the two spectral Gypsy women who had accosted me on the docks.

"Mother," said the second, her voice more attuned to American intonation, "perhaps we are intruding on the gentleman's privacy."

"Nonsense, men in such straits are always in need of female companionship," replied the mother.

Whence had these two figures come? Veiled as they were, and clothed in dark, muted fabrics, they seemed harbingers of intrigue, perhaps danger. I had heard no door open, no resultant increase in the volume of the merrymakers indoors. Were they dropped from the heavens or had they materialized from the now-impenetrable fog?

"You must excuse my appearance. I didn't hear you approach," I sputtered, straightening my hair and clothes.

"It is we who must beg forgiveness for startling you. We came up the stepladder, from the hold—there."

The older woman pointed down the length of the misty deck, but the passageway she indicated was, of course, invisible to us.

"At least you are of this earth." I laughed.

"Of this earth, yes, though not of this country. I am Alix L'Espanaye and this is my daughter Camille. From Corsica."

"Edgar Poe. Of Baltimore. Soon to be of Richmond. It is a pleasure."

As soon as the formal introductions were completed, both women simultaneously dropped their veils, and I was astounded and delighted to observe that they were both exceedingly beautiful. Indeed, such was their commonality of visage that the mother was at first indistinguishable from her daughter.

But as we talked, and I availed myself of the opportunity to examine their faces more closely, I saw they were each possessed of strongly distinct features. Camille, the daughter, was, as befits a young woman, more prone to smiles and laughter, and her mouth bore the permanent traces of merriment; the mother's laugh lines were there, though dormant—it had evidently been years since they had seen much use. Camille's lips were full and petulant, forever parted, her mother's subdued, more classically feminine. Camille's face was rosy, rounder, insistent and impatient; her mother's pale, withdrawn, arched and aristocratic, full of knowledge that promised both pleasure and pain.

Taken together, they represented a beauty to which I was unaccustomed. It was dark, velvetine and tempestuous. Their hazel eyes, their coal black hair, their nearly contemptuous features spoke of a life lived to excess, of passions sought after, experienced, then discarded in favor of new ones. They were not genteel, refined or ladylike. They would be ill at ease in society's ballrooms and parlors. They were not faithful, helpless or graceful faces. They represented everything Virginia was not, yet they were undeniably feminine!

I posed them a question the dictates of polite conversation demanded, but whose answer I already knew: "Would you care to join me inside?"

"Oh, no," responded Madame L'Espanaye. "What have we in common with such dignified drinkers? The company of a man who drowns his sorrows physically is infinitely preferable to that of those who do so figuratively." She smiled and indicated the now-empty valise which lay on the deck at my feet.

"Madame, you have merely witnessed a moment of psychic housecleaning. The habit has long been extinct, I assure you."

"No matter," laughed her daughter. "Mother feels a man's vices are directly proportionate to his talents. I must say, I quite agree with her."

Following this statement, Camille subjected me to a positively indecent perusal, more in the manner of a buyer examining a horse than a young woman making the acquaintance of a gentleman. Her forwardness did not go unnoticed by her mother, who punished her with a murderous glance before taking my arm and leading me in a leisurely stroll along the deserted deck. Camille, her advances momentarily frustrated, was forced to hurry after us, thrusting herself into our conversation whenever possible.

They seemed anxious to talk, and as the prospect of a lonely overnight voyage was exceedingly depressing, I was glad of the company. In speech that demonstrated the painstaking care that she had taken in learning to express herself in English far better than most Americans, Madame L'Espanaye described in vivid detail their traumatic arrival in the United States—her struggle to adapt to a foreign culture; Camille's rebelliousness at her mother's reluctance to part with certain French customs; and their nomadic, penny-pinching way of life which had taken them to the seamier quarters of a dozen great American cities.

A wife at sixteen, a mother at eighteen and a widow at twenty-one, Madame L'Espanaye had emigrated to America with her eleven-year-old daughter in 1830, eight years after the death of her husband. I longed to know more about this enigmatic pair, but I sensed a deep reluctance, bordering on fear, to further discuss the circumstances of their departure from France, and I therefore turned the conversation to lighter matters.

So involved did I become in comparing our tastes in music, art, literature, food and the like, I paid but little attention to the fact that we had forsaken the chilling mist outdoors for the comforting warmth of the ship's empty dining room. In this pleasant conversational manner the night passed quickly as we fortified ourselves with coffee and mineral water. My fear of being confined to my packing crate of a stateroom was wholly unwarranted.

Towards dawn, as the waiters who had abandoned us at midnight returned groggy and exhausted to their breakfast stations, we were still talking.

My initial impressions of the two women had not changed. I was fascinated by Madame L'Espanaye's worldly assertiveness (even drawn to it), and Camille's loving, calculated rebelliousness. These two women without men, thriving in a foreign, hostile society, their faces full of seductive promises and limitless experience, were endlessly intriguing.

Though our conversation was innocent, the feelings that stirred within me were not. A gratuitous combination of schoolboy awe and lust sharpened the most routine of comments into double-edged flirtatiousness. As an antidote I attempted to fix the beautiful face of Virginia in my mind, but failed.

"But on one point I am unclear," I interjected at last. "How, amid such adversity, thwarted by language barriers and so on, were you able to support yourselves?"

"Mother is very gifted," responded Camille enigmatically. Then she smiled conspiratorially, her face a halo of suggestive warmth. "And I am learning to acquire those gifts."

"In what way gifted?"

"Oh, in her ability to see where others are usually blind."

I was still mystified.

Madame laughed at my bewilderment, and brazenly leaned forward, resuming control of the conversation.

"We are not used to receptive audiences. That is why Camille is being deliberately vague. Back in Corsica I enjoy a reputation as a prophet—a seer as you may call it. Here in your country, such employment is scarce, because American credulity is equally scarce. But, nevertheless, there are those who are willing to pay to learn their future."

"You are a fortune-teller, then?"

She nodded her assent.

I leaned back in my chair, assessing this curious bit of information.

"Fortune-telling is not a common calling here in America," I said. "I don't believe it is taught in the universities. May I assume this is a hereditary talent?"

Camille and her mother exchanged secretive, significant looks.

"In the mountains of Corsica live people who have carefully avoided the modern world. There, such arts flourish, and are accorded a respect not found elsewhere. I spent a good deal of time among these people—when I was younger."

"And do you see anything noteworthy in my future?"

Madame L'Espanaye paused, countering my flippancy with a suddenly serious expression. She grasped my hand firmly, and ran hers over the back of it, touching only the upended hairs. She then smiled slyly at her daughter who had lapsed discontentedly into a pout.

"Of course, a ship's dining room is hardly suitable for a full, effective reading. . . ."

"Of course."

Madame L'Espanaye continued her wordless massage of my hand. Though I was surprised and not a little disappointed that she did not close her eyes or lapse into a trance, her concentration did seem considerable. Camille gazed at me as though gauging my responsiveness, then at her mother whose face was expressionless.

"Though specifics are unfortunately beyond us for the moment, I do detect an enormous sympathy passing from your hand into mine. Were we not mere shipboard acquaintances, whose lives are destined to follow divergent paths, I would be tempted to characterize our meeting here tonight as highly significant."

She shook her head as though to clear her thoughts, and released my hand.

"But surely you cannot expect an educated man such as myself to treat this soothsaying of yours with anything more than amused skepticism? It is merely an entertainment devised to render an otherwise tedious voyage more enjoyable."

Madame's eyes pierced mine with a sudden, galvanic intensity.

"We shall see, Monsieur Poe. We shall see. Times and circumstances change, do they not? And with them, opinions. Perhaps even *your* opinions!"

Three

Following our disembarkation at Richmond, and the jovial farewells customary among fellow travelers, I plunged headlong into life and work in the city of my boyhood, giving only occasional thought to the two curious L'Espanaye women.

I took up modest lodgings at Mrs. James Yarrington's boarding-house, a comfortable and hospitable building, conveniently situated across the green from Capitol Square, at the corner of Twelfth and Bank Streets. Mrs. Yarrington's table was bounteous, her rooms warm and secure, the rent of nine dollars per week reasonable and her guests quiet, if uninteresting. My domestic life thus satisfactorily arranged, I turned my complete attention to the *Messenger*, so that I should quickly be able to send for Virginia and mother. With the five-hundred-dollar annual salary I was to receive from my employer, Mr. White, and additional money I expected from contributions to other publications, I anticipated for my little clan a life by no means luxurious, but at least free from the insistent threat of poverty and hunger.

The offices of the *Southern Literary Messenger* were at the corner of Fifteenth and Main, in the heart of Richmond's commercial district. The neighboring businesses were of little interest—save one: My stepfather's trade store, Ellis and Allan, where I had labored as a boy under John Allan's harsh guardianship, was immediately next door. Three times a day I was forced to pass by this bitter reminder of the discord that existed between my guardian and myself until the day of his death.

In the sparse, dusty offices of the *Messenger*'s three-story brick building, on the second floor above the throaty, coughing rumble of the printing presses, I carried out my duties as assistant editor, correspondent, literary critic and contributor, under the conservative guidance of my employer, Thomas Wylkes White.

White was a stocky, priggish, whiskered gentleman whose careful and unadventurous editorial work had won him a firm and not altogether unjustified reputation in southern literary circles. As the days unfolded, and we settled into our familiar routine, our relationship continued to be one of quiet, mutual respect, but we seldom assumed a first-name standing. It was forever apparent that the *Messenger* was Mr. White's publication, and although my opinions were not without a certain weight, they would always have to bow to his should a disagreement arise.

My creative powers unfortunately dozed, awakened only when one of my condemnations of America's literary anemia necessitated the use of a particularly scathing metaphor or allusion. For several weeks I was thus occupied; loneliness kept at bay by hard work and long hours.

For the first time in many years I was regularly salaried, fed, clothed and housed, and since my arrival in Richmond, I had not given in to the temptations of drink. As my criticism gained acceptance, and my literary reputation grew correspondingly, the friends and acquaintances of my youth who had spurned me following the break with my stepfather welcomed me back into their parlors and dining rooms. Not a day passed when I was not accosted on the street with the offer to take a julep, a coffee or a meal. Following a salary increase from Mr. White and the satisfactory conclusion of talks with Mrs. Yarrington, I sent to Baltimore for mother and my secret wife, anticipating their arrival within the month. In short, my life had taken a long-overdue turn for the better, in which no personal obstacle seemed insurmountable.

But then, slowly, ineffably, a state of mind and soul began to steal over me which I can only term *perverseness:* an unholy alliance of depression, desire, restlessness and the irresistible urge to do precisely that which will cause the most harm and unleash within one the deepest unhappiness.

This condition is not discussed in classrooms or even taverns, is not discoursed upon in textbooks or novels . . . yet as a governor of human action it has no equal. What man has not stood at the brink of a precipice and, because his reason so violently deterred him from jumping, all the more seriously entertained the notion?

It was thus, that on a certain evening after work, I made my way from the offices of the *Messenger* into the few densely populated blocks that crowd the shore of the James River. Darkened by day from the odoriferous belchings of coal and tobacco factories, this fearful quarter grows still darker after nightfall, when its troubled, drunken denizens hold court. In the dockside slums and taverns, nothing is expected of one; indeed, the *politesse* and self-control demanded on the "outside" are here considered encumbrances.

I knew that by stepping into this sordid, twilit world, I was gambling with the happiness and future of both myself and my little family—yet, precisely because I knew it to be wrong, I plunged onwards *and* downwards.

Among the literary and merchant classes of Richmond, life proceeds at an unhurried and dignified pace. But here, amid hawkers, vendors, sailors and beggars, the pulse of life is accelerated, as though everyone is hounded and pursued. In this quarter of narrow, cobblestoned alleys, crowded open markets, cheap and rambunctious public houses, people are forced into a life of frenzied suspicion. Not a single piece of business is transacted without a sharp, worried look over the shoulder, a door is never closed without a sidelong glance to make sure one is not being followed. The public pie is so small and shrinks so quickly that everyone knows he must hurry if he is to get a piece of it. And once he has it, he must guard it with his life, lest it be stolen from him uneaten.

I was not, however, the sole representative of Richmond's healthier classes who, for one reason or another, felt compelled to dabble in dissipation. As I stepped into a smoky tavern whose corners undoubtedly masked countless varieties of licentious behavior, I spotted John Fergusson, a large, ruddy-complected printer for the *Messenger* who fancied himself a poet; Barrow Reece, a likeable, arrogant, nervous, narrow reed of a man with an even narrower intellect who was a newspaper reporter for the *Virginia Argus;* and Rob Stanard, a rational, reasonably successful businessman and boyhood friend who had somehow become a steady member of Fergusson's drinking clan.

"So, Edgar," shouted the boisterous Fergusson above the bar's clamor, "join us for a drink, damn you!"

"No, John. You know what the stuff does to me."

"Well, what do you want down here then, Edgar?" retorted Reece. He motioned expansively around the tavern. "Don't tell us you like the society."

"If I know Edgar, that's precisely why he is here," laughed Rob, and I joined them, relying on Rob's natural tact to prevent the conversation from taking any unpleasant turns.

"I'll sit down, but I shan't drink," I finally replied.

"So, what's this I hear about your sudden fit of intemperance?" laughed Fergusson.

"You should try it yourself, John. It might make our magazine legible for a change."

"I start making it legible when they start accepting the poems I give them."

This good-natured badinage continued at an unhurried pace without touching on anything of real interest or import. As the hours passed, my three companions grew intoxicated, while I became restless and anxious. I grew dizzy, watching the drams of brandy pass from hand to hand, the throats tipped back in unison as toast after toast was drunk to the health of various colorful and cooperative women the three purported to have known.

My vertigo and thickness of head became steadily worse. Time after time I was offered a drink and time after time I refused, until at last, a strong draft seemed the only thing likely to restore my balance and composure.

And so I drank. Just a drop, to sober up.

I felt no immediate ill effects, and so I dove into the evening's main attraction with fervor. I am not by nature a social drinker or even a willing participant in society—but to an observer, such as myself, who likes to mix dreams with the day-to-day, a head full of brandy can be a powerful inducement to reverie.

Though surrounded by friends and acquaintances, I passed the better part of the evening alone, lost in my own alcohol-tinged fantasies.

Sometime during the dirgelike passage of the hours between midnight and dawn, Barrow prevailed on us to accompany him to a certain house in the area, where he promised "diversion of an intriguing nature" was to be had.

"This is a ridiculous hour to run about calling on people," I objected, not willing to disturb my current melancholy.

"As a matter of fact, Edgar, they should just be opening for business about now," answered Barrow, examining his pocket watch.

"What sort of business is it, Barrow? I'm a married man, even down here," said Rob.

"Nothing adulterous in it at all, my dear fellow. But let's be off. I've taken the liberty of making appointments for the four of us."

Barrow would say no more, despite insistent questioning from the three of us. He smiled mischievously and paid his bill, exiting nonchalantly as though it were of no interest to him whether we accompanied him or not. I knew that quite the opposite was true; Barrow was a man who was never fully alive unless he was imparting some piece of tantalizing gossip or information to an eager audience. I also knew that three more curious men than Rob, Fergusson or myself were not to be found in Richmond; so in a flurry of flustered activity, we settled our accounts and, grabbing our coats and hats, rushed out into the now-deserted streets after

Barrow, whose wiry, wraithlike form was just disappearing around the corner.

Until that evening I thought I had penetrated to the heart of Richmond's underworld. But the squalid, festering, cheerless streets through which we now followed Barrow were sufficient to sober even the most worldly among us. The houses barely qualified as such, stacked upon each other like so many packing cases. The streets flowed with refuse and sewage—this fetid river often serving as a pillow for the drunk and homeless who made the streets their abode.

The alleys and byways were empty, but each of us had the distinct feeling that a thousand suspicious faces examined us from the dubious security of tenements and shacks. Every few minutes, the sepulchral silence of the neighborhood was pierced by a disembodied scream of terror, or a groan of pain, both of which seemed to be generated by the air itself. We three looked at each other uneasily, then, drawing our collars up against the dampness, hurried after our guide.

We caught up with Barrow as he was knocking at the door of a nondescript wooden house squeezed in between two equally unremarkable dwellings at the end of a cul-de-sac. There was a long pause while we waited for a response, and Barrow quelled our attempts to question him with an impatient wave of his hand.

The dread that had until now gnawed at the three of us gave way abruptly to amused surprise, when the door of this wretched and undoubtedly cramped home was opened by an elderly, reasonably well attired manservant, who bowed respectfully if somewhat drunkenly.

"Ah, Mr. Reece. Won't you and your guests please come in?"

"Thank you, Jarvis—These are my friends, Mr. Poe, Mr. Fergusson and Mr. Stanard."

The servant bowed again and disappeared into a closet with our coats, reemerging with a burning taper which gave us the first glimpse of our surroundings. We were standing in a narrow anteroom which was barely large enough to accommodate the five of us. Had a hat rack been added to the furnishings, one of us would have been obliged to wait outside. The room was decorated with trappings of foreign origin—dark tapestries, armorial trophies and unidentifiable stringed instruments. There was an inescapable dreariness to the place, which even the poorest of Americans generally go to some lengths to dispel. But not so the mysterious inhabitants of this house—it was almost as if they had gone out of their way to infuse their waiting guests with a sense of gloom and foreboding.

"Now, my dear Barrow, we've been kept in the dark long enough. What in God's name is this all about?" I asked, and my comrades heartily joined me in my supplication.

"Gentlemen, please. The experience will be all the more rewarding if you allow it to unfold in an unpremeditated manner. Trust me!"

Our further entreaties fell on deaf ears, and we reluctantly gave ourselves over to Barrow's care once more.

"Thank you, Jarvis. We'll go in now."

The servant opened an adjoining door to us, then withdrew into the shadows. We followed Barrow into a room furnished in a nearly medieval opulence. Under the glare of daylight it might have taken on a tawdry appearance. But in the phantasmagoric flicker of ten or fifteen wall candles, the rich damask wall hangings, gilded portraits of deceased poets and the arabesque shapes of furniture seemingly chosen for uneasiness rather than comfort, it spoke of wealth accumulated in exotic and mysterious ways.

Following Barrow's lead, we each stretched ourselves out on one of the long, plush couches which were scattered about the room at some distance from one another, as though to discourage talk. At the head of each couch was a carved end table upon which rested a candle and a glass containing a half inch of what appeared to be a particularly dark Madeira wine.

"Gentlemen: to a pleasurable and informative evening."

Rob, Fergusson and I looked over from our couches to see Barrow tentatively sip from his glass. He coughed once, and blinked rapidly, then as though all life had passed from his body, his head fell heavily back on the couch.

A broad and nearly incorporeal smile crossed his face and he turned his head towards us.

"Come on, you three, drink up. They're coming!"

Who "they" referred to, none of us knew. But we were too curious and, indeed, almost too tired to question our guide further, so with mutual shrugs, we drank hesitantly from our glasses.

The brown liquid which then passed my lips was certainly not wine. By its bitter, medicinal taste I could form an educated guess as to what I had just drunk. A look at my two fellow novitiates, who had proved somewhat more zealous than I in their first sips, confirmed my suspicions. They lay back on their couches, nearly motionless. Further contemplation of their condition was made impossible as I too fell back into a position of almost indescribable comfort. Whatever agitation or uneasiness the evening's events had stirred up in me seemed suddenly calmed. I felt as though an irritating and long-lasting internal pain had at last been healed.

Then I heard the footsteps.

Through a curtain two figures emerged—but they seemed to approach us from a great distance. Across a yawning abyss trudged the two forms—obscured by clouds and darkness. I could see them moving, yet they seemed to make no progress. What sort of people were these who walked but did not move forward?

I shut my eyes, as though mentally to shrink the gap between us, but to no avail. My eyes were now wide open and the two forms, moving with balletlike precision, continued their inexorable crawl towards me.

Then, in a second, they were directly before me, staring down at me with the detached curiosity of surgeons.

"There's nothing like tincture of opium to free the mind of unwelcome earthly associations, eh, Monsieur Poe? You are now ready for your first clear, untarnished glimpse into the future."

In an instant, my senses penetrated the dark mist that seemed to pervade the room, and I discerned the faces of Madame and Camille L'Espanaye!

four

I cannot say that I was surprised to again encounter the fortune-teller and her daughter under such unusual circumstances. Indeed, I should have been surprised to have met them in the light of day, on a street, in a restaurant or shop, anywhere where more prosaic reunions usually occur. But given my drugged condition and my almost preternatural surroundings, their presence seemed more than appropriate.

"It is a pleasure to see you again," I murmured, halfheartedly attempting to rise and offer my hand. "It is quite a coincidence that Barrow brought me, of all people, to your door."

"Relax, Monsieur Poe. Lie back down," replied madame as Camille busied herself collecting the glasses from which we had drunk the laudanum. "You should know by now that we never deal in coincidences."

"You appear to have had little trouble finding work in Richmond," I observed. "I'm quite curious about your little business here—"

"We can easily talk later," interrupted madame. "But for now, just put your mind and body at ease and turn yourselves over to our care."

"Yes, Edgar, for God's sake. I'm touched that you appear to know each other, but let them get on with it," interjected Barrow. The opium seemed to have had less of an effect on him than on Rob and Fergusson, who lay dazed and motionless on their respective couches.

"Camille, give Mr. Reece a sip or two more to quiet his impatience!" ordered madame.

Camille left the room briefly, returning with a teaspoon of laudanum, which Barrow downed with quiet satisfaction.

"As you seem to be the only disruptive influence here, Monsieur Reece, we'll start with you," declared madame.

"That's fine with me," muttered Barrow.

As Madame L'Espanaye drew up a chair next to Barrow's couch, Camille went from taper to taper, quietly extinguishing them until the only light in the room came from a single candle which burned next to madame. From our darkened corners, the rest of us watched the mysterious activity which began in the dim cone of light that illuminated the fortune-teller and her client.

She took Barrow's hand and ran her fingers gently over it.

"You haven't been writing," she scolded. "Why is that?"

"Hate the job. I've told you," answered Barrow.

She then passed her hand over his forehead, but it was a touch more business-like than sensual. I recalled the manner in which she had touched my hand the night of our shipboard encounter. Was she deriving information from the mere touch of his skin? Perhaps there was a firm foundation behind her methods.

"But you won't quit. You think about it constantly, but you are afraid to give notice."

"Why?"

"You know why."

"No, I don't."

Her hand traveled from his forehead down underneath his chin, where it began an exploratory massage.

"Don't look at me, Monsieur Reece. Look at nothing. Listen to nothing."

There was a lengthy pause during which Barrow seemed lost in thought.

"My uncle was influential in my obtaining the position. I'm afraid to lose face with him."

"Liar!" shouted madame. Her hand, as though disgusted by the feel of his skin, which was now sweaty and agitated, dropped back in her lap.

"These sessions are useless, unless you reply truthfully."

"It is the truth!" protested Barrow. "My uncle is an important citizen. His anger is something to be avoided!"

"You despise your uncle, Mr. Reece! He is of no consequence to you, therefore his anger is meaningless. Do you think I can't feel that?"

Barrow was slowly losing his composure; he began to bite his lip as Madame L'Espanaye took both of his hands in hers and rubbed them vigorously, her eyes shut as though sight would rend her insensitive.

"Shall I tell you why you are frightened of quitting?" she asked, the level of her voice rising.

Reece seemed suddenly stoic and exhausted. He shook his head. "No! There is no need to bring it out. Not in front of everyone. I know why."

Madame snapped her fingers and Camille appeared from the shadows with a wet towel; she placed it carefully on Reece's forehead, which had grown red and feverish.

"These damned sessions . . ." Reece stuttered. He attempted to articulate an additional epithet, but failed and appeared to fall asleep.

"I'm sorry, Monsieur Reece. This is no carnival act here, as you well know. It is often a matter of chance whether the product of our time together is prophecy or revelation."

Madame L'Espanaye turned towards me and smiled.

"As you can see, Monsieur Poe, he was not prepared to take me into his confidence, thereby making any serious prediction impossible. It is regrettable that your first experience with us was so painful for your friend."

"He's not quite a friend," I replied. "More of an irritant. But tell me, what did you find out?"

"Simply that Monsieur Reece's lack of confidence in his writing ability is not unjustified. I judge that much of what he contributes to his paper is unoriginal—stolen from another writer. He is hesitant to leave a job he considers unfinished."

"A plagiarist!" I exclaimed. My respect for Barrow as a man of letters, never very high, plummeted as I considered the miserable quality of the writing the poor sod had chosen to plagiarize. "Your methods astonish me! No tea leaves, no crystal ball!" I observed.

As a man of reason, I could not help seeking a rational explanation for their powers, but as a man of imagination I found myself praying there was none.

Camille floated ghostlike over me and cautioned me to silence, addressing me for the first time.

"Mother has asked me to tell you that, by your questions, you become agitated and thus defeat the purpose of the laudanum. Try to relax and give free rein to your senses."

After these few words of advice, Camille withdrew to join her mother who was now talking to Rob and subjecting his face and hands to her unique ethereal scrutiny. By now, concentration such as I had brought to bear on the conversation between Madame L'Espanaye and Barrow had become impossible and I gave myself over to the telescopic effect the tincture of opium was having on my mind and my senses.

My mental state had by now reached a plateau of sorts. The environment was still subject to distortions which rendered it borderless and infinite; but these distortions had become so pervasive and commonplace that I now considered them normal. Indeed, it became impossible to imagine the world otherwise.

When I suddenly felt the warm touch of a hand on each cheek —one the mother's, one the daughter's—long-submerged feelings of sensuality began to prick at the usually dull and ignored regions of my body!

Madame and Camille L'Espanaye had turned their prognostic attentions completely towards me. They appeared as though viewed through the wrong end of a telescope, and their voices seemed not to issue from their mouths but from the bottom of a deep well.

"Monsieur Poe, I hope this will not prove confusing to you, but Camille will be assisting me—I am passing my prophetic skills on to my daughter. From certain of my more interesting subjects, she can gain more experience than with dozens of less—promising—cases."

I didn't reply.

I couldn't reply. My lips were sealed, as though cauterized by the intense heat generated by the two exploring feminine hands.

"You begin to sense, Camille," instructed madame, "the variations in temperature that occur on his face?"

"Yes, Mother, it *is* hotter here"—I felt her hand on my forehead —"and much cooler down here." She descended to my chin.

Stroke for stroke, caress for caress, the hand of the daughter matched that of the mother, until I, too, began to sense the hot and cold spots on my face—minute, scarcely noticeable variations that I never imagined existed.

"You see, Monsieur Poe," explained Madame L'Espanaye, as the gentle investigation of my face continued, "we practice a certain form of . . . I don't know the word in English . . . *phrénologie.* As you may know, the *phrénologiste* believes that the formation of one's skull is indicative of that person's unique mental faculties— well, so it is with a person's hands and face. The hot and cold spots of these most expressive parts of the human body correspond directly to certain aspects of the individual's character. By combining a little *logique* (for example, the fact that Monsieur Reece's calluses are diminishing tells me he has not been grasping his pen in his usual overly intense manner) with questions that cause these spots to change temperature, it is often possible to deduce what a person is thinking or if he is telling the truth. The laudanum, in addition to freeing the subject's thoughts, heats the face slightly, making our task somewhat easier.

"The rest is primarily the power of suggestion," continued madame. "If one knows the subject's thoughts, which at this point are primarily of the future, then one can with a fair degree of certainty predict what that person will do. It is the unforeseen acts of God that prevent my predictions from being completely accurate."

During this explanation, the women's hands never ceased their exploration of my face, often with the fingertips, then again with the palm, occasionally descending as far as my neck.

But now, their hands seemed to leave a trail of heat behind them —if there were cold spots still to be found on my face I was no longer aware of them. I felt pleasantly feverish, almost delirious. My face and hands were the objects of their attention, but it was my entire body that responded to their caresses. These were certainly not the same businesslike touches they had employed on my three companions!

"Now then, Monsieur Poe, you are employed with the *Literary Messenger*," began madame.

"Yes . . . yes, that's marvelous. How have you deduced that?"

"Oh, we subscribe to a number of periodicals. Your name is on the title page, I believe." Mother and daughter laughed quietly at their little joke, then continued their telepathic interrogation.

"And you are happy in your work?" was the next question.

"Yes, as a matter of fact, things are going quite smoothly for me now," I replied.

Madame pressed my wrist lightly, where both she and I detected a slight, nervous flutter.

"Monsieur Poe, you are not being quite frank with us."

"Oh, I suppose not. My editorial freedom is not as great as I had hoped for. White is a stuffed shirt."

Both the hand of Madame L'Espanaye and that of Camille delicately traced the outline of my mouth. Never had I experienced such inflammatory caresses, never had the mere touch of a beautiful woman, indeed, two beautiful women, kindled the restlessness of Eros into actual flames. Their sensual ministrations brought the laudanum in my head to the boiling point!

Madame L'Espanaye moved her hand across my face again, but with seemingly greater concentration. She returned to certain spots several times, undoubtedly making her curious temperature comparisons.

"Monsieur Poe, a career shake-up is imminent," she declared suddenly. "A move, perhaps."

"Impossible," I muttered. "I've been at the job only two months."

"Monsieur Poe. There is so much tension on your face, such inconsistencies. This question is at the center of your feelings. Camille, feel this."

I felt, but did not see, Camille obey her mother's command, running her fingers across my cheek and over the surface of my closed eyelids with lascivious effect— I longed for her to continue.

"You see, Camille, Monsieur Poe is extremely agitated—one can detect it instantly from his skin. Here is a line of questioning worth pursuing."

At the word "agitated," I opened my eyes to see Camille withdraw her white-hot hand from my face and blink her eyes—slow, languid flutters of her shadowy, lacelike eyelids. I saw madame respond to Camille's flirtatious gesture with a look of stern disapproval. She moved deliberately between Camille and me and pressed forward with her questioning.

"Are you happy with your readership?"

"Happy? I don't even know them. They are names on a list. Dollars in the bank. I never correspond with them."

"And I think you would prefer stars in the heavens to those names on a list. A man like you can never be satisfied with local notoriety. It is only a matter of time before you forsake the narrow circle of your readership here in Richmond for a broader one elsewhere."

I closed my eyes and digested this astounding piece of prophecy. It was true—my readership was uniquely southern and my aim had always been to create a literature not only national, but worldwide in scope and theme. But to leave Richmond, when I had barely established myself and, indeed, still awaited the arrival of my family—that would be impossible. As I pondered this question, my head swam dizzily. I felt a hot, tender hand cradle my chin and the glass of laudanum was once again brought to my lips.

"Come, Monsieur Poe"—it was Camille speaking now. Madame L'Espanaye seemed to have vanished—"just a sip or two more. The evening has scarcely begun."

I was powerless to resist. I felt the bitter brown liquid trickle slowly, almost drop by drop, down my throat. I saw Camille's soft, yet determined lips descend to mine. We exchanged nearly invisible kisses and though I could sense her arms encircling me, it was as though I were embracing a ghost. Was she there or did I imagine her? I was solid and she was not. I could receive, but I could not give. In the dark, opiate hush of the room, the only sounds not absorbed by the thick wall hangings were the sighs of relaxation and enjoyment periodically emitted by Camille and the provocative rustle of parting lace and crinoline. So voluminous were the folds of her dress that my hands and mouth encountered the hot, soft surface of her skin only occasionally. I was being led as though blind, I responded as though trained. Camille was so adept that those portions of the body not ordinarily devoted to passion were alive and bristling with longing; the hairs of my moustache crackled like fireworks as her tongue brushed over my lips, the backs of my hands flamed with a heady phosphorescence as she closed her legs on them.

Our passion was steady though unfettered, a flight of fancy more than an erotic journey. It continued unabated, dreamlike, without resolution.

Then, a second, more demanding presence descended on us like an eagle blotting out the sun. Madame L'Espanaye, her figure bordered by the gilded aura of a thousand candles, slowly approached the couch where we lay entwined and waved Camille aside with her customary authority. But in matters of love her maternal demands went unheeded. Camille continued to kiss, to caress, to lead me through a vaporous, intoxicated dance.

Madame L'Espanaye, her orders ignored, knelt by the couch,

her ravenous, beautiful face moving towards me and away from me—her hand gliding across my face, drying the skin made slippery by her daughter's kisses.

We moved, embraced, touched and kissed with a voluptuousness only found in paintings—wordlessly—our bare skin beaded with sweat, prismatic in the candlelight. The interval between touch and response was stretched to the infinite, so that it became possible to wander endlessly within the space of a single caress.

Then, suddenly, as the lips of both mother and daughter approached my face simultaneously and the tips of their agile tongues lightly touched my closed eyelids, their heads flew back from my face, as though their necks were broken, and a climate of fear and foreboding invaded the room.

"Did you feel it, Camille?" asked the trembling Madame L'Espanaye.

"Yes . . . I did . . . it was horrible," she replied.

Both women rose to their feet, shivering, withdrawing from my couch in terror.

"What is it?" I called out across the void. "What are you frightened of?"

"The cold," replied madame. "Can you not feel it?"

"I feel no chill. Quite the contrary."

Madame L'Espanaye, filled with renewed courage, slowly returned to me and took both my hands in hers, while the still horrified Camille remained in the background.

"Do you feel here, Monsieur Poe? They are frozen. In a state of shock. Nearly devoid of life."

She had taken my hands and placed them over my eyes!

"But I feel nothing. No difference," I cried, now suffused with a growing sense of dread myself.

"Nevertheless, these are not the eyes of a normal, satisfied soul. The eyes are the most prophetic of your organs. monsieur," explained madame, the pressing need for rational and calm explication tempering her fear. "They tell me that you will witness some horrific misdeed—or yourself become involved in nefarious pursuits!"

"Perhaps the coldness you detect is merely the physical manifestation of some mental torment," I suggested. "It need not have a counterpart in day-to-day reality."

Madame shook her head grimly and gazed significantly at her daughter who had retreated to a far corner of the room, where she stood quivering with fear and cold, her palms pressed against the wall.

"No, no, Monsieur Poe. I have been doing this for twenty years now—and I have seldom received so intense a physical communication from another human being. I am certain that a misadventure of ghastly proportion awaits you—as preposterous as it sounds!"

I grew genuinely uneasy, as madame withdrew to comfort her terrified daughter. Why had she claimed that my eyes seemed nearly frozen, devoid of life? What did such an unfavorable verdict about the eyes reveal about the man himself? Was I to take this to mean that the often-sensed blackness of my soul was creeping slowly to the surface, through the channel of my eyes?

"But why did you react so violently?" I queried. "Why does this coldness have such a strong effect on both you and Camille?"

Madame L'Espanaye and Camille approached me again, slowly, with trepidation. The mother's face had tightened to such an extent that I half feared her skin was permanently stretched out of proportion. I had never been in the presence of such awesome, unwavering, almost painful concentration.

"Because you are not destined to be the only participant in the nameless horror whose approach I sense. Camille and I will form the center, around which this atrocious adventure will revolve!"

Madame would delve no deeper into the nature of the "horror" she had prophesied, despite my persistent questioning.

"It will be necessary to see you again, Monsieur Poe—and now that we are residents of the same fair city, it is not at all unlikely that our paths will cross. But for now, I am exhausted and not a little frightened. Consequently, my efforts would prove useless," she insisted.

David Madsen 46

With a weak, wilted smile, the shattered Camille bade me good-night and then, as though to cap the evening with a final touch of intrigue, turned with a swirl of her gown and disappeared silently through the damask curtains her mother held open for her.

The room now seemed empty and oppressive, and I noticed to my surprise that it had grown light. My body, confused from the laudanum-induced assault on its five senses, had not kept pace with my mind, which had been considerably sobered by the recent events. It was thus with great difficulty that I raised myself from the couch and staggered to my friends, attempting to rouse them from their opium sleep.

Rob later informed me that Madame L'Espanaye's predictions concerning his future were thankfully unalarming, though also quite unremarkable. Fergusson, it seems, had lapsed into profanity just as madame approached him, then passed out entirely. Would that I had fared so well!

Madame L'Espanaye, herself haggard and nervous, handed me my black overcoat and stovepipe and advised me to let my colleagues sleep. Agreeing to this, I was led from the bizarrely appointed chamber to the door.

"You're sure my friends will be fine, then?" I asked as I opened the door and was greeted by the cries of merchants and workmen, already well into their day.

"Of course. They'll sleep another few hours and then wake up and go about their business in the usual manner. You needn't worry."

"And Camille?" I asked.

"She will be fine—when she has slept. You must understand; though she has assisted me at several sessions, she has never experienced such a reaction from a subject. She will not soon forget it."

"And yourself?"

I gazed into madame's face, rendered innocently seductive by the sharp light of the morning.

"Only once have I received so strong, so chilling a message from the future."

"And the result?" I asked breathlessly.

She smiled almost nostalgically at me and tilted her head in a gesture of acceptance.

"It was unspeakable, absolutely unspeakable!"

"And you feel the same dire fate awaits me?"

"Us, Monsieur Poe, us. And though another session is called for to more fully illuminate this mystery, that should not be so very difficult. The first session was quite easy to arrange."

"Arrange?!"

"I apologize if the nature of our—services—has compromised you. I assumed that you knew, as do all our clients, what you were involving yourself in. I told you, we do not deal in coincidences here. When I discovered that Monsieur Reece was an acquaintance of yours, I prevailed upon him to invite you. Next time you will come of your own volition."

She smiled again, kissed me lightly and withdrew into her mysterious home—a calculated, tantalizing enigma.

My mind raced as I threaded my way through the neighborhood's narrow streets, occasionally losing myself until I recognized a landmark from our stroll the previous evening.

I struggled to sort out the events of the night, the real from the imaginary. Though I came to a complete stop in my walking, and closed my eyes as tightly as possible, I could not keep the two categories separate. The sensual events of the evening, so nebulous, so luxurious, so different from anything I had ever experienced, took on a sordid, unforgivable aspect in the light of day.

I was an adulterer; I had hideously violated the sanctity of my marriage, before it was even consummated!

This avenue of thought grew too awful to contemplate, so I turned my attention to the one fact I felt to be undeniably true: Both madame and Camille saw something ghastly in my future, and the intensity of their reactions seemed eloquent testimony to their firm belief in the eventual truth of madame's predictions. The session had proved remarkably free of carnival fortune-telling paraphernalia: the Gypsy folklore and incantations which are the stock-in-trade of the many occultists who prey on the superstitions of more gullible "customers." Could there, then, be a shred of truth to their dire divinations?

I pondered this at some length, until I eventually found myself across the street from Mrs. Yarrington's. I must have presented a curious sight to passersby as I abruptly stopped and, turning my back on my lodgings, frantically sought to arrange my disheveled appearance. My clothes, wrinkled and in an extreme state of disarray from a night spent in them, I straightened as well as I could; my hair, tousled and dirty with perspiration, I combed with my fingers; and my eyes, undoubtedly sallow and sunken, I hastened to revive by splashing them from a convenient fountain.

Despite my hurried toilet, I surely advertised the sleepless night I had spent in the company of women, alcohol and laudanum. I grew at once fearful and deeply repentant as I stepped across the street to meet the carriage which was at that moment rolling to a stop in front of the boardinghouse, bearing as its passengers mother and Virginia!

Five

Despite the clamorous creak of metal against wood and the clatter of horses' hooves on cobblestone, Virginia's cry of "Buddie" seemed to me as pure a musical note as the commercial thorough-fare was likely to hear. Once I had reached the side of the carriage and brought my little wife down to me, I instantly resolved that last night's shameful encounter would not be repeated. Here was a soul worthy of devotion and protection, and I hoped that her cheerful company would be the inducement to make me a complete and willing homebody.

Perhaps I was now satiated, perhaps the fascination for things worldly and exotic that the L'Espanayes had stirred within me was now appeased. Though I had lain transfixed, wondrously alive in their presence, I could never, given a thousand years, have summoned up love for them. Love I reserved for Virginia and for her innocence. She was the one vessel into which I could pour my dwindling reserves of lucidity, purity and tenderness. And because such innocence was tragically absent in my own soul, I now saw that I sought it through hers.

"But, Buddie," exclaimed Virginia, breaking our embrace and looking me over curiously, "what is the matter? Did you sleep in your clothes?"

Mother's stiff, worried expression formed a perfect complement to Virginia's question. Mrs. Yarrington and my fellow boarders had assembled at the dining room windows and were examining us, as they chattily sipped their morning coffee.

"Well, yes, in a manner of speaking," I improvised. "I awoke just before dawn and, finding sleep impossible, dressed and went for a walk. My sleeplessness got the better of me and I'm afraid I took a little nap on a park bench. . . . You've known me to have sleepless nights before."

"Well, yes, but you've usually overcome them with a hot drink and a good book," answered always practical mother.

"Yes, yes, I know . . . I apologize for my appearance. I didn't expect you this morning."

"We didn't expect to arrive so early either," answered my wife. "But there was a cancellation on the earlier ship, so we gladly took it."

Virginia glanced at her mother whose knitted brow indicated she was still contemplating a question or two. But then, in one of her increasingly frequent displays of haughty, girlish independence, Virginia took my arm, expertly gathered her pleated dress about her and executed a thoroughly ladylike about-face.

"Now come inside and have some breakfast, Buddie, before you take sick, you little child." Chin perceptibly raised and without a glance backward, she defiantly led me indoors, leaving mother to supervise the unloading of their baggage.

Our first breakfast together under our new roof was a trying experience. We three sat at the long dining room table and under Mrs. Yarrington's well-meaning, yet prying leadership, the other guests amused themselves by questioning us.

Mrs. Yarrington was a substantial widow in her late fifties with thick, carefully tended curls that seemed ludicrous piled atop her solid, masculine physique. She was a staunch defender of all things southern and feminine, though her pretensions to the latter were sadly imaginary.

Now that she had under her roof a complete family of southerners who had sampled life in the more industrial North and found it not to their liking, her happiness was boundless.

Her guests, largely male, were refined and slow moving, capable of deriving an hour's conversation from a single, mawkish sentiment. Though by no means well-to-do, they were skilled at giving the impression that money meant very little to them. These men held positions that somehow never required their presence at any office before ten, and thus their morning meal often lasted two hours or more, filled with dull and aimless conversation that was greedily devoured by Mrs. Yarrington.

The introduction into their sluggish society of Virginia and mother, two unknown elements, animated these gentlemen to a considerable extent, and my wife and mother were forced to endure a barrage of mundane and sophomoric inquiries.

Mr. Biggins, Mr. Chadwick, Mr. Iverson and Mr. Rawley had long since given up conversation with me; I was usually taciturn and introverted in their presence, and I broke into the proceedings only when I felt the discussion might prompt an inadvertent use of the words "wife," "husband" or "married." My fears were groundless, as mother and Virginia played their roles admirably, and left the men and Mrs. Yarrington with the impression that they were "charming, intelligent and delightful creatures."

Nightfall in the Capitol Square area of Richmond was a pleasant experience, redolent with the languorous southern atmosphere Mrs. Yarrington understandably extolled. The commercial traffic was gradually replaced by quieter, less numerous after-dinner strollers who in turn vacated the streets once it was dark. The streets then remained for the most part empty until ten or eleven, when after-theater carriage traffic was brisk for another hour or so. There was then the most welcome, undemanding silence imaginable, an especially scarce commodity in the seamier maritime quarter of Baltimore that Virginia and mother had just left behind.

The two rooms given Virginia and mother were on the second story at the front of the house, overlooking the square. They looked as though they had been decorated by someone's grandmother, furnished like all boardinghouses in a style that is perpetually outdated.

The women had used the day to unpack and redecorate; mother's talent was such that within a few short hours she had managed to overcome the staid mustiness of the rooms by the careful addition of a few personal articles and the clever rearrangement of the museumlike pieces already present. The tension my slovenly appearance had aroused dwindled away as the day wore on.

That evening we enjoyed a peaceful reunion in the privacy of these rooms; I read aloud from my most recent story, "William Wilson," while Virginia perched on the arm of my chair and mother knitted a mysterious article of clothing which would eventually find its way into our household in one form or another.

"This is how I want us always to stay," sighed Virginia, during a pause in my reading. "Buddie always creating and always reading to us in the darkness like this . . . with the world forever a comfortable distance away."

"As long as the rent has been paid, it can stay as far away as it wants," joined in my aunt.

"And why shouldn't it be? Eddie is indispensable to Mr. White."

"The question *is*, my dear, whether Mr. White is indispensable to me."

"Now, Eddie," interjected mother in admonishing tones, "we are finally settled again, we're together, which is the culmination of everything we've dreamt about since your leaving Baltimore, you're surrounded by old friends if you should ever decide to take advantage of them. Let the rest of us catch up to you before you unleash that ambition of yours further."

"Yes, Buddie," cooed Virginia. "Why can't you just rent another room here for your ambition, see that it's well fed . . ."

"And stays in at night," chastised mother.

"Both I and my ambition are perfectly happy here," I said reassuringly. "Your presence prompts me to work harder than ever. My days are unfortunately Mr. White's, but my evenings are yours and I see no reason why that should ever change."

"Nor do I," chimed in Virginia. "Now, continue reading!"

"Yes, go on, Eddie. When you stop, I lose the rhythm of my knitting. Continue please . . . at blanket speed."

When I finally rose to return to my room for the night, the kiss my wife and I shared was longer and more fervent than usual. Mysteriously, expectantly, as though seeing me for the first time, Virginia ran her delicate hand across my face, then drew back, wearing a perplexed expression, as though she detected the presence of another woman's hand.

Mother did not look up from her knitting during this—perhaps she could sense that the kiss was a major step in our evolution from cousins to man and wife. As I shut the door behind me, my last glimpse was of Virginia chewing her fingernail, her face eclipsed by the wavering shadow cast by the candle, tilted to one side in childlike petulance, as though an evening's play had been interrupted by a mother's call to dinner.

The other boarders were not early risers, but neither did they keep long hours. As I reclined in the ponderous darkness of my own room and thought over the events of the long day and the previous evening, I was wrapped in silence, interrupted only by the dull murmurings of mother and Virginia preparing for bed on the other side of the thin wall that separated our rooms.

Though I could not distinguish the words my wife and mother exchanged as they bade each other good-night, I could follow their progress to bed, by the sounds they made: the padded creak of footfalls, the rustling of linen as sheets and blankets were turned back, the chiming of crystal as water glasses and pitcher were set out on the nightstand, the slap followed by a hissing caress as a pillow was fluffed and, finally, the mixed sighs of fatigue and irritation as a tired body sought a comfortable position in which to fall asleep.

The bed nearest our common wall had been claimed by Virginia; that much I could tell from the timid creak of the springs which would have protested more vociferously had they been subjected to mother's greater bulk. By the muffled bump that occurred when my wife accidentally rolled against the wall, I knew she had pushed the bed directly up against the wall, a perfect complement to my own which rested flush against the thin paneling.

I undressed carefully and quietly in the moonless shadows, shivering with a newly sensed mixture of fear and awareness. I lay down shyly and gingerly, as though my bed were made of the most fragile glass. The beat of my heart had accelerated and my skin seemed suddenly possessed of a heady life of its own. It was as though my bed and Virginia's had been forged into one with only a thin wooden veil marking the boundary that separates husband and wife. I wondered if she felt as close, as thrilled, as frightened as I. Was each movement of my body transmitted through the wall to her in the same manner as her twistings and turnings manifested themselves to me?

I rolled against the coolness of the wooden wall. I found myself wishing it were Virginia's body, yet at the same time I was grateful that it was not. Better this barrier between us than the uncertainty of a passion that would surely prove destructive, both to the child Virginia was trying to leave behind and to the woman she was hoping to become. But where and what was the dividing line between girl and woman? Was it an age or a state of mind? If an age, was it twenty, which meant my wife would not be a woman for six years? Was it fifteen, the age she would attain next year? Was it fourteen, her age now? As for Virginia's state of mind, it altered every hour on the hour. It was subject to weather conditions, passing traffic, an item read in a news magazine, a chance comment overheard on the street. Virginia seemed more and more a creature of inconsistency (perhaps that is the ultimate sign of womanhood), equally comfortable in a salon full of grown ladies, or on a swing with girls her own age. For the moment, I decided to let the dividing line assume the form of the inch-thin wall that partitioned the bed I imagined we shared.

From across the deserted square, the bells in one of Richmond's innumerable churches churned their soporific message—it was midnight. My body, temporarily energized by its proximity to Virginia, was slowly giving in to its true condition: exhaustion. My mind craved sleep. In its kaleidoscopic interior, indistinct images blundered through an opiate residue, seeking preeminence: the frail form of Virginia; the gossipy boardinghouse residents; the militant Mrs. Yarrington; and, dominating them all, the face of Madame L'Espanaye as it sought to kiss me but was pushed away by jealous, disembodied eyes that could only belong to her daughter, Camille.

With my eyes clamped shut to prevent any further acquaintances from squeezing their way in, I kissed the wall opposite where I knew Virginia's face rested and fell instantly asleep.

"Buddie, is it really necessary that we keep our marriage a secret any longer?"

The three of us had requested breakfast in our rooms the following morning, in order that we might privately discuss our future in Richmond. Mother's stern nod at me following Virginia's question indicated that she, too, felt a certain amount of truth telling was now in order.

"Yes, my dear, I'm afraid it is," I began reluctantly. "You see, in order to buy your passage here from Baltimore, I had to do a good deal of borrowing, from friends, relatives, anyone who was anxious to reestablish their friendship by an extension of credit. This was looked on as charitable on my part—the concerned nephew taking pity on the financial difficulties of his aunt and cousin. Now, if I suddenly announced that we were married, I'm afraid I would seem quite the selfish fellow. That I was borrowing on my own behalf. That would certainly do my career—and our happiness—no good."

Mother attempted to counter Virginia's glumness: "It's only for a little while longer. We can still be seen everywhere together. We need not take the deception too far."

"Yes, darling, as a matter of fact, it would be better if people *did* see us together—let them guess and gossip, let them see a courtship develop before their eyes. It will be like playacting."

This last rationale would have placated my dear wife only a few months ago—but now I regretted it. To her, it was a subtle reminder that I still thought of her as a child. Hurt that I could not accept her entirely as a woman, she succumbed to her child's penchant for pouting and picking at her food. She no longer spoke directly to me or her mother, whom I sensed she perceived as my partner in this conspiracy, but glowered peevishly into her eggs and toast.

"But I don't want to play at marriage."

I stood and walked to her chair, attempting to hold and console her, but she drew away furiously, upsetting the tea service in the process.

"Now look at this mess, Virginia," scolded mother.

"I don't want to look at anything. I don't care if I spilled your old tea. I'll spill lunch and dinner too, if I want!"

Virginia turned her face, chalky and tear stained, towards me. I was ready to grant her anything.

"Buddie," she whimpered, "I adore you—I would do anything for you. I don't want to be difficult, but *please* don't make us continue in this way much longer."

"We shan't. I promise you. Only for a few more . . ."

"A few more . . . ?" she asked.

". . . weeks." I smiled. "It will be a whirlwind courtship. You see, Virginia, I can't afford to have very many people angry with me right now. Not people who can help me later with my writing."

She scoffed. "Then, if necessary, we can help out. Sewing. We can move and take in boarders again. I could learn to cook. Or you could do other work . . ."

I bent over her and took her hand in mine, smoothing the stray hairs that her tears had caused to stick to her cheek.

"What you are saying, darling, is impossible. As long as I am alive, a dollar will not cross my hand unless I earn it with my pen! A priest does not dabble in masonry, a writer steers clear of trades that might interfere with his concentration. And nothing addles the brain like a full day of business. And now, I'm late for work. I promise, we'll announce as soon as it is humanly possible."

Virginia stared at me, attempting to summon up the love she knew was necessary to banish her disappointment and skepticism. Further conversation seemed inappropriate, so I kissed the two women, receiving from mother a furtive nod of reassurance. Draining the last of my coffee, I hurried away, feeling at once guilt ridden for having hurt Virginia, yet exonerated by mother's apparent understanding of my position.

As I glanced up at the window while awaiting an opportunity to cross the street, I was for the first time intimately conscious of my need for both these women. Without either one of them, my life would have been an unbalanced, lonely affair, governed only by the mercurial dictates of ambition and literature. As I strolled past the shopkeepers washing their windows, swatting the dust from their striped awnings, and uselessly polishing their brass nameplates, I vowed that Richmond would soon be treated to the sight of Edgar Poe publicly courting his young cousin. I swore to deal with public opinion with a swift and uncompromising step: a wedding, with the reception to be held in the parlor of Mrs. James Yarrington's boardinghouse, Capitol Square, Richmond!

Six

"Overly harsh . . . unnecessary . . . they are respected citizens . . . vitriolic beyond reason . . . this should be watered down . . . this is simply too, too much! . . ."

Such were the comments that my employer, Mr. White, had made in the margins of the latest batch of reviews I had turned into him the previous week, reviews that were shortly due to be sent downstairs to Fergusson so they could be included in the next issue of the *Messenger*. There was scarcely a line of attack, a registry of indignation, or an expression of disgust to which White had not taken exception.

Throughout the changing fortunes of our association, I had been the target of an occasional upbraiding, but never had he launched such an unmitigated assault on my critical abilities. I angrily grabbed the sheaf of reviews from the hands of the nervous messenger boy and stalked into White's small, poorly ventilated office.

The prig was seated behind his miniature oak desk, whiskers dutifully carrying their load of breakfast crumbs, printer's ink and glue, gleefully opening envelopes containing the checks of newly won subscribers—a task he firmly reserved for himself. The office's one grease-smudged window admitted little light, and it was never opened—White evidently maintained that comfort was not consistent with meticulous work.

His waistcoat was unbuttoned, his tie loosened, his sleeves rolled up in striking contrast to the public posture of propriety and appearance he liked to cultivate. The manner in which he habitually tucked himself into the narrow space between his chair and his desk gave one the impression he was fat, whereas in reality he was quite reasonably proportioned. His office was remarkably prosaic and free from the normal affectations of a literary man, such as degrees from obscure European universities, pipes, liquor and, of course, books. I believe White was intimidated by the things; for a man to muster the patience and dedication to produce three or four hundred pages of prose was akin to sorcery to White, and it was my opinion that he bore an unhealthy and therefore uncritical respect for authors.

"Well, Edgar, I see you've read my notes on your work," he began cheerily. "Glad you've decided to approach me on the subject yourself. That way our little meeting avoids the unpleasant connotations of an employer censuring an employee."

"I can think of no more unpleasant connotations than those carried by your condemnations of my reviews," I retorted, refusing his offer of a chair.

"Tut, tut, Edgar. You're being oversensitive."

"It's impossible to be overly sensitive where one's writing is concerned."

"But it is where business is concerned. We are in the literature business here, Edgar. We must sell subscriptions in order to pay you and the other employees. Surely I needn't lecture you on basic economics."

"As I recall, our subscriptions have increased considerably since I assumed my duties."

"Very true, because a certain style and quality of writing has come to be expected. But this . . ."

He motioned to the stack of my most recent reviews with contempt.

"You no longer find quality in my writing?" I asked.

"Quality, yes. But little else. Evenhandedness seems to have vanished from your writing, Edgar. Take this, for example: 'Miss Hollingshead's 'Afternoon Games for Girls' should never have seen the light of day,' or this, '. . . there is a quality of epic tedium to be found in Longfellow's poetry that is sadly passing for profundity among his diverse and deceived readership.' There are those who think Longfellow is quite a writer, Edgar."

"I am not forcing them to dismiss Longfellow."

White was growing impatient. His whiskers bristled like the needles of a porcupine as he motioned expansively around the confines of his cluttered office.

"All of this rancor, this ill feeling just begets more of the same. We are here to extol literature and fine writing, to sing its praises and campaign for its growth."

"If you will glance over the work I've done here, Mr. White, you'll find that good literature is praised and bad writing is justly condemned."

"But in such terms! I quote, 'De Farquar deserves deportation to Africa, where his scribblings will connect with the audience for which they were designed.' Or this, '. . . evidently Morrison's years of writing sales slips for customers in his dry goods store convinced him he possesses a talent for literature. As far as this reviewer is concerned, he's still dealing in dry goods!' "

Despite himself, White chuckled at this last sentence, then, embarrassed at his approval of my wit, resumed his chastising demeanor. He filled his lungs with the office's musty air, and expelled it in my direction, slamming his hands down sharply on a stack of manuscripts, scattering papers and a fine cloud of dust.

"What I want is moderation, moderation, moderation! With a capital *M*. Give me a surfeit of moderation, Edgar, and your reviews will still emerge as thoughtful and provocative. Now, they are downright dangerous!"

"What you are after, Mr. White, is not moderation. It's mediocrity. With a capital *M!* You brought me into this office with the understanding that I would have editorial freedom, but now you've seen fit to go back on your word. Well, I'll go back to my office and give the Miss Hollingsheads of this world the benefit of the doubt. But with one word, you've undermined whatever loyalty I feel towards this publication. Should a better offer arise I will feel compelled to take it!"

Seething with indignation, I snatched my reviews from his hands and made for the door.

This creative disagreement between Mr. White and myself proved to be the first of many. Added to my professional worries was the tension we three lived under at home, as we reluctantly continued to mask from friends and acquaintances our true marital status.

But my peace of mind was periodically interrupted by something else as well—a force, not a fact; a sensation, not a material inconvenience. The problem was simply this: Ever since the scandalous night spent with Madame and Camille L'Espanaye, passion had evolved within me to a living, breathing, insistent urge! And this passion had assumed a mind of its own, and was even now going about its insidious work.

I had, of course, during my youth and my brief, unhappy career as a cadet at West Point, embarked upon transient flirtations with many women, had cared for them and even convinced myself that I loved two of them.

These relationships were necessarily cerebral and passionless; the society in which I was raised contained few women unencumbered by those clinging parents and relations who exercised imperious control over their daughters' lives. Thus, an attentive young suitor had best be convinced that the object of his affections would forever remain so, because the investment of time, energy and frustration necessary to run the parental gauntlet was so great as to almost preclude any further amatory fortune-hunting. I knew many a young man, who, having fallen prey to the charms of a Richmond girl, successfully withstood the onslaught of inquisitiveness and meddling, indecision and insult, unleashed by the girl's parents, only to find that his affection had been exhausted along with his patience. The young men in question usually foreswore womanhood forever and remained callous, sardonic bachelors the rest of their days.

But I was of the opinion that the male psyche is equipped to contend with only one true female obsession per lifetime, and I had formed mine as a child, when I first met my cousin, Virginia Clemm. Throughout my maturation she had evolved from a bright, dainty sisterly and play companion to a devoted, worshipful cousin and finally to a beautiful, admired young woman. So constant was our proximity, so intimate our sharing of feelings and frustrations as children and adolescents, that when we were apart, my ability to enjoy the company of other women was clouded by her presence in my thoughts.

She came, in time, to represent for me everything female; she was the standard by which I measured every woman, girl or child whom I met.

Thus, when we became man and wife, it seemed more the fulfillment of a preordained chain of events than the culmination of a courtship.

But of all the emotions aroused in me throughout the history of our companionship, physical passion was the last to emerge—and the strangest. I was ashamed that it had been drawn out of me not by my wife, but by two women whom I knew only briefly and by chance. I was terrified that it might, like alcohol, prove my superior, coercing me into again compromising my marriage—either through the lure of another night in the gaslit underworld of Richmond, or by forcing me to declare my passionate intentions to a wife I was certain was not yet capable of such a relationship.

One night, as I lay unhappily awake, gazing at the wall that separated us, I heard the faintest of whispers emanating from Virginia's room.

"Buddie, can you hear me?"

"Virginia!" I fairly shouted in my exuberance.

"Sssshh. If mother wakes and finds me talking to a wall . . ."

"I'm sorry, but I'm surprised that you are not asleep."

"Oh, it's impossible. Mother snores like a lion when she's had a trying day—and I keep thinking of you. Can you see me?"

"See you? How should I be able to see you when I can barely understand you?"

"There's the slightest of cracks in the wall. Here."

I searched for the spot she had indicated, but could find no breach in the barrier between us. I jumped out of bed, carelessly tossed the blankets aside and, retrieving a candle from my desk, returned to the wall. I played the dim light across the clapboard slats, praying that I would be rewarded for my trouble by a glimpse, no matter how narrow, of my beloved's face. But my expedition proved fruitless, despite Virginia's whispered directions.

"I can see nothing," I said at length.

"But I can see you, Buddie, and I can see that you've lit the candle and are now playing the perfect fool trying to find me."

I paused to consider my situation—hunched over on the bed, my head pressed against the wall, squinting as though looking through a telescope, I must have more closely resembled an anxious bricklayer inspecting his workmanship than an adoring husband straining to communicate with his wife.

"I can see the left half of your nose and part of your mouth— you are smiling now—and the button of your collar. Shall I give you a kiss?"

"You had better make it a thin one."

I heard my wife's characteristic giggle, followed by a wet crackle as she planted a kiss on the wall.

"Were you working tonight?" asked Virginia.

"Trying to. Three hours, two bottles of ink and four inches of candle—all for one paragraph. And a gloomy one at that."

"And why . . . Ssssshhhhh!"

I froze—as though I were an intruder in a room and was fearful of waking the person I sought to rob.

"What is it?"

"Mother! She's turning in her sleep. I thought she was listening. It's fine now. Do you love me, Buddie?"

"Of course I do."

"Why, then, is your writing continually so depressing? Some of the things you go on about—I just can't understand where they come from."

"Happiness has no effect on my writing— There will always be a cloudy, dark side to me no one can ever illuminate."

"Not even me?"

"Not even you—though you come the closest."

"But I seldom see this side of you. Oh, I know you are depressed about Mr. White now and again, or about your salary, or about something you have read, but never so gloomy and miserable as those tales of yours."

"And you never shall see that part of me! It comes out only in my tales— And remember, they are imagination—only imagination."

"Buddie!"

"Yes."

"Buddie, I'd like us to be married. Officially. I know I've asked you before. You know how much I love you. I feel so—so lucky, like a schoolgirl who suddenly marries the teacher she's always been in love with. You make me feel like such an adult. It's what mother and I both want. To be established, for us to be treated like every other couple. I, for one, have grown tired of your friends bending down to me after dinner and offering me sweets, as though I am only amused by toys and not by conversation."

I realized that the time had indeed come to grant her her wish —that all practical and professional considerations had become not only selfish, but outmoded. It was my darling Virginia's happiness that was of the utmost importance and there, in the trembling darkness, our lives kept apart only by a thin wooden paneling, I possessed the opportunity to make her realization of that happiness complete.

"Virginia?"

"Yes, Buddie. Hurry, I'm falling asleep again."

"I *do* want to marry you again."

"Honestly?"

"Honestly. With flowers and a ceremony and friends and a honeymoon. And our names in the paper!"

"Are you on your knees?"

"As close as I can manage."

"Then let it be as soon as possible! Buddie, Buddie, I'm going to die of happiness!" Then she added in a throaty, conspiratorial whisper: "Shall I come to you now? I won't creak the boards, I'm wearing stockings."

"No!" I exclaimed, a shade too enthusiastically. By endorsing our second and legitimate wedding, I had brought the specter of the marriage bed one step closer. But why, in view of the sensual frame of mind in which I now found myself, did I attempt to divert the flow of passion when I sensed it setting its course on Virginia? Other men had wives, surely many of them were as young and angelic as mine. And why, despite the presence and warmth of a woman with whom I was in love, did I voluntarily, and not without some degree of relish, permit my desire to settle on the faces and figures of the two Frenchwomen?!

"Buddie!" whispered Virginia impatiently.

"No . . . you had better remain there. Mr. Chadwick is a sleep-walker. There's no need to throw caution aside at the last moment. Just try and get some sleep now. Dream of me if you can."

"And of our wedding. Good-night."

"Good-night," I replied, but only with my voice, for my mind was already elsewhere. I stood and carried what remained of the candle to my desk where I dejectedly watched it drip onto the pages of the manuscript I had begun that evening. I went to the window and parted the lace curtains mother had sewn to adorn my room.

The street was deserted save for a solitary inebriate who was preparing a bed for himself on a park bench.

I closed the curtains and watched the candle expend itself with an ignominious sputter. The wax had hardened, covering the page I had written with graceful, concentric gobs of tallow. Everything seemed hopelessly foreign and out of sorts: the pauper in the square; the gentle, natural swirls of wax on a page of obsessive morbidity; and the dear, sweet child in the next room who irration-ally longed to deliver her innocence into my dubious care.

Like a predator stalking his prey in ever-tightening circles, I subtly altered my path home from work on a daily basis. I told myself it was coincidence that saw me veer off the main thoroughfare into the neighborhood in which the L'Espanaye women lived. I concocted excuses for the slow, meandering pace I set while walking down their street. I told myself there were other reasons for standing guard before their windows, motionless and invisible in the early-evening darkness.

And of course I was fooling no one, not even myself.

Madame and her daughter were exotic, perhaps overindulgent, slightly insatiable, certainly mysterious and most probably capricious and untrustworthy. They were prostitutes as well as prophets. They were things Virginia could never be, things I would not wish her to be or, indeed, ever allow her to become. Yet, they represented a breed of woman towards whom, despite all considerations of morals, manners and judgement, I was magnetically drawn.

My fascination with the two dark beauties had grown into an obsession—the need to assuage desires long held captive by the strictures of my chaste marriage, overwhelming!

I began to call on the L'Espanayes regularly. The visits, over which I had for so long agonized, were accepted by mother and daughter as the mere culmination of prophecy. There was never any doubt in their minds that I would return.

I saw them alone and in the company of other men. I saw them together and separately. Our program was always the same: The evening would begin with laudanum, my dosage increasing steadily until I found myself partaking of over a thousand drops per session. Then, Madame L'Espanaye, aided by Camille, whose competence increased with ease and rapidity, would guide me through her personal, curiously sensual brand of phrenology.

But our sessions were never as revelatory as they had been that first evening—Madame L'Espanaye attributed to our growing intimacy her inability to mold the blackness she saw in our futures into definable shapes. But though her prognostications lacked detail and definition, she never wavered from her conviction that a nameless, insatiable horror lay waiting in ambush, concealed somewhere in the months, the weeks, or perhaps even in the days ahead of us!

I grew attached to the two women on more than a professional level, and my affections were wonderfully reciprocated. We never saw one another in the daylight hours; we would meet only well after nightfall, in the dim, lamplit underside of Richmond.

The knowledge that I had deliberately taken a lover—had taken *two* lovers—did not shame or cripple me. Though it may seem woefully cruel to the happily married reader, I began to look on my involvement with the L'Espanayes as the only manner in which I could stem the tide of wickedness I knew abounded in me, and divert it from Virginia.

And so I filled the darker half of my soul with the L'Espanayes, just as the lighter half had been filled with my wife. A divided man, I had evolved into a human battleground between two opposing forces—and I vowed to keep them forever apart.

Seven

"Mrs. Maria Poe Clemm takes pleasure in announcing the marriage of her daughter, Virginia, to Edgar Allan Poe, noted editor and literary critic, on the sixteenth day of May 1836 at the boarding-house of Mrs. James Yarrington, Capitol Square, Richmond."

"Putting an end to temptation at last, eh, old boy?"

Barrow Reece surveyed the marriage announcement mother had happily written, upon learning of my resolve to proceed with the legitimate wedding, and leaned confidently back in his upholstered desk chair. The comparatively lush appointments of Barrow's office at the *Argus* always tended to invade his personality, lending him a slightly sumptuous, superior air.

"I expected it would be beyond you to comprehend the genuine affection I feel for Virginia. Just run the notice, please."

Barrow raised his eyebrows in irritated agreement. He began an exhaustive, overly meticulous search through the drawers of his desk.

"Of course, Edgar. Just let me procure one of our standard forms. I hear she's a lovely girl—some of my associates have seen you together. I have to rely on secondhand information—as a journalist I'm naturally opposed to it, but since an invitation to visit has never materialized . . . I will be invited to the wedding?"

"Naturally. No party is complete without its drunk."

As Barrow laboriously copied the marriage notice for the printer, I stood to survey his collection of books.

As we were so engaged, the door to Barrow's office opened and a young printer's apprentice escorted in a gentleman who wished to see Barrow.

"Sorry to disturb you, Mr. Reece, sir, but this fellow wishes to place a personal announcement. . . . He's French, or something. I thought you'd better see him."

Barrow puffed himself up slightly.

"Of course, Steven. I do have a working knowledge of the tongue. Thank you."

Steven discreetly departed and Barrow turned his attention to the caller, whom I observed behind the shelter of a first edition of *Tristram Shandy*. He was perhaps in his mid-forties, tall, large boned, confident, evidently a man accustomed to occupying a position of authority. His Mediterranean face was graced by a thin, manicured moustache that seemed slightly out of place, like a sprig of parsley on an empty dinner plate. His hair was thinning and thatched with gray, but it did not detract from an appearance that undoubtedly would be considered handsome by many ladies. He introduced himself in a thickly accented, slightly scratchy voice.

"Good afternoon, monsieur. I am Inspector Lucchino Contadina."

"Barrow Reece, and good afternoon to you, sir." Barrow winced as the two exchanged handshakes. "God, what a grip. And this is Edgar Poe, one of our city's literary lions."

Contadina nodded politely in my direction and I returned the gesture, but it was obvious that he was uninterested in anything but the purpose of his visit. He accepted Barrow's offer of a chair and lit up a thin, fragrant cigar.

"Now, sir," began Barrow, "my assistant tells me you wish to place an ad in our paper. I'm considered somewhat of a cosmopolitan and your name strikes me as Italian."

"It is Corsican, sir."

"Ah yes, Corsica, that jewel of the Mediterranean . . ."

"It is nothing but a blood-stained rock, monsieur."

"Well, even the humblest of stones can be polished into the rarest of gems, wouldn't you say so?"

"I would say such discussions are best left to the cafés."

"Quite right. Excuse me." Barrow threw an embarrassed glance at me, but I pretended not to notice as I delved deeper into Laurence Sterne. "We're so starved for international news here in Richmond that I get carried away. Now, about this advertisement."

"I have a copy of it here, monsieur. Perhaps you can assist me with it. You see, my English . . ."

"Nonsense, your English is superb. Where did you learn it?"

"An Englishman and I were very close once. He taught me."

"How nice. And you taught him French?"

"No sir, I taught him cooking."

Barrow smiled at this retort, then read the notice through once to himself, asking Contadina for an occasional clarification. As he read, his face underwent a curious evolution from studious, professional interest, to curiosity and finally to a blanched, bloodless look of shock. He set the notice slowly down on his desk and, loosening his collar, went to the window, which he threw wide open.

"What is it, Barrow? What is the matter?" I asked, my interest piqued.

Contadina, equally surprised at Barrow's reaction to the advertisement, merely stared at the editor, dumbfounded. Barrow shook his head vigorously, in the style of a drunk attempting to banish a hangover, and walked slowly back to his desk.

"What is it, monsieur? What troubles you?" asked the concerned Corsican, starting to rise to his feet.

"Yes, Barrow. What does the notice say?" I insisted.

"It's a personal notice. . . . He is searching for two women . . . two *French* women, to be exact. A mother and her daughter. Madame and Camille *Verneuil!*"

I immediately understood Barrow's amazement. Here was another coincidence worthy of Madame L'Espanaye and her daughter. It seemed no set of circumstances was too bizarre or incredible when it concerned the two women! But as we breathlessly awaited Inspector Contadina's story, a particular statement of madame's occupied the center of my thoughts: "We do not deal in coincidences." I determined to keep this admonition in mind as I listened to the Corsican.

"You seem startled, gentlemen. Do you know them, by any chance?"

"If you don't mind, Mr. Contadina, I'd like to get a few details before I run this notice. We have to be fairly scrupulous about everything we print, as I am sure you realize."

Contadina nodded his understanding. He reached into his pockets, extracting several official-appearing documents which he handed over to Barrow.

"These are my identification papers, Monsieur Reece. You are quite right to be suspicious."

Barrow perused the papers, his brow knitting as he strained to decipher the finely printed bureaucratic French that covered the documents.

"Well, this all seems to be in order," declared Barrow. "I see you are attached to the Marseilles *préfecture* of police. That is growing into quite a nest of criminals, according to what we read over here in the papers."

"I am kept busy, yes," agreed Contadina.

"I'm sure you are. Now, then, I presume you seek Madame . . . Verneuil and her daughter in connection with some police business?"

"Indirectly, yes."

"Are they wanted for some criminal offense?" I asked, fascinated by this opportunity to illuminate their nebulous pasts.

"Good heavens, no," responded Contadina. "It is merely my duty to inform them that a rather significant legal case in which they were involved has been brought to a satisfactory conclusion. I have succeeded in tracing them to Richmond, but as to their exact whereabouts in your fair city, I am confused. Hence the rather unbusinesslike personal notice."

"They fled France under unusual circumstances, did they not?" I asked, recalling the reluctance the two women had shown to discuss their arrival in America.

"Then you *do* know them?"

Barrow nodded. "Yes, I believe both Mr. Poe and myself have had the pleasure of making their acquaintance. Although we know them as Madame and Camille L'Espanaye, the coincidence is too great to be dismissed."

"That is understandable, that they would change their names. Anyone would, under the circumstances. But I am here to tell them that the need for flight and deception is over. They can return to their native Corsica in complete safety."

"I'm intrigued as to the nature of this case, which required the two women to flee France, not to mention the fact that the busy Marseilles police were able to spare you for so long. I think my readers might be interested in this whole affair," declared Barrow, already searching for paper and pencil to take down the gallant inspector's every word.

"They might at that. It *is* a fascinating history, I must say. My role in it was not at all minimal," replied Contadina, swelling with pride.

"Ah ha! You see, Edgar, there's not a man alive who's averse to getting a little press coverage, especially when it paints him in a heroic light."

"Barrow, why don't we wait and get both sides of the story. I'm sure the two women will have something to add."

"Capital idea, Edgar! We'll put 'em all together in a room and just let them reminisce. It will make an outstanding story. I can already imagine the lead-in: 'A decades-old passion, stretching back to a tiny Corsican village, its houses shuttered against the prying eyes of foreigners under the pretext of beating back the advances of the noonday sun . . .' That little suggestion just might be worth a free subscription to you, my boy."

"If you really wish to show your gratitude, you'll cancel the one I have now," I suggested.

Barrow, unperturbed by my sarcasm, returned the inspector's

identification papers and stood, indicating that the interview was at an end.

"Well, inspector, that was a damned good bit of police work, I must say, to have traced the two women thousands of miles, name change and all."

Contadina accepted Barrow's compliment with a graceful nod of his head.

"And now, that quite marvelous detective work has been crowned by a bit of old-fashioned luck. You've just saved yourself the price of an advertisement. Come along, Edgar. Let's all pay a call on Madame and Camille Verneuil."

As our hack hurried through the dismal maze of streets that fed into Richmond's waterfront, I found myself anticipating with relish the impending encounter with the L'Espanayes, despite the fact that my wife awaited me anxiously at home.

Arriving at the women's dockside dwelling, we jumped from the hack, paid the driver handsomely for his haste and stepped to the door, taking precautions to avoid stepping on the head of a loathsome drunk who regained consciousness only for the moment it took him to look us over and reassure himself we were not the police. Our initial knocks went unanswered, prompting Barrow to rap more vehemently.

There was an answering squeal, as though from an infant, and the three of us looked at each other in puzzlement. Another moment passed, then the door opened cautiously and a young, poorly dressed woman with matted, prematurely gray hair poked her head out and examined us suspiciously. I craned my neck over her shoulder, hoping for a glimpse of the two Corsican women.

"What are you wantin'?" she rasped, blowing hair out of her eyes with a contemptuous flutter of her lower lip.

"Do you live here, madame?" asked Barrow with his customary bluntness.

"Well, if I don't, I'm in fer trouble when the owner comes home. Of course I lives here, and so does my baby daughter and my husband who's away to work at the moment, if it's him yer wantin' to see."

"Excuse me," I interjected, hoping to win the woman's confidence with the politeness Barrow inevitably failed to employ, "but my associates and I were under the impression two women, a mother and her daughter, lived here."

"Did. Not no more."

An unavoidable disappointment fell over me at this reply. "I see. And do you know when they vacated the house?"

"Day we moved in. Three days ago. Beautiful women, too."

"Did they leave any word as to where they were bound?" asked Contadina impatiently, fitting himself as far into the doorway as the woman would permit.

"Not to me they didn't."

"Perhaps to your husband?"

"I pray not!"

The child began to cry from somewhere within the house. I felt an intense sympathy for this young woman whom poverty, marriage and motherhood had made a crone while still in her twenties.

"We don't want to disturb you any further. But there was a manservant . . ." I continued.

She hesitated, concerned at this line of questioning. "Mr. Jarvis," she said finally.

"You knew him?" asked Barrow, startled.

"Everyone knows old Jarvis. If you're from this neighborhood, he's talked your head off more than once about his servant days to your well-to-do Virginians. But now he drinks and he can't find a job for the life of him. Spilled hot garlic butter on a blueblood's baby—blinded the poor kid. You can't get work if something like that gets around."

"Except down here," observed Barrow.

"Down here? Who would have money down here to pay a butler?"

"The L'Espanaye women did," I answered.

"Exceptin' them. My husband and I always thought that was curious— You've got to be up to something no good if you live down here when you can afford to live elsewhere."

"Do you know where we can find this Monsieur Jarvis?" asked Contadina.

"If the sun's up, at his place, dead drunk. After dark, there's no telling."

"Where would his place be, madame?" continued the inspector.

"Down on Harkness Street. Ask anyone. Now I got to get back to my kid—and my house."

"We appreciate your help, ma'am. Give her something, Barrow —for her trouble."

Barrow stared at me incredulously, as the young wife and mother bit her lip in the anticipation of a gratuity. People down here had long since passed the point of being too proud to accept charity.

"Go on, Barrow. Pay her, for God's sake!"

Barrow grumbled a protest, but rather than appear a fool, even before this poor woman whom he would never see again, he dug into his pockets and produced a handful of coins, three of which he gave to the woman. I threw him a stern nod and he reluctantly doubled the sum.

"Thank you, sir. You seem like nice enough men all right." She then lowered her voice to a whisper and looked up and down the street to make certain she was not being overheard. "I thought you was the police. . . . You see, we don't pay no rent here. . . . We found out the two women was moving out . . . and being from poor circumstances . . . You won't say nothin'?"

We assured her her secret was safe with us.

"Well, good-day to you, then. And that Jarvis . . . he's forgotten this mornin' what he knowed last night. But if you do see him" —her demeanor softened slightly—"maybe you can save him from himself." The woman nodded a curt farewell and shut the door.

Barrow looked at me in bewilderment. "Well, Edgar?"

"Harkness Street?" I suggested.

Barrow sucked in a breath of the street's unhealthy air and exhaled it in exasperation, contemplating his options.

Contadina was growing impatient—and anxious.

"I'm frankly worried, gentlemen. There is a lot more to all of this than either of you suspects. The sooner we locate and question this Monsieur Jarvis, the better—for Madame Verneuil and her daughter."

"Do you really think they're in some kind of danger?" I asked.

"I cannot say yet—only that their sudden departure worries me."

"Well, if *you're* worried, *I'm* terrified! Harkness Street it is, then," exclaimed Barrow, leading us off down the street at a brisk clip.

Harkness Street was not a street at all; it was bedroom, dining room and bathroom to many of Richmond's disenfranchised.

The shacks and shanties that proliferated in the area had converted the once-broad boulevard into a quilt of smaller, one-way streets and dark, congested alleys. Even at midday, little light penetrated the stifling cloud of industrial smoke that blanketed the neighborhood. And now, close to dusk, it was positively funereal. Here in the omnipresent shadow of smokestack and chimney, Richmond's day laborers and factory hands lived, worked and died. Children played games against the sooty brick walls of the same buildings in which they would eke out their livings when they reached their mid-teens. There was no respite or escape from the night-and-day rumbling of hundreds of nameless pistons and pumps, which manufactured products whose purpose their makers would never know. The walls of the workingmen's taverns and public houses pulsated with the steam-driven heartbeat of industry—one learned to drink one's ale in rhythm with the generators.

As we threaded our way through this quarter of both despair and productivity, questioning the locals about the manservant Jarvis, I was overcome with the dreadful premonition that we were witnessing a way of life that was to be the norm, rather than the exception. We could see the resignation to anonymity already written on the faces of the workers who trudged by us on their way home from the factories, and on those of the children, who would soon inherit their fathers' hopelessness.

A teenage dock loader soon put us on the track of our Mr. Jarvis, and we located his address with little difficulty; it was the only wooden house in a neighborhood of brick storehouses and loading yards. Barrow led the way into a cramped and dingy hallway that echoed with the activity of the building's residents. We perused a dirty and oft-rewritten directory which indicated that Jarvis (and surprisingly a Mrs. Jarvis) resided on the first floor, in a room at the back of the house. As we made our way down the corridor, we became aware of a clamor and a chorus of shouting that accompanied some sort of frenzied activity that was occurring behind the building.

Doors flew open as we passed them and the apartment house's tired and impoverished tenants, most in the middle of their evening meals, rushed into the hallway and out the back door, pushing us aside in their eagerness to discover the source of the excitement.

While Barrow and I stood in bewilderment at the center of this heated commotion, Contadina's professionalism in times of crisis immediately asserted itself. The gentleman who had been so even tempered in Barrow's office was transformed into a dashing, militaristic figure who was at his most comfortable when shouting orders.

"I fear we're too late. I shall take Jarvis's room, you two must find out what is behind all the excitement." He charged off purposefully down the hallway in the direction of the servant's room, without waiting to see if his orders were being carried out.

Contadina was obviously accustomed to being obeyed, and in our position, we could do little else but follow the crowd.

One man, a stained napkin still tucked tightly into his collar, shouted back at his family, presumably still gathered within their apartment at the dinner table. "It must be old Jarvis again. That's him a-yelling, no doubt about it!"

There was a hoarse, drunken yelling that carried over the shouts and epithets of the crowd, but it was slurred and unintelligible. Had Jarvis gone mad? If so, it seemed to be a nightly occurrence.

We burst through the door and, among the other concerned curiosity seekers, hurried to the backyard of the house. Barrow and I were surprised to find ourselves on a rise overlooking the James River, which lay at the bottom of a steep slope, some five hundred feet below. Moored at the docks, I could see a series of freight barges on which were routinely loaded the manufactured goods produced in the factories that surrounded us. The backyard of the rooming house was evidently a storage area for one of these factories, and great piles of metal and miscellaneous piping—perhaps the factory's output for the recently concluded workday—were neatly stacked about the yard, ready for shipment the following morning.

Two miniature railroads, whose task it was to transport goods down to the river, rose from the docks up the steep slope to a loading platform that had been erected in the yard.

All this, which has taken minutes to write, took only seconds to absorb. I led Barrow through the jostling, shouting crowd to the edge of the precipice, where for the first time we could see what had occasioned such worried excitement.

The L'Espanayes' former servant was the center of attention; he was drunk, angry, tearful and pathetic. He carried a serving tray on which were precariously balanced an empty bottle and two glasses, and he seemed to be in the midst of a perverted performance of his calling. Through some ill-understood quirk of balance, his drunken weavings did nothing to upset the tray—it seemed to remain calmly horizontal. He was screaming—at first his words were impossible to decipher, but as I leaned closer and familiarized myself with his inebriated speech patterns, they grew gradually intelligible.

" 'Mr. Jarvis,' he says, 'you ain't fit to work no more,' he says. . . . 'You just tell me what I want to know,' he says. . . ."

As I examined the faces of the crowd, I realized that they were here out of a communal concern for the manservant's well-being —perhaps afraid he would slide off the cliff or frightened that he would wander into one of the surrounding factories and grind himself up into pipe or rivets. But as his black, bent and tattered form raged against the broad, gray snake of the James and the roiling panorama of an impending thunderstorm, he fended off their concern with an arsenal of unused railroad spikes. A well-wisher or an acquaintance would approach him, offering a supportive arm or encouraging words, and he would reach behind him and hurl one of the black ten-pound nails with malicious accuracy, pushing the crowd back.

"I've been with the best," he yelled. "You people want dinner, you'll wait 'til dinner is served." He squinted at the crowd, evidently having difficulty distinguishing individual faces as darkness began to fall.

"He knows me very well," whispered Barrow in my ear. "I'm going to try something."

I nodded in agreement and watched as Barrow stepped out from the ragged crowd, removing his hat and overcoat as he went and holding them at arm's length, as though to offer them to Jarvis.

"Who's that down there? Why don't you come any closer so I can see you?" barked the servant.

"It's me, Jarvis—Mr. Reece. I've come for a session. Would you please take my coat and hat?" As he spoke, Barrow walked forward deliberately, one slow step at a time.

Jarvis's eyes were fire red, his perspiring face taut, like a sweating racehorse's flanks. He circled Barrow suspiciously.

"Jarvis! Where are madame and Camille?" commanded Barrow.

"Why does everyone want to know? They are in their rooms, damn you!"

"No, they are not. And who is everyone?"

"Everyone is everyone—every bleedin' one. Him that drank with me especially!"

As Barrow stalked the servant, they came perilously close to the cliff, and Barrow, sensing the impending danger, shifted his line of approach, forcing Jarvis away from the edge.

"Can I have my drink now, please, Jarvis?"

"Certainly, sir. Though I have served better than you, I've met worse."

Jarvis poured carefully from the empty bottle and offered Barrow a glass filled with nothing but air. Barrow pretended to drink, grimaced and cautiously beckoned me to join him. I came slowly forward and offered my coat and hat to Jarvis.

"You remember Mr. Poe, Jarvis. He once came with me to visit your employers."

Jarvis nodded his recognition, then courteously took my garments and dropped them to the ground. I took the glass from Barrow and raised it to my nose—the smell was unmistakable. Jarvis had evidently drained a full glass of laudanum, more than sixty times the dosage Madame L'Espanaye had customarily served her clients and certainly enough to kill a fair-sized man! It was a miracle he was even alive.

"Who gave you this to drink, Jarvis?" asked Barrow.

"He did."

"Who?" I implored.

"He, the one that asked for the women like you done. I drank one on me own and he forced the second one . . . made me drink more and more all the time, askin' me questions . . ."

"Who was he?"

Jarvis lapsed into sad contemplation, gazing out across the river to the tranquil Virginia forests beyond, now turned black and uninviting with the flight of the last stray shards of sunlight. We seized the opportunity to grab him, one on each arm, causing him to drop the tray and glasses, which shattered. The crowd cheered the success of our rescue efforts and happily pushed forward.

But Jarvis panicked.

In his panic he possessed a strength Barrow and I could not hope to match. He easily broke free of our protective hold and ran haphazardly along the edge of the cliff, his boot slipping in the dirt that the constant passage of heavily laden wagons had broken down into loose, fragmented tufts. We gave chase, the crowd pressing desperately close behind us.

"Who was he, what did he look like? Where did your employers go?" shouted Barrow, as we pursued Jarvis towards one of the rail lines, whose terminus was marked by a pudgy assembly of unused, empty ore cars. No longer sure of where he was, who we were or what course of action to take, his brain undoubtedly a puddle of opium, alcohol and hopelessly jumbled impressions, Jarvis abruptly halted his flight and stood stock still, his arms outstretched as though he were a performer acknowledging applause.

"You've been so bloody kind to me—such lovely people to work fer . . ."

Suddenly, he tumbled over backwards in a somersault that would have pleased a seasoned gymnast, and disappeared.

In that instant, Barrow hesitated—either out of terror or the conviction that the manservant was dead—but I did not! I knew the slope was steep, but that it would slow the fall of a man tumbling down it until his progress was eventually halted by an impediment of some kind. I vaulted over the edge and, braking my descent with one arm, slid towards Jarvis who had, as I predicted, come to rest, lying across the rails of the abandoned transport line. Whether he was alive or not was impossible to determine. I moved gingerly towards him, confident that, upon reaching him, I would be able to prevent him from falling any farther until a rope could be lowered to us.

"Edgar, Edgar! Move away, move away!"

Barrow's cry from above was echoed by the crowd, but I paid no heed as I suddenly detected movement in Jarvis, proof that the resilient manservant still breathed.

"Edgar, move, damn you! For God's sake, if you value your life, move away from the rail. We can't hold them any longer!"

"Monsieur Poe! Please do as he says. Let the man go and save yourself." Contadina's thickly accented shout now joined Barrow's hysterical cries.

As I reached the form of Jarvis and reassured myself that his heart was still beating, no matter how weakly, I looked up the side of the hill and, terrified, beheld the reason for the crowd's awful anticipation. In his fall, Jarvis had knocked loose the wheel blocks that held the mine cars secure, and now they were prevented from hurtling down the slope only by the combined strength of Barrow, Contadina and the other members of the crowd.

I took firm hold of Jarvis's hand, struggling clumsily to drag him off the rails and out of the path of impending disaster. But the unconscious man's weight seemed to have trebled! I felt the muscles in my back stretch with pain as I fought to pull Jarvis towards me. But I succeeded in moving him no more than two or three inches. I attempted to stand, intending to lift the manservant bodily off the tracks, but the insecure footing combined with the steepness of the slope pulled my feet out from under me.

From above there were loud groans, the sounds of bodies straining and metal rubbing, counterpointing my own unsuccessful efforts. Then, a great wrenching reached my ears, followed by deep, thunderous exclamations of disappointment. These sounds were almost immediately erased by a hurricane of wind and whining, as the miniature train of coal cars, so toylike and unassuming when stationary, was transformed into a guiltless executioner.

I had barely time to throw myself clear of the tracks before the runaway cars were upon the poor manservant. Though his body lay directly in the path of the train, it was not slowed appreciably. I watched in horror as his prone form was scooped up by the lead car and pushed effortlessly down the slope until, as the angle of descent began to increase, his body was expelled onto the rocky escarpment with all the force of a musket shot!

As the coal cars clattered harmlessly to a halt on the level surface of the dock, silence returned to the hellish scene. More than a hundred feet below me, Jarvis's battered, lifeless form was sprawled across two sharply pointed rocks, his arms outstretched, his face gazing heavenward.

Spurred on by his impression of Contadina as a lonely, dedicated crusader, Barrow was determined to solve the death of Jarvis, which we both believed to be connected with the disappearance of madame and Camille, and to publish a step-by-step account of his progress in the *Argus*.

Before he was called away on business to Washington, he led me through a detailed interrogation of the L'Espanayes' other fortune-telling clients, with negligible results. A search of Jarvis's room was equally unsuccessful. The identity of the man who had forced Jarvis to consume the fatal dose of laudanum remained unknown.

Our investigative efforts thus proved fruitless, and I attempted to force the entire mysterious affair into the back of my mind.

Two things made this impossible.

One was the erotic awakening I had experienced in the company of the women. I found myself now in a near-permanent state of arousal, yet their disappearance had made the consummation of my insistent desires an impossibility.

Secondly, the bizarre nature of Madame L'Espanaye's predictions made intriguing food for thought. What was the "horrific misdeed" she had spoken of? What were the "nefarious pursuits" in which we were to become involved? Was the death of Jarvis the culmination of these prophecies? I prayed that this were true, but somewhere within me, in those unnamed organs that are sensitive only to darkness, I knew it was not.

I felt that the hand of predestination had swept all power of decision making out from under me—that I could return to normal, domestic pursuits and conduct my life according to my own desires only until Fate chose once again to intervene in the person of Madame L'Espanaye and her daughter.

I attended Jarvis's funeral a week before my second wedding. Barrow was still in the capital on business, consequently I was the sole mourner.

A tired priest read impatiently from the Bible, then gathered his overcoat about him and hurried away before the first spadeful of earth was thrown onto the coffin. Two shadows fell across the poorly maintained pauper's field, which was surrounded by immature, nearly naked cedar saplings: the diminutive, barely discernible spire of the chapel and the insinuating bulk of a factory smokestack.

As I walked down the lonely, overgrown path towards the main road, I met a frail figure hurrying towards the grave, poorly protected against the rising winds that buffeted the cemetery by a frayed, flannel shawl. The figure's eyes stared intently into mine —it was the woman who had moved into the L'Espanayes' home and who had hoped that we might save Mr. Jarvis from himself. I felt ashamed, plagued by the knowledge that I had failed her.

"Good afternoon, ma'am. I'm truly sorry to meet you again under such woeful circumstances."

"Them's the only circumstances there is, mister," she replied in the same worn, dispirited voice. She did not sound angry—merely resigned.

"Well, I'll never forgive myself that I was unable to save Mr. Jarvis. He undoubtedly was possessed of a good heart."

"He was rotten, if you want to know the truth of it. Still, he was a man, wasn't he?"

I nodded agreement, attempting to be sympathetic.

"Shall I walk you home, ma'am? There's not much to see. They'll be finished up there soon."

But the woman was not listening to me. She gazed up at the gravediggers who were idly tamping down the ground with the broad sides of their shovels and sharing a keg of beer.

"You had better come along now," I urged again. "Your husband will have started to worry about you, I expect."

She fell out of her reverie and examined me as though I had lost my senses.

"My husban' . . . ?"

"Yes, your duty's to him, not to this dead man here. Now, come along."

I took her gently by the arm, but she resisted with surprising strength.

"Why they are one and the same, you damned fool! And if he is worrying about me now, that's the first I heard of such a thing."

She left me stunned and stalked resolutely up the path towards the grave. I realized that further consolation on my part was useless; this woman had her own methods for dealing with tragedy.

As I passed through the rusted gate that guarded the entrance to the cemetery, I was surprised to see Inspector Lucchino Contadina seated on a nearby bench, gazing up at the silhouettes of the grieving widow and the gravediggers. I turned and walked over to him.

"Why weren't you up at the funeral?"

"Oh, I was, in my own way, Monsieur Poe. I prefer to observe such things from afar. In my profession, one attends more funerals than an undertaker. The ceremonies, the hollow words of the priests—they have lost all significance for me."

"I suppose you've got a point," I agreed. "It is a nice gesture that you have come to pay your respects, even though your style of doing so is somewhat unorthodox."

Contadina stroked his moustache, plastering the odd stray hair to his lip with a delicate gesture of a wetted finger.

"It is a rather depressing picture to leave Richmond with. Still, I felt compelled to be at least mentally in attendance."

"You're leaving so soon? May I ask why?"

"I'm quite certain the Verneuil women are no longer here."

"How can you be sure?"

By way of an answer, Contadina nodded somberly up at the grave where Jarvis's widow, now left to her own devices by the departed gravediggers, was kneeling before the headstone in prayer.

"Have you a notion as to who is behind this horrible crime?"

"I have my suspicions, Monsieur Poe. But a great deal more evidence is needed before they can be called anything but suspicions."

"Then you must go to the police with what you know! This may be a Corsican affair in origin, but a death has occurred on American soil, and the killer is still at large. He may strike again!"

Contadina shook his head in condescension and, rising to his feet, placed a fatherly hand on my shoulder.

"Would you really prefer it if I went to the Richmond police? Encourage them to ask questions, to raise suspicions, to summon witnesses, yourself most certainly included? *Naïve* may be a French word but it does not describe all Frenchmen. We both know the nature of the Verneuils' profession, and we both know you would not be so well acquainted with them had you not taken advantage of their . . . services."

I nodded my rueful agreement to his sound logic. "I certainly don't intend going to the police. And Barrow has been called away on business. He's much too busy to play police inspector."

"Yes, it's all for the best, monsieur. Leave these things in the hands of those best able to deal with them. Well, I'm afraid I must return to my hotel. I hope to leave this evening. It has been a pleasure making your acquaintance, despite the unfortunate turn of events."

Contadina extended his hand and I shook it vigorously, encountering the iron grip Barrow had spoken of.

"But where will you go? Where do you suspect that the Verneuil women have gone? The country is endless."

"I have relied on my wits and coincidence to bring me this far. I trust neither will turn her back on me without good reason. *Adieu*, Monsieur Poe. I look forward to reading of your literary fame. It would please me no end to then be able to count you among my acquaintances."

Contadina slipped his hands into his overcoat pockets and set off at a determined clip down the rocky, foot-worn path back towards the center of town.

My mind, weary from grappling with the hundreds of unanswered questions that plagued it, returned to the tragedy whose pitiful conclusion Contadina and I had just witnessed. Though I was unable to aid Mrs. Jarvis in her most trying hours, I was not prevented from vowing vengeance on whatever person or force had intruded in the lives of this couple. I was unaware that the saga of the late Mr. Jarvis and his exhausted, yet nobly durable wife formed only a tragic prelude to the horror that was yet to come.

Eight

Wedding preparations were at the center of my thoughts for several days following the funeral. I had informed mother and Virginia of my involvement as one of those who had tried to save the unfortunate man, fully expecting the local newspapers to report on the death. I, of course, did not mention my now severed connections with the L'Espanaye women or the opium-clouded hours I had spent in their company. But Jarvis's passing was deemed of no importance by Richmond's journalists, nor by the police who, following a cursory investigation, ruled his death an industry-related accident.

If Virginia was the perfect picture of girlish and absentminded anticipation, the day before the wedding found mother displaying her military talents to their fullest advantage. With friendly imperiousness she supervised the preparation of the wedding meal, locking horns occasionally with the equally stubborn Mrs. Yarrington over the menu; directed the decoration of the parlor, which was to be the site of the actual ceremony; fussed with the seamstresses over Virginia's wedding gown, which she herself had helped design; and pored over the text of the sermon, to be delivered by the Reverend Amasa Converse, an oaken, frustrated pioneer and editor of the *Southern Religious Telegraph.*

And when it came to subterfuge, mother proved again to be an efficacious and extremely willing accomplice. With Thomas Cleland—a likable, athletic young man who had recently moved into Mrs. Yarrington's and with whom I had struck up a conversational friendship—acting as surety, mother, Virginia and I swore to the county clerk that Virginia was a full twenty-one years of age and thus eligible for the marriage license the gullible public official gladly issued us.

Maria Poe Clemm was an independent and often intransigent woman. As a widow she had learned self-reliance and had acquired financial acumen; as the mother of a frail and quietly demanding daughter, she had learned both compassion and patience. Yet, for all of these respectable and attractive qualities, she was not satisfied with her life, even during those rare periods when the physical and financial health of herself and her dependents was sound.

She was an incurable romantic and armchair adventuress who often fell asleep at dawn, buried in sensational and exotic novels. Through my publishing and writing, I was her contact with the literary and artistic worlds.

She believed a bond stronger than blood had existed between herself and my true parents, Betty and David Poe, both of whom had been actors. With their deaths from consumption when I was three, all living connections with the world of art and imagination had been dissolved. Now, through the second marriage between Virginia and myself, one that could not be questioned or undone, Maria Poe Clemm would be eternally joined to me and my universe of dreams and speculation. She therefore treated my literary career with a respect and reverence equal to my own and brought to our household a clear-headed, sober sense of duty that I often lacked.

The night before the wedding found us with the myriad preparations complete, sitting exhaustedly but contentedly in the
women's parlor on the second floor. The room had grown considerably more comfortable and homelike, as mother and Virginia
almost daily purchased an odd knickknack or picture (usually one
of the accurately but dispassionately rendered hunting scenes that
were then in vogue among English painters and their American
imitators) to dress up their surroundings.

Virginia and I sat next to each other on a flowered couch mother
had purchased from the relatives of a deceased boarder, while
mother herself drank tea sitting on a stiff, upright chair in which
the deceased had been required, because of a fractured spine, to
spend all his waking hours.

"Eddie, would you care to read to us this evening?" asked
mother, breaking the silence that had reigned for the last half hour.

"I think not. The project I'm currently involved in will hardly
make a good bedtime story," I replied.

"Oh, what is it, Buddie? Tell us, please," begged Virginia.

"It's all rather scholarly. . . ." But I could see that no amount of
protestations on my part could absolve me of at least a brief summary of my treatise.

"If you insist . . . It has to do with logic and deductive reasoning. . . ." Almost as soon as I began, I noticed Virginia's face fall
in disappointment.

"*And* police work," I hastened to add, regaining my dear wife's
flagging attention. "You see, the sciences of probability and logic
—what might happen and what set of circumstances could have
conspired to make a given event take place—have been talked of
endlessly by philosophers and mathematicians and what have you,
but they have never really been brought to bear on practical enterprise. . . ."

I paused to assess the effect my words were having on my wife
and mother, and as they appeared highly interested, I continued,
if only for the benefit I might derive from stating clearly my position to a layman.

"It seems to me that the mental processes we deem analytical, or deductive, if you will, could play an important part in the solution of various crimes if they were employed properly by our police. As things stand now, our lawmen react to crime with depressing drudgery and predictability. Suspects are chased, apprehended, questioned to death, released, rearrested; people are beaten and brutalized. It is often only sheer force or even accident that leads an officer to the criminal, usually months or even years after the actual commission of the act. I, on the other hand, hold that through the proper training of the mental faculties we all possess, the solution to a given crime can be arrived at with an ease and rapidity that would astonish and certainly embarrass the best of our contemporary police. The powers of logic, if honed to acuteness, would permit a person to view the given crime from the distance I feel is necessary to accurately determine what has happened. All too often, our incompetent police officers delve so deeply into a problem that they fail to notice the most obvious and often most revealing aspects of a crime."

I continued for several minutes by citing certain unsolved crimes, with whose details I had familiarized myself, thanks to the *Virginia Argus* files Barrow had permitted me to examine, and listing the various steps I believed should have been undertaken towards their solution.

I was finally roused from my dissertation by the gentle pressure of Virginia's head, as it fell to my shoulder. The slight jolt momentarily awakened her, she gazed fondly into my eyes for a moment, then once again succumbed to sleep.

I immediately felt ashamed at having spent the night before our wedding boring my wife to the extent that she fell gratefully asleep.

"Mother, I'm awfully sorry. . . . It is a special night, and I'm afraid I failed to treat it as such," I whispered.

"Nonsense, Eddie," replied mother as she drew the shades and extinguished all but one candle.

"I admit that, to us, your essay does not possess the drama and excitement of your stories, but our girl is usually very tired these days. You may have noticed, it's more than she can do to stay awake for twelve hours running."

I nodded. "Is she still ill?"

"She's always ill, Eddie."

Mother sighed sadly and caressed her daughter's forehead with a wistful seriousness.

"She coughs all day—doctors come and go, they prescribe this for her color and that for her lack of energy . . ."

I was stunned. "But why do I never see these doctors? Why have I never been told of these visits? She never coughs inordinately around me!"

"She won't have you worry. They come during the day when you're at the office, so you won't know. She insists."

"But what a struggle for her—to appear constantly healthy when she's around me! Well, I won't have this. We'll hire the finest doctor in Richmond if necessary."

"Eddie," mother scolded, "the finest doctor in Richmond is quite beyond our means." Then she added hesitantly, "That's why I worry so when you tell me you've been quarreling with Mr. White. If we lose that income, we may lose Virginia."

"And the doctors can determine nothing?"

"Beyond the fact that she has a constitution of glass, they have told us very little."

I lapsed again into stupefied silence. My Virginia, my angel, deathly ill, yet unwilling to burden me with the knowledge!

"We don't know what it is that threatens to take her from us, Eddie, but we do know what keeps her alive, what sustains her mentally and physically. It is you, and her conviction that you will in time be regarded as one of the century's great writers. If you knew how she worships and adores you, how highly she speaks of you to friends and acquaintances, how she defends you and fights for you in conversation . . ."

"Enough, enough! I can bear this no longer. I need time to think. Our lives at present are insupportable, if Virginia is as you describe her. I can only blame myself for being such a stranger to her."

I stood up gingerly so as not to awaken Virginia, then I reached one hand under her legs, extended another beneath the small of her back and carried her fragile form through the dark room to her bed. The metaphor suggested by my cradling her still figure was inescapable. Though I could detect the warm blood still flowing through her tranquilly sleeping body, I nevertheless was seized by a ghastly sensation that I was an undertaker, delivering a meticulously embalmed corpse to its resting place in the casket. I covered her with blankets and a quilt, kissed her lightly and turned to mother.

"We will not tell her I know the extent of her illness. But together we will strive to banish it by offering her the most secure home possible and by protecting her from the vices and evil that proliferate outside the door!"

Mother nodded in stern agreement, then leaned ominously towards me. "That is all well and good, Eddie. But you must see to it that this evil, as you term it, does not accompany you home one evening and slip in the door behind you!"

As I sat dejectedly in my own room, the last remark of mother's continued to haunt me. The mere fact that she deemed it necessary to warn me of bringing disaster down on our house unnerved me. Could she have known of my involvement with the fortune-tellers, and that unfortunate night in which I had succumbed to the temptations of alcohol and opium and had for the first time tasted the sensual pleasures of those experienced and wanton women?

It appeared that though I could successfully mask the baser of my desires from Virginia, mother would not be so easily deceived.

I told myself that my own lapse into impropriety was securely confined to the past. It could not return to tragically insinuate itself into my life. The only deception I would need to perpetrate in the future would be the concealment of the occasional profane thought or yearning from Virginia, but never the act itself. I knew now that Virginia's very hold on life depended on the purity and propriety of my behavior and on my continued and, it was to be hoped, amplified success as a writer. But was my love for her strong enough to break the hold Madame and Camille L'Espanaye still held on my imagination?

I wrestled with these unsettling thoughts as I executed several circuits of my room: past the small, spindly desk that held the only heirloom I thought valuable, a handsome inkstand and sandcaster, given me by my stepfather; past the spartan wooden chairs that called to mind the harsh accoutrements of my room at West Point; the bookshelves that buckled precariously under the weight of half-completed manuscripts; the narrow bed and porcelain wash-basin; and finally past the locked carpetbag that held my most treasured possessions, which now included a small, unlabeled bottle that I had rescued from Jarvis's room on the evening Barrow and I had searched it.

I sat at the foot of my bed and stared with apprehension at the carpetbag and the thing it contained. I thought back on my experiences with laudanum the nights of the fortune-telling sessions.

There had been no nexus, no centrality to my thoughts; yet the entire experience had been somehow curiously liberating and confirmatory; I recognized an artificial complement to the natural state of mind in which I often found myself.

The tincture of opium, undoubtedly a profound shock to many who employed it, had proven a welcome and recognizable extension of my own imagination. And the opium intoxication carried with it none of the nightmarish aspects of an alcoholic stupor.

It seemed, therefore, to initiate a benign, painless period of energetic reflection, provided one was in the proper surroundings to fully enjoy the experience (an extremely important proviso, to which the lamentable death of Jarvis bore witness!).

The soundlessness of the room was stifling.

The burdens beneath which I labored were overwhelming.

My pen and mind had become leaden, clogged with a troubled lethargy.

I had no glass but I found a teaspoon mother had left behind while clearing my afternoon coffee.

I estimated the teaspoon could comfortably contain over one hundred drops of whatever was put into it.

And presently, I began to dream, to imagine, to fear, to travel:

My cousin was deathly ill.

She had been consumed by fever since the night of our wedding. Our chamber, situated in the very heart of my ancestral home, had proven too hot for her. At first, we extinguished the nightly fires, but she still burned with an inexplicable sickness that could not be placated. The windows were then left open, despite the snow-storms that raged out-of-doors—but to no avail. Still, the debilitating fever reigned, and the efforts of the country's most skilled physicians to contain it proved fruitless, until they finally stopped coming altogether. She changed in color from alabaster to blood red. She would not eat cooked food, she would drink only ice water. Her weight diminished daily, until she was little more than a willowy ingot. Yet, from beneath the weight of the fever that now exerted immutable dominion over her once girlish, laughing personality, she was still able to summon love for me.

And it was out of this love that I relented and allowed my cousin to spend the nights, when the fever was always the most unendurable, in a cooler, damper part of the castle. As the anemic sun departed gratefully from the frozen, treeless landscape that surrounded our home, I and two servants, whose unrecognizable faces seemed to me different each day, carefully carried my beloved wife from her room of velvet, gold and porcelain to the soundless stone cavity whose frigidity offered her respite from the crippling fever.

Down cramped, spiraling staircases, whose rough-hewn stone walls still bore bloodstains from the wars that had for centuries afflicted my homeland, we transported my perspiring bride, in silent, mournful procession. After an interminable descent, the staircase at last gave out into a broad, torchlit expanse of room, at the center of which rested a great stone bier. The rest of this hideous bedchamber was featureless. The builders of the castle had been practical people who realized that the finer points of design would be lost on the eventual tenants of this room—the dead!

Each night seemed to me a funeral, each morning a resurrection, as I bore my cousin to the only room in the castle that was cold enough to combat the scalding fever that possessed her—my family mausoleum! On the immense stone slab, which had been intended as a temporary resting place for the recently deceased while awaiting final interment in the individual crypts, we nightly laid my wife, on a thick bed of blankets and quilts.

I saw to the immediate needs of her comfort, then dismissed the servants who gratefully retreated to the more hospitable upper reaches of the castle. We would then talk idly about sunnier climes, about friends and splendid picnics out-of-doors, about verdant pastures and horseback riding—the delightful aspects of a life we would never return to. Soon, a wisp of a smile would cross her face and I knew she had fallen asleep to the comforting presence of hopeful thoughts. I bundled my overcoat tighter against me and began the long ascent of the staircase, each night fearing that the morning would find her dead.

But what of my own life? What enterprises occupied me while my wife fought her battle with death? I had no position, no friends or acquaintances, our wedding had been attended only by servants and my wife's relations who hailed from a distant part of the country. The only human contact apart from my wife was with the various servants who tended my vast, crumbling estate. Yet, even they did not live with me, but resided in a squalid, obscure village located at some distance from my home. The view from the arched, iron-barred windows of my bedroom was bleak: Icy, serrated teeth of snow and rock perforated the otherwise gray, featureless horizon. Of human activity or habitation there was no sign. On occasion, I watched my servants arriving or returning home, but so winding and confusing was the road over which they traveled, it proved impossible to pinpoint the direction in which their village lay.

How had I come to live such a torpid, hermetic existence?

I did not know!

I knew that a series of ambiguous, dimly recalled events must have transpired, causing society to render a verdict against me. Or was it I who deemed society intolerable and unfit? I was unsure.

The result was the same. Men and their ways, their pleasures, businesses, differences of opinion, their arts, their work, their emotions, had become eternally estranged from me.

But there was one human quality—call it a failing if you will—that lingered in my soul and persisted in making its presence known despite my solitary existence—desire! I had attempted to banish it, plunging into numerous esoteric and bizarre researches in the extensive family library. But it, like the fever that had overcome my wife, rose unexpectedly and insistently from a nameless pit inside me and soon began to dominate my thinking.

While my wife nightly languished in a premature death chill, I slept fitfully in our broad, canopied bed, obsessed by her frail, finely proportioned form and the horrible fever that had made impossible the consummation of our marriage. Passion, never an overwhelming presence in my personality, now threatened, by its denial, to expunge all other considerations from my mind. I became nearly delirious with longing, quaking and shivering with lust. I threw my servants from the house after laying in a substantial store of provisions—I did not want to be observed in my sordid, compulsive state.

Eating became an act of passion. I consumed great quantities of food and drink: venison, pork, game, barrels of wine and ale. The weeks passed in agitated anticipation, and during my wife's waking hours, it grew nearly impossible for me to hide from her the extent of my sensual preoccupations.

I now carried her nightly to her subterranean bed myself—but so all-consuming was my physical craving that I took no notice of the considerable effort necessitated by the lengthy, downward climb and the exhausting return trip upstairs. A month went by, then two months. And my wife deteriorated; the fever seemed to have reached its peak intensity and now, as though it had a mind of its own, it concentrated on a steady, though unspectacular effort to burn her up. She wasted away slowly but inevitably, almost, it appeared, in a direct ratio to the passion that grew within me daily, tightening its salacious grip.

And then one night, I could endure it no longer!

It was in midwinter, a few days either side of the shortest day of the year, I can't recall which. The sun had made a brief, fitful appearance, then, like a suitor who gives up the pursuit of his beloved, had dejectedly disappeared from view. My food and drink supply had dwindled to the point that I had forced rationing upon myself; the roads to the village were closed by heavy snowfall, making further shopping impossible. The library was dark due to a candle shortage. With nothing to occupy my mind but thoughts of my beloved, I paced nervously through the cold, empty house.

At length, as the small hours of the morning drew on, my wanderings through the castle, which was as large and labyrinthine as many a small village, brought me to the foot of the stairs which led down to the mausoleum. A thin taper burned weakly in an iron holder just inside the doorway, casting a worried, baroque shadow on the steps. Unsure if I shivered from the cold, or with dread at what I knew was about to happen, I grasped the torch in one hand and began the slippery descent to the crypt.

At first, I took a step at a time, remorse and indecision combining to retard my downward progress. But ultimately, the picture I had formed in my mind of my beautiful cousin, lying vulnerable and chaste upon the ancestral bier, blotted out all moral impediments to the course of action I was bent upon.

But how to explain, how to justify this most despicable of perversions? My lengthy period of self-imposed isolation? The strain of living with a mortally stricken wife? No, there could be no exoneration. From the veiled, only dimly understood shadows of our psyches, strange and virulent obsessions emerge; motiveless, random and inexplicable, they strike!

And they are impossible to deny!

The mausoleum was, as usual, cold and gloomy. I noticed that two candles had burned themselves out during the day; with the supply line to town indefinitely cut, fresh tallow was unavailable, and I calculated it would only be a matter of days before my wife's bedchamber would be plunged into total darkness.

She lay as always, still and seemingly undisturbed, the fever temporarily held in abeyance. I approached her slowly and played the taper upon her quietly sleeping body. She had earlier tossed off the blankets, perhaps in the throes of a nightmare, and was now protected from the room's exceeding chilliness only by a thin, nearly translucent silken nightgown. Her femininity, slightly diminished by the fever's destructive advance, was outlined by the torch, vividly visible beneath the silk that clung tightly to her.

Leaning gently over her, I swept my hand lightly along her body, from the ankle, across the surface of her smooth, almost childlike leg which became a fuller, more womanly thigh, over the slightly rounded plumpness of her stomach, up to the tender lassitude of her breasts.

She remained motionless. She was still sound asleep, the merest trace of a smile gracing the gentle curve of her face. Encouraged, I replaced one of the expended candles with the taper I had brought with me and threw my overcoat onto the floor, offering some unexpected warmth to a rat that had scurried out of a fissure between two stones. With despicable care, I silently climbed onto the bier and lay down next to my cousin. For a moment I lay motionless, trying to still my heart. Then I began to examine her intimately, curiously and lovingly—but still, she did not stir. There was nary a flutter from her eyelids, nor the slightest, involuntary twitch of her lip, as I brushed her face with the softest of kisses. Her slight breasts did not heave or respond with alarm as I tasted their flesh through the silk; my lips followed the course already explored by my hand and I moved with the same curious combination of dread and fascination with which I had descended the stairs to the mausoleum.

There!

Had she moved, however slightly?

Was she dreaming of me even as I slid the nightgown up from her legs and folded it carefully at her stomach?

No, she still slept peacefully.

Perhaps it was just as well. For I now moved with a single-mindedness that was inalterable, driven by a passion too long sequestered in the confines of the mind. There seemed no longer anything perverse, or obsessive, about my actions. To an observer, the sight of a husband bending over his sickly wife with the intent of taking her, as she lay sleeping, the very life slipping out of her body even as she dreamt—the entire tableau lit by dim, dripping, nearly dying tapers—would have seemed indescribably ghastly, an enormous, painful thorn in the side of Nature herself.

But to me, even the morbid surroundings of the tomb could not dissuade me from knowing her fully. My own clothes disappeared quickly and fell to the cold floor.

I kissed her, grasped her, caressed her, my heart quickened as I sought to learn, to discover, to satiate this longing once and for all. She did not protest, she did not awaken, so profound was her sleep. Into the darkness of her body I vanished, now blinded by my surroundings, my movements accelerated and involuntary. I pushed against her breasts for support, but they yielded to me in their softness, and I grabbed the edges of the bier, scraping my hands on the stone's harsh surface. My wife shuddered spasmodically beneath me and I called her name loudly, but my voice only echoed uselessly. My rhythm achieved the speed and regularity of an athlete's heartbeat, and as I peered into my wife's cold, chalky face, vainly searching for a sign of recognition, I felt myself erupt and collapse simultaneously.

It was done.

I felt changed, damaged, both victim and victimizer.

But before I could further contemplate the consequences of what I had done, something so horrific, so grisly and so abrupt occurred that it rendered insignificant all that had preceded it!

My cousin, my wife, this dying tendril of womanhood, was seized by a sudden and uncontrollable fit and with a strength seemingly summoned from beyond the grave, sat bolt upright, pushing me easily aside. Her eyes, blind to the world, fixed me with a frozen stare.

She then collapsed roughly back onto the bed, her head falling at a sharp angle across her thin, pallid arm.

I ran in terror from the crypt, stumbling and falling against the rough stones as I fought my way back to the surface of the earth.

From my long, compulsive nights of poring through ancient medical and occult texts, I instantly recognized the awful significance of what I had just witnessed . . . the final, agonizing muscle spasm of a body that had been dead for several hours!

Nine

At dusk, on a narrow, infrequently traveled thread of road an hour outside of Richmond, our coach rushed beneath a gnarled archway of leafless branches. In this colorless, uninhabited part of the state, night did not fall from the heavens; rather it seemed to unroll itself across the countryside, like a heavy, smothering blanket that made one struggle for breath.

Virginia pressed closer to me, as though for sustenance, her face intermittently spotted with flashes of gray sky that sparked now and then through the dense forest that surrounded us. I smiled as cheerfully as possible, then fell again into contemplating the unremitting dreariness of the scenery through which we passed.

The first day of our honeymoon was drawing to a lethargic, almost oppressing close, following a ceremony and reception that had proven to be everything Virginia had hoped for. The wedding was a simple affair, flooded with flowers sent by out-of-town well-wishers and attended by our closest friends and acquaintances.

The downstairs parlor had been cleared of the usual clutter of furniture and elderly tenants who usually sat so still they might as well have been furniture. Wooden, uniform chairs from the dining room were brought in to accommodate the guests in three orderly rows facing the podium.

We were married by the Reverend Converse in a ceremony that was moving and elegant, devoid of the frothy and soporific prose wedding guests are so often forced to endure.

As I kissed Virginia and placed the wedding ring on her cold, pale twig of a finger, she seemed happier and prouder than I had imagined she could ever be. While she accepted the congratulations of our guests, she reserved for me a look of gratitude, love and deliverance—her long period of insecurity and uncertainty seemingly at an end.

Following a lengthy and surprisingly elaborate meal, punctuated by toasts that grew progressively more drunken and raucous as the afternoon wore on, my wife and I extricated ourselves from our high-spirited guests and climbed into a comfortable coach that had been retained for us through the largesse of mother and various friends.

As our driver snapped the reins on the two impatient horses with a disarming vehemence, my wife and I said our most difficult and strained good-byes—to mother. I'm sure that it was only out of her well-developed sense of pride and what is proper that she refrained from inviting herself along on our honeymoon.

Fortunately, our driver's insistence that we cover as much of our journey as possible before nightfall proved more successful than mother's considerable efforts to detain us, and we pulled into the boulevard on schedule.

We were southbound, heading for Petersburg, a small town about thirty miles from Richmond, where we intended to pass our two-week honeymoon on a secluded estate recently leased by Barrow Reece. Barrow was still traveling on assignment for his paper, and he assured us we could make full use of the house and the forested grounds. Using the house as a base, Virginia and I planned to pay courtesy calls on several journalist colleagues in the area whose acquaintance I had made through my work with the *Literary Messenger*.

Barrow's house lay a mile outside of Petersburg and we were to leave the driver in town, while we rode out to the estate alone, the coach remaining at our disposal for the duration of our honeymoon.

Perhaps it was the enclosing darkness, rendering the mind susceptible to suggestion, that caused me to speculate that evening upon the curious sympathy that exists between life and dreams. As I watched the contented, nearly dozing form of Virginia bob roughly with the irregular shudders of the coach, her beautiful, rounded visage seemed indistinguishable from the pallid death mask worn by the unearthly heroine of my opium dreams the night before. Had the laudanum acted on my abilities to perceive the illness that grew within my wife, sharpening my sensitivity to it? Or had the knowledge of Virginia's miserable condition, recently gleaned from mother, so impressed me that it invaded my subconscious, molding my dreams to conform with the truth?

Still more frightful to contemplate was the perverted course taken by the obsessed lover of my dreams. Did this hideous coupling of passion and death foreshadow the role physical love was to play in my own married life?

There were no immediate answers to the questions with which I wrestled. I saw only that my most recent opium experience had corroborated that which I had for many years accepted as unshakable fact: Truth resided neither exclusively in the conscious or unconscious worlds. But this elusive truth could be captured and momentarily illuminated only by the writer who was prepared to cross those borders of the imagination arbitrarily erected by the moribund tastes of our publishers and actively supported by an unadventurous reading public.

Dedicated to becoming just such a writer, I realized with stunning clarity that a crisis of imagination was currently brewing at the *Southern Literary Messenger*, brought on by the growing inflexibility of my employer, Mr. White. Following our honeymoon, I intended to plunge into the battle for editorial control of the *Mes-*

senger with renewed vigor and, if my efforts proved fruitless, to seek a more rewarding position elsewhere.

Barrow's house was smaller than I had expected, considering he had once described it to me as an "estate." It would be more accurate to characterize the abode as a country cottage—it was a squat, unpretentious building, surrounded by a thick, insulating pine forest. A small stone chimney rose from behind the cottage, dominating a sloping slate roof that was choked with moss and twisted vegetation.

A dilapidated wooden porch extended along the house's northern face and was decorated with wooden planters and flower boxes that were so stuffed with plant life they seemed to have taken root themselves.

The interior was spartan and functional, yet comfortable. The furniture was country craftsmanship: the chairs, bookcases, cabinetry and tables simply carved from local woods. A great oaken bed dominated the corner of the house farthest from the door and was piled high with blankets and quilts, obviously designed for warmth, not appearance.

"Well, I'm afraid, 'estate' is somewhat of a misnomer," I exclaimed once we had lit the numerous, strategically placed candles and had examined our temporary domicile. "But we shall be happy here, nonetheless."

"Oh, Buddie, it's perfect. There's even a desk for you to write at."

"Undoubtedly unused, if it belongs to Barrow," I snorted.

"Well, I think it's marvelous," Virginia persisted. "I don't want to see another rooming house, or a tottering, complaining old guest for two weeks."

"I trust you shall have your wish. We *are* rather isolated here. Why don't you explore a little further and I'll fetch the trunks."

Virginia turned her attention to making the bed and I went outside to stable the horses and carry in our luggage.

Standing in the clearing, inhaling the dominant odor of pine tinged with the evening dampness that was finally manifesting itself, I felt gratefully cut off from society. Our little cottage seemed an island of tranquility in an inhospitable world, a light-filled retreat to which we could return each night. Though I knew the legitimization of our marriage would not prove a complete solution to the problems we faced, I did look forward to a sequestered fortnight, free from the complicated and virulent events in which I had recently become involved.

It was to be our first night alone together.

As children we had passed many a night in the same room, when I, as a guest, was given the extra bed that stood in the room occupied by my youthful cousin.

Later, as man and wife, our deception had necessitated separate bedrooms. But now, that need had dissolved along with the need for public dissemblance.

Virginia had systematically extinguished each of the candles in the house with a gentle, frolicsome breath, until only two remained lit—one which rested in a scratched pewter holder on a nightstand next to the bed, and a second which burned fitfully on Barrow's desk where I was engaged in making some hurried notes on my current treatise. She lay now in bed, blankets and comforters stacked mountainously upon her timid physique, anticipating her impending participation in the ritual others referred to in polite, hushed conversation only as: "the wedding night."

"Buddie," she prodded, "put that business away and come here."

I could not rightfully delay. Convention dictated my course of action. The terms of the marriage contract, adhered to by many couples with grateful, oft-postponed abandon, demanded fulfillment.

I blew out the candle on the desk and walked hesitantly over to sit on the edge of the bed.

"Do you usually sleep in your coat?" demanded Virginia.

"I'd like to talk over a few things first."

"We can talk all night if you wish. But won't you please come to bed first?" she implored.

How could I ignore her childlike supplications? I removed my overcoat and hung it next to my hat, exposed for the first time to the unseasonable chill that permeated the cabin. I changed quickly into my nightshirt as Virginia gazed at my momentarily exposed nakedness without the slightest indication that she was shocked or in any way surprised by the sight. Involuntarily holding my breath, as though I were a sailor about to abandon a ship, I dove beneath the voluminous covers into the cavern of warmth and security Virginia had created in the bed.

"Well, what is it that's so important, Buddie? I'm awfully sleepy."

I fussed with the pillows for a silent moment. The words were proving as difficult to pull out as a broken cork from a bottle of brandy.

I cleared my throat: "Now that we are married . . ."

"Now that we are finally married, the worst of our problems are behind us."

"I certainly hope they are."

"Oh, I'm not half as naïve as you must think. I know that we shall always have difficulties."

"But there is something very important that's weighing heavily on my mind, Virginia. It is a problem that comes with marriage; marriage does not eliminate it."

She shut her eyes and smiled sleepily. "I can't imagine what you are talking about."

She yawned vigorously and shifted her position so that for the first time I could feel the entire length of her body as it conformed to mine. I recoiled involuntarily as her nearly frozen toes brushed my ankles.

"My God, your feet are like icicles."

"They are always cold. I have such poor circulation. I could wear stockings, but a friend of mine told me that she heard a husband doesn't like it when his wife wears stockings—especially on their wedding night."

"Oh, where did your friend learn this?"

"From her older sister. She's married."

"What else did this friend tell you about the wedding night? And a man's tastes?"

"That was all. I wasn't very interested in the subject then."

"And how long ago was that?"

"A year ago. Before we were married for the first time. She was only ten."

"Are you interested in the subject now?"

"Of course . . . I have to be."

I paused, before asking my most important question, assessing the curious nature of our relationship. We were both enormously comfortable in each other's presence, we were both deriving pleasure from the proximity of our bodies as well as our hearts. The difference in our ages, especially Virginia's youth, scandalous to the unknowledgeable observer, did not appear to figure at all in our feelings for one another. Yet passion and desire, such strong emotions in my thoughts and dreams, were curiously absent that first night in the marriage bed. It was as though Virginia herself were a purifying agent. For the moment, I felt as innocent and as virginal as she.

"I know you often discussed marriage with your friends. But did mother ever talk seriously to you about it?" I asked.

"Well, of course! What a question. We talked about nothing else day and night."

"I mean, in a more specific sense . . ."

"Buddie, whatever is on your mind?"

"I was wondering if she ever told you, for example, what it would be like once we were sleeping together, as true man and wife?"

Virginia stared at me earnestly, trying to fathom the motives for my questions.

"She said we would be unbelievably happy."

"That's all?"

"What do you mean 'that's all.' That's everything, isn't it?"

"Well, yes, of course that's everything. But . . ."

"Then turn out the light and let's sleep. You're not making a bit of sense."

"It has been quite a day."

"I fear it has been too much for you. I'm glad this is the last of our weddings. I doubt you could stand the strain of a third." She laughed. She blew out the candle and buried her head in my shoulder. A moment passed, then Virginia quivered slightly as her muscles relaxed, and I knew my wife was asleep.

Our situation was unbelievable.

Virginia apparently knew nothing of the physical nature of marriage. Had mother deliberately neglected her education to such an extent? If so, what possible reason could she have had? What could be behind such an obsessive desire to preserve her daughter's virginity so long, even longer than society deemed healthy or normal? Virginia was no more prepared to assume the role of a wife than was a five-year-old child!

Yet, I was undeniably relieved.

She expected nothing more from our relationship than I felt prepared to give. In one fleeting moment of candor, the terrors of consummation had been set aside. Virginia could remain pure and unspoiled. I could not be held accountable for my failure to fulfill desires she did not even possess. Until I could exorcise my tendency towards dissolution, the danger that it would flow from me into her during the act of love was temporarily held in abeyance.

I fell peacefully asleep on that, the first night of our official married life, satisfied that a delicate and potentially dangerous situation had been avoided.

The first week of our honeymoon passed enjoyably. We spent our time cooking together, reading and writing, going for lengthy, silent walks through the neighboring forests and calling on various colleagues who ranged in character from the ingenious to the deadly dull.

On the evening of our second Saturday at the cottage, Virginia and I were drinking our after-dinner coffee, cutting the pages of Barrow's unread copy of *Pickwick Papers*, the first novel by the English writer Charles Dickens, when we heard the rattle of galloping hoofbeats approaching the house.

"Ah, our first visitor," I observed, rising from my chair and going to the window. I drew back the curtains in time to see a caped and top-hatted figure hurriedly dismount, tie his horse to the porch railing and anxiously approach the door. I had barely time to walk to the door myself with the intention of admitting our nocturnal guest, when he burst in, loudly and unceremoniously.

A startled Virginia dropped her coffee cup to the floor, shattering it and in the process spilling a sizable amount of the hearty liquid on her dress.

"My apologies, madame, if I frightened you. But I was in something of a hurry, and I am accustomed to entering my own house without knocking."

"Barrow!" I exclaimed. "Whatever brings you back here in such a state? . . . not that it's not good to see you again."

The journalist removed his stovepipe and carelessly attempted to straighten his hair, tousled from the wind.

"How's the coffee, then, Edgar? I could use a cup," he panted.

"It's a bit weaker than the sewage you usually brew, but it's warm. Have you met my wife, Virginia?"

"It's an honor, Mrs. Poe. And congratulations on your marriage. Edgar speaks of you constantly. As a matter of fact, his devotion to you makes him somewhat of a bore in men's society."

Barrow bowed gracefully and shook Virginia's hand with the utmost delicacy.

"It's always a pleasure to meet one of Edgar's esteemed colleagues. And it's very generous of you to let us stay in your house. It's been a wonderful week."

"Oh, it's not over yet, let me assure you," Barrow qualified, as he took the cup of coffee I poured for him and sat gratefully down on one of the straight-back chairs at the kitchen table.

"I've merely returned to fetch some important papers. I'll be out of your hair before you know it."

"Nonsense," Virginia replied. "You stay as long as you wish. This is, after all, your house."

"And this is, after all, your honeymoon." Barrow gave me a lecherous wink. "No, I'll be on my way shortly. But I would like to discuss some business matters with your husband, if you don't mind my monopolizing him for a few minutes."

"Of course. If you gentlemen have business to discuss, I'll close my ears."

I could tell from the gravity of Barrow's expression that it would be for the best if Virginia were not to overhear our conversation. He seemed troubled, his movements nervous. His demeanor was one of deadly serious concern, a concern I had never seen him bring to bear on so mundane a matter as business.

"That won't be necessary, darling. We'll go out for a stroll. The exercise will do me good."

"As you wish. I'll continue my page cutting. This Mr. Dickens certainly keeps one's hands busy."

I donned my overcoat and joined Barrow in the cold, moonless night, the filmy cloud-covering blotting out all but the brightest stars.

We set out on a slow circumnavigation of the clearing, as I pressed Barrow to explain the conditions of his unexpected visit. We paced in silence for a minute, then Barrow turned to face me.

"Did you read last Wednesday's *Argus?*" he asked.

"Why, no. We've been cut off from the march of progress— purposefully, I must admit, since our arrival here last Friday." I did not add that it was never my habit to read the *Argus*.

"It's just as well. In any event, that issue carried a rather lengthy article, or exposé, if you will, written by me. The next day, I noticed I was being followed."

"Followed?"

" 'Observed' might be more to the point. By someone in a black hackney drawn by a chestnut gelding. But the deuce of it is, Edgar, I can never get a clear look at who's inside."

"Coincidence . . . imagination."

"I wish it were so. But whoever is responsible makes no effort to avoid being seen by me. Only when I approach the hackney does it pull away so that the identity of its passenger remains a mystery."

"What do you make of it?"

"I'm convinced it's part of a plan to unnerve me, to dissuade me from publishing any further such articles."

"You had better tell me what it is you're involved in, Barrow."

"I'm afraid you're involved in it as deeply as I, Edgar. That's why I've come. It has to do with the L'Espanayes!"

We sat down on the damp stump of a tree, charred from a bolt of lightning that had recently struck it, and I anxiously begged Barrow to proceed with his story.

"This all begins with the death of Jarvis. I was affected by it more than you can imagine," he began, "especially considering the low opinion I know you have of me."

I attempted to refute Barrow's assertion, but he waved my objections aside.

"Please don't deny it, Edgar. I'm not hurt. As a matter of fact, I tend to agree with you. I do have a reputation for callousness, if you will. But my strongest feelings after Jarvis's death were those of guilt—guilt and the desire for atonement. . . . Do you remember the night of our first fortune-telling session? Well, this is very difficult for me to admit, but madame learned that many of my articles were plagiarized."

I nodded meekly, feigning ignorance.

"My conscience was slowly getting the better of me. I determined to mend my ways, and for that reason, I could not leave the paper, as much as I hated it. From that point on, I vowed to make up for a less-than-illustrious past, first by using my paper as an instrument of justice to apprehend the malefactor responsible for the manservant's death. And in so doing, publish an original series of articles of which I could be justly proud."

"Highly admirable."

"As you will remember, our search of Jarvis's room yielded nothing noteworthy."

I considered the bottle of laudanum, of the discovery of which Barrow knew nothing, then motioned for him to continue.

"Consumed as I was by this ambition, I did not conclude my investigation then and there. My wish to leave that poor woman who occupied the L'Espanayes' rooms in peace prevented me from questioning her any further. I had by that time formed the opinion that our two Frenchwomen were extremely secretive, and I highly doubted whether I could uncover anything substantial in their rooms. That led me back to Jarvis, and that night I returned to his room.

"My second search of his meager abode proved more fruitful. I discovered, secreted within a primitively hollowed-out windowsill, a key. As it did not fit any of the locks in the building, I assumed it to be the key to a trunk or some similar possession. Finding nothing of this description in his room, I headed for the basement —where my efforts were finally rewarded. I discovered in a corner, buried beneath the motley possessions of the building's tenants, a small trunk which the key easily opened."

Barrow paused in his story. The drama of the narrative was not lost on me, and as he noticed my reaction, he continued with a heightened sense of the melodramatic.

"Contained in the footlocker was an apparently random collection of papers, documents, newspaper cuttings and hand-scribbled notes, most of which were in French. I quickly realized they were not Jarvis's, but the property of the L'Espanayes!"

"Jarvis was a thief?" I exclaimed, mystified. "That's not at all in keeping with the character of the poor man we knew."

"But it is in keeping with his miserable station in life, my dear Edgar. A poverty-stricken alcoholic, living from hand to mouth, employable only by those like the L'Espanayes, who for one reason or another wish to avoid the traditional sources of domestic help in Richmond. In short, a desperate man! My thinking is that, by purloining the odd document, Jarvis felt he could eventually accumulate evidence against the women's customers, who were often drawn from Virginia's upper and influential classes. It would certainly do such men no good to be thought of as dupes in the hands of foreign charlatans, not to mention prostitutes."

"A blackmailer, then. But one for whom I can feel nothing but pity," I said.

"A potential blackmailer," Barrow reminded me. "We have no evidence that he actually put into use his secret cache of documents. . . ."

"Come, come, let's have it. What did they say, for God's sake?"

"The material in English was inconsequential: bills, correspondence with merchants and creditors, what have you. Obviously Jarvis was not bilingual, and I suspect he had not yet translated the other papers. Of course, I did."

"And?"

"And what we have are French newspaper accounts of the escapades of one Mario de la Costa, a notorious Corsican bandit who, it seems, recently escaped from prison."

"Corsica again!"

"Exactly! Banditry and violence are a way of life for the Corsican hill people. Entire families, even generations, are involved in long and widespread feuds which usually result in bloodshed. For centuries they have resisted change, whether ruled by Britain, Genoa or France. Periodically, the French government dispatches squadrons of soldiers or police to deal with these devils, in their feeble and certainly deluded attempts to demonstrate control over the island. This de la Costa was captured during one such foray, several years ago. Quite a battle took place and he managed single-handedly to kill several soldiers before he was ultimately subdued."

"A very colorful story, but its relevance to us is still not apparent."

"It will be. Captured along with de la Costa were a mother and her three-year-old daughter, who had been abducted from their mountain village by the bandit more than a year earlier!"

I sat for a moment in stunned silence. Madame L'Espanaye and her daughter had been kidnap victims? A most intriguing and unexpected twist. The picture, no matter how bizarre, was now a good deal clearer.

"Perhaps the shame and scandal that resulted from their year spent with the bandit made life so unendurable in their community that they were forced to flee to America," I suggested. "It would be the same in the backwoods townships of Virginia. Gossip is malicious the world over."

"That is one theory, to be sure," replied Barrow enigmatically. "However, the fact that Madame L'Espanaye was so diligent in her collection of news stories concerning de la Costa, and the fact that according to the papers, she spent more than a year in the bandit's custody without once attempting to escape, speaks to me of something else."

"She must have fallen in love with the fellow!" I deduced.

"Precisely! In my article I claimed that this de la Costa had arrived in Richmond, perhaps due to a rather obvious trail left by Madame L'Espanaye, and was involved in Jarvis's death."

"Why, she may have even had a hand in his prison break," I added. "Some paid accessory on the inside. But what of our dedicated Inspector Contadina?"

I did not fully expect to have my inquiry answered. Thus far, Barrow had been most impressive to me. I found myself growing jealous of the bold and perceptive moves he had made towards the solution of this mystery. He was more or less putting into physical practice those powers of deduction of which I was at the moment merely writing. But he must eventually reach an impasse, and I calculated that the trail of evidence he had followed was now at an end.

"According to a newspaper printed in the Corsican capital of Ajaccio, and dated only days after de la Costa's capture, the leader of the police assigned to apprehend the bandits was one Inspector Lucchino Contadina!"

I was now armed with enough facts to draw some logical conclusions, and I moved happily from the role of listener to that of theorizer.

"Inspector Contadina has, of course, been sent to recapture the escaped Mario de la Costa, hoping the two women will lead the way," I began. "De la Costa and Madame L'Espanaye had most likely agreed on a date and a place for a rendezvous, but the good inspector's arrival has made that an impossibility. Somehow, madame learned of Contadina's presence, and vacated her rooms. And, this brute, de la Costa, in order to find them, questioned our poor Mr. Jarvis by plying him with laudanum, unmindful of the consequences. It stands to reason that a man who would kidnap a woman would not be above murder to reclaim her!"

Barrow stared at me intently, as though he were waiting for me to reach an obvious conclusion. Not wishing to be outdone, I continued at a stammer.

"Then . . . your follower, or observer as you put it . . . is more than likely de la Costa."

Barrow slapped his thigh vigorously and jumped to his feet.

"Ah ha, Edgar, I knew you'd fall into that trap! But does Mario de la Costa read English? How would he know of my article naming him as a suspect in the death of Jarvis? No, no, my dear boy," gloated Barrow. "I'm afraid we must look elsewhere. Who knows I am employed by the *Argus*, for example? Who would be able to recognize me on the street? And, most importantly, who would stand to profit from my decision to abandon my investigation?"

Barrow paced about the darkened clearing, stretching his tired limbs while he awaited my rebuttal.

But I had none. My mind raced, searching in vain for evidence that would divert Barrow's suspicions from Madame L'Espanaye. His logic was alarming in its implication, but for the time being, nearly incontrovertible.

Madame L'Espanaye was in love with a killer; and she now appeared willing to take extreme measures to ensure that he remained free!

Ten

We returned indoors to join Virginia, where the three of us spent the remainder of the evening in idle discussion. We prepared a hot meal for Barrow and he was prevailed upon by Virginia to pass the night with us. An improvised bed was made for him by pushing two chairs together and he soon took advantage of it, falling asleep in his clothes before we had finished washing the dinner dishes.

"Buddie?" asked Virginia as we prepared ourselves for bed. "Mr. Reece seems awfully worried. Don't you think you might ask what's troubling him? Maybe there's something we can do."

"It's nothing so very important. We've already discussed it. It's a business matter of some urgency, that's all," I replied.

"But you always told me business has no effect on him," she protested. "And when he arrived, he seemed positively unnerved."

"Well, I certainly can't answer for him. He explained to us that he returned to fetch some documents."

"But if they were so important to him, why did he not immediately look for them? Since his arrival, he has been content merely to eat, gossip and sleep, with never a thought to those important old papers of his."

I kissed Virginia, attempting to dissuade her from this line of questioning.

"Darling, I think I shall call on you to compose a chapter in my essay on deductive police work."

"Buddie, I'm serious and all you can do is chide me. I'm worried about your friend, that's all, and I can't understand why you're not similarly concerned!"

"If he needs my assistance, I'm quite sure he will ask for it. Now, I think that's all the discussion the matter merits." My voice rose to an uncharacteristically authoritative level, as I climbed into bed next to Virginia and blew out the candle.

As she crept closer to me in the darkness, I felt that I had settled the question. I embraced her and held her to my chest, once again thoroughly ashamed of my lies.

"Buddie," she whispered, a few moments after I had thought her to be asleep.

"What?"

"Buddie, tomorrow I'm going to ask Mr. Reece to tell me what's bothering him. Sometimes a woman is more successful in getting a man to say what's on his mind."

"He won't tell you anything! . . . nothing of interest, at any rate. I can't understand why you're being so insistent about this rather mundane affair. It's certainly not like you."

"Because I feel that for the first time you're not being honest with me. And that's not like *you!*"

Her words stung me. It was quite sad and quite true that I was not completely honest with her. But what I found even sadder was that it was not the first time, as she imagined.

I visited the parlor of Camille and Madame L'Espanaye in one of my many dreams that night. I lay on the familiar velvet couch and drank heartily from the laudanum Camille offered me. Madame began her incisive, provocative questioning, probing my feelings about deceit and infidelity, as though seeking to unmask me as she had Barrow.

Her hands explored my face, searching out the variations in temperature she hoped would indicate a source of deep-rooted guilt. But I was conscious only of heat—of burning, searing spasms that rippled through my body, as though it had been struck by lightning. There was not a limb unaffected, nor an organ that did not scream with pain, begging to be released from the body that encased them.

But it had not been so unbearably hot before!

There had been relief, isolated cool spots. Never had my eyelids burned red into white—it was as though my eyes were wide open, and I was staring stupidly at the midday sun through a telescope.

But I touched them, at the risk of burning my hands, and found they were clamped tightly shut.

And last time there had not been screams of terror, certainly not those I recognized as Virginia's.

And last time there had not been smoke!

I awoke violently from my dream to find the heat was not imaginary. Virginia, sweating profusely, her face contorted in fear, was shaking me awake.

"Buddie, we're on fire, we're on fire!" she screamed.

I looked hastily around the cabin. It was colored magenta and orange by flames that feasted on the dry wood of the cottage's exterior. Through both the front and the back windows, the view was equally horrific—the cabin was surrounded by fire!

I jumped from the bed and ran to rouse the slumbering Barrow. I shook him violently, yelling into his ear. He eventually rolled grumbling to the floor, where the shock of his fall jolted him instantly to his senses. He surveyed our perilous situation in a matter of seconds, then jumped to his feet.

"Good Lord. It's all around us. Have you tried the door, Edgar?"

"It's useless," I yelled, the noise of the fire matching the heat in its awesome intensity. "If you open anything, you'll admit the fire!"

"Buddie, is it the forest that's on fire or just the cabin?" asked Virginia. Her question made perfect, deadly sense. If it was only the cabin that was ablaze, an escape route could perhaps be worked out. But if we were at the center of a forest fire, then our prospects for survival seemed dim indeed.

"There's no way of knowing. We can only pray it's just the cabin that's affected," I replied, pressing my terrified, quivering wife to my bosom. My own heart beat vehemently in a terror that was every bit as profound as Virginia's, and I doubted that I comforted her much by the gesture.

Barrow was frantically stalking the room, deep in thought, shedding his clothing piece by piece. The heat had become nearly unendurable and Virginia collapsed to the floor. I rushed to the porcelain water basin and emptied its contents on her face, without effect. Her face was as hot as the walls themselves.

"Is there no way out of here, Barrow? A basement, perhaps?"

"Not that I know of," he responded, "but it's certainly worth a search!"

Without hesitation, we tossed furniture and rugs carelessly aside, looking desperately for the slightest sign of a trap door in the floor that might lead to a cellar whence escape could be effected. As we worked, I kept one eye trained on the window, watching the upward progress of the insatiable flames. Where before, slight glimpses of the darkened sky could be discerned through the crimson, there was now just fire and more fire, a solid, impregnable barrier.

We found nothing to bolster our rapidly fading hopes. Numbed by the heat almost to the point of pain, our searching became agonizingly slow, labored and hopeless. Virginia had not spoken, or even moved for several minutes, though her heaving breast told me she still breathed. As Barrow and I crawled from corner to corner, examining every last crack in the floorboards with demented perfectionism, burning shards of the cabin wall began to splinter and fall to the floor, where we stamped them out as well as we could.

The walls were too hot to lean against, so we lay lengthwise on the floor, attempting to extract from it the relatively cooler relief its surface offered. My thoughts were disparate and unfocused. I suspected I was going to die, but there came no revelatory review of my life.

I glanced over at Barrow who was attempting to speak to me.

"Edgar," came his hoarse, exhausted call. "There's a weak . . . spot . . . the ceiling . . . I started to repair it after the rains . . . didn't finish . . . we can break through."

Somehow we struggled to our feet, although it seemed to require a tremendous effort, our bodies hardly responding to our commands.

Together, we pushed the kitchen table across the floor, disregarding the burning pieces of wall that fell to our feet with increasing regularity, to a spot directly in front of the chimney in the back corner of the house. Barrow and I then wrested a substantial length of shelving from the wall and while he used it as a battering ram to puncture the ceiling, I recrossed the burning floor to retrieve Virginia.

I picked her up with surprising ease—she seemed to have shed all her weight—and carried her back to where Barrow worked in muted agony. As he chipped away at the ceiling, my fears that the roof was also aflame were dispelled. As chunks of sod and freshly milled wood fell onto our upturned faces, renewed strength and willpower flooded my body.

The hole was now broad enough to admit light, and despite the intensity of the fire, I thought I detected a star sparkle momentarily through the gap in the ceiling, before it was filled with Barrow's body. Using the individual stones that comprised the fireplace as footholds, he inched his way up the wall, until, by supporting himself with two arms on the outside surface of the roof, he vaulted completely through the hole and onto the roof itself.

"Hand Virginia up next and hurry, man! The flames are already to the edge of the roof," Barrow screamed down to me, his voice scarcely audible above the hellish roar of the fire.

I climbed onto the table and, mustering whatever strength remained, I handed Virginia up to Barrow, as one would hand a sack of flour to a granary worker, her flesh boiling and her delicate, silken nightgown saturated with sweat.

He grasped her by the hands and pulled her up foot by foot, while I pushed as well as I could from beneath. She finally disappeared through the hole entirely, and I hurried to effect my own escape.

The stones of the fireplace were by now virtual roasting coals, and the skin of my hands and feet hissed, blackened and tore away, much of it sticking to the brickwork. But the pain only served to hurry me, and with a final exhortation to my reserves of stamina and determination, I too pulled myself through the hole to the comparative freedom of the roof.

At first glance, the situation outside was hardly reassuring.

The flames on all four sides of the cottage had surmounted the eaves of the roof and now reached to eye level. To gain complete safety, I saw we should all be called upon to leap through the flames to the ground twenty feet below!

But Fate held one shred of fortune in her hand for us. The fire extended only a few feet from the cottage—the clearing surrounding the house and the forest itself were untouched. If we survived our jump, we would be saved.

It was a fantastic and unforgettable scene; I cradled the unconscious Virginia in my arms, as the flames enclosed us in a fiery rectangle. The noise, as of a dam bursting, contrasted sharply with the serene, demi-sphere of the heavens which formed a natural lid to the cauldron in which we were trapped.

"Come on, Edgar. It's now or never," said Barrow, rousing me from my reverie. I stood, supporting Virginia, whose eyes momentarily opened, observed but did not appear to register the horror of the scene, then closed again.

"I was doing some gardening out back—the ground will be the softest there," explained Barrow. I nodded and carried Virginia to the rear of the house, where, without further ado, Barrow wrapped his arms tightly about his body and, taking a running start, hurtled through the flames and disappeared into the darkness.

I could not see past the fire to his landing spot, so it was impossible to know if his leap had been successful. I lifted Virginia, more weighty now, slightly off the roof and held her to me as tightly as my dwindling strength would allow. Shutting my eyes, which burned fiercely nonetheless, I ran as fast as the burden I was carrying would permit and leapt through the flames out into space.

I immediately opened my eyes and, for the brief second I was in flight, I could see the dark plateau of the ground rushing up to meet me. I was shocked, then immensely relieved to see Virginia tumble free of my grip and fall into the waiting arms of Barrow who had strategically placed himself so as to break her fall as much as possible. Nevertheless, the weight of a falling body, no matter how slight or frail, is still considerable and he was pushed brutally onto his back, striking the dirt with a breath-shattering jolt.

Virginia, aroused by her sudden flight through the night air, was uninjured, and she fell tearfully into my arms. Barrow, short of breath, slightly bruised, but wonderfully alive, smiled knowingly at me. The three of us retreated deeper into the coolness of the woods, where we then turned our attention to the little cabin which was now hopelessly lost to the fire.

"Is there nothing we can do to stop it?" I asked.

"Not a thing," replied Barrow. "It looks as if it'll burn itself out by morning."

"And all your possessions, your documents?" asked Virginia.

"All of my valuable papers are in my Richmond rooms. There was nothing really important . . ." Barrow caught himself in his own lie and turned away from Virginia to survey the flaming wreckage of his cottage. She ignored his slip of the tongue, and became the picture of well-intended concern.

"I shall never be able to repay you for helping Buddie save my life," said Virginia. "I'm afraid I was little help to you."

"It's payment enough that we are all still alive," observed Barrow ruefully. Following this matter-of-fact statement, our rescuer collapsed in a pile of leaves and, burying his head in his arms, fell into a well-deserved sleep of exhaustion. Virginia and I soon followed suit, carving for ourselves in the cool leaves a comfortable niche in which to pass the night. We fell asleep almost immediately, lulled by the steady hissing of the burning cabin—nothing more than a comforting campfire, now that it no longer posed a threat to our lives.

We awoke towards midmorning and our glances fell immediately on the cabin. Nothing was intact save the chimney which was stained by soot a deep gray. The remainder of the tiny wood-framed building was an unrecognizable morass of blackened spars and splinters, tossed together seemingly at random.

As we dejectedly approached the charred remains of the cottage, I stopped abruptly, distracted by a curious sight amid the rubble. I bent down and, sifting through a pile of ashes, uncovered a round, yellow object buried in the ground.

"Hello!" I yelled. "What's this?" Virginia and Barrow hurried over, bending down to discover the source of my consternation.

"What is it, Buddie?"

"Don't tell me you have found something spared by the fire?"

"I'm afraid so. Spared by the fire because it started the fire!"

Virginia and Barrow exchanged curious glances.

I halted their questions abruptly and, pocketing the small object, set out on a laborious examination of the perimeter of the cabin, bending over from time to time to examine the ground. They followed my course with exasperation, as each time I bent over, I muttered to myself, rooted in the ground like an animal searching for a buried bone, placed an object in my shirt pocket, then continued my stooped investigation.

At last tired of gazing over my shoulder as I worked, they collapsed on the ground at the edge of the clearing in frustration.

"When you are through going mad, Edgar, kindly tell us, then we can think about heading back to the town," called Barrow. I merely smiled cryptically and continued to fill my pockets.

Satisfied that I had pressed my investigation as far as possible, I joined Virginia and Barrow.

"What have you found, Buddie? You're not being very fair!"

"Yes, Edgar, enough of this dramatic dissembling. Let's have out with it, man."

I sighed, feigning failure.

"It was nothing, after all. I thought I had discovered a clue as to the origin of the fire, but unfortunately I was mistaken."

"Well, it's a mystery to me. There was no thunder or lightning at all last night," observed Virginia. She grew quietly contemplative and I stood and ambled over to the narrow driveway which led to the main road. As I had expected, an inquisitive Barrow soon joined me.

"What is it, man? I know you've found something. I won't say a word to Virginia."

"All right, all right. I just didn't want to arouse any undue suspicion until I was sure of what I had discovered."

"And are you sure now?" he asked.

"Without question."

"And your conclusion?" asked Barrow again, still skeptical.

"The fire was deliberately set!"

Total silence greeted my declaration, but rather than staring at me in stupefaction as I had expected, Barrow gave me a melancholy nod of understanding.

"The evidence supports my theory." I withdrew some of the contents of my pockets and handed them to Barrow: three round, uniform candles which had all burned down to stubs an inch or two high. Barrow examined the candles with bewilderment that soon gave way to rage and then, I thought, to a faint trace of recognition.

"And there are a score or more of them still in my pockets. They were most likely treated with kerosene or some similar substance to enhance their combustibility. I found them buried in the ground, equidistant from one another around the entire cottage, at points that were just beneath what used to be the edge of the floor. It would seem the arsonist arrived under cover of darkness and set his trap while we were asleep."

Barrow held the candles in his hand and paced about the clearing, seething with a private rage, his face taut and immobile.

"Now, Barrow, I believe it is *your* turn to supply *me* with some sort of explanation. I saw the look on your face when I took out the candles. You recognized them from somewhere."

He did not reply, but remained fixed in his stance.

"Barrow, an attempt has been made on our lives, for God's sake. I demand to know about those damned candles!" I raised my voice as much as I deemed advisable, glancing over my shoulder to assure myself that Virginia could not overhear our conversation.

"Barrow!"

He turned abruptly to face me, his eyes as hot and dangerous as the fire that had consumed his house.

"They're altar candles," he shouted. "And one of the most common forms of revenge and murder in the villages of Corsica is the setting of fires with altar candles!"

Eleven

I occupied a comfortable chair, I had a cup of tea in my hand and a freshly brewed pot lay within easy reach, as I settled back in the familiar environment of Barrow Reece's *Virginia Argus* office, so that we might plan our next move.

The morning after the fire, Barrow, Virginia and I had found our frightened team of horses grazing in a nearby meadow and, tying them and Barrow's own horse to our coach, had made our way into Petersburg. Virginia and I, still in our nightclothes, warmed ourselves by the fire in the Petersburg Inn, while Barrow went in search of more suitable attire. From there we relied on public transportation to return to Richmond. Virginia had naturally been told nothing of our suspicions concerning arson and had gratefully returned to Mrs. Yarrington's, disappointed, as I was, that our honeymoon had been so violently abbreviated, but thankful we had both survived the ordeal.

Mother took the news stoically, exercising her considerable strength and temperance to ensure that neither Virginia nor I brooded too long on our narrow escape. My wife soon enough put the episode behind her and began her tentative entrance into the genteel society of Richmond's married ladies, although she still reserved the better portion of the afternoon for play with her ever-widening circle of young friends. It amused me to imagine the collective eyebrow raising that must have greeted Virginia's announcement, "Excuse me, ladies of the Historical Society, but I am expected at the swings."

I resumed work at the *Messenger*, met by the hearty congratulations of employer and colleagues. Tuesday, my second full day at work, I arranged to leave midway through the afternoon so that I might keep my appointment with Barrow. And now we were sequestered in his office, with orders passed throughout the building to leave us undisturbed.

I first read the text of the article which we believed had resulted in the fiery murder attempt. It named Mario de la Costa as a suspect in the death of Jarvis and summarized the background of the "affaire L'Espanaye," as Barrow had begun calling it.

"Barrow, I know that you understand my position in all of this. Aren't you afraid that your public police work might cause the authorities to reopen their investigation? I can't be connected with Madame L'Espanaye, either publicly or privately."

"The day the Richmond police admit they've been less than thorough, I'll retire in wealth to the country. They think I'm a harmless crackpot, Edgar. I've offered them information before— on countless cases—and they want nothing to do with me. It's my investigation, and mine alone. And don't worry, your name will never grace these pages unless it's beneath a stanza of poetry."

Somewhat reassured, I asked Barrow how he intended to follow up his first article.

"I'm going to refrain from publishing anything until I've got something shocking and revealing—something that will really make my audience sit up and take notice. In the meantime I'm going to press the search for our Corsican fortune-tellers. I'm convinced they're the key to this entire puzzle."

He slapped his open hand on his desk to press his point.

"I've got a reputation to revive and a newspaper to put on the map. I'm clever, resourceful and hardworking. But I'm a plodder. I need your intellect, Edgar. Are you with me, or not?"

"Very well, very well. My intellect is at your disposal. Provided said intellect can be exercised here in your office. I'm as anxious as you to see the killer of poor old Jarvis brought to justice, not to mention whoever nearly ended our lives in that fire. But I am equally anxious to return to the care of my family and the further-ance of my career."

"Understood. What *are* your views on the fire, by the way?"

"I presume you recall the great profusion of small candles which decorated the rooms of Madame L'Espanaye?"

"Naturally. I was never there a night when they were not lit in great abundance. And whenever one burnt out, it was immediately replaced from a seemingly endless supply."

"Then we know it was not a problem for the women to obtain the weapons on short notice . . . *if* murder was on their minds. Do you recall mentioning to them the location of your forest . . . estate?"

"I do not recall *not* mentioning it. That is, it would be impossible to remember every subject I touched on in the many hours I spent in their company. As you know, I was often unconscious of what I was saying."

"Well, then, I suppose one could make a case for the women's involvement in the fire . . . though for my part, I can't imagine it!"

"I took the opportunity of making a few inquiries in Petersburg, when I went in search of clothing for us, Edgar. More than one person recalled noticing a black hackney drawn by a chestnut geld-ing the night of the fire. The evidence mounts rather steadily, does it not?"

"I would hesitate to term it evidence, Barrow. We have certain logical suspicions, but they are sorely in need of substantiation."

"Come, come, Edgar," chastised the indignant journalist. "You can't see the nose in front of your face. You're smitten with the L'Espanaye women, and you can't bring yourself to admit that they might be guilty of attempted murder—much less attempted murder on behalf of a lover!"

I walked rather than rode home from the *Virginia Argus* offices, in an effort to gather my dismembered thoughts.

There was, of course, a degree of truth in what Barrow said. But he would never know what Madame and Camille L'Espanaye had come to represent for me. Whether they were courtesans, prostitutes or prophets was to me a matter of little significance.

My attachment to them had been born in the darker, demonic recesses of my soul and I was hopelessly attracted to them, almost as if they had been my own fictional creations. There was nothing they could do on this earth, in this life—no law they could break or moral barrier they could tear asunder—that would diminish the voracity of my obsession. To be joined with them was to be connected to the Underworld.

Barrow understood none of this. For him, my decision to pursue or not to pursue the case was simply a matter of deciding for or against my family. For or against Virginia. For or against what he held to be an everyday extramarital infatuation.

He could not guess at the divided nature of my being or how Virginia and the L'Espanayes each represented the two opposing forces that fought for control of it.

Prior to our parting, Barrow and I had resolved that I would play a secondary role in the investigation, devoting what time and effort my duties as a family man would allow. And, of course, I stood ready to rush to Barrow's side should any emergency arise.

But I did not anticipate being called on to perform much more than an occasional piece of armchair police work. I knew that the greater proportion of my energies would be devoted to combating a nearly irresistible longing to strike out in search of Madame and Camille L'Espanaye myself!

A week of domestic tranquility passed, then two, during which there was no word from Barrow. Our routine was as before, pleasant yet unvaried: breakfast with the other guests, a morning's work, lunch with Virginia and mother, an afternoon's work, then perhaps a stroll through the evening air or an occasional play. Virginia and I, as man and wife, had been given a larger room with a double bed, and my cousin devoted a good deal of her time to its decoration. My room was given to a retired military man whose sole pleasure in life lay in regaling the other retired military men who called on him with his rather mundane exploits in the last war with England.

Though I strained to conceal it from Virginia and mother, even from myself, the placid, secure evenings at home were growing a trifle numbing in their predictability. A definite longing for change and excitement was quietly sown within me and slowly began to grow.

Furthermore, life was deteriorating rapidly down at the office. Mr. White found it increasingly necessary to censure me for some literary "overindulgence," while I responded to his criticism with even greater license. I knew our differences were building to an inevitable and final confrontation, which I, as an employee, would lose. Yet I had compromised myself long enough by pandering to his juvenile, introverted sense of public taste. And by now, my editorial duties consumed such a large portion of my time that writing, both fiction and fact, seemed almost a pursuit of the past.

Thus, there was no alternative but to present Mr. White with my grievances.

I was admitted to White's office an hour after I learned of his refusal to print my latest story, "The Man of the Crowd." He was, as usual, steeped in his accounting pursuits, surrounded by stacks of unread manuscripts awaiting his mercurial approval.

Rather than allowing him to mellow my mood with his usual cheery greeting, I threw the red-inked copy of my manuscript on his desk with such force that the remains of his breakfast seemed to become dislodged from his whiskers.

"I cannot possibly, by the remotest stretch of my imagination, continue to work for you under such repressive conditions," I shouted.

For at least a minute, White impassively continued to do his accounts, not even bothering to glance up at me. My mind worked with the tactical dexterity of a chess player, as I considered rebuttals to the various persuasive arguments I expected White to deliver.

But evidently, he had been preparing for this scene as long as I. He raised his head only an inch or two, just enough as was necessary to meet my gaze. He spoke calmly and with great authority.

"I understand, Edgar, and I am prepared to accept your resignation."

Though White's matter-of-fact statement took me quite by surprise (to be frank, I had hoped for him to protest a little more vociferously that I was indispensable to the magazine), I fell into a mechanical series of remarks which poured from my mouth with unthinking rapidity.

"Very well, then. Consider this my resignation."

"I accept on behalf of the *Messenger*."

"I shall clear out my desk at once."

"If you please."

"There's the matter of back pay."

"I've already settled it with the bookkeeper."

"Shall I prepare some remarks for the editorial page concerning my departure?"

"No need to trouble yourself. I've someone working on it now."

I breathed out loudly—a sigh of regret, laced with the indignation I felt at having my resignation accepted so rapidly and efficiently.

"I do apologize for letting you know on such short notice. So near our first-of-the-year deadline."

"Edgar, I've been expecting this for some time, so it does not come as quite the shock you had expected or, I dare say, hoped for. We've plenty of unused manuscripts in our files that can fill the void this issue, though it will mean settling for second best."

I was galled at my inability to cut short our conversation and go about my business. But try as I might, I could not overcome my feelings of sentimentality for the old man and his magazine.

"Though no longer your employee, I trust you will always consider me your friend?" I ventured.

White rose from his chair and offered me his swollen, ink-stained hand, which I shook robustly though I could not bring myself to look him directly in the eye.

"We shall never agree, Edgar. But we should not let our differences of opinion interfere with any future correspondence. Should you ever require advice or criticism . . . you may call on me!"

Though he proved headstrong and arrogant to the last, I must admit that I was impressed that day by the enduring qualities of Mr. White and the *Messenger*. He possessed a solidity and blind optimism that made him a perennial survivor.

I hated him for his ideas, yet respected him for his ability to stand by them.

White curtly dismissed me, then returned to his subscriptions.

As I entered my office for the last time, the floor began to rumble, as the presses beneath my feet went to work on the first edition of 1837—an issue from which my name would be conspicuously absent. Yet, as I collected copies of the eighty-three reviews, six poems, four essays and three stories that had appeared in the *Literary Messenger*, my regret dissolved into anticipation of the future. My reasons for leaving had not been changed or diluted by my final encounter with Mr. White. The *Messenger* was still a provincial publication with a distinctly southern perspective, whose writers were locally honored, revered by old maids and abhorred by schoolboys.

This would simply not do for an author desirous of making the world his theater.

I did not return directly home from the office. The reason for my intentional tardiness was simple—I did not wish to meet mother straightaway and so be forced to break the news of my resignation to her immediately. The budget of our small family was almost entirely in her hands. I had neither the time nor the aptitude for the management of accounts, whereas mother took naturally to business matters. Though it was my work that supported us, it was mother's prudent use of my salary that was responsible for our comfortable, though by no means sumptuous, lives. I feared a strained and difficult dialogue between us when she learned that my salary was no more, and I preferred to wait until the following morning when I should feel fresher and more energetic.

I therefore took my evening meal out, as was my habit when approaching deadlines forced me to work on into the evening, and later went for a lengthy, contemplative ramble along that pastoral section of the James River which flowed through Richmond's, southernmost suburbs. As the hour grew late, both foot and barge traffic thinned until I was quite alone. I then turned around and retraced my steps towards the center of town.

Entering Capitol Square, I was gratified to see that the lights in mother's room were out and that she was already asleep. I entered the darkened house and, taking a candle from the stand in the entry hall, I climbed the stairs as quietly as possible. Glancing briefly at mother's door, I made my way slowly down the corridor in the opposite direction towards the room Virginia and I shared. As I was about to open the door, I heard the surreptitious lifting of a latch, followed by the creak of an unoiled hinge. Then, from behind me came mother's sharp, demanding whisper:

"Eddie, come here!"

I turned to face her, the embarrassed expression on my face hidden from her by the darkness of the hallway.

"I'm tired, mother. White's been a slave driver with that deadline. May we talk tomorrow?"

"I think we'd better talk now."

"Please . . ."

"I sent a boy around to the *Messenger*. We were invited unexpectedly to dinner, and I had hoped you could join us."

"We'll talk now," I breathed in exasperation, walking down the corridor to join mother in her room.

I was surprised to see that the bed had not yet been slept in and was equally surprised and not a little insulted to notice mother's favorite chair pulled up to the window, affording her a comfortable view of the street below. She now sat in this chair, turning it to face the center of the room, while bidding me to occupy the straight-back desk chair she used when attending to her correspondence.

"Watching the comings and goings of nocturnal Richmond?" I asked, hoping to take some of the wind out of her sails by beginning our conversation on the offensive.

"Yes, and they can be most interesting."

"I think I'd best explain my decision, mother. It's not as rash as it sounds."

"Knowing you have been contemplating such a move for several weeks, I do not find your resignation rash. Ill considered and selfish is more like it," retorted mother.

"But it was impossible for me to grow any further there as a writer. I've said as much to you on several occasions."

"And I thought we agreed that, for the welfare of our family, a little patience and endurance on your part was called for."

"I've worked for that vain little man and his monthly for over a year. I call that endurance!" I was by now on my feet, angrily pacing the room, furious that mother was questioning my decision making with such persistence.

"Eddie, please calm down. I'm not attempting to dissuade you from whatever artistic course you've set for yourself. I only ask you to keep us uppermost in your mind."

"I am thinking of you, damn it all! Would you like to be known as the wife and mother of a second-rate, local writer with no prospects? It's absurd. Richmond is stifling all of us."

"Oh, and where were you thinking of moving us to now?"

"I'm not sure. New York, Philadelphia. Somewhere in the North where I'm appreciated. I've already sent out several inquiries, and I have become fairly well connected up there through my work with the *Messenger*."

Mother shook her head in disgust and impatience.

"Eddie, I don't like what this affair foretokens. I see a future in which Virginia and I are carried from city to city, like so much luggage, while you attempt to carve a name for yourself across the entire country."

"But I have ambitious literary plans! Even as I work on more prosaic pieces, a large, innovative project is never far from my thoughts. Does ambition also fall under your definition of selfish and ill considered?"

"When it comes at the expense of your family, yes, it does. Now you know I believe in your talents and I am convinced you will one day occupy a position of distinction among the world's greatest writers, but if I am to help you, if I am to hold this family together, then I feel I have a right to an opinion on something as momentous as this."

"Hold this family together? If it were not for my writing you would not have a penny to hold this family together."

Mother also jumped to her feet and brought her fiercely indignant face to within a foot of mine.

"And if it were not for my management of your salary, you would squander every cent you earn on drink!"

"I haven't touched a drop of liquor in months!"

"I'm beginning to think that's no advantage."

Our voices were raised to near-shouting level and there now came at our door and on our walls a series of loud, admonishing knocks, accompanied by angry reminders as to the lateness of the hour.

The interruptions of our sleepless fellow-tenants served to slow the pace of our argument, which had threatened to become boorish and insulting. We retreated to our respective chairs, where I loosened my tie and collar while mother mopped her sweat-flecked brow with her handkerchief.

Our quarrel had been painfully inconclusive. I saw that my reasoning would forever be incomprehensible to this woman. My decision to seek more fertile literary fields elsewhere, which had so pleased and excited me earlier in the day, was now proving to be the cause of familial bickering and, to judge by mother's sullen, defeated countenance, pain as well.

For the first time in many a week, I found myself craving artificial consolation: not the fanciful, emotionally taxing escape of laudanum, of which I still had an ample supply secreted in our rooms, but the numbing, stuporous oblivion of alcohol.

Twelve

I know not for how long I remained drunk and dissolute.

Following the altercation with mother, I returned dejected to the streets and made my way via hackney through the respectably slumbering neighborhoods of Richmond's upper classes to the brazenly drunken, uproarious tavern district. Before long, in the company of hard-drinking strangers, quick to declare themselves my best friends, I was near blind with despairing intoxication.

My memories of individual taverns, bartenders or other people with whom I must have conversed are thankfully obscure. I recall seeing the sun rise and fall two or three times in rapid succession, as though it were painted on a magician's deck of cards. But whether it was day or night, I was dimly conscious of one abysmal fact: I had renewed my servitude to alcohol with a vengeance! I languished in the streets and bars, starting petty, pointless quarrels with policemen and passersby, eating breakfast at dinnertime and dinner not at all. I did not consume great quantities of drink, indeed my constitution could not have withstood the steady flow of liquor my newly won alcoholic friends regularly imbibed. Yet, so susceptible am I to even the smallest glass of brandy, I was constantly and irredeemably drunk.

At night, in an infrequently traveled alley behind yet another nameless public house, I lay in a stupor. My back rested against the moist, moss-infested brickwork and my legs managed to cross at once the two streams of mingled sewage and rainwater that coursed through the narrow thoroughfare, filling the wagon-wheel tracks.

At either end of the alley, I could see the neighborhood's shabby residents pass beneath the streetlamps, going about their evening business. As I struggled to maintain consciousness, I noticed to my left a human figure come between me and the streetlamp, blotting out my view of the boulevard as it slowly approached. Like a schooner closing in on a harbor, this person made her way towards me, the many folds of a loose-fitting dress billowing outward like sails.

This dark, intimidating figure hovered over me, then lowered her white-capped head to examine me.

Though I viewed everything through a fine haze, I could still discern the livid, scolding face of mother. I felt her work-hardened hands slap at my cheeks in an attempt to revive me.

She spoke to me angrily and authoritatively, but it was as though I were deaf. I grumbled incoherent replies to what I imagined were her questions, but she gave up conversation in disgust and momentarily disappeared from my field of vision. She reappeared in a matter of seconds with another figure—this time a man, burly, gruff and unusually strong, as he lifted me from the gutter and into a hackney coach with ease.

I was soon aware of a ringing in my ears and I realized it was the wind. Our carriage hurtled through the sparsely populated streets of Richmond with alarming speed. I raised myself up on one elbow, and from my vantage point in the back seat I could see mother exhorting the driver to greater speed. The wind and the chill night air gradually combined to clear my head. As houses and streets rushed by me in dizzying succession, I could hear mother addressing the chauffeur at the top of her lungs: "Please keep us moving, take any streets you wish, the fare is no object. We must sober him up before you return us to Capitol Square!"

I leaned forward into the front seat, struggling to balance myself against the unpredictable jolting of the coach over the cobblestones.

"How is Virginia? Does she know anything?"

"She's perfectly fine, considering her husband was called away on business so shortly after her marriage!" she retorted angrily.

She had, as usual, arranged everything in my absence. My wife would never know of this period of dissipation.

To my surprise and confusion, I awoke in my own bed at midday.

Riding over the usual sounds of the street were the strident, excited screams of girls at play. I raised my head and looked out the window to the yard below, where Virginia and several of her friends were entertaining themselves with a game of tag.

I collapsed back into my pillows and attempted to clear the muddiness from my mind. Despite the enervating throb of my headache, the events of the previous evening began to sort themselves out: Mother and I had sat in the deserted parlor in embarrassed silence until we knew Virginia was asleep. Then I had managed somehow to return to our bedroom, remove my clothes and fall asleep without alarming my wife. For the moment, my deception was a success—yet I knew that before the day was out, I would be made to account to mother for my drunkenness and flagrant disregard for my family.

Following a lengthy bath and a shave, I felt somewhat restored and I spent the afternoon ordering the manuscripts and files that I had brought home with me from the *Messenger*. Our family dined together twice and it was as though my absence (which I learned had lasted two and a half days) had gone unnoticed. Virginia had believed without question mother's lie concerning my business trip and when I informed her of my resignation from the *Messenger*, she accepted it with total understanding and equanimity. By nightfall, I had even broached the subject of a move to my wife. Though disappointed at the prospect of leaving Richmond, she was prepared to undergo whatever was necessary to further my literary ambitions. I noticed a twinge of jealousy on mother's face, as my wife, by promising to abide by whatever decision I would make, undercut her own authority.

To an observer our leisurely evening of reading and parlor games would have seemed tranquil enough. But as the hours crept past, I knew by the tautness of her face that mother's anger towards me simmered unabated. I myself shivered internally with dread at our upcoming confrontation.

I longed for relief from my psychic discomfort, for something to happen that would break the crippling tension of the evening. Had I then known how hideously Fate was to intervene, I would have prayed to God that the evening continue indefinitely.

Shortly before eleven, mother, Virginia and I were finishing a hand of cards. As the older guests had tottered off to bed, and the younger, gayer guests had not yet returned from town, we were alone in the parlor. As we contemplated our cards in silence, there came the sharp report of boot steps in the foyer and into the parlor walked Thomas Cleland, the fellow-guest, well liked by all of us, who had served as surety before our wedding.

"Evening, Edgar, Mrs. Poe, Mrs. Clemm."

Cleland, a tall, finely proportioned young man who seemed to grow on an hourly basis, removed his hat and bowed politely to the women. Mother, who had a strong liking for politeness in those younger than herself, smiled and greeted him effusively.

"How do you do, Mr. Cleland?"

"Fine, thank you, ma'am. Just on my way up to bed, but I thought I best give this to you first, Edgar. Found it in the mailbox. It must have just arrived."

Cleland handed me a sealed envelope bearing my name, marked "urgent." My heart stopped as I recognized Barrow's handwriting. I knew that when Barrow said "urgent," he was not exaggerating. Though he had remained incommunicado for two weeks, I was certain that he had not been inactive. Something was afoot!

I did not wish to alarm mother or Virginia, so I thanked Cleland calmly and bade him good-night.

I stood foolishly with the letter burning a hole in my hand as Virginia and mother craned curiously towards me.

"Well, what is it, Buddie?" asked my wife.

"It's only a message from Mr. White," I lied. "Most likely unimportant."

Virginia stood and pressed herself affectionately against my back, reading over my shoulder.

"But it's marked 'urgent.' Aren't you going to open it?"

"Well, yes, I suppose I had better."

I tore open the envelope and read Barrow's tersely scribbled message: "COME TO THE ARGUS AT ONCE—EXTREMELY URGENT!"

"He wants me to come down to the office," I explained. "Something about the new issue. Guess the old boy's having difficulty getting along without me."

"Now?" asked mother angrily.

"Yes, I'm afraid so."

"But, Buddie, you just got home," complained Virginia. "You never spend any time here!"

"I won't be long," I replied, gathering my overcoat and stovepipe. "You go up to bed and I'll be along shortly. It's probably nothing. You know how White is."

Neither my lies nor my kisses served to cheer Virginia in the slightest, but as I rushed out to hail a carriage, I consoled myself with the fact that my wife assumed this nocturnal escapade concerned only an inconsequential business matter.

At length I succeeded in hiring a cab and as the driver skillfully drove his team of horses through Richmond's residential streets towards the commercial district, I wondered what revelation awaited me in Barrow's office. For I knew without a doubt that he had uncovered some extremely important information concerning the L'Espanaye women and their two determined pursuers.

My driver reined the horses to a halt in front of the *Argus*—a large, two-story brick building flanked by an alley on either side. I paid and released my driver. The midnight air was warm, wilted and lazy. Breathing deeply of it, I felt refreshed and even nourished.

As I approached the front door, I was surprised to see that not a single light burned in the building, and as I searched through the window, among the vague, ominous shapes of the printing presses for a trace of my colleague, I shivered involuntarily. The inevitable clock tower chimed in the distance and as I looked up and down the street, I saw not a trace of human life. Having worked late many a night myself, I knew that these business districts emptied out completely at six o'clock and that by nine in the evening, they were gloomy, deserted and unfriendly.

For no apparent reason, other than a dimly perceived sense of dread and foreboding, I refrained from knocking at the front door and set out on a short, exploratory ramble around the building. The two sides that fronted on the alleys were unremarkable facades, broken only by iron-barred windows which were too far above eye level to permit a glimpse of the interior.

The rear of the building was an enigma. A saddled horse was tethered to a pole and a battered, grimy door stood open a fraction of an inch. I felt the stallion's flanks, which were heated and sweaty, as though he had been recently and energetically ridden. I pressed my ear against the open crack in the door and was rewarded with absolute silence.

I felt leaden and hesitant. While outside, the choice to fetch assistance was still mine; once in the building, I would have no option but to deal with the person or persons within.

But I scolded myself for such childish suspicions—the horse may have been borrowed by Barrow and he had undoubtedly returned from some urgent midnight errand and was even now lighting a lamp to work by. I was fabricating a turgid melodrama from what were easily explainable circumstances. Filled with new resolve, I boldly opened the door and stepped into the darkened ground floor of the *Virginia Argus*.

I quickly realized that the ground floor, which I had never entered from the rear, was composed of but one room. Dark as it was, I had no immediate need for a lamp since the entire place was dimly illuminated by the streetlamp that burned outside the front window. I made my way slowly nonetheless, down a narrow causeway bordered on my left by a low row of desks and counter tops where the type itself was probably set, judging by the broad outlines of several gently slanting desk tops, and on the right by the grotesque, insectlike shapes of the printing presses.

"Barrow," I whispered, "it's Edgar. Are you there?"

There was no answer. I continued my gradual progress to the front of the building, feeling with my hands where my eyes were useless. They had become as accustomed to the darkness as they would, and I now realized a lamp would be necessary if I were to distinguish any further details.

"Barrow!" I repeated, this time in a louder tone of voice, but still without response.

I peered into three small adjoining offices, separated from the main room by thin wooden partitions. They were empty.

Having completed a cursory examination of the ground floor without discovering even the slightest evidence that Barrow had been there that evening, I groped my way past the three tiny cubicles to the stairs which led to the second floor. The service door to the stairwell, usually open during working hours, was locked, preventing access to the second story. I sat on one of the printers' tall, three-legged stools and contemplated my next course of action. Several minutes passed as I sat motionlessly, attempting to unravel this most recent mystery.

Gradually I began to grow tense in the unfamiliar, shadowy surroundings. My charged nerve endings began to cry for relief. I was reminded of winter afternoons I had spent as a child on a hill overlooking the James, my eyes tightly shut, sensing on my skin and bristling arm hairs the impending changes in the weather. I felt that, now, such a change was imminent. The air had remained static and heavy for too long. Like cymbals poised to deliver the final, cacophonous beat of a symphony, events hung momentarily arrested, almost as if they begged me to effect my escape while it was still possible.

There was a sudden, barely audible shuffling and a groan of exertion as though someone were lifting a great burden. A blurred, human figure rushed at me from the impenetrable shadows cast by the presses and, knocking the stool out from under me, hurtled the length of the building and vanished out the back door. I heard an incomprehensible shout and the rhythmic, echoing clatter of hoof-beats.

To my horror, I found myself on the floor, face to face with the motionless form of Barrow Reece!

I was bruised and slightly dazed by the sudden fall, but the sobering sight of my unconscious colleague instantaneously restored my strength and reason. I conducted a hurried search for a lamp and, locating a sturdy lantern, bent over Barrow to examine his condition.

He lay on his back, his left arm twisted behind him unnaturally. Holding the lamp next to his face, I saw that his features were waxen and pale, still warm to the touch.

I slapped him gently in a feeble attempt to revive him. I spoke his name repeatedly and shook him by the shoulders in exasperation. Then, in a sudden moment of painful understanding, I saw that the broad, troughlike brown band that stretched across his throat and that I had assumed to be a sort of muffler was in actuality a deep and fatal cut!

I recoiled from the wound in revulsion, dropping the lantern carelessly to the floor. Bending over to retrieve it, I paused momentarily to consider my own narrow escape—I had been in the same room with the murderer! I had foolheartedly blundered into the building, perhaps surprising the fiend in the very perpetration of his crime, and had sat on my stool, thoughtfully and patiently, like a schoolboy doing penance, not three feet from where the vicious killer had concealed himself!

Barrow lay dead at my feet, brutally slain for his part in an intrigue that had grown pervasive and malignant. I had often considered Barrow a fool, had mocked him behind his back, had laughed at his childish arrogance and pretensions. But he was a tenacious man, not easily defeated. I knew that through sheer courage and willpower he would have eventually solved the murder of Jarvis, no matter where the trail led. We had grown from colleagues into friends, and now, as a friend, I was overcome with the need to avenge this new murder—his own. It was my duty to carry on with the investigation he had begun. "L'affaire L'Espanaye" now demanded my immediate and undivided attention.

Conquering my terror at being closeted with a corpse, I forced myself to think calmly. What was called for was a systematic, rational perusal of the office, employing the tenets of logical deduction I had outlined in my treatise. Here was the ultimate proving ground for my theories—they would never find a more urgent or personal application!

After a moment's struggle, I was able to force the lock on the stairwell door and thus gain admittance to the upstairs offices. There was a staggering amount of material to examine, and I pored over files, documents and reports, even back issues, as briefly yet as thoroughly as possible. The results of my reading, both upstairs and down, were negligible. I uncovered nothing to help me illuminate the riddle of Barrow's murder.

I therefore turned to the most distasteful task of all—the examination of the corpse itself.

The weapon was, of course, gone. Barrow's pockets contained nothing more than the average southern gentleman's day-to-day appurtenances, none of which seemed relevant to my investigation.

But as I brought the lantern closer to the body and played it about the floor and the ghostly iron legs of the printing presses, I found several small, black objects scattered about, like so many rectangular, uniform pebbles. Upon closer examination I saw they were individual letters of type that had either recently been set or prepared for setting, judging from the amount of wet ink that rubbed off onto my hands. Barrow had evidently been preparing an already written item for publication and had been interrupted by the arrival of the killer. If, by combining the scattered letters, I could somehow re-create the message Barrow had intended to print, I felt sure a major step towards the illumination of the night's disastrous events would be taken. I had solved puzzles, rebuses, anagrams and conundrums of far greater complexity, both as a recreational pastime and as replies to challenges sent in by the *Messenger*'s readers.

I therefore began a meticulous, grimy scrutiny of the ink-stained floor of the office, tracking down as many of the individual letters as I could, emerging from my efforts with a large handful.

I quickly looked through the type stands for a board that had been recently disturbed, hoping that by plugging the dropped letters into already existing sentences the nature of Barrow's baffling article would be revealed. There was only one board that contained any letters at all—the others were completely empty. These letters were still wet with ink and I was certain they had once formed a portion of Barrow's article. But there were no more than a dozen, and they were scattered about the board in such wide disarray that my cryptographic task was made all the more difficult. There were no simple, partially constructed sentences missing, only a letter here or two letters there—entire words and phrases seemed to be missing—and they would have to be assembled from scratch with the letters I found on the floor.

Unaware of the passage of time, I set to work diligently in the phantasmal glow of the lantern, combining, inventing, scouring my mind for words and connective phrases, but creating, for the most part, incomprehensible gibberish.

An hour passed, perhaps two or three, as I attempted to bring the full force of my ratiocinative prowess to the puzzle at hand; yet as the night wore on I found myself continually and morbidly distracted by the presence of Barrow's corpse at my feet, whose bloodless flesh appeared yellow-green in the dim light. A sentence would appear in my mind, a way out of the grammatical maze in which I wandered, but it would be instantly obliterated by a single, piercing glance at Barrow's cadaverous face.

But then, as the dawn began stealthily to infiltrate the building, the body itself provided the most elucidative clue of all!

I had previously noticed the awkward position of the body, but had paid it little heed. Barrow had tumbled to the floor on his back, his left arm pinned awkwardly beneath him, at such an acute angle that I knew it was broken. I could vividly imagine the twisting, agonizing effort he had made to grasp the arm that held the knife to his throat. He lay now perpendicular to the desk at which

I worked, his head at my feet, his own feet lazily pointed towards the opposite wall. I deduced that he must have turned from his typesetting to face his attacker, who was even then coldly administering the coup de grâce. The assassin had then withdrawn the knife and Barrow, momentarily reeling backwards, had dislodged the letters from the printing block as he slid lifelessly to the floor. If such was the case and he had fallen against the letters and their fresh coat of ink, then some image of the message they spelled out might have been transferred to Barrow's clothing!

I immediately set about the gruesome task of overturning his body. He seemed to have gained weight in death, a cementlike heaviness that gave me the impression he was molded to the floor. In movements as clumsy as they were ghastly, my boot heels slipping on the ink-slicked tile floor, now more slippery still with a fresh glazing of blood, I managed to turn the corpse on its front, taking care to avoid breaking the arm any further. As fascinated as I was repelled, I brought the lamp to within a few inches of Barrow's white-shirted back and found that my fantastic surmise had been correct: In infinitesimal, barely legible newsprint an uneven message appeared—the last news story Barrow Reece ever wrote:

THE CITIZENS OF RICHMOND MAY SLEEP SOUNDLY IN THEIR BEDS TONIGHT, BUT THOSE NEW YORK CITY DWELLERS WHO VALUE THEIR LIVES HAD BEST CHECK THAT SHUTTER LOCK TWICE BEFORE RETIRING. THE CORSICAN FORTUNE-TELLER AND HER DAUGHTER—NO STRANGERS TO VIRGINIA'S UPPER CRUST, WE'RE TOLD—WHO ATTRACT VIOLENCE AS A FRESHLY BAKED TART ATTRACTS FLIES, ARE ON THEIR WAY TO THAT METROPOLIS ON THE HUDSON, THIS PAPER LEARNED TODAY. AND IN A RELATED, HIGHLY REVEALING DISCOV

I was paralyzed with disappointment and frustration!

The "related, highly revealing discovery" would not be known —at least not that night. Barrow had either been interrupted in mid-sentence by his killer, or the remainder of the message had imprinted itself on his black trousers, where it could not possibly be deciphered.

The handwritten, original text of the newspaper article was now almost certainly in the hands of the murderer, and all the important, incriminating evidence it contained—the evidence that had cost Barrow his life. How did Barrow know the L'Espanaye women were bound for New York? What had he learned about the escaped bandit Mario de la Costa? Had he perhaps made contact again with Inspector Contadina? And above all, what was the discovery he had been about to reveal?

I was now faced with two unsolved murders and a mysterious murder attempt. I was unsure whom to suspect or whom not to suspect. But I knew who could provide me with the answers: the same women who had predicted the "horrific misdeeds" that were occurring over and over again with terrifying regularity.

And those women were now to be found in New York City!

I covered Barrow's body with the only blankets that were at hand—the massive blank sheets of newsprint that would ironically carry his obituary the next day.

My mournful work complete, I trudged down the narrow corridor between the presses and the printers' desks and emerged into a smoky, overwhelmingly oppressive dawn.

Thirteen

I was forced to walk several blocks through the still-deserted streets before I found a hack. The driver, rudely awakened, grumbled and spat an incessant stream of tobacco as he conducted me homeward. I alighted in front of Mrs. Yarrington's just as the streetlamp was being extinguished. The lamplighter winked at me, muttering some aphorism about what a gay party city Richmond was, and continued, singing, on his rounds.

To my relief, it appeared that not a soul in the house stirred. I climbed stealthily to the second floor, almost expecting mother's door to open as it had the night of my resignation. But she was apparently fast asleep and I entered my own bedchamber unimpeded. Virginia also slept soundly in the semidarkness that was slowly succumbing to the gray, meager illumination of the dawn. I disrobed silently and slipped into bed beside my wife. She stirred minutely, executed a succession of satisfied chewing motions with her mouth, then fell again motionless, dreaming in rigid serenity.

Though physically and emotionally drained from the terrors of the evening, I found sleep impossible. As I watched the minute-by-minute progress of daybreak and waited for Virginia to awaken, I contemplated the awful uncertainty of my situation.

Though in the eyes of the law, and in my own mind, I was guilty of complicity in Barrow's murder by not immediately informing the police, I had my family to think about. The fact that I was present at the scene on the night of the crime could prove exceedingly uncomfortable for me. The nature of my visit would be probed, a line of questioning established that might eventually connect me with the L'Espanaye women and my dalliance with them. And once such information was in the hands of the police, it would be but a matter of hours before one read of it in the newspapers.

As it was, his body would shortly be discovered by the first of the *Argus* employees to arrive for work and the police would be duly notified. As a colleague of Barrow's, I might eventually be summoned by the police to shed what light I could on the murder, but of that I was unafraid. The horror of my friend's violent death could not be kept from my wife's delicate ears, but my role in it certainly could.

Prevented as I therefore was from unburdening myself before the law, I was the only person with sufficient information to conduct an informed and ultimately successful search for Barrow's Corsican murderer!

As I was making mental plans for this investigation, exhaustion finally overcame me and I fell into a dreamless sleep, just as the sunlight, dappled and patterned through lace curtains, chased what remained of the long night's darkness into the inaccessible corners of the room.

I was brutally awakened, scarcely an hour later, by a series of loud, pummeling knocks at the bedroom door. Virginia and I both sat bolt upright in shock and stared at each other.

"Who can that be, Buddie? What time is it?"

"I don't know. It's still early. Who is it?" I called. "What do you mean by knocking our door down at this ungodly hour?"

"It's Steven, sir. From the *Argus*. Something awful has happened!"

I looked at Virginia to see if she was aware of the manner in which I trembled, anticipating the young apprentice's next few words. But she was focused on the disembodied voice at the door with the earnestness of a theatergoer—interested, but not fearful.

"What is it, Steven? What has happened?"

"It's *Barrow*, sir," replied the voice, still in a high-pitched trembling tone.

"What about him, for God's sake?"

"He's dead, sir," was the response, now dull, lifeless and pained. "Murdered in the office. They just now found him."

Virginia did not scream or burst into tears or collapse in a faint. But she began to shiver, as from a sudden chill, and I embraced her, warming her with my body. Her shivering grew more frantic, nearly epileptic, and I felt my own body begin to shake as well. She fell backwards from her sitting position, rocking the bed with her contortions.

"Virginia, Virginia, what is it? Please, please stop! Stop it!"

She now began to cough, but it was a cough so violent, so uncontrollable that I feared it would strangle her. Her body was no longer her own, as it shook back and forth in the throes of a dictatorial, choking pain. Her hands flew to her chest in a desperate attempt to quell what appeared to be the source of her agony.

"Mr. Poe! Are you all right in there? I've got to go."

"Steven, send for the doctor at once," I managed between breaths, as I struggled to prevent Virginia from throwing herself off the bed.

"What is it? What's wrong?"

"Just send for a doctor, damn you! My wife is dying!"

Following the doctor's departure, mother and I maintained a vigil beside my wife's bed throughout the day and night, and well into the next morning.

Her condition was serious but stable and she rested comfortably, having succumbed to sleep.

The physician's impatiently rendered diagnosis, though something of a relief, had been sadly incomplete. He believed Virginia to be severely rheumatic, a condition which was aggravated by influenza, though he did not rule out the possibility that the reverse might be the case. The doctor had applied cold compresses to her forehead and had eased her choking cough with a particularly vile, viscous liquid, the odor of which even now permeated the small room. Leaving us with an assortment of painkillers and nostrums, and a complicated schedule for their administration, he had departed with the stern recommendation that Virginia be spared shocking or surprising news of a negative nature.

He also left behind the bill for his services. The total figure was a shock and surprise all its own.

Fortified by hot tea and occasional light meals provided by the thoughtful Mrs. Yarrington, mother and I stood watch over my stricken wife and earnestly planned our future.

"I won't dwell on your recent intemperance, Edgar," she began, "but will get right to the point. I'm afraid that the recent turn of events makes your intended move nigh impossible."

"On the contrary, mother. It's more imperative than ever."

"And how so?"

"Primarily from a financial standpoint. I have decided on New York. It's a larger, more progressive city than Richmond, with a greater number of magazines and periodicals, and therefore greater opportunities for employment."

"But the strain on Virginia . . ."

"I'm not talking about catching a steamer tonight, for God's sake. As soon as she is well. May I remind you of her vow to accompany me. She possesses a faith and conviction it is my fondest wish that you shared."

"Eddie, I share her faith—perhaps my own belief in you is even greater. But the instability, the rashness, the fear of the unknown is what frightens me. We'll be strangers in New York, hopelessly out of place as southerners."

"But I have connections there," I protested. "I can obtain letters of introduction. In addition, the salaries will be higher. I don't need to remind you of the doctors' bills."

Mother shook her head in grim agreement. She grew silent, absorbing the logic of my reasoning. But her wrinkled brow and her pensive manner did not, I knew, indicate her acquiescence—merely her attempts to formulate additional arguments.

She stared into Virginia's sleeping visage, which still bore the traces of her recent ordeal.

"It seems too much to ask of her—and us."

"Richmond has nothing for us anymore, mother. The awful events of last night should serve as a tragic reminder that we no longer belong here."

Maria Poe Clemm seemed close to tears. She removed a handkerchief from her dress and dabbed at her eyes, which were moist though not yet tear filled. Barrow's murder had been confined to the back of our minds since Virginia's seizure, but now the gruesome specter of my colleague's death returned.

"Perhaps a fresh start is all for the best," she admitted wearily.

"Of course it is!" I rejoined enthusiastically. "New York is a large, bustling city where there are plays and concerts and museums, a thousand diversions to put these horrible events behind us. And a city where I can make a respectable living—as a writer!"

"I suppose I could take in boarders again. Our financial status *is* miserable, Eddie. You must be aware of that. With no regular salary . . ."

"All the more reason for a hasty departure."

Mother gave me a sharp look of disapproval.

"As soon as Virginia is well enough to travel," I hastened to add, gazing down at my sleeping wife.

"Then you must curb your drinking. You may mask your weaknesses from Virginia, but I am not so easily fooled. There will come a time when I will conspire with you no longer."

Mother's words stunned me. Never before had she so outspokenly condemned me.

"The humiliation I feel is more than enough to turn me into a teetotaler," I replied.

"Excellent. Then your humiliation, no matter how painful, has not been in vain."

The discussion for the moment concluded, we turned to our own thoughts as we watched over Virginia. My motives for the move to New York were as diverse as they were numerous: career advancement, financial stability, the murders of Jarvis and Barrow, and the erotic magnet personified by madame and Camille. All of these currents were equally strong within me. I wondered if I would prove strong enough to endure their collision. . . .

Virginia seemed to be the picture of health.

The headland of Norfolk receded in the sunlit Atlantic haze, as our steamer steered a course for the main north-south shipping lane and our ultimate destination—the city of New York, a voyage of nearly three hundred miles.

Despite the stiffness of the offshore wind and the increasing choppiness of the waves, the fresh sea air appeared to be working wonders on Virginia's normally chalky complexion, tinting it with a healthy and uncharacteristic ruddiness. Though the three of us believed Virginia's illness to be serious and deep-rooted, the voyage, the change of scene and the out-of-doors provided her with a much needed mental lift.

I joined my wife at the stern of the ship and together we watched the Virginia coastline disappear from view. Mother was below decks, stricken with a mild attack of seasickness which had set in as soon as we stepped aboard.

"Do you regret your decision to leave?" I asked gently, my arm encircling her waist.

"I must admit, I did question it up until the very last moment. But now that we are at sea, I find myself looking ahead rather than behind," she replied.

"We must console ourselves with the future," I agreed. "After . . . after the funeral . . . Richmond seemed to me cold and uninhabitable."

She pressed herself against me, begging with her body to be embraced.

"Are you cold? Shall we go inside?" I asked.

"In a moment."

She looked at me, suddenly anxious and worried.

"Buddie, do you promise to take care of us in New York no matter what happens? I'll be lost there, you know that."

"But of course. I would never have undertaken this move if I didn't feel confident that I could provide for us!"

"This is very difficult to talk about, but . . . I want you to understand that every ounce of courage I've ever displayed for you has been false. I've tried so very hard to appear confident and strong, but my youth weakens me, Buddie. . . ."

"Is that why you have never told me about the doctors' visits, the medicine, the—illness?"

She nodded "yes" to my question, smiling ruefully as would a child caught stealing chocolates.

"I've nothing to offer you other than my strength, Buddie. I barely understand your writing, I've no head for business, I certainly don't add to your stature in society by being an entertaining conversationalist—I don't understand half the words your colleagues seem to employ as a matter of course . . ."

"As a matter of *show,*" I interjected.

"And, in addition, my continual illness can be nothing but a burden to you," Virginia concluded.

"But I demand nothing of you, darling. There's no preconceived role that I long for you to fill. Only that you are always at my side."

"All the same, I wish I hadn't abandoned my harp playing. I'm sure you would enjoy coming home at night to a little music. But I'm afraid singing will be out of the question for quite some time."

"You amaze me. The things that enter that fourteen-year-old head of yours. While laughing gaily on the swings with your friends, your mind is grappling with the problems of the world."

She chuckled at her own expense and kissed me playfully.

"Perhaps I do worry too much. Still, I find it more and more difficult to play all afternoon while I know you're working so very hard, just to pay the doctors."

"But, Virginia, you're being silly. I would be working just as hard if I were single and had no family to support. I'm lucky that I am paid for my writing at all. Think of all the frustrated would-be Mrs. Brownings there are sequestered in the parlors of America who will never realize a penny from their scribblings."

"Nevertheless, I am going to exercise everything in my power to recover speedily, so I can be a help to mother," she declared with a freshly summoned determination. "Now I'd like to go below or this chill will make all of my talk seem foolish."

Happy that Virginia now viewed our move to New York with courage and optimism, I escorted her to our small quarters below decks, marveling all the while at the contradictions this girl embodied. So frail and sickly at times that I was forced to carry her upstairs to bed, yet possessing the inner strength to keep the full extent of her illness a secret for so long: a child in body and frequently in mind, yet plagued by the doubts, frustrations and ambitions common to all adults.

Our steamer made rapid northward progress as we slept.

The *Independence* was one of the first packets to ply the sheltered coastal waters on a regular schedule, and one of the fastest. On one record-breaking voyage from Boston to Fall River, Massachusetts, she had maintained an average speed of nineteen knots, a feat so astounding it was made much of even by the conservative southern papers.

We awoke following a surprisingly sound night's sleep in a cabin that lacked the luxurious rosewood paneling and full-length mirrors of the first-class staterooms, but was nevertheless quite comfortable. We treated our voyage on the *Independence* as an adventure, exploring the three decks with childish curiosity, pausing every few hundred steps to allow mother to do battle with her ever-present queasiness. She was a woman who welcomed the progress of science and invention, and she refused to allow a temporary bout of nausea to prevent her from fully experiencing one of the country's genuine technical wonders.

We visited the engine room, where a great copper boiler that resembled a giant soup kettle generated steam to a single massive piston, which in turn pushed the side-mounted paddle wheel. The ship burned both wood and coal, and though many of our fellow passengers expressed fear of sailing on a vessel that had a fire burning in its interior, we did not feel the slightest uneasiness.

The ship came to represent for us the spirit of hope and anticipation that gradually flooded our veins as we approached the city that was to be our new home. Though not by temperament a technical man, I was not immune to the spell cast by this marvelous vessel of the future, and by the time we entered the crowded, vibrantly alive harbor of New York, I was positively giddy with an excitement I had thought it impossible to recall.

New York and its 250,000 inhabitants were suffering from the worst depression in that city's history!

The first evidence of the severity of the financial plague that had descended on New York came as the three of us disembarked at the Beach Street boat slip on the Hudson River. From out of the throngs of shoving, shouting porters, who spoke a multitude of languages but little English, I had chosen a bright, hungry-looking teenage boy to transport our baggage to our new home, a small cottage in lower Manhattan.

I engaged his services with silver; he gave me my change in lighter-than-air metal tokens that had, to a large extent, replaced coins!

"But what can I buy with these worthless coins?" I had protested in indignation and surprise.

"Nuthin' much," responded the boy matter-of-factly, as he hefted our overpacked trunks onto the small of his back, and from there onto a trailer coupled to his hackney. "But then, there's not much to buy, is there, sir?"

The depression, I later learned, as I too fell victim to its tragic circumstances, had in part been initiated by natural disaster. On December 16, 1835, the "Great Fire" had started at the corner of Hanover and Pearl Streets, in the heart of the city's financial district, and had burned more than six hundred buildings over a seventeen-block area, including the Merchants' Exchange on Wall Street.

The insurance companies were consequently bankrupted, and a massive rebuilding program got underway. Land speculators caused the price of downtown real estate to soar unrealistically, even beyond the reach of the wealthy. The market was destroyed, initiating the fearsome depression which touched the lives of each and every New Yorker in a different, but ultimately tragic, manner. The general opinion was that President Jackson's chaotic and unfeeling economic policies would ensure the depression a long reign.

My family climbed into the hackney side by side and we set out on a kaleidoscopic route through lower Manhattan Island.

The densely packed buildings and people of New York far surpassed even the most overpopulated districts of Richmond. Our progress through the narrow streets was extremely slow; the average New Yorker seemed to consider the street his own personal sidewalk, and little attention was paid to vehicular traffic. Our driver uttered fearsome oaths unbecoming his youthfulness, as he cracked his whip and shouted at pedestrians and other carriages who obstructed his progress at every turn. For the most part, these victims of his wrath, whether gentlemen or scullery maids, responded in similar language.

Mother, Virginia and I grimaced at each other, and the two ladies covered their noses with their handkerchiefs. I had to agree that the stench was nearly intolerable, as there appeared to be not even the most rudimentary standards of sanitation. I later learned that there was no garbage pickup—the bankrupt city government could not afford it. Consequently, the city was continually piled high with garbage and filth: a feast for the pigs who materialized out of thin air to take their meals in the streets, and a vomitous nuisance for the citizens who were compelled by their aldermen to "voluntarily" clear the boulevards of refuse once a week.

As we rode away from the docks towards the center of the city, our speed gradually diminished until we came to a halt altogether. The alleys and byways had now become the exclusive domain of carriages, hackneys, fiacres and public stages, unlike the pedestrian-choked streets we had recently seen. The result was even more absurd: Endless lines of wheeled vehicles had brought traffic to a standstill. As the motion of each individual carriage depended on the movement of every other, progress seemed impossible.

"What has happened?" I called to our young driver above the din of a thousand angry, swearing passengers and drivers. "Why aren't we moving?"

"It's noon," replied the boy, as though it were obvious. "This here's the heart of your commercial district. Banks, insurance companies, what have you. They all go home for lunch. From noon to three you can't budge. It's called the 'rush hour.' "

"How long will we be stranded?" asked mother.

The boy shrugged nonchalantly.

"Depends. If they get the streets cleared up to the north, maybe in the next half hour we can be on our way. If not . . ."

The boy's unfinished sentence was disheartening, to say the least.

But, mired as we were, a perfect opportunity to survey my adopted city presented itself. Leaning back restfully in the rolled leather seat of our carriage, I watched the eccentric and variegated life that swirled around us.

As our driver had pointed out, the principal business of the district was business. I counted no fewer than twenty-two banks and financial institutions in my immediate field of vision, their presence subtly announced by the gold plaques that graced their doorways and the harried, dark-suited businessmen who gathered in worried conclaves outside their offices.

Ragged hawkers, vendors, fishmongers and novelty performers were in great abundance, pestering the flustered money men to partake of their wares, and being generally rebuffed.

Men, women, children; Orientals, whites, Negroes, Slavs; poor, rich or middle class—no occupation, social standing or race seemed unrepresented here—an eddying, tumultuous living carpet on which the bankers and financiers appeared to tread with deft immunity.

As I continued my fascinated perusal of the city, an uproarious series of shouted protests attracted my attention to the sidewalk on my left. A curious caravan of brightly painted wagons, drays and carriages, accompanied by pedestrians of all sizes, dress and description, had forced its way out of the road and onto the footpaths. It was a carnival of some sort and, having grown impatient with the sluggish flow of traffic, it was attempting to circumvent the impediment by taking to the sidewalk.

Indignant bankers and lawyers, as well as beggars and hucksters, were shoved rudely aside by the cursing gaggle of carnival performers. Great, swarthy men wearing obviously false beards sat at the head of buckboards carrying all manner of rudely painted, slapped-together paraphernalia. There were tents, divination parlors, houses of horror, cages containing tired and ragged jungle beasts, and a particularly menacing baboon or orangutan. At their sides sat outrageously adorned women, many of whom were midgets preening with all the ludicrous self-deception of overweight prostitutes. On foot, helping to push the wagons over obstacles that slowed their progress, were drab laborers, men and women alike: the underpaid, sweating retainers whose services were required to move the shabby entertainment from camp to camp.

I watched the carnival's progress with pity and curiosity, marveling that it continued to exist in such depressed times, until a freshly painted canvas-covered wagon passed by us, exposing to my view its two dejected female passengers.

There could be no mistaking the dusky, ever-arrogant faces of Madame and Camille L'Espanayé!

I was jarred from my stupefied immobility as our carriage sprang suddenly forward and the traffic began to flow again. I saw Camille lift her face from its nest in her hands and execute a feeble wave, before her mother swiftly defeated the gesture as the wagon withdrew into a teeming, shadowy alley.

Lost in contemplation, I merely nodded at mother's and Virginia's exclamations of relief that we were finally moving again.

I had forgotten how magnetically beautiful the two women were! How the heat of their presence welded them to one's imagination! Could they really have been directly involved in the attempt on the lives of Virginia, Barrow and myself, or in the grisly murder of my colleague? Was it perhaps this aura of criminality that made them even more attractive to me?

It was not long, however, before my thoughts of sensuality were replaced by the sobering reality of the dangerous task I had sworn to undertake. Barrow had certainly been correct in his surmise that the case would lead to New York. But nothing could have prepared me for the thrill of seeing the two women my first day there!

Fourteen

The lodgings we had engaged at the corner of Sixth Avenue and Waverly proved too cramped for the three of us and our fellow boarder, Mr. Gowans, and shortly after our arrival in New York, my small family was once again forced to move. Our new home at 113½ Carmine Street was a two-story Georgian, which, though somewhat dingy, proved more acceptable.

One walked up four steps from the street and entered a small hallway which gave onto the kitchen, the dining room and the parlor. The second story contained three bedrooms and one bathroom. Virginia and I were happily able to secure one of the two rear bedrooms which proved infinitely quieter than that facing the street. Above and below, for storage purposes, were a small attic and a damp but spacious cellar.

Though the interior of the house was dark and less than impressive, the exterior of 113½ Carmine Street, with its freshly painted shutters, finely crafted iron railings, sharply sloping roof and newly repaired chimney, was not at all unsuitable for a young author on the rise. Our neighborhood was in transition: Immediately to the south was the most crowded and squalid of New York's immigrant districts, rife with crime and poverty, whereas to our north lived the city's intellectual and professional classes, whose success in their chosen fields was easily measured by the facades of their houses. Though financially I belonged to the former group, I considered myself otherwise a member in good standing of the latter—and thus our situation was ironically appropriate.

We lived as before, with the exception that mother and not Mrs. Yarrington was now mistress of our household. She managed the cooking and cleaning as effectively as ever, aided by Virginia whenever her health permitted. Gowans, who had moved with us, was a jovial gentleman in his sixties, who found it impossible to keep his opinions to himself. He performed the more masculine chores and provided a welcome and educated addition to our meal-time conversation.

Once we were settled, I plunged into the search for a position with one of New York's many prestigious periodicals.

But though I felt my credentials were impressive, and indeed I had developed a small reputation in the Gotham literary world, employment was not immediately forthcoming. Day after day the situation was the same: Armed with copies of my stories and reviews I would arrive at the offices of a magazine only to find it closed until further notice, a victim of New York's ever-widening depression. Those publications that still held their heads above water were running limited editions, had fired half their employees and were in no position to pay for new manuscripts, let alone take on a full-time editor.

The only periodicals that thrived in the midst of the financial chaos were those offering mindless gossip and dreadfully optimistic poetry. A public that did not know where its next meal was coming from had no time, it seemed, for intellectual nourishment. These tawdry publications, which pandered to the lowest level of public taste, employed overworked and underpaid staffs of oily, artistic cripples who only in times of great distress could be considered authors.

Despite the failing financial health of my family, I would never deign to join their ranks!

On a dreary Friday afternoon, with snow threatening, my last hopes for permanent employment were dashed. A small literary publication in Jersey City, recently founded by a group of Princeton graduates, had advertised for an editor, and I had taken a ferry across the Hudson to inquire after the job. Though I was hospitably welcomed, I was disappointed to learn that the only remuneration offered by the magazine's youthful founders was room and board. So desperate for employment had I become, I even asked to be shown the room. It was a small, leaky chamber on the fourth floor, and hardly suitable for family life.

But my failure to find work did not prove to be the unendurable burden that I first imagined. My commitment to my own fiction was vigorously renewed. From my involvement with the L'Espanaye women, and my subsequent investigation into the deaths of Jarvis and Barrow, an idea had grown in which I placed great faith. Coupled with my nonfictional inquiries into the science of deduction, this idea contained, I felt, unlimited and innovative potential. Though not yet ready to see the light of day, it had the effect of sparking my literary imagination and I was able to focus on more immediate work. And so, as the depression raged around our little house like a contagious disease, I sought solace in my imagination.

But after several days I found my thoughts straying from the paper that lay in front of me to madame and Camille. The single-mindedness with which I had sought employment had not removed the need to see the women, merely displaced it temporarily. Even as I marched along the thoroughfares of New York, shuttling from office to office, I had kept one eye wide open for signs of a traveling carnival.

I was finally unable to write at all. Immediately after breakfast I would perform as many of the household chores as mother would permit, in an effort to delay confronting the stack of blank paper prominently displayed on my desk. But ultimately, towards eleven, there would be nothing for me to do but sit down at my desk. And once there, the mental energies that should have been devoted to fiction were diverted to the Corsican fortune-tellers, and the web of intrigue and murder that surrounded them.

One morning I finally capitulated, throwing my pen down in disgust, toppling a bottle of ink onto the pages I had found impossible to cover with words.

I strode determinedly and loudly upstairs, angry at my inability to write, anxious to proceed with my investigation, yet fearful of the effect that investigation would have on our family.

The room Virginia and I shared was a good deal less comfortable than our accommodations in Richmond, but this was made up for by the fact that through an adjoining door we had access to a bathroom which we were required to share with only one fellow boarder, Mr. Gowans. On a clear day, the view from the bed out the back window was truly exceptional: The gabled rooftops of New York, topped by a colorful jumble of drying laundry, extended to the flat, white-crested waters of the river. One could watch the semaphore men signaling to the hundreds of vessels that weekly made their way in and out of New York's crowded harbor. The overall sensation was one of commerce and energetic activity. One could not hope for a more encouraging environment for one as ill of health as my wife.

As I entered the bedroom to fetch my overcoat, Virginia was seated upright in bed, cheerfully drinking from a cup of tea mother had prepared.

"So, Buddie, has another job prospect presented itself, or are you merely taking a walk to clear your mind?" she asked as I donned hat and gloves.

"There's a slight chance that I might have a position. But I wouldn't become too excited if I were you. It will lessen your disappointment if nothing comes of it."

"Still, one never knows. Come here and give me a kiss."

I bent over and offered a perfunctory kiss, which she returned with surprising ardor.

"I kiss quite well for someone who is supposedly ill, don't you think?"

"You're not so ill, darling—only weakened slightly from the voyage and the tedium of our second move. You'll be up and about before the week is out."

"You've no idea how glad I am to hear you say that. Mother treats me as though I've one foot in the grave already. I offer to help her iron, or fold the clothes, but she'll have none of it."

"Aaaah. Mothers never change. If anything, they grow more protective."

"Still, I've convinced her to let me help with the sewing. I think we can bring in a little extra money if we both work as seamstresses. That's something I can do in bed, at any rate."

"That's a capital idea," I agreed enthusiastically. "Not that we're in dire need of money right now, but you can always use it to buy yourself something nice. So, I must be off."

"Come here and give me another kiss. I want to feel you next to me."

I did as she asked and she anxiously extracted every ounce and inch from me that she could, her hands searching beneath the thick woolen cloth of my overcoat for the contours of my body.

My response was less than passionate—indeed, compared to her I was positively anemic. As I bade her good-bye, and she gazed after me in disappointment, I reflected on Virginia's freshly awakened passion and its curious effect on me. Though I was sure she was quite ill internally, her appearance and her behavior did not reflect it as much as usual. Less chalky in complexion, more talkative and aggressive, she struck me at that moment as strangely unattractive. As bizarre and as inhuman as it sounds, her improved health was to me decidedly unerotic!

I crisscrossed New York, from the towering lairs of the city's uptown aristocrats to the slung-together hovels of the poor. Everywhere the reaction to my question, "Have you seen a traveling carnival hereabouts?" was one of surprise, giving way to pity that a grown man seemed so desperately in need of such childish diversions.

But on the third day, my diligence was rewarded. In a dreary neighborhood not far from the East River docks, I reached an open square teeming with activity. At once I recognized the raggle-taggle tents, wagons and gaudy attractions of the traveling road show to which Madame and Camille L'Espanaye belonged.

Upon venturing onto the grounds themselves, I searched the well-attended carnival for familiar faces. My biggest fear was that the two women had succeeded in joining forces with Mario de la Costa, an alliance for which I would have been no match. But, recognizing no one in the crowd, I had no choice but to press on.

I moved with trepidation through the maze of cheaply adorned, loudly touted attractions: tiny, hand-painted stages on which sword-swallowers and fire-eaters performed to the enthusiastic ac-claim of New York's gullible poor; orange and red tents in front of which Arab chieftains promised untarnished glimpses into forbid-den practices of the East; a series of dubiously secure cages in which were imprisoned a sorry lot of wild animals including a somnolent lion who was stubbornly resisting a trainer's attempts to anger him. They were all well attended; in times of trouble only the most undemanding forms of entertainment are palatable to a public longing to escape the miseries of day-to-day life.

Turning a corner, I suddenly found myself before the blue cov-ered wagon in which I had seen the two women. Decorating its stretched-canvas roof were all manner of occult designs and insig-nias, primitively rendered in broad, almost childlike strokes of gold paint. A handmade series of wooden steps led up to the rear door of the wagon, but the mysterious activity within was masked from the public by thick, tightly drawn curtains.

I paused, and as I considered my next move, I briefly examined my surroundings. The nearby attractions were worthless, save for two: a fire-eater who roasted potatoes with his breath and then sold them to hungry customers (because of the dual nature of this at-traction, he was blessed with an inordinately large proportion of the audience); and a caged orangutan who was at that moment carefully shaving his trainer with a lethal-looking straight razor. This beast, as tall as a man and covered all over with stiff, reddish hair, possessed a highly expressive face and was capable of a range of emotions that would have been the envy of many of the city's so-called professional actors.

I stood before the women's wagon transfixed—fear and nervousness washed away by the sensual, forbidden glow that seemed to emanate from within.

At that moment, a tall man with rough and twisted features emerged from the wagon and addressed a few remarks over his shoulder to an unseen person inside. He turned and fixed on me a harsh, probing stare, then strode down the steps and hurried off into the crowd. I gazed after him curiously for an instant, then my attention was drawn back to the wagon's entrance.

In a movement I'm sure was habitual and uncalculated, but which at the moment seemed to me the height of drama, a thin, beautifully pale, braceleted arm reached out from the secret confines of the wagon and swept back the curtains.

Madame L'Espanaye stepped out onto the top of the handmade staircase to survey her tawdry realm.

Though her coal black eyes widened, betraying her surprise at seeing me standing before her, she made every effort to remain as calm as possible.

"My dear Monsieur Poe," she said at last. "It seems that once again the wonderful hand of coincidence has brought us together."

"How unlike you, Madame L'Espanaye, to express faith in the power of coincidence. I'm afraid I share your disbelief in it now myself. I took great pains in finding you."

Before she could reply, Camille emerged from the wagon behind her mother, and bringing her hand to her mouth, emitted a short, somewhat exaggerated cry of surprise.

"Monsieur Poe! I am happy to see you, indeed, though I can't imagine what could bring you to New York."

"Have you forgotten the prophecy delivered by your mother the night of our first fortune-telling session? 'You will become involved in nefarious pursuits.' Well, those pursuits have proven nefarious indeed, and they have led me to your door! And now, Madame . . . *Verneuil*, we have matters to discuss, and it will be most advantageous for you and your daughter to discuss them with me rather than with the New York police."

Madame, momentarily flustered by my knowledge of her true name, turned away from me. I stepped closer and pressed my case.

"I know a good deal more about you than you suspect, but quite a bit less than I need. We must talk." Then, in a whisper audible only to us three, I delivered the coup de grâce. "For example, your whereabouts on the night Jarvis died, on the night Barrow died, *and* on the night I and my wife nearly died would be of great interest to me."

Camille looked quizzically at her mother, who cautioned her to silence. Though the daughter was as beautiful as before, the flight from Richmond had aged her. Now, more than ever, the two resembled each other. Gone forever was the striking facial contrast between innocence and experience.

Madame's haughty, aristocratic profile was turned towards me, as she stared into the distance in shock. Her face grew by degrees whiter and paler. The face that was always so beautiful, so coldly confident, looked as though it was about to crumble into a thousand pieces. She reached out her hands and clutched the tiny wooden banister next to her, tightening her grip with unflinching concentration.

I had not expected so vehement a reaction to my interrogatories. Could our suspicions have been correct? Were these two refined, desirable, determined creatures capable of murder?

"You are quite right, monsieur," Madame L'Espanaye said at length. "A confession is long overdue." She turned towards me, the blood entirely drained from her beautiful visage, her lower lip trembling from a profound inner weariness. Camille's arm encircled her mother, supporting the now-tearful woman.

"It seems like a thousand years since I've spoken the truth."

I waited in the doorway across the street from a small, weathered building that was distinguishable from those immediately adjoining only by the relative newness of its drab paint. The two women had found it impossible to elude the watchful eyes of their employers, and consequently it had been decided that we would meet in their rooms when the carnival closed for the evening. I held in my hand a purse containing their life savings—collateral I had demanded to ensure their presence.

Aside from one other block of apartments, the neighborhood was one of storage and light industry: by day choked with loud commercial traffic, by night still as a cemetery. The only nocturnal reminder of the business that thrived in the area was the ever-present smell of tobacco from a cigar factory that did a brisk business three blocks to the north.

It had been dark for well over an hour when the gray-shawled figures of Madame L'Espanaye and her daughter turned the corner and made their way up the singularly dreary, deserted street to their building. I stepped from the shadows and crossed over to join them at their door. They nodded briefly, then wordlessly led me inside and up a winding, dilapidated staircase. On each landing, as we tromped loudly past the apartment doors, gnarled, suspicious faces appeared, examined us with disdain, then retreated abruptly inside. Neither madame nor her daughter greeted their fellow tenants; a permanent air of hatred and mistrust seemed to reign throughout the building.

Once inside their apartment, however, an entirely different feeling came over me. Their lodgings were warm, inviting and almost sensually cramped. Though their hasty flight from Richmond had evidently necessitated leaving behind many of their exotic furnishings, they had made do admirably with secondhand furniture, low-hanging lanterns and hand-sewn cushions and pillows.

"You must pardon our tardiness, Monsieur Poe. There was considerable excitement at the carnival. The ape which you have seen near our wagon . . . it seems he has escaped, vanished," Madame L'Espanaye snorted with mild laughter. "Everyone is quite concerned."

"I take it you are not?"

"It can only mean less competition for us. Now, if I may suggest that you choose a comfortable seat . . . I'm afraid that our story is a long one."

"I hope that it will prove as illuminating as it is lengthy," I replied.

As I watched the two women moving about their home, preparing tea and changing into more comfortable clothing, I was acutely aware of the fascination they still held for me.

"I would like to begin by expressing my sorrow that you and your colleague have become entrapped in this vicious affair," began the mother once we were all seated—the two women side by side on the chaise facing me.

"I'm afraid your apology is poorly timed. Politeness at this late moment strikes me as highly inappropriate. What I was hoping for was information—concerning a certain midnight visitor to Barrow Reece's *Virginia Argus* office, or a suspicious fire set at Mr. Reece's secluded cabin, or . . ."

Madame L'Espanaye halted my recitation with an indignant wave of her hand.

"Monsieur Poe, if you please. Spare the details for the moment in the interest of clarity. I don't quite understand what it is you're trying to say."

"The details are everything!" I lashed out angrily. "Detail one: Your former manservant, Jarvis, died from an overconsumption of laudanum which had been forcibly given to him by someone anxious to learn your whereabouts. Detail two: Barrow Reece was violently murdered because he was investigating Jarvis's death and was about to publish some revealing information concerning the poor man's killer."

Camille suddenly began to sob and she buried her hands in her face.

"And you believe that I played a part in these crimes?" her mother asked, genuinely shocked by my intimations. "But this is incredible!"

"Either you or that damned lover of yours, Mario de la Costa!"

At the mention of de la Costa's name, Camille abruptly ceased her crying and fixed her gaze on me.

"De la Costa my lover?" Madame L'Espanaye began to shake her head as a thin smile of contempt appeared on her lips. "I am indeed astonished at the waywardness of your delusions, my dear sir. For a person of your intellect to have erred so grievously is reassuring to those of us who also make mistakes in judging human nature."

Both mother and daughter had regained their composure and it was I who was now placed on the defensive, forced to substantiate my insolent accusations.

"You have not been corresponding with him since his prison escape? You have not been planning for years to join each other here in America and continue the affair that began during your captivity? And did you not flee Richmond because Inspector Lucchino Contadina had arrived on the scene and you feared leading him to your beloved's hiding place?"

"*He* is here as well?" asked Camille.

"Where is Lucchino?" asked madame. "We must contact him at once. Aside from you, he is our only ally."

"I'm no ally as yet, Madame L'Espanaye."

"You will be when you learn the truth. But I don't understand, Monsieur Poe, why you have involved yourself."

"There are the unsolved deaths of two innocent people. Let that stand as reason enough for now. I assume you are pleading either innocence or ignorance regarding these deaths?"

"We are, at the most, guilty by association. But we certainly never expected, nor did we cause, any of the violence you describe. I swear to you this is the first we have heard of these murders."

Camille heartily nodded her agreement.

"Then I suggest that if you earnestly wish to put my suspicions to rest, you unburden yourself before me . . . there is a great deal left unexplained and we cannot act until I know more. I've already survived one attack on my life, and I've no wish to provoke another through ignorance."

"Our name is Verneuil, not L'Espanaye," began madame. "This name we took only upon our arrival in America, I suppose in part to bury the memories of the tale I am about to relate. I lived with my husband, Henri Verneuil, in a small village in the Corsican highlands. It was said that he killed two small children belonging to the de la Costas, a prominent family from a neighboring hamlet. Do not appear so shocked, Monsieur Poe. The killing of the children was an act of revenge for an even greater atrocity committed by the de la Costas against our family—although I will admit that no one remembered exactly what it was. It is a way of life with us —no one likes it, no one publicly condones it, yet no one steps forward to change it. Indeed, men turn bandit in order to preserve this mad institution. You must understand that, once you are committed to the vendetta, you are committed to performing an act demanded of you by a thousand years of history. When one backs down, one inherits not only the shame of one's family but the scorn of one's ancestors.

"So you can understand that following the death of these two children, it fell upon the de la Costa clan to retaliate. Mario de la Costa, a fiery, brazen sort of fellow who was already building up a reputation for lawlessness among the local police, was the eldest son and therefore it was his duty to see that a suitable revenge was extracted. The obvious course of action—the murder of my husband, Henri—was made impossible when he died from influenza. Therefore, this lunatic de la Costa kidnapped Camille, who was but three at the time, and myself, and fled with us to a remote hideout in the mountains, where he had assembled a formidable gang. These bandits made a routine of robbing the island's French officials and couriers, and distributing whatever goods they stole among our poorer citizens. He was, consequently, less of a brigand than the sensation-seeker French papers claimed.

"Either out of love or humanity, Mario de la Costa could not find it within himself to kill us. He was under no pressure from his gang, who preferred my cooking to their own, and he was beyond the influence of his family. Nearly a year passed, a year in which I was ultimately forced to submit to de la Costa's advances—in order to save ourselves. I eventually succeeded in contacting the police in Ajaccio, by bribing one of de la Costa's lieutenants with certain favors.

"One winter morning, shortly before dawn, we were awakened

by gunfire, and within minutes all of de la Costa's henchmen were either dead or captured, and we were delivered into the hands of Lucchino Contadina, leader of the detachment of police sent to rescue us. At the trial, I said only what was necessary. But don't think for a moment that I did not witness crimes sufficient to sentence de la Costa to the guillotine. I merely held my tongue. Too many had already died."

Madame shook her head in exhausted remembrance.

"With us Corsicans, love is not the strongest emotion. . . . Still stronger is the power of revenge. As he was led away to prison following the trial, de la Costa's clansmen, rather than offering him words of comfort or encouragement, spat at him, swore at him and callously turned their backs on him. He had failed in his mission to carry out the vendetta! His last words to me were not those of one lover to another—they were those of killer to intended victim. He vowed to escape, to seek us out wherever we were, and murder us. Contadina, Camille and myself!

"For the imprisoned Mario de la Costa, the simple lust for revenge slowly supplanted the demands of the vendetta. We had caused him to be humiliated in front of his clansmen, we had brought death down on many of his gang and we were responsible for his imprisonment. Twice he escaped, and twice he was easily recaptured. But on the third attempt, he somehow, perhaps only through the incredible strength lent him by his obsession, made his way across France to Marseilles, where he boarded a boat for Corsica. He was discovered at last, unconscious from exhaustion in a barn less than a kilometer from the house Camille and I shared!"

"I'm curious. Did you ever tell de la Costa's fortune while you were his captive?"

Madame Verneuil merely nodded, as though she were ashamed of the fact.

"And you detected, and I quote, 'a strong, chilling message from the future'?"

Again, she agreed silently.

"Then Mario de la Costa was the subject whom you described

to me that night of our first session together. The man whose fortune you characterized as unspeakable."

"That is correct, Monsieur Poe. And it is unspeakable, indeed. So unspeakable, in fact, that it has not yet played itself out!"

She collapsed back in the chaise, momentarily drained. In response to her rather ominous declaration, I looked worriedly around the room, as though to verify that we were alone and surrounded by four sturdy walls.

After a minute or two of silence, I begged for Madame Verneuil to continue her narrative. "What about our Mr. Contadina, then?"

"Oh, we kept in close contact. What with the business of the trial and its rather painful aftermath, we saw a good deal of each other. I last saw the inspector on the night de la Costa was recaptured so near to our home. Above all, he seemed an ambitious and effective official. If anyone is capable of following de la Costa here, it would be Lucchino Contadina.

"Soon thereafter, I fled to America with my daughter. I knew that it would only be a matter of time before de la Costa escaped from prison and was successful in his murder attempts. And now, almost miraculously, he is here. We saw him, together, on the streets of Richmond! We had read of his fourth escape, kept a close watch on him through the French papers, but we never dreamed that it would be within his power to follow us. We left Richmond immediately, and joined the carnival you saw us with today."

For several minutes, no one uttered a word.

I was shocked by the implications of Madame Verneuil's story —so precisely detailed, so sincerely told that it could not be anything but the truth. The bandit Mario de la Costa sought the women not out of love as I had at first assumed, but out of an obsessive desire to murder them: a strange and virulent desire that had its origins in a decades-old, nearly forgotten Corsican feud! And Contadina, whom I had assumed Madame Verneuil loathed, was our only ally against the deadly, duplicitous de la Costa!

Fifteen

As I digested Madame Verneuil's astounding story, Camille glided into the kitchen and returned with three glasses of a familiar opaque liquid.

"I suggest we take immediate steps to contact Mr. Contadina," I said, trying my best to ignore the temptation represented by the laudanum. "Unless I have underestimated the worthy inspector, I would venture to say that if you two are in New York he cannot be far behind. We might use the same method he used in attempting to contact you—a personal announcement in the New York papers. Their circulation is quite extensive."

"If I may suggest a more effective means of contacting Monsieur Contadina . . . ?" offered Madame Verneuil.

"But of course," I replied.

"I am acquainted with a gentleman of some standing in New York's Corsican community, by the name of Renzo Gentinetta. He is a man from whom the city can conceal little, and he is familiar with our curious story, thanks to several . . . visits he has paid us. If Contadina is here, he may know it."

"And where might I find this Gentinetta fellow?"

"There is a tavern located in one of the city's poorer neighborhoods, known as La Maquis—a gathering place for our countrymen. Gentinetta is a frequent patron."

"I shall head there straightaway. In the meantime, I think it advisable that you two remain on your guard—stay indoors as much as possible. De la Costa knows you are here, thanks to Barrow's enterprising journalism. It is only a matter of time before he learns your address. Where our Monsieur Contadina possesses skill and intellect, de la Costa possesses an equal portion of desperation. It is anyone's guess which will prove the stronger weapon."

As my statement dangled in the air, I stared at my laudanum glass in confusion. I had accepted it automatically, as one accepts brandy and water from a hospitable host. It was a foregone conclusion that I would drink from it.

Why had I not the strength to say no?

"Come, come, Monsieur Poe," chided Camille, taking my hand and bringing the glass to my lips. "Take it, if only to help dissolve the remainder of your suspicions about us. We have a long road ahead and it may be awhile before we have a similar opportunity."

Camille's mother smiled her seductive agreement, and the two women raised their laudanum glasses in a toast.

"To the success of our friends, and the defeat of our foes."

As we brought our glasses together, they seemed to spark as they made contact; and a ghost of playful depravity appeared in the four black, feminine eyes that met mine.

I sipped gingerly from the liquid, testing it for strength, taste and effect. A world of dangerous work awaited us and time was in short supply; yet all I could imagine, all that I wanted to imagine, was a lifetime spent in the sensual sanctuary of these nearly entombing rooms.

It had happened so quickly, so naturally. That we three would find ourselves together in these chambers was never anything less than inevitable. As the landscape dissolved into haze, the two women came towards me. All memories of home and hearth vanished as their dark, demanding faces filled my vision.

I had begun my relationship with them by accident. I had not been charged by passion or lust (or even by an overwhelming desire to know my future), yet I found myself needing them as an alcoholic craves his daily ration of whiskey. They gave freely of themselves, they willingly bestowed pleasure on the lowliest man who called at their door. With those for whom they cared little, Madame and Camille Verneuil were the most ardent, inventive of lovers; the attentions they bestowed on me, a gentleman of whom they appeared genuinely fond, were almost inhuman.

The laudanum, with the sluggish insistence of a worm burrowing towards a freshly buried coffin, crawled through my five senses, working its characteristic sorcery with my perceptions of time. All men dream of a creature who lives for nothing but pleasure: a woman for whom life holds no meaning other than the invention and practice of erotic pastimes; a woman who will make love constantly and repeatedly, even though the man knows he will never be able to physically match her. Under the influence of the laudanum, with its ability to telescope each passing second into a millennium, I sensed that the two women would be mine forever, eternally passionate, through life, death and beyond.

"We must contact Gentinetta . . . immediately . . . tonight if possible . . ." I heard the words I was speaking, but could not feel my lips form them. A hand glided behind my neck and lifted my head off the couch, as though I were a sick man being offered medicine by a solicitous nurse. It was not medicine that met my lips, but another mouth, and I felt a tongue push its way through my teeth, which parted easily to admit it. It began to lick the inside of my cheek—I shut my eyes and imagined—like a child dreaming of the places spoken of in bedtime stories. I saw the tongue: a dancing, dark red pyramid pirouetting from cheek to cheek, skating dizzily over the ice-sharp surfaces of my teeth.

I was no longer conscious of sight or sound; I sensed only a searing, curling wetness on my face, on both cheeks; it descended slowly, eddying unpredictably down across my throat.

Two diaphanous, nearly unidentifiable silhouettes were painstakingly devouring me. The wet heat that had been incubated on my face was now everywhere. Hands landed on my body with the delicacy of fine mist and wound themselves around and around, first my torso, and then each of my legs. I felt enveloped, wrapped up, yet still the hands continued in ever-widening circles, raising the hairs on my legs.

I turned to my left and opened my eyes. I was horrified to see three motionless human figures lying bundled up on the couch in violent disarray, as though all their limbs had been simultaneously broken. I recoiled momentarily in shock. I flayed randomly with my left arm—a mouth followed it, kissing the length, engulfing the fingers one after another.

There was laughter, a choking, sucking giggle. From somewhere below came a guarded, throaty chuckle that vibrated within me.

From the three corpses?

Then my own laughter joined that which was already drifting away. Our clothes, silently, unknowingly shed, lay afloat on the chaise!

"What a fool that morbid mind can make of you," laughed some-one.

I smiled my agreement and turned back, pressing my cheek against another. In tandem, as though welded together, our two faces descended to a third face and kissed it from end to end.

Then, with a precision so complex it seemed random, Camille and I left the disappointed mouth of her mother and joined our-selves together. In fits and flurries, in brief skirmishes between recognition and intoxication, we heated each other, stabbing with our hands and tongues as though combatants. She fastened on to me and pulled me into her, her hands rippling over my back to ensure the completeness of our coupling.

A quivering, gelatinous chill bored upwards from the center of our bodies. Then, to counterpoint the almost unbearably pleasur-able coldness that bit at our legs, stomachs and breasts, needle points of heat began to erupt on my back, in no discernible pattern, but with startling voracity. As Camille tightly cradled me, swerv-ing and slipping beneath me, her mother attentively bit and kissed those portions of my body not consumed by her daughter.

I was entirely pierced by pleasure!

One by one, my extremities were lost to my thoughts. With each breath, now clipped and panicky as though I were struggling for air, I slipped further and further away from consciousness. The two women pulled me over a precipice, and I hurtled downward into bottomless darkness, clutching tightly onto their bodies for support, shuddering with a terrible pleasure.

Suddenly, I noticed that the door seemed to be moving, undulating slowly as though it were made of liquid. It was buckling and heaving, its normallly straight and angled outlines curved and trembling.

It was opening!

I was conscious of a slow, meandering cry of terror welling up from somewhere deep inside of me. It grew focused, demanding, and entirely uncontrollable. I sensed it flowing up my throat like a backwards waterfall, and as it escaped my lips, I was no longer sure if I heard it resound in reality, or merely reverberate in the muffled unconsciousness that finally claimed me.

I am not sufficiently versed in the effects of tincture of opium to ascertain exactly how long I remained asleep. I awoke in total darkness, confused as to my whereabouts. I lay motionless for a moment, waiting for my eyes to accustom themselves to the gloom.

I waited in vain. Not a shred of illumination pierced my vision. Nor could I hear the slightest noise, or detect any movement. I was sealed off somewhere, a prisoner. I felt as though I had been prematurely entombed.

I felt around me and above me, tentatively at first, as though I were afraid my hands might encounter the pine panels of a casket.

No, I was not encased in anything. I was free to sit or stand, to move about if I wished—or if I dared.

My worst fears thus proven groundless, I was no longer as afraid, merely bewildered. Though I felt clearheaded and free from the effects of an alcoholic hangover, my memory was a useless appendage. I could not recall where I had been my last waking moment. With my arms I executed broader, more exploratory motions; my right hand scraped across a wooden floor, played briefly with the edge of a frayed carpet, then encountered an empty glass, which lay on its side. I was in a normal, everyday room filled with everyday articles. My left hand moved more quickly, feeling in the air for a table leg or something equally recognizable, but encountering instead human flesh!

As my hand groped across the skin, I grew more and more uneasy. There was a decidedly bizarre aspect to this flesh. It was too cool; indeed, it seemed to grow more frigid by the minute. It did not move or react to the explorations of my hand.

With a shudder, the truth dawned upon me. It was dead flesh!

My hand flew back to my side and I stood up rapidly, backing away from this horror until I collided roughly with a wall. I fumbled in the darkness for a lamp, dreading the fearful sight that awaited me, yet dreading even more being left alone in the dark with it. I finally succeeded in locating and lighting a stout candle, which I played about the room until the corpse slowly took form in the shadows, dead limb by dead limb.

And as I recognized the face, the last few hours came flying back to me in crystalline, intimate detail.

Camille Verneuil lay dead at the foot of the chaise where she had entertained me, her naked body blotched with bruises and flecked with blood. Her mouth was frozen in a firmly set grimace of determination, mirroring every ounce of strength she had summoned to resist her killer. Her brilliant black eyes, the only feature of her body that seemed to still bear traces of life, were wide open, holding a look of startled recognition.

I brought the candle nearer her body and bent as close as I dared. Stretching from ear to ear was a deep cut, similar to the wound that had killed Barrow. Camille's blood had dried a rusty brown, giving the wound the appearance of a leather neck band. Her blood had flowed profusely indeed, running in torrents down the smooth path between her breasts, collecting in a pool on her stomach. In the mournful silence that reigned throughout the apartment, the intermittent dripping of blood from her body onto the floorboards seemed an intolerable din.

I turned away, revolted, to face an even more repulsive sight: Madame Verneuil's body lay across the room, face down on the floor, her arms outstretched in supplication, reaching vainly for the doorway into the kitchen. She had obviously tried to reach the next room ahead of her murderer, perhaps hoping to close the door on him. But he had finished his hideous work with the daughter, and had closed in on the mother, reaching her seconds before she could effect her escape. Her once-noble fingers stretched out from the hands towards the door; they appeared so long it seemed to me that they had grown, fed by the terror that had overcome her.

Her body, which had glistened so seductively in the candlelight when alive, now seemed to absorb the scanty illumination my candle offered, darkening morbidly before my eyes. I knelt down next to her and gingerly attempted to turn the body over in order to examine the wound.

What next occurred was so unexpected, so bizarre, that not a night has gone by since when I have not seen it replayed in my mind in unforgettable detail!

As I attempted to lift Madame Verneuil, there came a nauseating splash, as though a heavy parcel had been dropped into a pool of stagnant water. I had succeeded in turning her body onto its back, but with the head I was not so successful. It remained where it was, face down, and totally severed from the body!

I collapsed onto the floor in a sitting position, struggling to remain conscious. I shut my eyes but they fought my commands, forcing themselves open, compelling me to witness the carnage I had somehow survived.

I needed to think; action was called for—immediately! But never had the simple art of connecting one thought to another seemed so impossible. I staggered to my feet, dressed hastily, and walked across the room to the kitchen, sliding on the blood like a novice ice skater. I poured a pitcherful of water over my head, letting the cold liquid cascade over my features in an attempt to restore my faculties.

I then pulled back the curtain and peered down to the streets. They were dark and empty. It was obviously well after midnight and evidently the women had not screamed loudly enough to arouse either the neighbors or the police. The end must have come swiftly and silently, their screams of terror stillborn in their throats.

But why was I spared?

Did the killer hope that I would sleep longer, long enough to provide the police with a handy culprit for the crimes?

Yes, of course, that had been his plan! The women would not report for work in the morning, their employer would send someone around to rouse them, he would report their curious lack of response, the police would be summoned and they would batter the door down to find me on the floor, my victims lying beside me.

I would be gone long before the police arrived—but how was I then to proceed?

Based on Madame Verneuil's startling narrative, I was certain that the murderer was Mario de la Costa—whose entrance I would have undoubtedly witnessed had I remained conscious a few seconds longer. But if I were to go to the police, report the crimes and my suspicions concerning the killer, would they believe me? Mightn't they detain me overnight, subject me to harsh, incessant questioning? Would they not contact my family, thus exposing my shameful relationship with the dead women? The shock of my adulterous behavior, so intoxicating a few short hours ago, would, I was convinced, kill my sickly, sensitive wife.

And if de la Costa were captured, would he not point an accusatory finger at me? He had, after all, found me at the scene of the crime.

I recalled how the building's other tenants had glanced at the Verneuils and me with such disdain, as we climbed the stairs a few short hours ago. Had they gotten a good look at me? Could they describe me to the police? The stairway had been dimly illuminated at best, but inquisitive neighbors often have the sharpest of eyes. Though they may have seen nothing, I could not afford to ignore the grim possibility that they too were capable of implicating me in the crime.

Either way I turned, my position seemed hopeless, the problem insoluble . . .

Unless . . .

Unless another suspect could be apprehended—someone who knew nothing of me and my involvement with the Verneuil women, someone who would find it impossible to defend himself against charges of murder.

I halted my pacing abruptly. I thought back on something Madame Verneuil had mentioned earlier that evening, and slowly a plan began to formulate in my mind. Out of my drug-laden lethargy a potential killer appeared: vicious, bloodthirsty, possessed of great strength, easily capable of perpetrating the awful murders for which I was to have taken the blame.

The scheme was almost too bizarre to warrant consideration. Yet if I handled everything properly, I could provide the police with a guilty party, and thus divert suspicion from myself while keeping my family innocent of my involvement in the affair.

Fear was now seeping through my body, as ground water slowly infiltrates a basement floor. But the fear brought with it fresh reserves of strength and determination, and I hurried into the living room, ignoring the corpses as well as I could while I put the first part of my plan into action.

In the once-comfortable, feminine rooms I created an inhuman chaos. I ripped curtains from the walls, tearing them apart with hands and teeth; the bedclothes I subjected to the same brutal fate, scattering the torn tufts of the sheets in all directions.

I emptied the contents of the women's two dressers and steamer trunks onto the floor. Whatever valuables I could find—coins, jewelry, a pitiful handful of banknotes—I displayed prominently about the room, hoping to dispel robbery as a motive for the slayings.

Drawers were pulled out, their contents thrown about the room, their finely crafted wooden frames kicked brutally into kindling.

I smashed a mirror, and with the jagged shards of broken glass, I shredded Madame Verneuil's hand-sewn pillows and knitted tablecloth.

Vases were hurled to the floor and shattered, the flowers trampled underfoot.

Our tea glasses I emptied, scattering handfuls of the soggy leaves around the bodies; the glasses I left standing intact on the table in strange contrast to the total destruction around them.

The impression I created, as I sat back to survey my handiwork, was not that of two women murdered for their money, or of rooms madly ransacked for treasure. It did not suggest a lover's quarrel in which a wronged husband impulsively murders his wife in a fit of passion.

It was a picture of irrational, unfettered bestiality!

I grew conscious of a gradual lessening of the darkness, of fine, parallel lines of light appearing on the bloodstained surface of Camille's skin.

Dawn was filtering in through the tight black slats of the shutters.

I stood up instantly. Accompanying the slow arrival of morning were hurried footfalls from the hallway outside the door. Someone had been awakened by the unholy clamor I had created, and was coming to investigate!

I padded silently to the door and assured myself it was locked. The footsteps grew louder, then stopped altogether and were replaced by sharp, demanding knocks.

"Mrs. L'Espanaye, Mrs. L'Espanaye! Are you all right in there?" came a hoarse, sleepy-sounding masculine voice.

"Hullo, hullo, it's me, Mrs. McCabe, your downstairs neighbor. Are you two all right in there?" called a female voice, probably the wife of the first.

They conferred in inaudible tones. I rushed to the window, lifted the glass as high as it would go, and with a great deal of effort, was able to throw back the shutters and gaze down into the streets. They were for the most part deserted, although lights were beginning to come on in the apartment across the street. Directly below, the ground was soft and muddy, but the drop was four stories and I doubted my chances of emerging from a jump intact.

"Mrs. L'Espanaye," called a third, more authoritative male voice. "It's me, Mr. Beans, the landlord. I think it would be better if you opened up. We can't have this kind of noise this time of the morning. We don't get enough sleep as it is."

Another whispered conference took place. Someone complained about the inherent risks of taking in foreign boarders, and someone else ventured the opinion that the police be summoned.

I was a mass of indecision. I could not bring myself to abandon the two women. Even in death, they exerted a powerful, intoxicating influence over me. They embraced the blood-soaked floor as they had embraced their countless lovers, their faces a mixture of terror and ecstasy.

I bent over Camille and ran my hand delicately across the cold curve of her hip, slowly caressing the dried blood that stained her thigh until it grew warm and liquid beneath my touch. I felt tears collecting in my eyes.

"Please don't make us break this lock, Mrs. L'Espanaye," cried the agitated Mr. Beans.

My confused thoughts were obliterated in an instant by the gruff cry of the landlord. Self-preservation leapt again to the forefront, and I returned to the open window as Mr. Beans, aided by the first voice, began to hurl his body against the door.

I looked desperately up and down the outer wall of the building, searching for an escape path. There were no ornamental outcroppings which offered a foothold, and aside from a lightning rod which hugged the wall and which, in any case, was well out of my reach, the building was entirely featureless.

Then, as the dull thuds emanating from behind the locked door grew more vehement, I saw my salvation emerge from down the block, out of the shadowy dawn.

A heavily laden, horse-drawn tobacco wagon was on its way to the nearby cigar factory with the first of the morning's deliveries. The horse was trotting deliberately up the street, the driver shivering from the predawn chill. Behind him, tightly roped together in parallel clusters, was a soft, thickly piled bed of freshly picked tobacco leaves.

As the door began to give beneath the steady onslaught of Beans and his assistant, I crawled onto the windowsill and balanced myself. Then, with great difficulty, I managed to lower the glass and close the shutters behind me, all the while perched delicately on the edge of the sill. The tobacco wagon rolled closer, its tired driver unaware that he was about to receive a passenger. Rapidly calculating the angle of my fall, and praying that my hasty judgment was sound, I leapt into space.

I crashed into the rear of the wagon with surprising force. The tobacco broke my fall somewhat, nevertheless, a jarring pain coursed through my body and collected in the balls of my feet. I did not strike the bed of the wagon squarely in the middle; rather, I fell feet first towards the rear of the load, immediately collapsing on my back. Before I could steady myself, I slid off the back of the tobacco wagon onto the cold, hard pavement.

For a dazed moment I lay on the cobblestones. But as I heard the wagon slow and the driver utter a confused exclamation, I rapidly regained my feet and hobbled from the thoroughfare into the shelter of a dark, garbage-strewn alley.

Sixteen

The carnival where Madame and Camille Verneuil had worked was still asleep. I entered from a side alley and wandered quietly across the muddied grounds. In the colorlessness of the predawn light, the gaily painted tents and wagons were drab and uninviting, rendering the depressed poverty of the road show more obvious than ever.

Outside of the tottering blue wagon belonging to the Verneuils, I paused and stared blankly, as though I expected the curtains to part and Camille to beckon me seductively inside. Too tired to register emotion, I walked on, coming to a stop before the cage that had contained the East Indian orangutan. It was empty, save for an oaken bucket of filthy drinking water and a rotting pile of some unidentifiable tropical fruit: obviously the escaped beast's breakfast.

His trainer was nowhere to be seen, nor was there a sign of any other carnival employee. Glancing around quickly to assure myself I was not being watched, I reached into the cage, snatched up two handfuls of the ape's coarse red hair from the floor and returned it to my pocket.

I tried to recall the beast's appearance: He had been massive, obviously agile with long, hairy fingers which I could imagine encircling a person's neck with ease. A wild jungle creature who, more than likely, could be easily angered. With grim satisfaction I concluded that the protests of two terrified women would render him absolutely furious!

I was disturbed in my thinking by the loud crack of a door slamming in the immediate vicinity and the cough of a heavy-set man who had not slept well. The carnival was beginning to awaken.

My business concluded, I crept away from the cage and struck out once more for the lodgings of Madame Verneuil and her daughter.

As I gazed on the women's building from the concealment of a nearby alley, I observed that each of New York's numerous law enforcement bodies was well represented. The watchmen, or leatherheads as they are known because of the leather firemen's hats they wear for identification, were milling about, gossiping with various constables and marshals, all as ineffectual as the curiosity seekers who had gathered in great numbers. They were peering up anxiously at the fourth-story window I had recently jumped from, watching the shadowy figures of policemen going about their business.

I waited impatiently, hoping for the crowd to thin out, but it showed no signs of doing so. Indeed, as the minutes crawled by, the ranks of officials and bystanders alike seemed to swell.

Too tired to reason or proceed with caution, I stumbled out of the alley and entered the crowd, stepping on toes and bumping into people, all the while muttering apologies. In short, I behaved as clumsily and as discourteously as everyone else, and in so doing, was able to make my way to the lightning rod that led down from the roof without attracting the least bit of attention.

I stared up at the fourth-story room and exchanged a few shocked exclamations with a destitute couple to my left. While we were engaged in a brief conversation, my right hand slipped several shocks of the orangutan hair into strategic locations along the short length of the lightning rod.

I nodded my respects to the young couple and turned away, my mission completed. As I reached the perimeter of the crowd and began to walk towards home at last, the nausea that rightfully should have overcome me the moment I discovered the murders began to manifest itself in heavy, oppressive waves.

As I entered our parlor, drained by what seemed like the longest night of my life, I was shocked to see two uniformed constables embroiled in earnest discussion with mother!

As they turned to greet my arrival, their expressions went from grim to deadly serious.

I started to shiver with genuine terror. Had they, contrary to my wildest expectations, already succeeded in connecting me with the double murder?

Before I could introduce myself, mother rose to her feet and stalked angrily over to me, her face a picture of stern sobriety.

"Eddie, where in God's name have you been?" She sniffed busily around my mouth, then stood back and planted her hands on her hips.

"You haven't touched a drop of alcohol!" she exclaimed in surprise. "Or else the art of distilling has progressed to such an extent that whiskey is now odorless."

The two officers stood at a distance, conferring in embarrassed whispers. Finally one stepped forward, and reluctantly addressed mother.

"I assume, ma'am, that this is the 'missing person' in question?"

"Yes, this is he, all right. I'm awfully sorry to have troubled you."

At this brief exchange, I breathed a deep sigh of relief.

"We'll be going, then," continued the constable. "I'm glad he turned up." The two officers executed clumsy bows and left quickly, obviously relieved to have avoided mother's dictatorial employ.

"Mother, I'm very touched that you would go to all the trouble of filing a missing person's report. But there was no need to go to such lengths. You see . . ."

"Damn your explanations, and damn your gratitude as well, Eddie. It never occurred to me that you were in any real danger. I just thought that if the police were to find you drunk in some alley, this time you might be shamed into a little reform."

I puffed myself up, straightening my soiled clothes as well as I could.

"Well, as you can see, and as you can smell, not a drop of liquor has passed my lips since you saw me last."

"That hardly explains a twenty-four-hour absence, sober or not."

"There is a small literary publication in New Jersey, *The Scribe* by name actually, and they advertised in yesterday afternoon's papers for an editor. Fearful that competition for the post would be stiff, I took the liberty of boarding a ferry without notifying you. I had hoped to return with the glad tidings that I had secured permanent employment.

"Unfortunately, by the time I arrived, which was well after dark, they had gone bankrupt, and were consequently no longer in need of my services. There being no later ferry, I was forced to pass the night in a local inn, where I had a glass of good, strong tea with my dinner before retiring at nine o'clock. I returned this morning on the eight o'clock boat. Owing to the fact that my room was situated above a particularly boisterous tavern that was open until dawn, I have slept very little, so if you'll excuse me, I'll wash and repair to my bed."

I offered mother a warm, affectionate kiss, and turned on my heels without waiting for a rebuttal. As I trudged up the stairs, I glanced over my shoulder to see mother mulling over my surprisingly sarcastic outburst.

When I entered our bedroom, Virginia was wide awake, anticipating my return. Ordinarily she slept as soundly as an infant; I could come and go at all hours without disturbing her.

But this morning was different. The bedclothes were in an extreme state of disarray, as though she had had a nightmare, or had lain awake for hours seeking a comfortable position.

There was a glimmer in her eyes, a symbol of something distant and foreign to her character.

"Buddie. We have to talk. Seriously."

"Not now, my darling. I'm exhausted. I've been to New Jersey and back in search of a job. The trip was totally in vain. I need some rest." I removed my clothes and, letting them fall to the floor, crawled slowly into bed. I wanted to be a youngster again, for sleep to be more than recuperative. I wanted to fall asleep with the knowledge that adult powers would attack and solve my problems before morning.

"Buddie, we don't have a proper marriage. I'm convinced of it. Are you listening?"

"Yes," I replied, already half asleep.

"Another married woman was here today. Looking for a room, which unfortunately we were not able to offer her. She seemed such a sweet woman. Her husband was away at work and couldn't come. But we talked quite a bit together."

"That must have been enjoyable," I said, feeling guilty that I was not able to converse intelligently with Virginia. But I craved sleep above all else.

"She told me of feelings she has. That I don't ever have. I couldn't sleep because I had to talk to you about them. It has to do with finally being treated like a grown-up woman. There's a terrible pressure inside of me, Buddie, a terrible pressure which none of you wants to recognize. Buddie . . .

Virginia's words echoed in my ears for a few more seconds until sleep descended upon me with a thick blanket of silence.

The *New York Evening Herald* devoted its entire front page to coverage of the gruesome double murder:

A CORSICAN FORTUNE-TELLER AND HER DAUGHTER WERE DISCOVERED THIS MORNING, BRUTALLY SLAIN IN THEIR FOURTH-FLOOR APARTMENT ON JOHN ST. MADAME AND CAMILLE L'ESPANAYE HAD BEEN DEAD FOR SEVERAL HOURS WHEN THEY WERE FOUND AT SEVEN-THIRTY THIS MORNING BY ANDREW BEANS, LANDLORD OF THE BUILDING IN QUES-

TION. CAUSE OF DEATH WAS DETERMINED TO BE A LOSS OF
BLOOD FROM SEVERE THROAT WOUNDS PROBABLY ADMINIS-
TERED WITH A KNIFE OR RAZOR.

THE APARTMENT WAS IN THE WILDEST DISORDER—THE
FURNITURE BROKEN AND THROWN ABOUT IN ALL DIREC-
TIONS. THE DRAWERS OF A BUREAU AND A STEAMER
TRUNK WERE OPEN AND HAD APPARENTLY BEEN RIFLED,
ALTHOUGH WHAT MEAGER VALUABLES THE WOMEN POS-
SESSED WERE STILL SCATTERED ABOUT THE ROOM IN PLAIN
SIGHT. THE KILLER'S MEANS OF ESCAPE REMAINS A MYS-
TERY, AS THE DOOR TO THE WOMEN'S CHAMBERS WAS
LOCKED FROM THE INSIDE AND ATTEMPTS BY POLICE OFFI-
CERS TO CLIMB DOWN THE BUILDING FROM THE OUTSIDE
MET WITH FAILURE. NOR WERE ANY FOOTPRINTS OR FUR-
THER EVIDENCE OF THE KILLER'S PRESENCE DISCOVERED IN
THE MUDDY GROUND SURROUNDING THE BUILDING.

TO THIS HORRIBLE MYSTERY, THERE IS NOT YET, WE BE-
LIEVE, THE SLIGHTEST CLUE.

A related story had this to report:

SPOKESMEN FROM THIS CITY'S GROWING CORSICAN COMMU-
NITY, RECENTLY AT THE CENTER OF VIOLENT RELIGIOUS
AND FAMILY RIVALRIES, EXPRESSED FEAR THAT REPRESSIVE
POLICE MEASURES WOULD FOLLOW THE DEATHS OF THE
L'ESPANAYE WOMEN, AS NEW YORK'S LAW ENFORCEMENT
OFFICIALS PRESS THEIR SEARCH FOR THE PERPETRATOR OF
THESE AWFUL CRIMES INTO THE HEART OF THE CORSICAN
NEIGHBORHOODS.

As mother, Virginia, Gowans and myself sat that same evening
at the dinner table, our boarder, openly fascinated by the crimes,
read aloud from the newspapers, relishing each and every dramatically delivered sentence. Virginia, moody and irritable, absorbed
the news with equanimity, while mother, much to Gowans's delight, blanched and gasped at each shocking particular.

My reaction, full of calculated astonishment, fell somewhere between those of Virginia and mother. I registered surprise and indignation, but attempted to exert a calming influence whenever Gowans mentioned that the vicious murderer was still at large.

"But with someone like that you never know," exclaimed mother. "His motives are so curious, and the crime is so inhumanely brutal. Perhaps he might strike again."

"Indeed he might, madame," replied Gowans, happily fueling her fear. "I would definitely term this a pleasure killing, and pleasure, as we all know, can be extremely addictive."

I, of course, knew otherwise. De la Costa was done with killing. Although his exact plans were unknown to me, I was certain they did not include murder.

"I would venture a slightly different opinion," I interjected. "Our murderer, temporarily satiated, will withdraw again into the anonymous ranks of society, until the urge to kill overcomes him again. However, he is no fool, judging by the miraculous nature of his escape." I gave mother a reassuring glance. "He knows the police here are at least familiar with his methods. I think we have seen the last of him in New York. I predict when he surfaces again, it will be someplace far away, where his next crime will again have the same numbing effect on the populace."

"You may be right there, my dear fellow," agreed Gowans through a mouthful of Irish stew. "However, have a listen to this. . . ."

"Please," objected mother. "I think we're familiar enough with the details of this crime, Mr. Gowans. Perhaps you'd be good enough to read quietly to yourself?"

Gowans cleared his throat in mock irritation, glanced briefly at Virginia, then nodded at mother in understanding. He immediately continued his reading, and not another word passed his lips during the meal.

I slept dreamlessly for nine hours, and awoke feeling at least physically refreshed. I had recovered somewhat from the shock of the terrible events of the evening before last, and was for the first time in twenty-four hours able to think with a modicum of logic.

But my mind was a jumble of contradictions.

I prayed that I had planted enough false clues to deflect police suspicion from myself, if only temporarily. Yet I still had no way of knowing whether the building's tenants had identified me or not. I could only wait.

But could I now morally terminate my commitment? Just what was the nature of this commitment? How much of my desire to see justice done, beginning with the death of Jarvis, could be attributed to a sense of moral rectitude, and how much to a consumptive desire to be reunited with the L'Espanaye women? Like consumption, this need had worked beneath the surface, never blatantly controlling me, yet subtly coloring all my actions.

But the women were now dead—the most terrifying of their prognostications had been fulfilled. There was a sense of completion in their deaths; the final link in the chain of murder which began with the deaths of Jarvis and Barrow Reece was now in place.

Yet the entire affair, from that first chance encounter on the Richmond-bound steamer, had taken on such importance in my life that to leave four people unavenged, one a close friend and two my lovers, seemed a criminal act in itself.

I knew that as long as de la Costa remained free I would be useless as a human being. As long as his mind was clear, mine would be clouded. The thought of this fiend returning to the pleasurable pursuits of daily life was intolerable. The picture of him sleeping behind unlocked doors, walking unconcernedly down city streets, eating, drinking and socializing without fear of reprisal or revenge, was more than I could bear.

Unless he was dealt with to my satisfaction, I could never experience a return to normality. I realized with painful clarity that Mario de la Costa had come to represent the chaos and disorder in my own life.

He had to be confronted with the horror of his own inhumanity!

The next night I found myself in the heart of New York City's immigrant district, masking my misgivings beneath a facade of grim determination, trying my best to look as though I belonged there.

I had forgone my normally strict standards of personal hygiene in order that I might appear at ease among Manhattan's downtrodden. My hair was uncombed, my face unwashed and unshaven, and I affected a bold, angry walk that I hoped would dissuade those groups of suspicious men I passed who more than likely had robbery on their minds. As I wandered through the crowded, cobblestoned alleys, past warming fires improvised from refuse, and beneath curtains of tattered, nearly frozen laundry, I attracted no more than a few curious stares.

I knew that as a single individual, my chances of apprehending Mario de la Costa were virtually nil. Now that his dreadful task was complete, he would be preparing to leave New York either by ship or by road. It was obviously impossible for me to keep watch on all the exits from the city—even if I knew what he looked like.

And so I was bound for La Maquis, the Corsican gathering place Madame Verneuil had mentioned. There, I hoped to find and enlist the aid of Renzo Gentinetta—and perhaps even that of Inspector Lucchino Contadina.

La Maquis was announced only by a hand-painted sign, and loud, argumentative voices coming from within. A group of black-shawled women were gathered outside the saloon, locked in heated discussion. I stopped and observed them from across the street. After a minute's further debate, one of the women was delegated to enter the bar, which she did only after considerable exhortations on the part of her companions. There followed immediately a violent argument in Corsican dialect inside the saloon, punctuated by the shrill screams of the woman who had entered. In a moment she emerged, shouting a barrage of insults towards whoever had forcibly ejected her. The women conferred for a moment, then in a group stormed off angrily down the street. It seemed that these Corsican women, like their counterparts everywhere, were engaged in an admirable yet hopeless attempt to promote temperance among their husbands.

I hoped my errand would meet with more success. I entered the sparsely furnished tavern and took a seat near the door. Though I endeavored to appear inconspicuous, my presence was as obvious as if a servant had announced my arrival. A group of eight men sat at dinner around a large corner table, and another, separate group was drinking at the bar. They examined me briefly over their shoulders, then returned to their respective discussions.

The tavern owner, a curly-haired, leather-skinned man of indeterminate age, came from behind the bar and approached me with reluctance.

"One drink is all I'd advise, mister," was his inhospitable welcome, delivered surprisingly enough in a thick English accent. "They don't like no one overhearin' 'em," he concluded, pointing with his head to the men conferring over dinner.

"What's an Englishman like yourself doing in this Corsican stronghold?"

"I'm not half as out of place as you, mister. And I've got me friends 'ere."

"Your friends are awfully secretive, don't you think? If they desire privacy, they should not conduct their business in a public place."

"Whatever gave you the idea this was a public place? Now, wot'll you have to drink?"

"I'll have brandy and water, please." The bartender nodded and withdrew. I had no intention of drinking my brandy. I had made a vow to abstain from drink as long as possible—I would need all of my wits about me in the days to come.

As I waited for my drink, I examined the bar's customers in greater detail. They all appeared to be Mediterranean in origin, and were most certainly from either the working or the criminal classes, or both. The drinkers at the bar were engaged in sporadic gossip—their main reason for being there was simply to drink. But the group of men gathered at the dinner table interested me the most. The hushed, deliberate tones in which they conversed were not characteristic of a group of friends gathered for an evening of food, drink and companionship. They had something more serious on their minds.

David Madsen 202

The tavern keeper returned with my brandy, for which I immediately paid—in case an emergency retreat would prove necessary.

"Does a fellow named Gentinetta ever come in here?"

The bartender glanced over at the diners, then back at me.

"Now and again," he replied.

"What about now? Is he at that table over there?"

The bartender eyed me suspiciously.

"If he were, who'd I tell him was askin'?"

"You would tell him a Mr. Poe is inquiring after him. I've come from a mutual friend, Madame L'Espanaye."

The bartender pocketed my coin without a word and walked over to the dinner table to see if any of his guests desired more wine. As he made the rounds, he stopped at the head of the table and whispered into the ear of a tall man who had been presiding over the meeting. The man looked up and regarded me with curiosity—and recognition.

It was the same man I had encountered leaving the women's wagon not two days earlier: the same deep-set eyes, the same rough-hewn face, so harshly lined it looked as though it had been sculpted out of wood. Suddenly, he beckoned me with a brief wave of his hand, and I stood and walked over to join them.

I stood self-consciously before this imposing Corsican, at the side of the table. The others made no effort to move over or offer me a chair. He stared at me silently and impassively—and I realized that the move was mine.

"I presume that I have the honor of addressing Renzo Gentinetta?" I began.

"Whether it is an honor or not, you may judge for yourself. But yes, I am Gentinetta," was his reply. "How may I assist you?"

"Well, you could offer me a chair, to begin with."

"The length of our discussion may not require it. Please, what is on your mind?"

Resolving to hold back no longer, I leaned into their midst and lowered my voice. "I'm searching for someone, a French police inspector by the name of Lucchino Contadina to be exact. I was told . . . by Madame L'Espanaye, that you might know how to find him."

"For what purpose do you seek this gentleman?"

I paused, attempting to dispel the tension that was coiling up within me. Was I correct in wanting to take this stranger into my confidence? Was I really prepared to reveal my involvement in a hideous crime, acting only on the recommendation of a dead woman?

I proceeded reluctantly, knowing I had no other choice.

"I know who killed the L'Espanaye women! With Contadina's help, I'm certain we can capture him!"

I stood back, waiting for the outburst of shock and surprise I had anticipated. But before the men could react to the news, their leader cautioned them to silence with a crash of his fist on the table.

"And how do you come to possess such startling information?"

"That's not important now. What is important is that he be apprehended without the New York police mixing in. And it is quite obvious that I am not equal to the task myself."

The leader looked to his followers for their opinions. One by one they responded with slow, affirmative nods of their heads.

"Please take a chair, monsieur. Your feet must be tired."

After I was seated, Gentinetta presented for my approval his·six fellow-diners, all substantially built, severe-looking individuals whose stretched, reddened faces told me they liked their drink. But the intimidating demeanor they prided themselves on was betrayed by a gentleness, just below the surface, that bespoke contented family lives.

"Anything you say to me, you say to all of us. For though I currently have the honor of presiding over our little *société* . . . or protective league, my voice is actually no stronger than that of the others. As a matter of fact, our meeting tonight concerns the very crime you speak of . . . and police reprisals against our community."

As Gentinetta spoke, I noticed that the bartender was ushering the tavern's other customers out the door, and that they were going quite voluntarily. He bade them a cheerful good-night and locked the door carefully behind them. He smiled at me briefly, then hurried over to the bar where he began the laborious task of washing and drying the night's glasses.

"That day of our chance encounter," began Gentinetta, "I did not dream we would see each other again . . . and on such a sad occasion. You knew the L'Espanayes well?"

"Yes . . . in a professional sense I did."

Gentinetta squinted at this reply, as though searching for a deeper meaning to my statement.

"They were fortune-tellers, after all. Their customers were many. I was but one," I explained. "And you . . . ?"

"You might say I knew them in a professional sense as well. This has all been a great blow to me."

"An outrageous tragedy, to be sure. All the more reason for us to act swiftly. This Contadina, do you know him? Can you find him?"

"Please. First I should know why this man is so vital to your efforts."

"Because he is the only one who knows what the killer looks like! He is familiar with his habits, his methods, his motives. He has followed this murderer across the length and breadth of France, across an ocean to America. Lucchino Contadina is the only man capable of capturing our killer, of that I am certain."

"And this killer. What do *you* know of him?" asked Gentinetta.

"Aside from some past history, very little. Only his name, Mario de la Costa."

The effect of my words on Gentinetta and his fellow Corsicans was immediate and profound. Hushed, excited whispers broke out around the table, accompanied by stares of disbelief.

"Mario de la Costa!" exclaimed Gentinetta. "Are you certain of this?"

"Quite certain. The name was given me by Madame L'Espanaye, herself."

Several moments of strained silence passed, broken only by the startling "pop" of two corks being extracted from fresh bottles of wine.

"This de la Costa has quite a notorious past," I continued. "A rather infamous bandit I believe, who . . ."

"Yes, yes, please, Monsieur Poe. I am quite familiar with this dreaded name . . . and all it implies," interrupted Gentinetta.

He turned away from me, and taking a newly opened bottle of wine, filled his glass, draining it in one swallow. His mood grew pensive and somber.

"The L'Espanayes spoke of you to me. Of your literary brilliance, your ambitious, inquisitive nature . . ."

"Then it seems we both come highly recommended."

"But the addition of de la Costa to this situation demands careful thought. If you will return tomorrow evening, we can discuss the matter further."

"I shall be happy to return," I replied. "But I must impress upon you the need for haste. If we do not act immediately, de la Costa will be gone and the women's deaths will go unavenged."

"They shall not go unavenged!" shouted Gentinetta. "I will make inquiries concerning this Inspector Contadina. If he is in New York, perhaps one of my comrades will know something. Until tomorrow, then . . ."

As I shook Gentinetta's hand and stood to go, I could not resist a parting admonition. "You realize, of course, that no mention of this case can be made to the police?"

"You appear to have some knowledge of Corsican affairs, Monsieur Poe. Therefore you must know of our mistrust of judges and juries, of our hatred for the police. If we do work together, it will be completely outside the law, I can assure you."

I expressed my satisfaction with this arrangement and, following a brief exchange of farewells, I made for the door, which the English bartender opened for me, as scrupulously polite and accommodating as ever.

As I departed, I glanced back at Renzo Gentinetta, already well on the way to finishing his second bottle of wine.

Seventeen

It was nearly midnight when I arrived home following my meeting with Gentinetta. I had told mother and Virginia that several unexpected job prospects had presented themselves, and that in all likelihood I would be home late.

I was therefore surprised to find mother still up, hunched over her writing desk in the parlor, rubbing her tired eyes with an ink-stained hand. As I entered, she turned towards me expectantly.

"Did you have any luck?"

"I'm afraid not," I sighed, taking a seat next to her desk. "There was no need to wait for me, I could just as easily have told you in the morning."

"No, no, Eddie, it's always best to receive bad news when one is too exhausted to think about it. Are there any further prospects in sight?"

"No, the outlook is exceedingly grim . . . but what's this?" I asked, indicating the papers scattered about her desk. "Thinking about plunging into the literary world yourself, are you?"

"These are our accounts, Eddie . . . or what is left of them.

Unless there is an unexpected turnabout in our fortunes, and I use the word loosely, we shall be on the street within a month!"

"What? But that's quite impossible! We have our savings; what about the sewing you and Virginia have been doing, the rent from Mr. Gowans? Surely our situation is not as desperate as you imagine!"

I snatched the stack of papers from mother's grasp and attempted to decipher the rambling array of figures which covered the pages. Mother just as impatiently grabbed them back.

"Don't be so naïve! I've gone over these for the last three hours. I mean what I say. And as for Mr. Gowans, he gave us his notice tonight. He will be gone in a week. He's moving in with some relatives in New Jersey. We should have to sew twenty-four hours a day to match what we took in from the rent of that room."

"We shall have to rent it out immediately then. It is as simple as that."

"If it were as simple as that I would not be in such a foul mood. We shall need a steady income as soon as possible. We have nearly depleted our savings with our day-to-day expenses alone."

I pulled my chair closer to mother, and took her hands in mine.

"Mother, I understand what you are trying to tell me. I believe I have been as diligent as humanly possible in my search for work. But for the time being, I have exhausted all possible avenues of inquiry. The editorial jobs are just not available in these troubled times. Good literature is the last thing on people's minds."

"Eddie, I know that. I realize . . ."

"But there is something at work inside me now. It must be given time to grow, to develop. It will be a radical departure from everything that I've written before, from everything *anybody* has written before! It could make all such financial discussions merely idle chatter. But it cannot be rushed or pressured."

"But in the meantime, Eddie, in the meantime . . ."

"Yes?"

"There are other jobs available. Every day I see a sign or two in shop windows. There are, despite everything, notices in the papers from employers seeking help."

"A job? A job!? You'd like me to find a job?"

"Sssssshhhhhh. Please be quiet, Eddie, for God's sake. Do you want Mr. Gowans to move out tonight?"

"You would like me to lay bricks for a living, stooped over like some wounded soldier, like some cripple? Perhaps you would prefer me to join the street sweepers, to make my living from other people's refuse? Or I could become a clerk in some dimly lit accounting office. Destroy my eyesight trying to set some well-to-do aristocrat's financial affairs in order?"

"Eddie, please!"

"Do you know what an effect such employment would have on my English alone? *Dos, dem, dere, ain't got no, nohow, I are, they is, we was* . . . Trying to play dumb in order to enjoy the camaraderie of my fellow workers!"

"Eddie, damn it," retorted mother, pulling her hands free of my grip, her voice now rising in anger as well.

"Stop playing the arrogant, temperamental artist for a moment and face the facts. We, your family, are in desperate need of funds. I am doing everything in my power to provide for us, but to continue living, we must have money. Surely someone of your considerable intellect is capable of comprehending this one admittedly unartistic, uninspiring, practical fact!"

I stood and paced the darkened parlor. I walked over to the room's one small window and studied the dingy thoroughfare that was Carmine Street.

"I believe in you, Eddie," mother whispered from her chair across the room. "I believe in your talent and this great work you say is evolving within you. And no matter how stubbornly you behave, you can never undermine that belief. But with Gowans gone, we shall be forced to pay the next month's rent entirely by ourselves. And there is just enough in our savings to cover it, after which we shall be entirely without resources. I'm wondering just how this belief of mine is going to feed our family."

I moved slowly towards the stairs, my customary mode of retreat whenever I was at a loss as to how to proceed.

"We still have a little time, mother, until the officials from the poorhouse come calling," I whispered with an obvious lack of conviction. "I promise that I shall use that grace period to find a solution to the distressing problems that confront us."

"So shall I, Eddie," she replied portentously. "So shall I."

I entered our bedroom that night to find the bed peopled by armies of paper cutout figures, fighting heroic, sweeping battles atop the bedclothes, under the command of their general, Virginia. She was, as had become her habit, wide awake despite the lateness of the hour.

"Buddie," she exclaimed happily as I gave her a kiss and began to undress. But then her mood darkened considerably, as she remembered something important that was preying on her mind. "This is growing depressing. I see you in the morning when I wake up and in the evening just as I am about to fall asleep, and not a minute in between. I feel like Princess Whoeversheis here," she said, rather spitefully tearing one of her cutouts into tiny pieces. "Waiting impatiently at home all day while her husband, the prince, has fun killing enemy knights."

"You're growing quite metaphorical these days, darling. Have you been reading over my shoulder again?"

"How can I read over your shoulder when you're never around to do any writing?"

Still partially clothed, I crawled into bed next to her, inadvertently crushing a division of her paper army.

"Buddie! Be careful, I worked on them all day."

I apologized, as I attempted to repair the damage.

"It doesn't matter," she declared suddenly, sweeping her cutouts off the bed with a contemptuous wave of her arm. "I just do such things to pass the long afternoons when I feel obliged, for mother's sake, to play childish games. She still expects that of me, you know."

"I presumed she liked to have you help with the sewing, even with the cooking occasionally."

"Nothing taxing," she scoffed. "You should see what she has me do: boil water, sew on a button—things a child could manage blindfolded."

"She still thinks of you as a child, Virginia."

"I know that she does! But the question is, do you?"

"I think she still considers me her child as well."

"Buddie!"

"You *are* barely fourteen," I reminded her.

"Fourteen and married! What are you trying to say, Buddie?"

"I merely wished to point out that your age is more than enough reason for mother, and others, to treat you as one would a child. Most people do not look beneath the surface, beneath your childish exterior, for example, to find the person living within."

"I do *not* have a childish exterior," she complained loudly.

She sat up in bed and examined herself in the vanity mirror across the room, turning her profile first to the left, then to the right, squaring her shoulders and stretching her neck in an attempt to add additional height to her tiny frame. A minute later she collapsed back against the pillows.

"It's true, I do look like a child. Why, I look the same as I did ten years ago, probably the same as I did the day I was born."

I reached behind her slight back, feeling the delicate protrusions of her spine beneath the silk of her nightgown, and brought her to me in a firm, comforting embrace.

"I remember you the day you were born—give or take a few months. Now that was a child. But now . . . well, it's certainly no handicap to appear younger than your age."

Virginia twisted against me, subtly transforming our embrace from one of solace to one of sensuality. I remained rigid and motionless, unwilling to return her increasingly ardent caresses.

"These hours together at night are the only time I'm permitted to feel like a woman, Buddie. When I'm alone with you, without mother scolding me and protecting me and introducing me to everybody as her 'darling little daughter.' But I wish I knew how *you* felt about me."

She kissed my face, my neck and my lips. She pulled me down onto the sheets, crushing what remained of her paper army, while she continued to cover my face with tearful, desperate kisses.

She seized my hands and guided them to her breasts, forcing me to caress them in a manner obligatory rather than erotic, just so the deed might be done. She was making love as though adhering to a minutely detailed schedule that she had drawn up in her mind; a synthesis of her own imaginative powers, and the word-of-mouth passed among her young, girlish companions.

It was not a matter of love or even Eros; to Virginia it was merely a physical step on an imaginary ladder—once you have yielded yourself to your husband, you are irrevocably, in everyone's eyes, a woman—age, state of body or mind notwithstanding.

The room filled with short girlish gasps for air—and sighs of frustration. Her hands stabbed at me, kneaded and pulled, seeking skin beneath clothing. But aside from a few clumsily returned kisses, I began to cool and withdraw, as the painfulness of our situation overwhelmed me.

We had long passed the point where I could rely on Virginia's ignorance of physical love to avoid consummating our marriage. While I was seeking employment and plotting my final, fatal liaison with the Verneuils, my wife's budding maturity had been preparing her for an erotic encounter she welcomed without clearly comprehending the full nature of what was involved.

She had changed since that first night of our honeymoon back in Barrow's cabin; she had developed an insistent, stubbornly sensual side that she equated with womanhood.

But I was the same. I was no more worthy, nor no less dangerous, to the inherent goodness Virginia personified. My soul was still a divided one, the darker half chained to murder, wickedness and adultery. Until I could break free of these corrupting bonds, I could not, in all conscience, gratify our desires.

To the reader accustomed to the normal progress of married life I am sure my attitudes and actions will appear bizarre, perhaps insupportable. But I grew physically terrified of our impending coupling and I shrank back from my wife, unwilling—or unable—to respond to her advances any further.

"Buddie, what is it?" exclaimed Virginia, sitting upright and slapping her fists down on the mattress. I moved to a sitting position on the edge of the bed, leaning protectively over my wife more in the manner of a hospital nurse than a husband and lover.

"Virginia, I know that we've spent very little time together recently. This seemingly endless search for employment has filled almost every waking hour. But it's a situation I intend to change, I can assure you."

"I know, Buddie—I don't mean to complain—but we're together now, aren't we? Why do you behave so strangely?"

"Because I feel strange," I replied. "I feel so tired, too tired to think, or to return your kisses. And in eight hours the great, blasted struggle begins all over again."

"We should change places, Buddie. You remain at home and have mother pamper and scold you—I'll go out in search of work."

"The scolding I could do without, but the pampering does sound inviting. Just to lie here in bed while mother serves me chamomile tea, hot soup and the papers two times a day."

"And I'd spend the day up here with you! Cutting things from magazines, organizing games and activities, feeding you from the spoon when you grew too tired to lift your hand to your mouth."

"I thought you were to be out on the streets, diligently seeking employment."

Virginia grew playfully despondent.

"Well, I'd just have to find a position that would allow me to work at home."

I removed the remainder of my clothing, donned my nightshirt and climbed into bed next to my wife, conscious for the first time in several weeks of how pervasively tired I really felt—almost as though exhaustion were a liquid that ran in my veins instead of blood.

I sighed and blew out the kerosene lamp which stood on the nightstand next to our bed. The smoke from the smoldering wick mixed with the pungent aroma of kerosene, and dissipated slowly into the air of the room. Though many found this particular smell offensive, to me it was a comforting, soothing aroma which I associated only with the act of slowly and contentedly falling asleep.

"Virginia, darling, you are growing into womanhood extraordinarily quickly as it is. I don't consider you a child, I honestly don't, and as for mother—well, I promise I'll speak to her about giving you a little more responsibility around the house. Perhaps it would be for the best if she were to treat you as more of an adult."

"I shall find out everything there is to being a woman, Buddie. And I will become one before your very eyes. An irresistible woman!"

But then, as she nestled her body against mine in the darkness, her determined demeanor softened.

"I enjoy these little secrets we two have from mother, don't you? It's at moments like these when I feel so close to you, so incredibly close."

Virginia turned over on her side and I moved behind her, fitting our bodies together like stacked silver spoons, wrapping my arms around her thin, fragile frame. As she settled into a comfortable position, she was wracked by a series of deep, shuddering coughs, an almost nightly occurrence. It was as if she were being required to pay for her comparatively healthy days with agonizing nights.

We bade each other good-night and Virginia fell almost immediately into a light, fitful sleep.

The next day began on a quiet note of hopefulness: From the back pages of the *New York Sun* the following notice confronted me:

> LOST: A VERY LARGE, REDDISH ORANGUTAN OF THE BORNEAN SPECIES. APPROACH WITH CAUTION. EXCEEDINGLY RARE. WILL MOST LIKELY SEEK REFUGE IN DAMP, WOODED AREAS MOST CLOSELY RESEMBLING HIS NATIVE HABITAT. A REWARD IS OFFERED FOR HIS RETURN TO CARNIVAL PAR EXCELLENCE, 24 HOUSTON ST., NEW YORK.

At least my culprit was making news; by the time he was finally captured I prayed that the evidence pointing towards his guilt would be ironclad.

I attempted throughout the whole of the late morning and afternoon to write, but accomplished little. Mother, on the other hand, was a maelstrom of activity as she trundled in and out of her room, furiously addressed envelopes at her desk and rushed in and out of the house on countless, inexplicable errands. All this was in addition to her regular household duties of cooking, cleaning and sewing. Virginia and I grew winded merely watching her.

That night after dinner, under the pretense of attending a conference sponsored by one of New York's literary magazines, I headed for La Maquis and Gentinetta's all-important decision.

The tavern appeared exactly as I had left it. Gentinetta's council was seated at the corner table, having just finished their evening meal; the English bartender was clearing their plates, and the same group of drinkers was hard at work at the bar. But from the doorway I noticed one difference—a major difference—between tonight and last night when I had first approached the Corsicans: An empty chair stood beside Gentinetta, awaiting my arrival.

"Come, come, Monsieur Poe, be seated," exclaimed Gentinetta, filling a glass for me from the bottle of red wine which lay always within reach. I took my seat and nodded my greetings to the others, who returned my gesture with their characteristic sobriety.

"You may be curious to know the reason for my hesitance last night," he began.

"I assumed you had private motives. You need not enter into them," I replied, toying uncomfortably with my glass of wine.

"But I would prefer to. In the interests of a successful relationship, it would be best if we were truthful with one another."

"Then by all means proceed."

"You see, Mario de la Costa represents for all of us a past we had assumed was forgotten—a bloody past, filled with feuds and vendettas, with violent battles in the Corsican hills between rival gangs. De la Costa led one such gang, I was the leader of another. Corsica is a small island, monsieur—our clashes were frequent—and costly."

Gentinetta's colleagues stared down at the table, as though in bitter remembrance.

"There came a time when de la Costa and I commanded the two most powerful—and feared—organizations on the island. I sensed a final war between us was imminent, a war that few would survive. My men, their families, had grown weary of the violence, the continual need for retribution that cost so many innocent lives. And so, rather than face certain death, we fled, and left whatever meager spoils there were to de la Costa and his followers. I led a small 'exodus,' you might call it, to New York. We have not done badly here, eh, *mes copains?*" exclaimed Gentinetta, gesturing broadly around the table.

A chorus of halfhearted agreement met this statement, then quickly subsided into melancholy.

"Until now, Monsieur Poe. Until the murder of our mutual acquaintances, the L'Espanayes. So you see, my reluctance to join you was not purely personal. How could I justify committing my comrades to a battle we thought settled years ago?"

I digested this astounding information as Gentinetta took a generous swallow of the red wine he so favored. Everywhere I turned I seemed to encounter the malignant shadow of Mario de la Costa. As the "affaire L'Espanaye" continued to widen, so did the circle of his sworn enemies!

"But the situation here is completely different," I replied. "We are many and he is alone. You are familiar with the city, whereas de la Costa is a stranger here!"

Gentinetta waved my remarks aside.

"There is no need for persuasion. As reluctant as we are to join an enterprise of this nature, the specter of de la Costa free in the streets of New York is intolerable. He is a blight upon the entire community. I and my men shall do everything in our power to find him. And once he is captured—he shall be punished according to the magnitude of his crimes!"

Choosing for the moment to ignore this ominous declaration, I pressed ahead. "Very well, then, I have a curious-sounding, but all-important request."

"Please," said Gentinetta, indicating his colleagues, who listened attentively.

"Is there an artist among you—one who can draw portraits?"

Bruno, a large, fatherly man, stood up rapidly with an almost military precision, as though he were a soldier volunteering for a dangerous mission.

Gentinetta nodded towards him, and there was an unspoken changing of position at the table, which ended with Bruno seated immediately to my left.

"If you will be so good as to guide this man through a rendering of de la Costa's likeness, we shall then distribute copies of this drawing among your men and their acquaintances."

Gentinetta beamed as he grasped my intention, and the bartender was asked to fetch pencil and paper. Bruno proved to be a most talented sketch artist, and very adept at following Gentinetta's instructions. The other men gathered anxiously behind Bruno's chair, and peered over his shoulder as he worked. Slowly, yet skillfully, a Mediterranean face materialized on the blank paper, a large-boned, well-formed visage topped by thinning gray hair and graced with an impeccably manicured moustache.

A shudder of recognition shook my entire body.

"This is quite impossible," I stuttered. "That cannot be Mario de la Costa!"

Gentinetta and his men loudly assured me that it was.

"If there is one face forever committed to my memory, it is his, Monsieur Poe. There has been no mistake!"

"But this is Lucchino Contadina!"

"The police inspector you wished me to find?"

"The very same!"

There could be but one explanation for this shocking revelation: Somehow Mario de la Costa had succeeded in impersonating Inspector Contadina, and had obtained or forged his identification papers. It certainly explained how, with apparent ease, the escaped felon was able to board a ship in France, sail across the Atlantic and slip past U.S. Immigration officials. As to the fate of the worthy inspector—one could only surmise.

The realization that the tall, confident man who had so favorably impressed me back in Barrow's office was none other than the murderer Mario de la Costa was more than I could face.

Barrow and I could have so easily curtailed his reign of terror then and there had we not been so gullible, so shortsighted!

"Well then, if you are certain there has been no error on your part," broke in Gentinetta, interrupting my troubled reflections, "our task has been made somewhat easier. We now have only *one* man to find."

Recovering my composure somewhat, I nodded my rueful agreement. "Now, we shall require the services of an engraver."

Before I could explain what I had in mind, Gentinetta stood and addressed his men at length in Corsican dialect. Following his remarks, the council themselves stood and, in random groups of twos and threes, left the bar. Through the window I watched them disperse, hurrying towards their homes; furtive silhouettes outlined against the tenements in the yellow glow of a streetlamp.

"By this time tomorrow night, their numbers will have tripled," declared Gentinetta proudly.

"Good Lord, they're not all comin' here, is they?" asked the bartender, who had overheard our conversation while clearing the table.

Gentinetta smiled and laid a generous stack of banknotes on the table.

"No need to worry, Haverlock—your wine cellar would not be equal to it. Come, Monsieur Poe. If you will follow me, I will show you our greatest weapon."

I shrugged and followed Gentinetta through a door into the restaurant's meager kitchen. I had at this point little choice but to let Gentinetta handle the first details of the investigation. He had access to an army of devoted followers, and now he was even talking of weapons. I was anxious to see the extent of his power.

He led me through the kitchen and into a storage room piled high with boxes and supplies. The Corsican moved deliberately towards the rear of the room and, without explanation, began moving a towering stack of vegetable crates, which he instructed me to arrange carefully nearby. As Gentinetta's stack diminished, and mine grew, a damp, moss-choked brick wall was gradually exposed. Gentinetta turned towards me and leaned against the wall, pressing his back into it with great effort. In a moment, the reason for our exertions became apparent: A group of bricks, approximately half the size of an upright man, slid inward as a single unit, forming a cramped, but nonetheless easily passable opening. Gentinetta waved me inside and I entered a dark, narrow space which I presumed to be the beginning of a tunnel. Wordlessly he reassembled the stack of packing crates in front of the hidden brick door, then pushed it back in place, enveloping us suddenly in total blackness.

A brief feeling of panic threatened to take hold of me, but before it could progress further, Gentinetta produced a tiny, flickering torch, which would have been useless out of doors, but which in our cramped, clammy surroundings seemed as bright and blinding as a fireworks display.

In front of me descended a seemingly endless tunnel which appeared to have been hand hewn out of the rock that formed its walls. It was no more than four feet high and Gentinetta and I were obliged to stand uncomfortably bent over, in the clumsy, lumbering posture of a gorilla.

Seeing my astonishment, Gentinetta was the first to speak.

"This is but one of hundreds, Monsieur Poe. In certain places where the tunnels join, there are rooms large enough for groups of men to assemble and talk."

"But where do they go? Who built them?"

"*Ils vont partout* . . . everywhere men need to go unseen. From house to house, house to factory—the entire neighborhood is connected by these tunnels. At any given time I can place a hundred men underground, ready to fight."

"It's almost inconceivable, an entire underground world that the citizens of New York know nothing of!"

"Some citizens, perhaps—but in the Bowery and the Five Points, in all of the poor areas, every man, woman and child is familiar with the tunnel system. They could draw you maps of it with their eyes closed. To survive, many of us live outside the law, carry on our dealings in secrecy. This is not the exclusive domain of Corsicans."

"But who decides who will use them? Who decides who has the right to pass and who has not?"

"These decide, Monsieur Poe," snarled Gentinetta, holding his rocklike fists up to the light. "All are free to use the tunnels when they wish, but when one group gets in the way of another . . . there are battles down here that rival any of the street fights you may have heard about aboveground."

"And the police?"

Gentinetta shrugged, as though to ask me, "What about the police?"

"They know of this system, surely?"

"They know of it, yes. They find an entrance now and then, but we change them faster than they can discover them. Every year new tunnels are dug and old ones destroyed. It is a brave police-man who enters our neighborhood aboveground; it is a foolhardy one who dares come down here."

"And these tunnels will lead us to a printer?"

"Certainly, monsieur. Everywhere that can be reached by road can be reached secretly by tunnel. Everywhere."

With a provocative smile, Gentinetta turned and, holding the torch aloft, led me down the winding tunnel, into his subterranean world.

As our tunnel descended at a gentle rate, we passed entrances to other tunnels: great gaping black holes that seemed to lead no-where. Occasionally, someone approached us heading in the other direction and we were forced to flatten ourselves against the damp rock wall to allow him to pass. Gentinetta exchanged suspicious glances with everyone he met, but no words were spoken. The gay, profane camaraderie of the street was certainly missing in these underground thoroughfares. Though the pedestrians who passed down these dingy corridors were safer here than above-ground from harassment by police and enemy alike, the gloomy, claustral surroundings instinctively heightened mistrust and sus-picion.

"I'm curious," asked Gentinetta as we continued downward. "What is it that drives you with such passion to chase Mario de la Costa?"

"A matter of honor . . . the desire to see justice done. My mo-tives are in many ways similar to yours," I replied, his question taking me somewhat by surprise.

"But the same could be accomplished by a simple visit to the police. Your conscience would be satisfied, and it would be so much less strenuous."

"For certain personal reasons, I wish to avoid publicity," I snapped.

"To keep your 'professional involvement' with the women a secret, no doubt."

"I fail to appreciate your tone of voice, Mr. Gentinetta. Surely the nature of my relationship with the L'Espanayes can have no bearing on the case as it stands now. And as for your own motives, can they really be as noble as they appear on the surface?"

"It is not my motives we are discussing here, Monsieur Poe."

"Yet for all your talk of honesty, there is a side of this affair that you have no intention of revealing to me. I do not blame you for it. We are still little more than strangers."

Gentinetta stopped abruptly and whirled around to face me.

"De la Costa and I are mortal enemies! I thought I had made that clear to you. Whatever else may be involved . . ." Gentinetta broke off in mid-sentence for a moment, the torch flickering uneasily across his face. ". . . is unimportant," he concluded, after which he turned and resumed walking.

For a silent half hour we progressed steadily downwards, passing no less than twenty other entrances. Then, the passageway leveled off for several paces and, happily, began a rather sharp ascent. Just when the tunnel grew so steep that I thought we would be obliged to continue our journey on hands and knees, Gentinetta led me into another narrow, perpendicular tunnel which, after ten steps, ended abruptly in a wall of wooden siding.

We stood in silence for a moment while Gentinetta allowed me to catch my breath. Then the Corsican executed a series of knocks on the wooden siding, which I correctly interpreted to be a variety of code. Seconds later, one of the upright slats of wood was pulled away and a pair of hands appeared, fumbling with the rest of the siding until an opening large enough for us to exit through was created. Squinting from the harsh lamplight, and swatting several layers of dark, red dust from my frock coat, I stumbled into a small, sparsely furnished print shop. A meek, bespectacled gentleman with a high, receding hairline and a chaotic, woolen beard stood against a small printing press, examining us with a humorous glint in his steely eyes.

We kept him waiting a minute while Gentinetta and I strutted about the office, pressing our hands harshly into our stiff backs, groaning a great deal and generally reveling in the luxury of standing upright.

There were no introductions. Gentinetta quickly explained to the printer what we wanted. He examined Bruno's sketch of de la Costa and scowled; whether he was displeased with the amount of work required to faithfully reproduce it, or with Bruno's artistry, was not readily apparent. We were instructed to return just before dawn, at which time we could pick up two hundred copies of the drawing. Gentinetta attempted to offer the printer something for his services, but he refused. The Corsican bowed courteously to the gentleman, after which I was led back into the tunnel, the entrance sealed carefully after us. The complete transaction had lasted less than three minutes and no more than twenty words had been exchanged.

As we made our way back to La Maquis, I outlined my proposed course of action to Gentinetta, who curtly nodded his agreement. In addition to systematic house searches and rigorous questioning of underground sources, guards armed with our homemade wanted poster would call regularly at each of Manhattan's docks and at the offices of the various freight and passenger concerns that offered service in and out of New York. Surveillance would be maintained, as strict as manpower permitted, along each road and bridge leading out of the city.

In less than six hours, as many as two hundred sharp-eyed Corsicans would take to the streets and alleys of Manhattan—their mission to apprehend the villainous Mario de la Costa, who with his acts of violence had brought shame upon his countrymen everywhere. They would find de la Costa, if he was still in New York. I prayed that I had acted soon enough!

Eighteen

Despite the misleading clues I had planted the night of the murders, police oppression of the Corsican community continued unabated. Democratic Mayor Cornelius Lawrence, facing an election and stiff competition from Whig candidates who promised (as do all candidates) to rid New York City of crime, had made it clear to High Constable Jacob Hayes that the apprehension of the Verneuils' murderer was of the highest priority. New York's calloused and "civilized" society, ordinarily unconcerned by crimes committed outside of their narrow neighborhoods, had taken madame and Camille to heart.

Never mind that they were prostitutes who nightly entertained the vilest representatives of the city's criminal classes. They were an innocent, unprotected mother and daughter and they had been killed in a manner the Knickerbockers deemed outrageous. They preferred their violent crimes to be clean and uncluttered, with a minimal loss of blood. They liked their murder victims to die of neatly and accurately targeted gunshot wounds, or of traceless, exotic poisons. They liked to see evidence of a clearly thought-out, justifiable motive—not the bestial, bloody, inconceivable attack that had been unleashed on Madame and Camille Verneuil.

And consequently, they cried out for retribution!

"The murderer must come from their own classes!" they said. "From those filthy, downtrodden immigrants who crawl unceasingly onto our shores with not a penny in their hands, only to take up valuable space for a few years before they die and are buried at taxpayer expense."

And Mayor Lawrence listened, as did Jacob Hayes, as did the constables and the marshals and the justices and the watchmen, all with their eyes on the reward the apprehension of the notorious murderer would fetch, and all with their ears open for the sounds of French on suspicious foreign lips.

But no one was looking at the evidence. How had the killer escaped? Where were his footprints? What about the reddish, coarse hair it was rumored a delivery boy had found behind a lightning rod leading up to the murdered women's rooms? What about the lack of motive, the inhuman chaos found in the bedroom?

And what about the two small articles I read over breakfast the morning after my second meeting with Gentinetta? Buried beneath such mundane *New York Sun* features as shipping news and winter road conditions were two officially discounted sightings of the escaped carnival orangutan: one from a professional pugilist who claimed to have encountered the beast while on a training run through a thickly wooded glade near the Hudson; the other from an independent freight boatman who swore he surprised the orangutan napping in the prow of his vessel. Both men laid claim to the reward, and both men were summarily dismissed from the offices of Carnival Par Excellence, whose investigation of the reports was unsuccessful.

I realized that unless the dim-witted New York police were confronted with incontestable evidence of the orangutan's guilt they would continue to press their search for a killer among the city's Corsicans. And if the wrath of Mayor Lawrence grew strong enough, and the blood lust of the voters increased to unmanageable proportions, an innocent man would be arrested, summarily con-victed . . . and executed. And without knowing it, without the slightest effort, de la Costa would have taken another life.

That same night the combined forces of the New York consta-bulary, in apparent reaction to the vehement editorials that had appeared in the New York papers that day, descended on the Bowery with nearly uncontrollable fury. In action resembling a military siege, several tenements were transformed into armed for-tresses. The area's residents, finally tiring of the continued police harassment, had decided to strike back. All that had been required was one bullet from the rifle of an impatient immigrant to provoke a fiery police counterattack.

The divisions between the city's various law enforcement agen-cies had broken down entirely; marshals and constables joined with bloodthirsty leatherheads in firing willy-nilly into buildings, at suspicious bystanders and even, on occasion, at one another.

By the time I turned the corner into the dingy avenue that led to La Maquis, total chaos reigned. One policeman lay motionless on the cobblestones, his blood mingling with the sewage that contin-ually flowed through the neighborhood in sluggish, slimy rivulets. Citizens were firing sporadically out of their windows at the police who knelt in small groups, taking cover behind ashcans, packing crates and carriages. A horse, panicked by the crack of rifle fire, broke loose from its tie post and charged down the street, scatter-ing the police to the delight of an audience who howled their appreciation from the rooftops.

The entire scene, bizarrely lit by the warming fires that burned continuously at every corner, was an uneasy mixture of Mardi Gras and the Battle of New Orleans. Though the hail of bullets produced insignificant results, I nevertheless retreated back around the corner and entered the alley behind the tavern, hoping to locate a rear entrance.

The narrow thoroughfare was crowded with prostitutes who haggled with impoverished potential customers, roving salesmen who attempted to sell their meager assortments of battered house-hold wares and scruffy, screeching youngsters with coal-blackened faces who played dangerous games with sticks, rocks and knives, running just out of reach of their tormented parents. In short, life here was proceeding at its usual imperturbable pace, despite the battle that raged not a hundred yards away.

I tried several doors before I was successful in locating the rear entrance to La Maquis. I stumbled through the darkness of a cluttered service room and made my way into the bar itself, where Gentinetta and his gang were in the midst of feverish activity. Now no sober, dinnertime discussion was underway at the corner table, no gossiping drinkers sat lethargically at the bar.

Indeed, there was no place available for one to sit and enjoy a quiet meal or even a drink. The chairs, bar stools and tables had been shoved across the wooden floor and up against the doors and windows. The Corsicans were evidently expecting a siege.

"What is it? What has happened?" I called, rushing over to Gentinetta.

"It's disgustin' and disgraceful, that's what it is," interjected the furious bartender, hoping to have found in me a sympathetic listener. "I'm lettin' 'em use me pub all these months fer their meetin's, and now they thought they'd turn it into a battlefield. Well, who's gonna pay for it?" he yelled, indicating deep scratches on the wood floor resulting from the tables which had been pushed about. "That's what I'd like to know, who's gonna pay for it?"

"*Calme toi!*" shouted Gentinetta. "We will take care of you when this is finished. We will take care of it all. You are as one of us."

"Who says I wants to be one of you? One of you is likely to get his head shot away!"

"You are either one of us, or you are against us."

The bartender surveyed the faces of the quick-tempered Corsicans that glowered at him, and he made the propitious decision. "I'm one of you, then," he sighed.

Following a further moment of hesitation, the bartender then joined the others in securing the tavern's windows and doors. Gentinetta grasped me firmly by the arm and led me into the relative quiet of the kitchen, where the gunfire, so loud and frightening in the tavern itself, was audible only as hollow, harmless cracks.

"The police have been informed that some underground criminal society meets in the neighborhood, plotting God knows what. It is only a matter of hours before our friends across the street exhaust their ammunition and a house-to-house search begins."

"Has there been any word?"

"None. We have distributed the pictures, asked the same questions of all our people—people whose survival depends on knowing the community's secrets. No one has seen or heard of this fellow."

"And the wanted posters?"

Gentinetta grinned mischievously and, reaching into a bake oven, extracted a stack of the reproductions for my perusal. Staring up at me in finely rendered, steely malevolence was Mario de la Costa, alias Lucchino Contadina.

"Your man does excellent work."

"Yes, yes, he does. It is a pity that his talents must be used for such things."

As I was about to question Gentinetta further, there came a chorus of anxious shouts from back in the tavern and a tremendous wrenching of wood. We rushed back into the bar to see the gang members leaning against the furniture, straining to hold at bay the hordes of policemen who battered at the barricade from the outside with thundering insistence. In the corner, Haverlock was seated in the one chair not committed to the fight, his head buried in his hands, bemoaning the violent fate that was about to befall his beloved tavern.

There came a deafening crash, and a cobblestone, still caked with the dirt from which it had been uprooted, hurtled through a window and skidded across the floor, coming to rest against the bar with a resounding thud. A rifle barrel appeared through the broken glass and fired a wayward shot at the ceiling.

The barricade was now very nearly breached. The police had evidently obtained some stout timbers and were thrusting them against the door with concerted effort. The chairs and stools creaked timidly as the door buckled ominously behind them. It was obvious that the Corsicans could not hold the door much longer, and they looked anxiously towards their leader for instructions.

"When I drop my hand," he shouted, "everyone abandon the door and make for the tunnels. By the time they succeed in crawling over all of this, we should be away! Monsieur Poe, please remove the crates that guard the entrance to the tunnel!"

I was on my way before Gentinetta could complete his sentence. I rushed through the kitchen, snatched the sheaf of wanted posters from their hiding place in the oven and headed for the storage room.

Once there, I hurried to remove the stack of crates that concealed our escape route, spilling their fruity contents onto the floor and, in my haste, dropping the wanted posters. I was still scurrying about, attempting to gather up the drawings, when Gentinetta and his comrades hurtled around the corner, heading furiously in my direction, shouting and jostling like a crowd of schoolboys released for the summer. I was rudely swept aside as the men collectively threw their weight against the pivoting brick door. One by one the men crawled through the tunnel entrance, urged on by a wildly gesticulating Gentinetta. I was the last to enter, before Gentinetta haphazardly reassembled the camouflaging crates and climbed in after me, sliding the brick door shut with one great, puffing effort.

Bumping clumsily against each other, we turned ourselves completely around and, hunching over in the now familiar apelike posture, we followed the retreating men, the progress eerily marked by the shadows cast by their torches.

We had not been running for more than a minute or two when we heard behind us angry shouting and the echoing clatter of boot heels skidding on wet rock.

"They've found the tunnel, damn them!" exclaimed Gentinetta. He swore loudly and rapidly in dialect, then shouted some unintelligible instructions down the tunnel to his men. Exhorting me to greater haste, he led our cramped, stumbling retreat into darkness with an urgency now bordering on fear.

For several minutes we continued downwards, our progress a

combination of walking, crawling and running. Our pursuers matched our grueling pace, their proximity marked by their torches which were now visible whenever the chase entered a long, straight stretch of tunnel. Gentinetta and I plunged onward, our world reduced to the twin tubes of darkness that separated us from the lights of the police and those of our companions.

At length the torches of our advance guard vanished altogether and I assumed they had entered one of the many side tunnels we continually passed. I turned to Gentinetta, partly in confusion and partly in alarm—without the reassuring light of the torches, no matter how dim, further progress seemed impossible. But my comrade appeared not to notice the suffocating blackness. He took my arm and, feeling along the rock wall with his hand, led us several footsteps further, until I perceived directly in front of us a soft pool of light on the tunnel floor, which seemed to emanate from the rock wall itself.

Puzzled, I broke free of Gentinetta's protective custody, and hurried towards the light, which grew brighter with every step I took. In a moment, its mysterious source was apparent. To my left, through a large man-made hole in the wall, I saw the torches of our gang, burning cheerfully within the confines of what appeared at first glance to be a large cavern.

Gentinetta pushed me through the opening and he and a companion sealed it with a large, finely chiseled slab of builder's granite. I turned from the doorway and, before I could register my amazement at the surprising nature of our surroundings, Gentinetta gave the order that the torches be extinguished. In a second, we were once again cast into total blackness.

All we could do was wait.

Through the foot-thick granite wall that protected us from our pursuers, we heard their muffled footsteps and unintelligible shouts. Though we could discern no individual words, their tone of voice convinced us that they were thoroughly confused. They came to a halt directly outside our place of concealment.

Through the thin cracks in the granite doorway threads of light momentarily appeared as the police searched for signs of a tunnel entrance, then vanished as they abandoned all hope of apprehending us. There followed some more worried discussion before the police retreated in the direction they had come.

Sighs of relief pierced the darkness, and as one by one our torches were relit, nine smiling faces took shape out of the shadows. While Gentinetta and the others gathered in groups to discuss the events of the evening in excited whispers, I stood to survey the miraculous chamber in which we had taken refuge.

Had I not known that in reality we were somewhere deep beneath the familiar streets of New York, I would have sworn we had somehow achieved admittance into the burial chamber of an Egyptian pharaoh!

I guessed the room to be approximately three stories in height. The upper reaches were shrouded in darkness, our torches being insufficient to illuminate the entire vast, vaulted room. Marking two higher levels were outcroppings ringing the four walls of the chamber, wide enough to permit the passage of several men. Into each of these outcroppings, at regular intervals, opened large, uniform doorways, their interiors foreboding, solid squares of black. The walls, the floor and undoubtedly the ceiling were constructed of gigantic, precisely engineered blocks of granite, each of which must have required the services of at least ten strong men to fit into place.

The entire room was distinguished by the sharp angles, pyramids and squares so familiar to us as Egyptian from the widely circulated picture books describing the work of English archaeologists. Drawings, paintings and hieroglyphics, which may or may not have been merely the figment of some American designer's imagination, had been drawn on the stone walls in neat, finely executed brush strokes.

"But what is this impossible place?" I asked Gentinetta.

The Corsican smiled, enjoying my bewilderment.

"We are beneath the intersection of Franklin and Center streets, Monsieur Poe. Not at all far from La Maquis."

I concentrated intently on this answer for a moment, trying to picture in my mind the intersection in question. I passed along both of those streets on an almost daily basis, but could recall no building whose exterior matched the exotic interior in which we now found ourselves.

"All I can call to mind is a great deal of construction work somewhere near that corner."

"Your memory serves you well, my dear Poe. The facade of the building whose lower level we are in is unfinished. You cannot tell from the outside what it will be. But down here . . ." He completed his sentence with a broad gesture up towards the tiered, doorless entrances and the wide ledges they opened on.

"But what are those openings? They have no doors."

"They will never have doors—only bars. They are cells! And the wide ledges you see will be lined with railings so that the prison guards may patrol their charges in safety!"

"The Halls of Justice!"

"Or as they are more commonly known, by police and criminal alike—the Tombs."

The Tombs! A more appropriate name would be impossible to find for the oppressive dungeon that was shortly to house New York's thieves and murderers.

The Tombs! I had read of it continually in the papers. Officially known as the New York City Prison, construction on it had begun two years ago in 1835 on a small, filled-in lake known earlier as the Collect Pond. The area's history was both bloody and distinguished: In pre-Revolutionary times it had been the site of hangings; more recently when it was still a body of water, early steamboat experiments had been conducted here.

Scheduled for completion in 1838, the "Halls of Justice," as the building was euphemistically known, was being constructed in the Egyptian style of architecture that had in recent months grown so popular, and it was thought to be a particularly fine example of that noble genre.

"You see, Monsieur Poe," explained Gentinetta, interrupting my musings, "as we are at constant odds with the law, it is unavoidable that some of our group will be confined here—and so we have taken the precaution of constructing this escape route."

"An ironic place in which to hide from the police," I agreed. "So close to the very seat of their power."

Gentinetta swelled momentarily with pride, and nodded to his men, who, permitted by their leader a little arrogance, beamed with satisfaction at the cleverness of their joke.

His serious demeanor returned, however, just as quickly as it had flown.

"As you can see, Monsieur Poe, the police have intensified their search for the killer among us Corsicans. With so many of them up there"—he motioned with his head towards the distant ceiling—"our search for de la Costa is made all the more difficult. As of yet we have found no trace of him. We must be free to operate, to circulate, otherwise . . ."

I smiled somewhat smugly, anxious to reassure them that this problem was already being dealt with.

"If my plans proceed as intended, you may not be troubled by the police for very much longer. I sense that an arrest is imminent!"

Gasps of amazement met my statement.

"I'm afraid we are somewhat confused. An arrest? Of whom?"

"Not 'of whom,' my dear Gentinetta. 'Of what!' "

This enigmatic assertion only compounded the Corsicans' bewilderment.

"In my attempts to lead the police astray, I have planted false clues and evidence. I am in the process of building up a case against a certain . . . individual. If all goes well, you shall soon read in the papers of the bizarre solution to the murders of Madame and Camille L'Espanaye! And then, neither of us need fear the police any longer."

Sensing that I would reveal nothing further, Gentinetta merely glared at me in frustration, nervously stroking his chin.

"Well, then, Monsieur Poe, I pray that your optimism is justified. I shall make the newspapers required reading for my colleagues. Now, if you have nothing further to tell us, I suggest we attempt to find a way out of here and return to our homes. My men have families."

"But I do have something further," I retorted. "There exists the possibility that your men have discovered no trace of de la Costa because he is in no position to leave a trail. We should first make a check of the city's hospitals and morgues. We will all seem quite foolish if de la Costa should undermine our efforts by dying an untimely death."

Reluctant groans of agreement met my suggestion and, dividing ourselves into groups of two, we bade good-bye to our unique and exotic sanctuary, carefully sealing the dungeon upon our departure.

Prevented from exiting the tunnel through La Maquis, we were forced to walk more than a mile farther before we emerged from the underground network through the side of an undeveloped hill overlooking New York harbor. The fresh night air was an invigorating relief to lungs that had been forced to subsist on the stultifying atmosphere below ground.

Like a broad black sash the East River wound out of the closely clustered uptown lights and emptied itself into the anonymous darkness of the bay. Despite the lateness of the hour, the harbor was choked with ships and barges, their leisurely progress marked by their running lanterns bobbing peacefully back and forth. It was a soothing tableau, but Gentinetta and I, headed for a long, grisly night's work, had no time to enjoy it. Instead, shaking the dirt clods from our clothes, we set off at a brisk clip for the city hospitals and morgues.

Four and a half hours later, exhausted from walking, our stomachs unsettled by the sight of so many dead and dying, we were forced to concede defeat. Mario de la Costa had neither died nor been taken ill—at least not ill enough to be confined to a hospital.

It had been a grotesque, nightmarish evening. While the ordinary New Yorker sleeps, the business of caring for the city's diseased and dying carries on unabated.

We had visited hospital emergency rooms, where physicians, red eyed from liquor and lack of sleep, were proving woefully inadequate in dealing with the vast numbers of patients admitted with knife and gunshot wounds.

We had shared coffee with a lonely morgue attendant in one of the city's wealthy neighborhoods, whose only duties were to dress the already immaculate, occasional heart-attack victims, who were wheeled in on spotless, sparkling stretchers, between the building's staid, Corinthian columns.

And in the Bowery, we had watched with horrified amazement as a score or more graying, decaying bodies, the recent victims of an outbreak of cholera among immigrants, were dressed and dispatched with mindless alacrity by a group of laughing, drunken teenage mortician's apprentices.

I felt vaguely guilty about my presence there, as though the dead would be insulted that I was eavesdropping on this final, most personal of rituals.

After a brief rendezvous with the other Corsicans, whose efforts had proven equally inconclusive, I parted company with my cohorts and trudged home, depressed by the negligible results of my investigation thus far, and anxious to wash the overpowering stench of death and embalming fluid from my hands.

That night, to my relief, Virginia was asleep when I returned. I slipped into bed without disturbing her, but was unable to find sleep myself. I lay awake for several hours, attempting to mentally reason out de la Costa's whereabouts.

In my view, a man in his situation had several alternatives. He could seek sanctuary with a friend or acquaintance, but as I had explained to Gentinetta, this was highly unlikely. He might have developed a cursory friendship or two over a quick glass of beer—but such new-found friends would not be likely to allow a suspicious-looking fellow-drinker into their homes for several nights.

Secondly, as a Corsican, he could seek refuge among his countrymen, relying on their sense of duty and patriotism to hide him from the police. But if he tried such a trick, I would soon know of it. I was sure that any society capable of constructing an elaborate, secretive subterranean world would immediately be aware of a stranger in their midst—and would inform Gentinetta.

Thirdly, he could attempt to leave New York, by ship or by foot or by stage. There again, I was hopeful that he would not escape the watchful scrutiny of Gentinetta's sentries.

A fourth alternative I considered less likely. De la Costa could go into hiding somewhere on his own: in some obscure sewer hole, in the attic or basement of an abandoned warehouse. But here again, I reasoned, he would eventually have to emerge if he were ever to leave New York. And unless he left by air—we would capture him!

Finally, equipped as he was with Inspector Lucchino Contadina's identification papers, he could volunteer his services to the New York constabulary, and we would have a most difficult time abducting him from their midst. As this last alternative appeared to offer the highest degree of safety, I was certain that de la Costa had considered it. I could not afford to ignore the possibility that de la Costa was now a member in good standing of the New York police force!

REWARD: JACOB HAYES, HIGH CONSTABLE OF THE CITY OF NEW YORK, HAS BEEN AUTHORIZED TO PAY THE SUM OF $100 TO PERSONS HAVING INFORMATION CONCERNING THE DEATHS OF MADAME AND CAMILLE L'ESPANAYE ON THE NIGHT OF MARCH 25. ALL PERSONS IN THE NEIGHBORHOOD ON THE NIGHT IN QUESTION AND WHO NOTICED ANYTHING AT ALL NOTEWORTHY ARE URGED TO COME FORWARD. INQUIRE AT CITY HALL. STATEMENTS TAKEN AT ALL HOURS.

The foregoing announcement, which appeared on walls throughout the city of New York the following morning, as well as on the front pages of the city's newspapers, afforded the ideal means of my appearing at police headquarters without arousing their suspicions. And, it provided me an opportunity to move forward in my campaign to incriminate the escaped Bornese orangutan in the L'Espanaye murders.

And so, immediately after breakfast, I hurried off to City Hall to pay a call on the New York constable's office—or to be more precise—a slightly inebriated, unshaven, rag-clad beggar went calling that morning. For underneath my customary knee-length black frock coat I was clothed in tatters I had rescued from a refuse heap behind our building.

I must have presented a curious sight indeed to the destitute citizens of our back alley, as I rummaged through the filth and garbage for the vilest-smelling, most desiccated garments imaginable, all of which I excitedly put on over my freshly laundered shirt and trousers. I then mussed up my hair, applied a fresh coat of dirt to my untamed moustache, and sporting a disreputable set of whiskers, hurried back to the main street, leaving my audience in stunned bewilderment. On my way to police headquarters I added the crowning touch to my disguise: a soiled, woolen cap which I picked up from the gutter and set on my head, pulling it low over my eyes in a further attempt to render myself unrecognizable.

Examining myself in the window of a shop I passed en route, I had every reason to be proud of my efforts—had I not known who it was lurking beneath that awful, cast-off rag suit, I would have been hard pressed to recognize myself.

I staggered up the stone steps of City Hall, a grandiose, recently completed structure that faced Murray Street between Broadway and Park Row. I attracted the curious, jeering stares of schoolchildren on a tour of New York's official institutions, but their teacher, anxious to spare her charges the sight of a broken-down old drunk, hurried them along, attempting to divert their attention with a brief description of the building's architectural attributes.

Once in the lobby I explained the nature of my visit to a uniformed officer, who, recoiling from me involuntarily, directed me to a numbered office at the end of a long, featureless corridor.

As I shuffled towards my destination, I made a point of mistakenly blundering into every office I passed, keeping a sharp eye out for Mario de la Costa. I was angrily ejected by each and every public servant whose work I interrupted, and finally, as my drunken activities began to call attention to me, I entered the office of a Constable Butterworth, to whom I was to give my information.

Butterworth, a young, anxious bureaucrat with an exasperated look, was seated behind a flimsy desk, awash in a sea of paperwork, his chin resting dejectedly in his hands. As I entered, the constable looked up and, despite my unwholesome appearance, he smiled, welcoming an interruption of the mindless activity in which he had been engaged.

"Yes?" he asked.

"I've come for the reward," I declared, bobbing from side to side. Noticing my unstable condition, the officer stood and, according me more courtesy than I deserved, offered me a chair.

Once I was seated, both hands clutching the sides of the chair in an attempt to maintain my upright position, Butterworth began to question me.

"Now Mr. . . . ?" he began, pencil poised.

" 'Mr.'? No one calls me 'mister.' "

"We require it for our records. It's merely a formality. We must have a name for the reward check, mustn't we?"

"You don't pay cash?"

"I'm afraid not."

"I can't take no check. I can't even sign my name. . . ." I stood, as though I intended to leave. Butterworth, hopeful of a break in the case and the commendation that would come his way, reached out a strong arm to detain me.

"It's all right. Sit back down. Fine, we don't require a name for the moment. If your information proves useful, we'll see what we can devise in terms of a cash payment. Now, what do you have for me?"

"I was walkin' down the street. . . ."

"What time was this?"

"I don't have no watch."

Butterworth ran his hand through his thick head of hair. I was beginning to enjoy playing my role, despite the fact that I was in the den of the enemy.

"Can you estimate? Did you see a clock at any time that night? Think back on where you went."

"Well, I bought a bottle of brandy at about eleven. At a neighborhood tavern. But I didn't notice no clock there."

Butterworth smiled at my admission and made a meticulous note. He sat back in satisfaction for a moment, staring down at his handwritten note, and the manner in which it perfectly fit into the box provided for it on the official information sheet.

"And how far had you gone, from the time you purchased the brandy to the time you were in the neighborhood in question?"

"I'd say half a bottle."

Butterworth grimaced.

"I don't suppose you have any idea how fast you drink?"

"Well, of course I do! There's a fact I can help you with. When I'm in form, and I was in form that night, I can drain one in an hour. That's on my own. If I were put into competition, there'd be a slight improvement in that, naturally."

"That would place you in the vicinity at half-past eleven. Now what was it exactly that you saw—or heard?"

"It was dark as a dungeon. I was walkin' along, drinkin' and thinkin' of nothin' at all, when I hears this horrible screamin'. It weren't human, because I never heard nothin' like it in my life and I heard a lot of screamin' in my life."

Butterworth leaned across the desk.

"What exactly did it sound like?" he asked.

My eyes widened in horror, and I began to gesture broadly with my arms, weaving back and forth in the chair.

"Like a beast of the jungle! High and mean, like no human could ever make. It froze me right to the cobblestones. A coldness took hold of me and I was scared, sir. So scared, I dropped my brandy and it shattered, wasting a whole half a bottle. When somethin' makes me waste drink, you can bet it was awful."

"Did you see anything? Could you determine from which direction these screams were coming?"

"You bet I saw something! The screams was comin' from the top floor of this here apartment building, across the street. I looks up and out of the window crawls this hunchback."

"A hunchback?"

"Yes, sir. I saw him. All bent over like a cripple, with thin, spindly arms and legs. He just stood on the window ledge for a minute, like a balancin' act in a circus."

"This is more than incredible, my dear sir. A circus hunchback, screaming like a jungle beast, balanced on a fourth-story window-sill. Had you been drinking *that* heavily?"

"Half a bottle of brandy. I don't call that drinking, do you?"

"I'm not sure. I've never been drunk to the point where I began seeing things."

"I wasn't seeing things! This here hunchback climbed down that lightning rod like you or I would go down a staircase. Then he jumped onto the cobblestones and disappeared."

"Down the lightning rod? That strikes me as impossible."

"It striked me as impossible too, sir. I went right back to the tavern and ordered another brandy. But I didn't see nothin' else that whole night, I haven't seen nothin' at all like it since," I said, allowing a hint of disappointment to creep into my voice.

Butterworth stared at his notes in confusion, attempting to ab-sorb my astonishing confession. There being no designated space on his forms in which to include stories of hunchbacks who climbed lightning rods, he took a separate, blank sheet of paper, and while I waited, appeared to write a brief summary of the events I had related. He then turned his gaze on me, examining me harshly with his youthful blue eyes, as though attempting to pen-etrate my disguise.

"I'm curious. If you are unable to sign your name, how is it you could read the reward notice?"

"A friend told me," I replied without hesitation. "When you sees somethin' like I seen, you tells your friends. It so happens that some of my friends can read. I promised I'd buy him a drink if I collected. He told me he'd heard you had an imported Frenchman, all the way from France, just to work on this case. I figured if you was gettin' that desperate, you'd be of a mind to listen to my story."

"I assure you, my friend, we are quite capable of handling this affair without the meddling of foreigners. Your friend may be literate, but he is not well informed. I know everything that goes on in this department, and we have no Frenchmen in our employ!"

I shrugged and fell silent.

"Now, sir, I believe our business is for the time being concluded. If you will kindly leave your address, we will contact you if your information proves useful."

"What? I bare my soul for you and I don't see a penny? How do I know you'll contact me? How do I know you won't keep the reward for yourself?"

As the level of my voice rose, Butterworth rose with it, motioning me to silence.

"Please, please be quiet, can't you?"

"It just strikes me as underhanded, that's all. Preyin' on poor citizens for information you're too lazy to go out and get yourselves, then not payin' a penny for it."

"All right, all right, I'll pay you now. Out of my own pocket."

Butterworth reached into his pocket, extracted several bills and handed them over to me, his voice diminishing to a whisper. "Here's twenty-five dollars. If your information proves valuable, you just come right back to this office. No, by that time you'd better come to the under-assistant constable's office, and I'll give you the entire hundred dollars. Agreed?"

I nodded, eagerly stuffing the money into my coat pocket.

Butterworth shook his head as I stood to leave.

"They should pay me. I now have the unenviable task of looking up and questioning every damned hunchback in New York!"

I tipped my woolen hat in sympathy, and left Butterworth's office before the youthful, ambitious officer could question me any further.

As I strode down the corridor towards the exit, I found it difficult to keep up my act as a disheveled intoxicant. I was elated. I had successfully planted an additional clue—Butterworth had seemed an intelligent enough young man—and I hoped that through the simple exercising of his mind he would begin to connect the hunchback to the earlier evidence I had provided the police.

Though I was skeptical about the young constable's assertion that he knew "everything that goes on" in the department, I reasoned that the arrival of a high French police official in their midst would have occasioned such interest, not to mention gossip, that even the lowliest clerk would have learned of it. Little by little, day by day, I was discovering where Mario de la Costa was not. It seemed likely that, through the process of elimination alone, we would succeed in hounding this fiend into a corner from which he would not be able to escape!

There was one further, most ironic explanation for the good spirits in which I found myself that morning. I carried in my pocket twenty-five American dollars, the payment for my abilities as a storyteller and an actor. It was more than I had earned as a writer for the last three months!

Nineteen

I returned to Carmine Street in the mid-afternoon to find it a scene of great commotion. Standing in front of our humble cottage was a passenger carriage to which was affixed a freight wagon heavily laden with furniture and personal belongings. Two sweating work-horses strained at the bit as though anxious to earn their keep. Mother and Virginia (wrapped from head to toe in wool—at mother's insistence, no doubt) were standing on the uppermost of our four stone steps, conversing with William Gowans and two women whom I did not recognize.

"Ah, Eddie," exclaimed mother as she noticed my approach. "You're in time for a rather regrettable farewell. Our dear Mr. Gowans is taking his leave of us today. This is his sister Melissa and her cousin Hyacinth."

I acknowledged the curtsies of two spinsters; they were nearly identical in their firm commitment to drabness of dress and person-ality. Not a stitch of color relieved the dull, gray monotony of their clothing, and not a spark of interest or humor appeared on their faces.

Gowans leaned close to me, and whispered dejectedly in my ear, "It's positively confounding to what lengths this damnable depression will drive a man. I can just imagine it—cooped up unto eternity with these sexless crones. Still, free rent is free rent." Noticing he had attracted the attention of the two "crones," Gowans slapped his hands together and busied himself with the knots that held his precious belongings in place.

Virginia slipped past her mother, and kissed me, taking my hand.

"Quite a pair, don't you think?" she giggled, and I was forced to agree with her. For the first time since I had met him, I felt pity for the long-winded bookseller. A lifetime spent with these two made my occasional nightmares of premature interment pale by comparison.

"It's a shame you have to leave us, my dear Gowans."

"Well, one gets used to adversity. My regular customers are dropping off like flies. No one wants to read books anymore. If you want my opinion, most people have got life figured out all wrong. The worse things get, the more a body needs food for thought. So what did I do? I stocked up on philosophy. Haven't sold one damned book. So, I'll send 'em all back . . . trade 'em in for something a little lighter when I open my new store. New Jersey folk never did go in for the classics. Just shows you you can't go on always living your life according to your own way of thinking."

Gowans planted an embarrassed kiss on Virginia's and mother's cheek, then extended a helping hand to his female relatives as they clambered onto the front of the buckboard and strained to make themselves comfortable.

He turned to me and gave me a quick slap on the back and a vigorous handshake before he too climbed aboard and took hold of the reins.

"Well, look after yourselves, now. And you, Edgar, as soon as something new of yours finds its way into book form, send me a dozen. We'll put on a window display that'll leave 'em talking."

"You've my word on that," I assured him, as he gave the reins a brisk slap. Mother and Virginia and I waved heartily as the over-burdened caravan lumbered out into traffic and began a slow crawl up the boulevard.

When the carriage had finally disappeared from view, mother handed me a sign reading "Room to Let," together with a hammer and nail, then she and Virginia returned indoors to prepare dinner. I stared blankly at this most tangible symbol of our financial diffi-culties for a moment. To affix this sign to our wall seemed to me like so much wasted effort—though there were many who needed shelter, the times were such that there were few who could afford to pay for it.

Several frustrating, uneventful days passed. La Maquis had been closed down by the police, though Haverlock, the proprietor, was engaged in an uphill legal battle to have it reopened, and the tunnel entrance in the storage room had been permanently sealed.

From our cramped headquarters in Gentinetta's one-room base-ment flat (also conveniently equipped with an escape tunnel), my Corsican comrade and I monitored the unsuccessful activities of our small army. Reports filtered in on an almost hourly basis, as messengers arrived secretly via tunnel or called at his door, dis-guised as merchants, delivery boys or charwomen.

The reports from the various far-flung outposts were depress-ingly similar—no one had uncovered even the slightest trace of the fugitive bandit. It was as though he had been absorbed into the structure of the city itself, his identity dissolved into pavement and cobblestones.

I began to despair of ever apprehending de la Costa. I began to wonder what it would feel like to abandon my efforts; to live with the knowledge that I had compromised my integrity, had failed to meet the greatest challenge of my life.

On all fronts my life was deteriorating rapidly. With Gowans gone, the burden of the entire rent was thrust suddenly on us and we three were without income of any note. Virginia and I were growing estranged, and I was unable to cope with her demands on my time and understanding. Mother had apparently given up hope in me, and was concentrating on some mysterious business scheme which had her writing and posting letters during her every waking hour.

And as for the great literary work which I had assumed would rescue us from our spiritual and economic malaise, I entertained little hope that it could be completed given my present oppressive state of mind.

And as though to cap matters, as though I were not satisfied with the downward progress my fortunes were taking, I had begun to drink again!

Then, one dull, uneventful afternoon, my ill-fated luck was instantly reversed by a seemingly unremarkable coincidence.

It happened as I was shopping.

Mother had contracted a touch of grippe and I had volunteered to perform her daily errands. In a densely populated open-air market, surrounded by haggling bargain-hunters, and stubborn, heavily accented greengrocers, I chanced upon Haverlock, the Englishman who had been the proprietor of La Maquis. Though I was a stranger to this bustling commercial district, he evidently was not. From a distance I observed him as he moved from stall to stall, selecting fruits and vegetables, many of which were exotic varieties unrecognizable to me, with the exacting care of a seasoned chef. He stopped now and again to chat amiably with the merchants, who all appeared to know him on a first-name basis. Feigning interest in an assortment of spices offered for sale by a yawning, bulbous vendor who seemed sorely lacking in the enterprise necessary to drive a hard bargain, I examined the Englishman curiously.

There was something puzzling about this man, in this context, but I could not determine what it was.

Perhaps I could not reconcile the delicacy with which he probed each piece of produce before he purchased it with the swaggering, boisterous manner in which I had seen him serve mugs of ale to his thirsty customers.

Perhaps it was the sight of a gruff, weathered tavernkeeper performing the chores one more normally associates with a woman.

Or perhaps, I decided at last, a smile crossing my lips, what I found so strange was that an Englishman should take such an obvious interest in the gastronomic arts. Distinguished in virtually every field of endeavor—social, political, scientific and literary—the English had yet to develop a reputation of any standing in the kitchen. Consequently, an Englishman who cooks is something of a rarity to our shores.

For a moment I turned over in my mind the significance of this seemingly most insignificant observation.

An Englishman who cooks, an Englishman who cooks? . . .

An Englishman who cooks!

I recalled that first meeting with Mario de la Costa, when I still knew him as Inspector Lucchino Contadina. In a moment of candid humor, he had explained that his knowledge of English resulted from a friendship with an Englishman—an Englishman to whom he had taught cooking in exchange for language lessons!

The coincidence was admittedly outlandish. But then, I reasoned, as soon as a coincidence is explained, it ceases to be a coincidence. And perhaps Madame Verneuil had hit upon a great universal truth when she asserted she did not deal in coincidence. I was certain an explanation lay behind Haverlock's presence in New York as the only English café owner among a suspicious, nationalistic society of Corsicans.

I had become so involved in my thoughts that when I finally elected to follow Haverlock, he was nowhere to be seen! Panicked that I had let him slip through my fingers, I dropped my grocery bag, scattering fruits and vegetables onto the cobblestones, and dashed madly about the marketplace. Enduring the oaths of enraged shoppers and the jabs of their umbrellas and walking canes, I made my way through the market and into the side street that fed into it.

There, turning the corner in front of a rotting picket fence, burdened down with groceries, was Haverlock.

I hurried down the alley in pursuit, and rounded the corner at full speed, nearly colliding with him! He had stopped for some dealings with a kitchen-ware salesman, but was deeply enough involved in negotiations for a copper kettle that I was able to slip back around the corner unnoticed.

A moment later, now armed with the kettle, Haverlock set off at a brisk clip, and I followed, exercising extreme care to appear as nonchalant an afternoon stroller as possible.

For nearly half an hour I followed the Englishman, who seemed to be taking a deliberately circuitous route in order to discourage just the sort of practice I was engaged in. We wound through construction sites, in and out of damp pedestrian tunnels crowded with lovers, into cacophonous workingmen's cafés and out the other side; we even boarded an omnibus briefly, though we traveled only two stops, and upon alighting, traced our way back to the spot where we had boarded.

As the afternoon wore on I grew certain that Haverlock's extraordinary meanderings could have but one purpose—to frustrate followers who hoped he would lead them to Mario de la Costa.

As we entered the lobbies of several nondescript apartment buildings, my heart jumped in anticipation. But each time we merely strolled down dimly lit hallways of peeling paint and scurrying rats, to emerge into garbage-strewn backyards.

But eventually, as the gray pall of a smoke-infested dusk descended on a dreary residential quarter, Haverlock and I entered a small park: its trees leafless and sickly, its grass brown and choked with weeds, its obligatory Revolutionary War statue already chipped and neglected.

At the far side of the park, Haverlock unaccountably took a seat on a bench and, extracting an apple from his groceries, began to eat it with quiet satisfaction.

I grew impatient and frustrated. I slammed my fist into my open palm, and the crack of skin on skin reverberated through the silent park.

Haverlock glanced briefly about, and I secreted myself behind the statue. He then returned to his eating, a process which he was drawing out with an imperturbable calm.

What was the deuced fellow about? Why had he led me through this labyrinthine chase only to plop himself down on a park bench and begin eating apples?

I peered across the street at the unremarkable block of brownstones that faced the park. I wondered which of these buildings, if any, was occupied by Haverlock.

Then I had my answer. Someone suddenly appeared at the second-story window of the building nearest the corner and, glancing down at Haverlock and his bench, vanished just as quickly.

Haverlock had been signaling to the face at the window!

I rushed up to the Englishman, abandoning all thoughts of concealment. Choked with rage, I grabbed him by the collar and lifted him to his feet, as flecks of chewed apple tumbled from his lips onto his chin.

"Here, here, what's this now?" he squealed, wiping his face and grabbing my wrists in an attempt to disengage my grip.

"What apartment is yours? Which number?" I demanded.

Haverlock merely stared at me. His expression, as mute as chiseled rock, sufficed to tell me he would never answer my questions. I removed my hands from him in disgust, then turned and dashed across the street and up the steps of the building.

The stairs were to my left as I entered. Rather than proceed immediately upstairs, I hurried down the length of a gloomy, yellowing corridor, then looked out the back door into the alley. I saw no one. If anyone had passed this way, he had disappeared into the impenetrable Bowery landscape and could not be followed.

I ran back down the corridor and, taking the stairs two at a time, dashed up to the second floor. Of the four apartments whose doors opened into the hallway, the two to the rear could be eliminated. Apartments C and D remained to be searched, and a knock at the door of C produced a disgruntled Chinese youth who was unable to understand my questions.

The door to D was unlocked, and I cautiously pushed it open and looked in.

The apartment was empty. I was standing in the living room, which was furnished adequately enough with articles purchased on a thousand trips to secondhand stores and estate auctions. I padded across a frayed, once-elegant carpet into the kitchen. A small wooden table was set for two, and a glass of red wine stood half-finished next to a recently opened bottle.

The bedroom contained two mattresses without frames, set against the far wall to accommodate two large chairs that took up more than their fair share of space. They were pointed at an angle so as to allow their occupants an unobstructed view of the park.

Between the chairs, on a delicately carved mahogany stand rested an ashtray and a partially smoked cigar, its owner so recently departed that it still smoldered slightly, filling the room with a faint, not unpleasing aroma.

As I stood absorbing my surroundings, I heard footsteps approach softly behind me. I turned to face Haverlock, who had entered, still clutching his bags of groceries.

"You just drove me only friend away—I hope yer proud o' yerself," he declared, collapsing into one of the armchairs. He looked at the burning cigar for a moment, then pressed it out with a wrenching, hateful gesture.

"It was he, wasn't it?" I asked. "Mario de la Costa. You've been harboring him here, keeping him informed of the progress of our investigation from information you gathered down at La Maquis."

"No 'arm in admittin' I was, I guess. He ain't comin' back now."

I sat down next to Haverlock as de la Costa must have done on many an evening. My disappointment at having been so near my goal, only to have it maliciously snatched away, was impossible to articulate—either in feelings or words. It seemed almost a predestined failure—one of Madame Verneuil's unalterable predictions.

"Had you no idea of the magnitude of this man's crimes? Did you never suspect that he was responsible for the murder of these two women—a crime which has outraged the entire city of New York?"

"We was mates, fair and simple. Mates don't as a general rule much mind what t'other done."

"Can you tell me where he's gone?"

"Just who are you to be askin' me these damn questions? You follow me home, you make yourself comfortable, you drive me friends away . . ." Haverlock stood and gestured towards the door. "I think it's about time for you to be leavin'."

"This isn't your tavern anymore, sir, and I'm not some belligerent customer you can casually eject."

"Well, I don't know where he's gone," admitted Haverlock, cooling considerably. "I'm not sure I'd tell you if I did, but that don't matter now."

The Englishman walked to his bed and produced a bottle from beneath the pillow. He uncapped it, availed himself of a long, deep swallow, then replaced it.

"I always sleep with my valuables within reach. I could've had a pistol under there for all you know."

"I didn't expect it. You took in a vicious criminal on the basis of an old friendship; he used you; and now at the slightest sign of danger, he's taken off. You're angrier at him than you are at me."

This did not set well with Haverlock. Wiping the whiskey from his mouth, he stormed about the room.

"We was cell mates! We spent five years together, two of 'em in the same room. You gets to expectin' things from a man after that much time goes by."

"Would this be in France?"

The relationship between Mario de la Costa and Haverlock was now painfully obvious. Back in the *Virginia Argus* office, de la Costa had in a candid moment admitted to a close relationship he had enjoyed with an Englishman. Until this moment, the bitter irony of their "closeness" had been lost on me.

"Yeah, in France."

"Quite a coincidence, your being cell mates. Fortunate even."

"Well, Mario was an escape artist. He'd been in that bloody prison ten years and had made as many escape attempts. I arranged for his cell mate to meet with an accident, then I moved in with him. I knew that he'd have no choice but to take me with him on his next escape."

"I trust you were not disappointed."

"Lord, no, I warn't. Our first attempt was a whopping success. We lived on the back roads of France for six months, and we loved every second of it. We went on to Corsica—Mario's old haunts, you know—and I landed me a job in some restaurant. Mario, bein' a felon and all, skulked about a bit, sayin' he had business to attend to, and I wouldn't see him for weeks at a stretch."

"Then, if I'm not mistaken, he convinced you to try your luck in America?"

"You're a damned sight smarter than you look, mister. He came to me and said there's no future back there, and before I knew what was happening, we was on a boat for America."

The Englishman sat on the windowsill and gazed over his shoulder down at the darkening park.

"By George, I remember the day we landed in Boston harbor clear as this glass here—New Year's Day, 1835. I took that as a right good omen back then."

"Do you have a Christian name, Mr. Haverlock? I'd like to call you by your Christian name if you'd permit me to."

"Eustace," he responded without so much as a glance in my direction. "My folks was upward-lookin' people and Eustace was the highest-minded name they could come up with. Thought it would ensure my entrance into the right kind of society. Lord, if they could see the people I was associatin' with now, they'd turn over in their graves."

"Eustace, I'm very interested in your story. I'd especially be interested to learn what transpired once you reached our shores."

Haverlock had totally abandoned his stubbornness. He moved to the bed and took the whiskey bottle from beneath the pillow, this time leaving it uncorked. The secrecy he had been obliged to maintain while serving as de la Costa's landlord had been an intolerable burden, and I sensed that in a way the flight of his only "friend" provided long-overdue relief.

"We traveled about the East Coast, taking jobs here and there. I wanted to establish myself, 'ave a go at me own business, but Mario wasn't at all for it. We eventually parted ways, and I wandered into New York and the café business, which was where my only experience was, outside of prison. Makin' Corsican friends was easy; by that time I almost thought of myself as one of them."

"You must have corresponded with each other during this time?"

"Mario wrote to me at general delivery every couple of months. But his letters never included a return address. Then a few weeks ago, I'm down at the post office to pick up me mail, and he's there in person! It was one hell of a fine day. Reminded me of that day we first landed in Boston. We talked about opening our own restaurant, of starting this and that kind of business. He said his wandering days was definitely over."

"Then the two Verneuil women were murdered, and he changed, grew suspicious, and distant," I surmised. "He devised a system whereby you might warn him of the approach of police or unwanted strangers . . . you could not have been oblivious of the facts!"

"I ignored 'em! They wasn't my doing. Of course I had my suspicions. Wot with the way the underground was comin' alive, you and Gentinetta conspirin' right 'n' left, and Mario talkin' of goin' back to France. But wot would you have liked me to do? Turn him in, me best friend? I knew wot kind of man he was—do you think he'd receive justice at the hands of those monsters? You don't betray a man, just like that."

"Is it better to let him go free? After what he's done?"

"I don't care wot he done. I don't care if his pastime is poisonin' babies. I'll not betray a friend. I got a clean conscience and a case of this whiskey in the cellar, and I'm able to sleep at night 'cause of it."

"Well, then," I snapped, "before you drift off into this untroubled sleep of yours tonight, give some thought to the misery de la Costa has caused."

I stood and curtly offered my hand to Haverlock. He made a halfhearted effort to shake it, then fell back against the wall.

"Mister," he called as I stepped into the hallway, "don't think too badly of me. I'm just a tired old tavern keeper who's 'ad it up to here with runnin' and hidin'. They took me livin', and now me friend."

"I'd think hard, if I were you, on what kind of a friend it is that runs out without a word, and leaves you to do the talking."

Leaving the dejected Englishman to his thoughts, I quietly left the flat.

Though I was naturally disappointed by de la Costa's narrow escape, I derived some solace from the fact that, like a hunter, I had flushed my quarry into the open. In a brief meeting with Gentinetta in his rooms, the Corsican leader and I agreed that with de la Costa on the run our chances of catching up to him were greatly magnified. His fatal mistake had been to run—had he stayed in Haverlock's flat and killed me, his sanctuary would have remained uncompromised. This solitary moment of weakness would prove to be his undoing!

I was not entirely convinced that Haverlock and de la Costa would not attempt to rejoin forces, so we dispatched a guard to the Englishman's flat. That done, I bade Gentinetta good-night and returned home, unaware that the final, harrowing act in the "affaire L'Espanaye" was shortly to play itself out.

Twenty

Our house was a scene of nearly funereal gloom.

Though it was six o'clock, there was no dinner on the table. Neither mother nor Virginia was to be found in the kitchen. Not a pan had been taken from the cupboard, not a vegetable or a piece of meat was anywhere in sight.

Though the early winter darkness had descended on the city, not a light burned in any of the downstairs rooms. I hung my coat and hat in the foyer, and stepped gingerly into the parlor. Were it not for the streetlamp which burned directly outside the window, casting a pale pyramid of light across the carpeting, the room would have been immersed in total blackness.

Something was desperately amiss!

I fumbled about for a moment before I managed to light a small lamp which rested on an end table at the head of our couch. Stretched along the length of the couch, her hair unkempt and her clothes disheveled, was mother, a brandy glass held lazily in her right hand! It was a scene more characteristic of my former dissolute ways than of the sensible, industrious foundation of our household. Yet there she lay in the gathering darkness, oblivious of my entrance, marooned in a private, mysterious depression.

"Mother," I whispered, kneeling at the side of the couch, "what in God's name is the matter?"

She turned to me with a gaze that was one of neither surprise nor welcome—it was suffused only with distress and loneliness. "This stuff is not at all bad, Eddie," she said, raising the empty glass. "I understand why it tempts you."

"Mother, I haven't seen you take a drink between meals for as long as I can remember. What is it? Is it Virginia? Is she ill?"

My question was answered by a mysterious crash from upstairs, as though glass were being shattered.

"She is not ill in the conventional sense of the word, Eddie. What I mean to say is that she is not in an extraordinarily weakened state."

"That would seem obvious. What is she doing up there? I must go to her."

"The door is locked. I have been trying for the last hour to gain admittance."

"In heaven's name, what is the matter? Have you two quarreled?"

There came at this point a series of resounding thuds, punctuated by Virginia's muffled squeals of anger and frustration.

"She sounds as if she's gone quite mad!" I cried.

"Pass me the brandy decanter, Edgar. My, this drink is a smooth one—you scarcely know you're drinking at all."

"I think I'll join you, mother." I poured each of us a glass from the decanter which lay on the end table—a wedding present from someone unaware of my alcoholism. It was testimony to the level of mother's dejection that I was able to imbibe in her presence without her registering the slightest word of protest.

"A group of her girl friends from the neighborhood came calling this afternoon. They were up in your room for several hours, locked in one of those serious discussions of life that only the young participate in. When her friends emerged, they threw me angry glances and, without so much as a word of good-bye or thanks for the tea I'd brought them, they flounced out of here like they were mistresses of the house and I was some unmentionable servant."

"Mother, the rudeness of a gaggle of schoolgirls is hardly reason for you to lapse into such a profound depression," I replied, relishing the relief each sip of brandy offered to my besieged nerves.

"And then my daughter descended the staircase and approached my desk with all the portentousness of the pontiff. And she accused me of negligence, of secrecy, of interfering with her growth, and I don't know what all!"

I instantly realized the significance of what mother was saying! I coughed with some embarrassment, choosing my words carefully.

"Her accusations were not unfounded, mother. It was your duty to prepare her for womanhood. She has been as ignorant and as innocent as a newborn babe. And as we agreed together, you and I, I thought it not my place to instruct her. And now she has learned it from her friends, under rather crude and unfortunate circumstances."

"But to call me those names, to chastise me with such vehemence. You did not see her face, Eddie—all bitterness and lines. I could not help feeling there was genuine hatred there."

"There was no hatred, don't be absurd. But she feels betrayed, as though by being kept in the dark, she has been unworthy of your trust. And now, God knows what silly, distorted facts those schoolgirls fed her!"

Mother smiled slightly, as she dabbed her tear-stained eyes with a handkerchief and took another generous swallow of brandy.

"They were more or less accurate. Apart from a few details. At least we needn't trouble ourselves on that score."

"Well, then, the situation is not nearly so desperate as you imagine. Virginia's accusatory manner will pass—it's just childhood stubbornness. You haven't lost her love, for God's sake."

"No, no. I haven't," she answered, raising herself to a sitting position. "But I've lost the relationship that has governed this house for the last fourteen years—that of mother and child. I confess I ignored her 'womanly education.' I admit that!"

I raised my hand to object, but mother continued.

"I even admit, Eddie, that I attempted to artificially prolong her childhood, to increase her dependence on me. But can you guess why? With womanhood comes assertion, and with assertion comes independence. And this is one family to whom independence would do more damage than it would good. Can you imagine striking out on your own like just another married couple?" she scoffed. "Do you think for a moment you could exist in this world, Eddie, without Virginia or myself? With that morbid temperament of yours, with your susceptibility to drink and self-pity and depression? Do you think yourself capable of earning so much as a dollar without the spiritual support your family provides you? And Virginia . . . with her nearsighted adoration of her husband, 'Buddie, the all-seeing, immortal poet.' Do you think she possesses the worldliness, the basic practicality to survive? This is not to mention a debilitating illness which sometimes renders her incapable of even feeding herself. She would follow you into Hell, Eddie, without so much as an inkling of her destination!"

"And yourself, mother. You haven't mentioned yourself."

Her voice lost its strident tone, and descended into quiet resignation.

"And I would be a useless old spinster, efficiently knitting myself into the grave. With never so much as a glimpse into that sublime world of art and ideas that you inhabit, Eddie."

I joined mother on the couch and sat for several minutes cradling my brandy glass, as I absorbed her frank and deeply felt comments. It was a truth somehow painful to admit, that neither of us could exist without the other. Try as I might, I could not imagine a life without either Virginia or mother. Mother's desire to keep our family welded together through preventing Virginia from crossing the threshold into womanhood was ill considered and underhanded, yet it was motivated by a profound understanding of our situation.

"We are quite a trio, aren't we?" I observed at last.

"You're not planning on deserting me for some grim garret or attic in a poor neighborhood?" she joked, slowly recovering from her depression.

"Good heavens, no. This new work of mine, which I seem to be continually reminding you about, *will* become reality, you needn't fear. It will lift us out of this poverty which makes the best of men pessimists. Our family numbers three, and will forever remain three!"

Mother was gradually regaining her usual equanimity, as she stood and straightened the cushions that had become rumpled under her weight.

"I think you had better go up and talk with her, Eddie. It's been quite a trying day for her as well." Then, noticing it for the first time, she snatched the glass of brandy from my hand and emptied its contents into a potted plant.

"A slight family crisis, and you go entirely to pieces!"

I recognized in mother's brave, argumentative front a desire to be left alone. Honoring her wishes, I kissed her on the cheek and headed upstairs for a confrontation with Virginia—the outcome of which I could only guess at.

If the downstairs had resembled a funeral home, our bedroom resembled the aftermath of an earthquake.

In her bitterness and frustration, Virginia had indulged her penchant for breaking things—with a vengeance it had never been my misfortune to experience. The vanity mirror had been shattered by an inkstand hurled with impressive aim. The vanity itself now resembled a massive, uncut diamond as the tiny shards of glass sparkled brilliantly, reflecting the amber light given off by our bedside lamp, which had somehow survived Virginia's temper. Bookshelves had been overturned and their contents lay scattered about the bedroom floor. A fern which she had carefully tended throughout our several moves had died an ignoble death, its delicate leaves crushed, its stalk uprooted.

The knowledge that the secrets of adulthood had been deliberately, conspiratorially withheld from her for so long appeared to have affected her more deeply than anything else in her fourteen years.

Her indignation was not misplaced.

I had played a major role in isolating Virginia from the normal progression of married life. Mother had played her part and sickness had done the rest. These three factors had combined to create the unique, sequestered creature that Virginia had become. Her womblike existence had been so total that it was no wonder she had reacted violently when that existence was suddenly punctured by the forbidden, wondrous secrets of womanhood her young friends had brought with them.

My frail, fourteen-year-old wife now sat fully clothed at the head of our bed, whimpering and breathing heavily, the spread pulled up protectively around her neck. Her eyes wore a glazed, ignorant look; she appeared not to have even noticed my entrance. Her cheeks and forehead were furrowed in torment, but there was a feverish glow to her features that had nothing in common with anger or emotional pain!

I strode over to her quickly, and she neither turned her head to follow my movements nor offered the slightest sign of recognition. I placed my hand on her forehead—it was scalding!

Her breathing was labored and painful. Each breath resembled an agonized growl as she strained from the deepest part of her chest to inhale and exhale.

"Virginia, Virginia, for God's sake. Can you hear me?" I screamed, slapping her sweat-soaked wrists.

She lay perfectly petrified for a second, then turned her face slowly towards me. She nodded her awareness of my presence, and with her last reservoir of strength, she guided my hand towards her chest.

"Your chest? It's in your chest? What is it? What does it feel like?" I continued to plague her with questions that demanded complex answers, even though I knew she found speech impossible. I stood abruptly and stared down at her in a stupid moment of indecision.

Then I turned and ran from the room.

I bounded down the stairs, tripping when I reached the bottom. My legs buckled under me and I went down, tearing the knee of my pants on an exposed nail. Screaming for mother, I righted myself and charged into the kitchen, where she was busily preparing the dinner her difficult afternoon had postponed.

David Madsen 260

I wrested a kettle of boiling water from her grasp, spilling its contents onto the floor. Grabbing mother by the hand, I fairly carried her out of the kitchen and up the stairs.

"What in heaven's name is the matter, Eddie?" she cried as she attempted to keep pace with me. "What kind of an argument did you two have, anyway?" I was too distraught and out of breath to reply. I wordlessly led her into our room, where Virginia lay as before. The only movement suggesting that this pale, wraithlike creature still lived was the bedspread rising and falling above her heaving chest.

"When did this happen?" mother said, as she executed the same clumsy examination I had performed moments before.

"She was already in this state when I entered. We didn't exchange a single word. She must have been stricken to such an extent that she was unable to call out!"

I surveyed the damage to the room again, the real reason for my wife's destructive rampage now readily apparent.

"She has been trying to signal us! She has been calling for help by hurling things against the wall. The crash we heard was a cry for assistance. And we ignored it!"

Mother looked at me, her expression every bit as grim as Virginia's.

"We must act immediately if we are to save her. Her rheumatic condition has deteriorated into something else. God knows what! You must go for the doctor. I'll go down to the kitchen and prepare the medicine he gave me on his last visit."

"But who is to stay with Virginia?" I protested. "What if her condition worsens? What if she stops breathing entirely?"

"I'll fetch the new boarder. I'm sure he'll cooperate when he understands the gravity of the situation."

"New boarder?"

"I was so upset earlier, I forgot to mention it to you. He arrived late this afternoon. A lovely, civilized gentleman . . ."

A door slammed out in the hall and footsteps padded anxiously towards us.

"That was the bathroom door. He must be coming."

The situation temporarily in hand, I bent over Virginia and placed a kiss on her forehead. Her lower lip twitched momentarily, as though she were attempting to smile. It was caked with dried saliva, and now, ominously, flecks of blood began to trickle out of her mouth: the first harbingers of a potentially fatal, internal eruption.

Impelled to haste by this distressing omen, I turned to leave and collided roughly with the new boarder. He had evidently been interrupted while shaving by the commotion we were creating and had hurried to investigate.

I suddenly felt myself losing my hold on consciousness. I reeled backward dizzily, as though struck by a blow. I seized the wooden bedpost and struggled to remain upright.

"Eddie, what is it? What's wrong?"

"Yes, monsieur, please, what is the trouble?"

Despite the generous portion of shaving soap that graced the chin of the new boarder, the face that stared down into mine in mock concern was instantly recognizable as that of Mario de la Costa!

Mother lifted me onto my feet by placing her strong, work-weathered hands beneath my shoulders. She shook me roughly, castigating me at the top of her lungs.

"Eddie, please, now is not the time for a fainting spell. Go and fetch the doctor. Your wife may be dying!"

"You go for the doctor, mother. I think it best. You've always had a better relationship with him than I," I managed to gasp at last. "I doubt that I should be able to rouse him from in front of his crackling fire . . . on a cold night . . . like this. I'll attend to Virginia's wishes."

"Very well," she replied, seizing a shawl from Virginia's dresser and wrapping herself hastily in it. "See that Mr. de la Croix prepares coffee for the doctor. He likes it strong!"

"Yes, mother, I will," I replied, still in somewhat of a daze. I continued to stare vacantly down at the floorboards, unwilling to gaze into the eyes I had hounded and despised for so long.

"I'll see that Mr. . . . . *de la Croix* takes care of everything."

"I'm sorry we have to get off on this footing, Mr. de la Croix," apologized mother. "But it is an emergency. I hope you understand."

"Certainly, madame," replied de la Costa. "I'll do everything that is asked of me. I'm quite handy in moments of crisis."

Mother subjected de la Costa to a haughty, head-to-toe perusal, and apparently satisfied as to his coolness under fire, hurried from the room to fetch the doctor. I raised my head and watched as the bandit wiped the lather from his face with a hand towel, exposing the hateful visage I had last seen but briefly, as it appeared in the upstairs window of Eustace Haverlock's flat.

"What is the meaning of this intrusion?" I asked. "What do you intend doing here?"

De la Costa raised an olive-skinned hand. "Monsieur Poe, there are matters of greater urgency than how I came to be here. Had we not best see to your wife's recovery?"

I looked again at Virginia, whose condition, though not any worse, was indeed frightful. She had fallen asleep at last, and I hoped she would thus be able to achieve some temporary relief.

"I trust you were not lying," I growled, contempt edging my voice, "as you have every step of the way, about your ability to make coffee."

"If you will but direct me to the kitchen? . . ."

"Down the stairs and through the living room."

It took every ounce of strength I possessed to refrain from wildly attacking the man. To allow this fiend into our bedroom, to permit him to perform routine household tasks in our own kitchen—in short, to be required to treat him as one would any other guest—was almost more than I could bear.

"How can you be sure that I won't summon help?"

"Because your wife requires constant vigilance. For you to leave her alone, in this, her greatest hour of need, would be tantamount to murdering the poor girl. One can see how desperate her plight is merely by looking at her."

"What qualifies you to go about rendering diagnoses?"

"One does not have to be a medical man to recognize consumption. My aunt was stricken with it at age twenty-seven, and died shortly thereafter!"

Following this dreadful pronouncement, the bandit turned sharply on his heels and left the room.

Consumption! The great white plague!

The mere mention of the word was akin to the reading of a death sentence. My brother had died of it at an early age, nursed diligently to his dying breath by mother. It was a disease feared coast to coast, class to class: a crippling illness whose progress was not swift and merciful, but lingering, and almost maliciously misleading.

Recovery was an almost futile wish held by all, but realized by few. But was it indeed consumption? Could it not be an unusually vicious bout of rheumatism? Was de la Costa lying, attempting to gain a spiritual advantage over me through inducing fear and desperation?

Mother would be back with the doctor shortly and the verdict would be delivered then. There was little to be gained now through wild and perhaps unwarranted speculation.

And so, as Mario de la Costa, the killer of four people, matter-of-factly brewed coffee downstairs in our kitchen, I crawled onto the bed next to my wife, covering us both with my overcoat as we awaited the arrival of the doctor.

"She's mildly consumptive, I'm afraid," declared Dr. Moloney, a cheerful, blatant sort of man who was much sought after due to his singular lack of reliance on medical mumbo-jumbo and obscure scientific terminology. "Another doctor would call it 'exaggerated rheumatism,' just to make the family feel better so he stands a better chance of collectin' his fee, if you understand me."

Dr. Moloney, de la Costa, mother and myself were gathered around Virginia's bedside, sipping the coffee the bandit had brewed, anxiously listening to the doctor's diagnosis.

"What is the immediate danger to her life, Doctor?" I asked.

"It is not so great at the present time, Mr. Poe. But she is going to take some real looking after, I'll tell you that. She's not to have free run of the house, climbing those stairs every five minutes and what have you. These kinds of attacks can come and go. And above all, she's to keep warm and well fed. Why, just look at the way that poor child is shivering."

Virginia was indeed shaking; though it was not a severe thrashing but a subtle, continual quivering that manifested itself in gentle undulations of the bedclothes.

"Can you come see her regularly, Doctor?" asked mother.

"It would be a pleasure as well as a necessity, my dear Mrs. Clemm. But for now, I'm afraid I must be going. I've another call to make, and I don't much relish the prospect of strolling these streets at a late hour. See to it that she takes the medication I've left for her."

"Of course, Doctor," I said, fetching his hat and coat. We bade Moloney a hearty good-night, and mother left the room to show him to the door.

We resolved for the time being to maintain a constant vigil at Virginia's bedside. I volunteered to stay awake the remainder of the night, with mother to relieve me at dawn. Mario de la Costa graciously offered his services, but they were refused by mother. I was sickened to hear her extend to the bandit her heartfelt thanks for his "surprising and most welcome charity."

I presided over Virginia for the next seven hours, during which there was little change in her condition. Towards dawn, however, her breathing grew more natural and when mother came in at six, I was confident that the most dangerous hours were safely behind us.

Exhausted from a worrisome, sleepless night, I trudged down the hallway to the room where mother had prepared a bed for me. As much as I craved sleep, I knew I would find none; Mario de la Costa was waiting for me, and he obviously had something urgent preying on his mind.

He was standing at the window, in the unflattering light of an overcast dawn. The room seemed unnaturally silent, as though it were aware of the dismal events transpiring down the hall, and had fallen into mourning. The mannequins on which mother fitted clothing for her customers stood against the wall in haphazard array, imparting to me the uneasy sensation that de la Costa and I were not alone.

"What is it? What do you want in my house?" I demanded, securing the door behind me.

"Yes, Monsieur Poe, make sure the door is closed, would you? It would not do for your family to overhear our conversation." He turned from the window and faced me squarely.

"How did you find my house?"

"Mr. Haverlock, my most trusted and loyal *ami*. He has of course kept me abreast of the efforts made by you and your comrades. He came to me one day with the news that Gentinetta had allied himself with a moustachioed—actually quite dashing— young writer who claimed to have known Madame and Camille Verneuil. I simply had him follow you home one evening."

"You planned to come here? Even before I discovered your hiding place?"

"Planned, no. But I realized that my safety with Eustace would not endure forever. A second haven would eventually be necessary. I think it quite ironic that it was your discovery of my room in Eustace's flat that drove me to your door. I had intended to facilitate my entry with a pistol, but the 'For Rent' sign made that unnecessary."

"And what are your plans now? Do you intend to keep us here as your prisoners?"

De la Costa leaned back in fatigue against the window, staring absentmindedly down to the street. It was obvious that he, too, was suffering from the rigors of his ordeal.

"I shall only require your hospitality for the next twelve hours. There is a ship sailing this evening for Le Havre. . . ."

"Well guarded by men in my employ," I reminded him.

"If they are indeed in your employ, they will follow your instructions tonight. You will permit me to board the ship without so much as a word of objection. I'll be armed, of course."

"But you are a wanted man on both sides of the Atlantic, de la Costa!"

"Corsica is my home. I know the island intimately, I can move about it as if invisible. And there are those who will conceal me if necessary—when they learn my quest for vengeance has been successful."

"But will they even remember what prompted your hideous quest? Many of those whom you seek to impress will be dead, either of natural causes or through one of those blasted vendettas themselves."

"They will remember. They *will* remember!" he spat, his voice rising ominously. "Honor is timeless!"

I shivered as I regarded this dangerous—and deluded—man. For fifteen years he had been driven by the conviction that the murder of two women would atone for the loss of honor he felt accompanied his arrest and imprisonment.

He was a cold-hearted, callous murderer; he should have elicited hatred and revulsion from me, but at that moment as he sat receiving the first tentative strands of weak sunlight, lost in the contemplation of his bloody past, I could only find him pitiful.

"Monsieur Poe, do you know what my first childhood memory is?" he said after a few moments. "It is of my father's body lying twisted on the stone steps of our house. He has been shot. A third hole graces his forehead, placed perfectly between his blue eyes, which are open, staring at a point far out in space. My mother is screaming and crying at the same time, but she is not mourning, monsieur. Do you know to whom she is appealing? It is not God. That will come later. She is appealing to me, a five-year-old boy. She is making me swear revenge on my father's corpse. My uncles and my aunts are standing in the background listening, correcting my mother when she mixes up the words of the oath. I am five and already a pledge for revenge has been extracted from me. I am already committed to the way of the vendetta.

"I was raised in anger. We were sealed into our houses at night, and I alternated sentry duty with my brothers, guarding our house from attacks by those families with which we were feuding. In times of vendetta there was no school, no fishing, no harvest. My mother, her pastime was the creating of *lamenta*—funeral poetry. Her verses were in such demand that she could have asked payment for them. The songs of my youth were the *vocera*, long, tragic songs improvised over a corpse. . . ."

"But you cannot excuse the deaths of four people—my innocent friends and acquaintances—by your childhood, your way of life, no matter how appalling it might have been," I insisted passionately.

"No, I do not attempt to excuse it. But I have been schooled in death as you have been schooled in literature. Therefore, do not expect me to feel sadness at their passing, or sympathy for your loss."

"And if the police recapture you?"

"A remote possibility, at best. However, I have escaped before . . ."

"And when you escaped the last time, you headed for Corsica with Eustace? There, you fulfilled this stupid scheme of revenge by murdering Inspector Contadina and appropriating his identity. I trust this crime, too, was carried out without your customary brutality?"

De la Costa shrugged modestly, as though acknowledging a well-played hand of cards, rather than a murder.

"Then, if I'm not mistaken, you decided that 'fortune' was calling you to the United States. But I'm curious. How were you able to trace the Verneuil women to Richmond?"

De la Costa stared intently at me. He tugged his sprig of a moustache, unconsciously twisting it into a tight, black spiral.

"I must say, Eustace proved to be a most talkative colleague."

"Mr. Haverlock told me nothing. These are merely my personal suppositions."

"They are quite accurate, to say the least. But I can't see what there is to be gained through this information. A prisoner, no matter how well informed, is no match for an armed guard."

"Let's just say that, as a writer, I'm intrigued by your case. And if your position is as advantageous as you deem it to be, then the information cannot possibly hurt you."

I recalled de la Costa's boastful nature from our previous encounter in the *Virginia Argus* office, and hoped he could be encouraged to talk.

My hope was fulfilled.

The Corsican stood and, warming to his subject, began to pace about the room. While he spoke, my mind desperately sought an escape from my predicament—a way in which I could contact Gentinetta, and so prevent this fiend from leaving the country.

"Since I had assumed Mr. Contadina's identity, it was a small matter to make certain inquiries at the Corsican shipping companies. I soon located the official who had written out madame and Camille's ticket—he was such a cooperative fellow that he was able to furnish me with a copy of their complete itinerary. Though I was several months behind them, it was only a matter of diligence to trace their course across France to Le Havre, where they had boarded a ship sailing for Boston."

"And Mr. Haverlock knew nothing of this mad plan of revenge, which was the true reason for your coming to America?"

"He was, as you say, 'blissfully ignorant.' When he first discovered that I intended to leave Corsica for America, he demanded to accompany me. At first I saw little use for him—I assumed he would only impede my progress. But as I reflected on the matter, I realized that at some point I might require his services, in one capacity or another."

"Then friendship had nothing to do with it?"

"Friendship had everything to do with it. Is not a friend one who offers you shelter in times of crisis?"

"I'm afraid Mr. Haverlock's attachment to you runs deeper than that. And now he realizes that he has been used precisely as Mr. Jarvis was used—and discarded. Had your ends required it, Mr. Haverlock would have proven just as disposable as the others."

"I will be the judge of the depth of my friendships!" he answered coldly. "We arrived in Boston. I sought out the carnival people at once. I knew Madame Verneuil would support herself in the same way she had in her native Corsica. I must say that I was surprised at the number of superstitious people to be found in this 'progressive' land of yours. I interviewed charlatans and magicians, sorcerers and fortune-tellers, but found no trace of the women I sought. Eustace and I joined a roadshow, serving as its cooks. In the evenings we would often camp outside the town where we were playing, and join with the other carnivals for feasting and festivities. I would make the rounds, always inquiring about a foreign-born fortune-teller and her daughter. You would also be surprised how many of *them* there are!

"The show traveled southward, through your states of Rhode Island, Connecticut, New York and New Jersey. One evening I heard from a fellow cook about a female fortune-teller who employed laudanum— I knew that I had found them!"

"Why did you not kill them immediately?"

"Because I had merely heard of them, I had not yet caught them. From this cook I learned the name of the carnival they were said to be traveling with. After Eustace and I parted company, I headed south, through Pennsylvania and Maryland. Several months elapsed, during which I continually seemed to be one city behind this elusive roadshow. Ultimately, I traced it to Richmond, but they were no longer in its employ, and no one I questioned had the slightest idea where the two women had gone.

"I grew despondent. The money I had earned as a cook was dwindling away, and I was forced to sleep in alleyways, on the riverbanks, anyplace where I could spread a blanket. I despaired at having come so close to the realization of my aims only to be defeated. And then one evening, in a riverfront pub I overheard several men singing the praises of two French fortune-tellers who were not above . . . prostitution if the money were proper. *Merci à Dieu* for the natural talkativeness of Americans, eh, Monsieur Poe? I followed these men to the Verneuils' rooms, and passed a nervous night in a damp alleyway waiting for them to depart. When they did, I called on madame and Camille, only to be told by their damnable servant Jarvis that Madame 'L'Espanaye' and her daughter had vacated the house. 'L'Espanaye!' A most appropriate *nom de guerre*, don't you think? The name of their village priest."

"I believe I can account for your movements from this point on," I interrupted, anxious to counter his detective work with some of my own. "Jarvis was either stubborn, as you assumed, or he was in reality ignorant of the women's whereabouts. By the time you realized he would tell you nothing, you had prevailed upon him to consume a fatal quantity of the drug.

"Then in the guise that had served you so well, you came to the offices of the *Virginia Argus* to place a personal announcement. There, you were temporarily elated that fortune had guided you to two people who were acquainted with the women, but you were just as quickly disappointed when you learned we assumed they were still in Richmond.

"You were more or less compelled to accompany us to Jarvis's home in order to allay our suspicions. I am curious, though, as to what prompted you to appear at his funeral. You surely were not concerned that I might think you callous for failing to attend?"

"If you will recall, our discussion outside the graveyard concerned your going to the police. I merely wished to dissuade you from such action, but as it turned out, persuasion was unnecessary. You had your own reasons for wishing to keep your . . . relationship with the Verneuil women a secret."

"But you didn't count on Barrow's tenacity. When he began to get too close to the truth, you decided to kill him too! I wonder, did you know that I and my wife were in Barrow's cabin the night you set it ablaze?"

De la Costa was taken greatly aback by this news. For a moment he seemed at a loss for words.

"I assure you I did not," he answered, recovering quickly. "Mr. Reece was quite alone when I followed him from town."

"In a black hackney drawn by a chestnut gelding!"

De la Costa nodded silently, wondering, I'm sure, how I came to possess such detailed information about his activities.

"And the article Barrow was about to publish the night you murdered him . . . ?"

"Quite simple, really. Through the Corsican press he had learned of Contadina's death and had deduced the obvious—he had discovered my secret identity. He had also learned the name of the carnival which madame and Camille had joined to flee Richmond. It was based in New York and he intended to follow it there. It was I, though, who ultimately made use of this information. I took to the road again and in a few weeks had located the women in New York. Can you imagine my surprise when I discovered you, Monsieur Poe, so tenderly cradled in their arms—so convenient a suspect for the New York police!"

"Then why did you not aid them in their investigation? You should have sought sanctuary with them, not with Haverlock or' myself. They would not have looked for the killer in their own midst."

"The explanation is ironic, to say the least. I, like hundreds of others, fell victim to New York's rising tide of crime."

"What?"

"I was robbed. Attacked on the street, and stripped of my money and personal effects—which included the official documents identifying me as Inspector Lucchino Contadina. Without papers, the police would have treated me as any other riff-raff. And now, somewhere out there is a bearded ruffian who carries with him all the authority of a high French police official!"

De la Costa glanced once more out the window, squinting at the sun which struggled to burn through the thick overcast.

"I'm going downstairs to take my breakfast now, Monsieur Poe. This description of my exhausting adventures has given me quite an appetite. Fortunately, my meals are included in the reasonable rent charged by your mother-in-law."

After de la Costa had departed, I collapsed onto the daybed, equally tired as the loquacious bandit, but infinitely more dejected; he had me at a distinct disadvantage and I saw no way to remedy the deplorable situation.

Scarcely a minute had passed, when de la Costa popped his head back through the door.

"Oh, and Monsieur Poe. You should bear in mind that any attempt to contact your friends or to leave this house will most certainly result in harm to your family."

Following this brusque threat, he slammed the door shut, and I heard his footsteps recede down the hall.

Twenty-one

The next twelve hours were the most agonizing I had ever endured!

De la Costa passed them in confident security while I boiled with rage at the hospitality shown him by mother. While I relieved her at Virginia's bedside, she cooked a hearty breakfast which the killer enjoyed immensely; she brought the morning papers and a second cup of coffee to the seat in which he was comfortably ensconced in our parlor; she questioned him as to his culinary likes and dislikes so as to be able to prepare midday and evening meals that would be to his satisfaction; she changed his sheets and towels and saw to it that a bowl of fresh fruit was placed in his room.

After the departure of Mr. Gowans, mother was taking no chances on losing another boarder.

I stalked angrily about the house, up and down the stairs, in and out of the kitchen, my mind continually straining to devise schemes whereby the Corsican might be tricked into submission.

I paced from room to room, keeping one eye on our villainous guest, and one eye on the clocks which were inexorably ticking away the hours and minutes in which I still had time to act.

I checked on my wife's health on an hourly basis. Her condition had stabilized and her shivering had subsided somewhat. She was still too weak to discuss what was really troubling her—the previous day's visit by her schoolgirl acquaintances—so she and I exchanged only the most superficial of comments.

I considered overpowering de la Costa, but the bandit cleverly made that impossible. He was continually seated or standing near mother, and he let it be known that his pistol was always in readiness. Any attempts on my part to wrest the weapon from his grasp would most likely result in his firing on either mother or myself— and I entertained no doubts as to his accuracy. On those occasions when I stationed myself at Virginia's bedside for any length of time, de la Costa would pay a call as the concerned boarder and, with the bulge of his pistol prominently displayed, pull up a chair next to mine.

As the afternoon wore on, I determined to call de la Costa's bluff. Towards three o'clock, while he lounged in our parlor, apparently lost in thought, I crept silently up the staircase and padded along the upstairs hallway towards the entrance to our attic. I entertained some wild notion of executing a daredevil leap from the tiny third-floor window onto the cobblestones below, after which I would run to the nearest omnibus stop and take it as far as Gentinetta's flat, where I would rouse the Corsican and his henchmen, and return to place de la Costa under arrest—all before the wily bandit would even notice my absence.

As it happened, de la Costa appeared behind me while I was still struggling with the attic door and, taking the key from my possession, gave me a mildly critical look before prodding me at pistol point back downstairs.

The situation remained static: as impossible as ever.

The darkness that descended on our house that night seemed to me one of overwhelming finality; never had twilight heralded a more malignant nightfall. As the oaken clock in our parlor dolorously chimed the hour of six, I could tell by de la Costa's increasing agitation that action was imminent.

David Madsen   *274*

Mother, our boarder and I partook of a quiet dinner at six-thirty. De la Costa was worried and distracted, as a man in his position was likely to be, but he still managed to find the presence of mind to compliment mother on her cooking. She beamed with pride, and shortly after the meal, she disappeared upstairs with Virginia's dinner, leaving me to clean up the kitchen.

As soon as we heard the upstairs bedroom door slam shut, de la Costa withdrew from his coat the longest, most fearsome dueling pistol I had ever laid eyes on!

"It is time we were leaving, Monsieur Poe. My ship sails at nine."

Taken by surprise, I could only stare at the weapon incredulously.

"This scheme of yours is half-mad, de la Costa," I gasped. "You'll never be able to book passage without a passport, without the proper papers."

"You have characterized all of my schemes as 'half-mad,' Poe, and they have without exception been successful. When we reach the ship, I will merely employ your papers. For the purposes of this transatlantic voyage, I shall become the struggling poet Edgar Allan Poe!"

De la Costa had, of course, planned for every contingency. It was foolhardy of me to suppose that a man who had spent ten years in prison plotting a single act of revenge would allow a last-minute miscalculation to interfere with his plans!

His intellect, when directed towards matters of deception and intrigue, was, I grudgingly admitted, considerable. I felt myself to be by no means an inconsequential opponent, yet I still lagged a step behind the cunning Corsican.

"Please, Monsieur Poe, you will have time enough for contemplation once we have completed tonight's mission. I will now accompany you upstairs where you will fetch the necessary papers and invent a reason for our going out that will be acceptable to your wife and mother."

At the moment, I could think of no alternative that would not cost me my life.

I led de la Costa out of the kitchen and through the parlor to the stairs. I paused for a moment, and with my arm poised on the banister, turned to confront the bandit.

"You are a hideous, pitiable human being, de la Costa—and I flatter you needlessly with such terms. You subscribe to an archaic, bloodthirsty code of honor which has no place in today's society. You track down and murder two women with whom you were once involved, you kill two other complete strangers merely because they proved an inconvenience. These are unpardonable crimes, to be sure, but they could have been accomplished with equal facility by a common thief, or by a temporarily crazed lover —by a thousand and one degenerates who plague this city. They kill once, perhaps twice; perhaps it becomes for them a vice or a habit, like a cigar, or laudanum. They have no idea that their actions create grief, misery or physical pain. They are unable to see the cause-and-effect nature of events."

"What has all of this to do with me?" he rasped, waving the dueling pistol impatiently.

"That is just the point—these dim-witted villains have *nothing* in common with you. You are an intelligent man, you perceive with undiluted clarity the awful consequences of your actions. Yet you seek for them justification where there can be none; you expect sympathy when by rights you deserve the gallows; you commit murder and disguise it as honor—this is what makes your crimes doubly despicable. You are a fraud, de la Costa, and four people have been needlessly sacrificed to the hollowness of your philosophy!"

De la Costa smiled. "We shall never see eye to eye, Monsieur Poe. We have too little in common."

I nodded my agreement. "I would rather die than have it otherwise!"

"Then since we are in accord, we have no excuse to delay any further. Up the stairs, please."

We quietly entered Virginia's room, and I bent over my sleeping bride in concern.

"She has a fever," mother notified me. "But it usually tends to rise in the early evening. I expect it to drop in the next two or three hours."

"Did she eat?" I asked, caressing her perspiring forehead.

"As much as could be expected. I will try to get something else down her if she awakens."

"Well, I expect there is little more that we can do for the present. Mr. de la Croix and I must unfortunately go out for a bit."

"Oh?" Mother seemed very curious.

"Yes . . . I don't much relish it, but . . ."

"Is it a matter of some gravity? You both seem quite anxious."

"No . . . no, Virginia's health is preying rather heavily on my mind. But we . . ." My imagination seemed suddenly depleted. I looked towards the bandit. Why didn't the fool concoct some excuse?!

"We are bound for the docks, Mrs. Clemm," he blurted out.

I coughed loudly. What in God's name was on his mind?

"There is a ship due to arrive from France this evening, carrying some more of my belongings. Your son-in-law has graciously consented to assist me in transporting them back to my room. I'm afraid they are more than I could comfortably handle alone."

"I see. Well, you had best bundle up, Eddie. I don't much like the sound of that cough of yours."

"Save your concern for Virginia, mother," I said, embracing her with an ardor I realized was quite unusual. What did I expect to happen tonight? I made a transparent attempt to conceal my nervousness, and after a suspended moment in which I stared at the sleeping figure of my wife, concentrating intently on her features as though I would never see her again, de la Costa and I beat a hasty retreat.

We took our hats and coats from the stand in the parlor, and bundled up tightly, as much to ward off the evening cold as to make ourselves difficult to recognize.

"Have you no belongings?" I asked the bandit, still hopeful that by engaging him in conversation I could gain time in which to invent an escape from my predicament.

"I have everything I need right here," he replied, smugly patting his breast pocket which I knew contained the identification papers he had taken from me.

There being little more to say, I walked slowly to the door, only to have my hand deflected from the knob by an insistent push of de la Costa's pistol. I glanced at him in puzzlement.

"Do you have a basement exit?" he asked.

"Well, there is a small service door that has been boarded up for years."

"Then tonight we shall open it. Your house may be watched—by the police, by Gentinetta and his friends, by I don't know whom. It will be safer if we leave via the cellar."

I shrugged and led de la Costa back through the kitchen to the basement door. Lighting a lantern which I extracted from the pantry, I opened the door and began cautiously to descend the shaky, long-neglected cellar stairs, with de la Costa never more than a footstep behind me. As we reached the bottom, and I stepped onto the damp, earthen floor, a sudden chipping noise arrested my progress. I stopped suddenly and played the lantern about the murky interior of the basement.

The walls were lined with shelves installed by the previous tenant, containing long-forgotten stores of bottled fruits, jams and preserves, ancient newspapers and magazines, and stacks of similarly worthless belongings he had wisely elected to leave behind. An empty steamer trunk, forgotten by Mr. Gowans, stood in the far corner, surrounded by mundane, miscellaneous articles whose sole destiny seemed to be to take up space in a series of basements and attics. There was nothing unusual, mysterious or even mildly interesting about the room.

Except for the noises—unexplained scratching sounds which were increasing in intensity in those recesses of the room beyond the reach of my lantern.

"*Mon Dieu*, what is that?" asked de la Costa. "Are your rats as big as everything else in America?"

"They surely cannot be rats," I replied, moving carefully in the direction of the noises. "But there is something alive back there—something that appears to be sealed in behind that wall!"

"I want nothing to do with this ridiculous affair!" exclaimed de la Costa, drawing his pistol. "You may investigate these disturbances at your leisure—tomorrow. Now, where is that service exit which you spoke of?"

Despite an overpowering curiosity, I was forced to abandon my investigation of the noises and guide de la Costa to the service door. It was a squat affair, wider than it was high, and it opened directly at street level, onto an alley behind the house. Fastening it were three large beams, which had been nailed to the door and the surrounding jamb in a Z pattern. While I held the lantern, de la Costa searched for an implement to pry the boards away from the wall.

As he looked, my attention continually wandered over my shoulder towards the back wall, behind which the scratching and chipping had become still louder, and more rambunctious. Was some animal, perhaps a dog, somehow trapped behind the brick-work? If so, how in God's name had it come to be there?

De la Costa managed to remove an iron hasp from Gowans's steamer trunk and, employing it as a lever, attacked the first of the three boards, removing it from the door with ease. The beams were old and mildewed, and consequently the nails served little purpose. The Corsican tossed the improvised lever aside, and began to tear at the boards with his hands.

At the same time the scratching gave way to a quieter, yet equally insistent jolting, which seemed more to indicate the presence of a man than a small animal.

De la Costa had succeeded in prying the last of the boards away from the door, and was now grappling with the latch, which had rusted over the years, and was as a result proving quite stubborn. He cursed under his breath, cutting his fingers and bruising his knuckles.

I looked discreetly behind me, not wishing to alert de la Costa to the rather bizarre spectacle that was unfolding less than ten paces behind his back: Chunks of mortar were falling away from between the brickwork, tumbling to the floor of the cellar as they were pushed from the inside. In the next second, one of the bricks itself became dislodged, crashing onto a scrap of metal with a sharp clatter.

De la Costa whipped around in alarm, and for the first time since I had made the villain's acquaintance, a genuine look of horror seized his features. With his back to the service door, his pistol pointed harmlessly to the floor, he stared in utter disbelief at a most unexpected and singular sight: Accompanied by a disembodied groan, an oblong section of the brick wall swung slowly outward!

Realizing that the ghostly noises which had so unnerved us were human in origin, de la Costa turned and hurled himself against the service door, snapping the rusted lock. The decaying wooden doors flew open; the cobblestones, glistening from the heavy evening mist, lay temptingly within reach.

De la Costa, pistol in hand, reached for the edges of the opening, intending to vault through the narrow space onto the street.

I grabbed for his ankles, dropping the lantern to the floor. We struggled in the shadows for a moment, de la Costa kicking wildly in an effort to break my grip. Panic had endowed him with extraordinary strength. As a fearsome Corsican oath burst from his throat, the killer wrenched free of my hold and scrambled out of the cellar!

Several seconds passed before I succeeded in clambering through the service door after him. A slice of moon had risen above the soot-stained rooftops, and through the low-hanging clouds cast a wan, colorless light on the deserted neighborhood. Though I looked in both directions, straining as I squinted into the distance, there was no sign of de la Costa.

I jumped back into the cellar and snatched up the lantern from the floor. Exposed to my thankful and astounded gaze was the face of Renzo Gentinetta, who at that moment was emerging from the newly created tunnel entrance!

"It's you! . . . But I . . . I had no idea this tunnel existed," I sputtered.

"I was unsure myself," replied Gentinetta, rubbing dust from his eyes. "Had it not been for Haverlock, I should never have known where to come. He gave me your address and I was able to locate the tunnel which led to your cellar!"

"Haverlock! He swore to me he would never betray de la Costa."

"Apparently your words were not without their effect. In addition, it seems de la Costa robbed our dear Mr. Haverlock of his last cent, in order to finance his trip home. It was the final indignity!"

"And your followers. Where are they?"

"There was no time to summon them. I left the moment I heard from Haverlock. Even now, we are wasting precious seconds. Where is he headed?"

"I'm afraid we are beaten," I replied. "He had intended to escape tonight via ship, but we shall never catch him."

"But we have him at a disadvantage!" Gentinetta protested loudly. "The streets between here and the river are an impenetrable maze unless one is familiar with them. We may be able to cut him off!"

The dejection I had experienced but a moment ago began to fade.

"Then lead on," I exclaimed. "And let us pray he becomes hopelessly lost!"

So saying, Gentinetta and I climbed once again through the cellar door, rounded the corner of the alley and set off at a brisk clip down Carmine Street.

"Had we not better engage a hackney?" I puffed, as I struggled to keep up with the vigorous pace set by the athletic Corsican.

"No, no," replied Gentinetta, his eyes focused on the distance. "It will only slow us down."

"Slow us down? But surely . . ."

"Save your breath for running, monsieur. Believe me, a carriage would do us no good whatsoever."

I soon learned that Gentinetta was quite correct in his insistence that we continue our pursuit on foot. Our route to the docks passed through the heart of Gentinetta's immigrant community, much of which was unfamiliar to me: the Bowery, Five Points, Shantytown, Murderer's Alley and the Den of Thieves. Here, in contrast to the mournful pall that descended on my neighborhood after nightfall, the streets were charged with a festive air.

It was a Friday evening and the poor residents of the area, released from the confines of the factories and sweatshops for a few hours, were intent on making the most of their freedom. The narrow, crowded streets were nearly impassable for us two pedestrians—a carriage would have been out of the question.

Despite the chill, scores were gathered on sidewalk and street, telling stories, singing and carousing, wine bottle and torch thrust in the air as though to mark their presence. Tables had been shunted out onto the street from ground-floor apartments, and impromptu card games, backgammon tournaments and brandy bars had been organized. The side alleys were filled with dancers, who, warmed by wine and scrapwood fires, gavotted frantically to the out-of-tune offerings of intoxicated violinists.

But no one had noticed a well-proportioned, moustachioed Corsican bolt through their midst like a flushed rabbit.

Undeterred, Gentinetta led me through the uproarious festivities, eliciting angry shouts from those whose activities our passage momentarily interrupted. Our progress was slow but steady as we wound through a maze of alleys and cramped, pedestrian walkways, Gentinetta holding to a seemingly aimless course—apparently the shortest distance between two points in the nonsensically laid-out streets of lower Manhattan.

As we turned the corner into a particularly boisterous, crowded avenue, we discerned up ahead a single covered hackney slowly fighting its way through the drunken throngs, its driver cursing and cracking his whip furiously.

"Who would be foolish enough to bring a carriage through here?" laughed Gentinetta. His laughter froze on his lips as the same thought struck us simultaneously: Could it be de la Costa?

With renewed strength, we wound our way snakelike through the jostling crowds, inching towards the hackney, which appeared to be completely stalled. Unabated, the driver continued his tirade against those in his way, while apologizing profusely to his unseen passenger. We had nearly attained the coach, when it began to move. Then, as though somehow sensing we were directly behind, Mario de la Costa himself leaned out the window and threw us a withering glance!

Enraged at the sight of his nemesis, Gentinetta seemed suddenly possessed of the strength and agility of ten men. As the shocked de la Costa exhorted his driver to greater speed, Gentinetta began to force his way through the crowd on the run.

"Gentinetta, no!" I shouted, grasping his intent.

But my advice went unheeded. Lifting a large, unsuspecting man from his path, Gentinetta executed a daring leap onto the running board of the moving coach!

As the carriage gathered speed, Gentinetta struggled with de la Costa, all the while straining to maintain his precarious foothold. De la Costa began to hammer viciously on Gentinetta's hands with some blunt object, attempting to break his grip on the door frame. The furious battle continued while the driver, fearful of losing control of the horses, screamed for the combatants to desist.

I bolted from the footpath onto the road, my path cleared by the carriage, which scattered pedestrians as it continued to roll even faster. Though I was once a record holder in the broad jump, it had been years since I had seen such strenuous exercise, and I quickly began to lag behind.

The carriage hurtled around a corner, seeming very nearly to tip over. For an awful moment, Gentinetta was lost to my view; but as I turned the corner myself, I saw that he was still clinging desperately to the coach, one hand grasping the wrought-iron door frame, the other tightening around de la Costa's throat!

My heart and head were pounding, my legs threatening to give out as I lost ground. The coach became for me little more than a receding black rectangle, with two pairs of wildly flailing arms extending from it.

I had all but given up the attempt to catch the runaway carriage, when I heard the loud report of a pistol!

Amid the screams and gasps of terrified onlookers, I saw Gentinetta thrown backwards from the carriage, his hands grasping in vain for purchase in the air. For the briefest of seconds, it appeared that he was suspended in midair; then, as the hackney hurtled onward with undiminished speed, Gentinetta plummeted to the cobblestones.

I rushed over to him, pushing aside the curiosity seekers who were gathering around his prostrate form. As I knelt beside him, I noticed a dark red stain slowly spreading across his chest; and pulling his outer garment aside, I saw with horror that his waist-coat was already soaked with blood! De la Costa's ball had struck Gentinetta squarely in the heart!

The noble Corsican's eyes were open, searching mine for signs of reassurance. Fighting back tears, I turned and shouted to the crowd at large, "Someone fetch a doctor, for God's sake!"

The fascinated onlookers returned my supplications with mute stares and merely waited, as though anxious for Gentinetta to die. A weak, quivering hand took hold of mine, and Gentinetta began to speak in a hoarse whisper.

"*C'est fini*, Monsieur Poe. Too late. Please, go after de la Costa."

"What, and leave you here to bleed to death in the streets?"

"Please, you can see for yourself . . . I'm dying. Will you not honor a dying man's last request?"

"But this is preposterous!" I protested, trying my best to stanch the bleeding with a pocket handkerchief. "You carry this too far, my dear Renzo. You are as obsessed as de la Costa."

"*Avec raison*, Poe. With good reason." His speech began to falter and I was forced to bend closer. The crowd had gradually grown respectful, as they became affected by Gentinetta's struggle for survival.

"Madame L'Espanaye was my wife!" he gasped.

I was struck speechless with disbelief. Gentinetta and Madame Verneuil married? It was almost too startling to believe, but ulti-mately, so tragic that I knew it must be true.

"Where's that damned doctor?" I cried, as I attempted to absorb this latest revelation.

"He's been sent for!" came a response from somewhere in the crowd.

"So you can see, *mon cher* Poe, de la Costa must not be allowed to escape."

"But how? Where were you married?"

"Here in New York. Six weeks ago. In a private ceremony," replied Gentinetta, his face now contorted with pain, his breathing marked by deep, agonizing groans. Though speech was becoming increasingly difficult, I sensed that he longed to make a clean breast of things, and so I allowed him to continue his story.

"You see . . . I met Madame L'Espanaye, as did many others, through her fortune-telling. She was threatened with . . . deportation. I am a naturalized American citizen, and so, we were married so that she and her daughter might remain in the country."

As he concluded this sentence, Gentinetta's body was wracked by sharp spasms of pain, and his knees jerked upwards reflexively.

"You'd best be quiet, Renzo. The doctor'll be here straightaway."

"It was a marriage of convenience," he continued, undaunted. "But though we lived apart, I slowly found myself growing to love her. Who knows what time might have brought?"

Gentinetta closed his eyes, as though trying to recover from the strains of speech. I searched in vain among the solemn, soiled faces that bent over us, for signs of the doctor.

But I knew he was beyond salvation.

Gentinetta's lips moved slightly, as he tried with his dwindling reserves of strength to convey a few last words.

"Find him, Poe," he declared at last, his voice now all but inaudible. "Find him—and kill him!"

Hardly had this last request for revenge left his lips, when an awful shudder rippled through Gentinetta's body, and he lay still.

For several moments, total silence reigned. Then, the onlookers began hesitantly to converse among themselves as they slowly drifted away to return to the pursuits of the evening. Somewhere in the distance, a violin struck up a dance tune, and the music echoed mournfully through the crowded alleys. Laughter was heard again, then jovial singing and shouting. By the time the last witness to Gentinetta's death had wandered off, the streets had returned to life.

With profound sadness, I watched from a darkened doorway as the lifeless form of Renzo Gentinetta was loaded onto a battered hospital carriage. It was purely a formality, I knew. The Corsican's stay in the hospital would be brief—just long enough for a clerk to make out an official certificate of death and obtain the necessary signatures. From there, it would be taken directly to the morgue. Would it be claimed? And by whom? I vowed to notify his fellow Corsicans, so that he might have a proper funeral service, and thus be spared the final ignominy of an unmarked grave.

As I hurried through a deserted industrial neighborhood that bordered the docks, I pondered his dying request: "Find de la Costa—and kill him!" To somehow prevent de la Costa from fleeing New York was my primary goal—that in itself would be difficult enough—but as for the latter . . . I knew that I was not the man for the task. If I was able to capture the bandit, I determined to turn him over to the Corsicans as planned, and to let them deal with him as they saw fit.

A barely perceptible sea breeze came up, coating my already perspiring face with a fine mist borne in from the harbor. I turned the corner onto Pike Street, dodging a solitary dray that shuttled by on some late-night assignment. At the mouth of Pike I stopped and, from the security of the shadows, surveyed the East River docks.

There were few signs of life. The pier immediately across from me was deserted, and two leather-headed watchmen, clubs in hand, strolled up and down its length, smoking cigarettes and loudly sharing some ribald joke.

Many of the ships docked along the twelve-block length of South Street could be dismissed at a distance. Only those rigged for sailing needed to be investigated; the others, their naked masts visible as black spires piercing the gray nighttime sky, were deserted save for skeleton crews, and would not put to sea for several hours, perhaps not for days. That still left five or six ships of all description, and so I hastened towards the nearest pier, where a large, square-rigged cargo packet was moored.

As I strode rapidly along the dock, hoping I might encounter one of Gentinetta's guards, I noticed crew members clambering onto the yards, beginning the laborious process of bringing in the sails. With disappointment, I realized that the object of my investigation had just docked and would certainly not be sailing that night. Frantically, I ran back along the pier, threading my way through shipping crates, steamer trunks and mountains of miscellaneous cargo, and charged down to the next ship—a fore-and-aft rigged, three-masted schooner.

I did not bother with even a cursory examination of the schooner —it, too, had arrived that afternoon, and it flew only two sails, broad thatches of white on a charcoal and gray background, hanging heavily in the nearly windless night air.

Brigantines, barks, sloops and barkentines were all lazily mired in the rippleless East River waters. An occasional lantern-bearing sailor could be seen scrambling along the yards, pulling in a topsail, a topgallant or a royal, visible only as a darting pinpoint of light against the tangled, manmade forest of rigging.

I grew dizzy running from pier to pier, never stopping long enough to absorb detail, merely noting from the corner of my eye the essential information: the pier itself, a long, rambling structure composed of stout, splintery beams; the thin belts of water that lay on either side of the ships; the prows of the packets, bluff bowed and apple cheeked; and the horizon beyond, an inseparable mixture of black water and the blacker hills of Brooklyn across the river.

One by one, each ship was eliminated as a possible escape route for de la Costa. Not one of the several vessels docked at that moment was bound for Europe. None at all were to sail that evening. And the sailors whom I questioned had seen no one answering to de la Costa's description.

Had he lied to me concerning his nine o'clock sailing? Had he in reality intended to lead me to some other destination? Or had he devised some alternative method of escape from the city?

Crestfallen, I collapsed on a wooden bench, unmindful of the cold Atlantic mist that coated it, and surveyed the somber expanse of New York Bay; a lifeless panorama that well matched the sense of loss I deeply felt. I had thrown everything into de la Costa's pursuit; together, Gentinetta and I had employed intellect, imagination and guile, yet we had not proven quick enough to capture our quarry. And now, I had followed him to the very tip of Manhattan, to the physical ends of my tightly confined world, and somehow Mario de la Costa had slipped over the edge, as if the earth were flat. Like a canoe moving slowly through calm waters, he had left no wake.

A hansom trotted along the far side of a small park which lay at my back. The inky waters of the bay lapped politely at the pilings, like a cat at his milk. Tired sailors awaiting sleep swapped lies in hushed tones from the decks of the ships, their conversation occasionally punctuated by a crisp splash as a drained bottle of rum was tossed overboard.

I otherwise contemplated my defeat in an environment of silence as the New York night descended, sheathing all objects, human and not, in its cold, conquering cloak.

The "affaire L'Espanaye" was once again reduced to its simplest terms: no Corsican posse, no vengeful ex-cell mates, no constables and no police—just Mario de la Costa and myself. Whether it was the all-consuming nature of my obsession, the desire to see de la Costa atone for the deaths of Gentinetta and so many others, or merely the fiction writer's hatred of inconclusive endings, I did not know. But I did know that despite my temporary paralysis, I was not going to return home with my task incomplete. De la Costa was out there somewhere, secreted away in some shadowy, impenetrable niche where both men and sunlight feared to tread. He was still in New York, of that I was sure. I had lived within his deadly aura for so long that I knew I would sense it when the villain passed beyond my reach.

Then, from out of the cobblestoned gloom, a black wagon, drawn by four proud, overworked horses rumbled momentarily into the light of a streetlamp. It passed quickly out of the dim yellow halo and again into shadow, bound for a pier somewhere in the distance. Yet in that instant of illumination, I recognized at the reins the eager, freckled face of one of the young mortician's apprentices Gentinetta and I had interviewed on the night we searched for de la Costa in the city's morgues.

And then I knew.

David Madsen   *288*

Twenty-two

Just beyond Battery Park, between Watts and Vestry streets was a small commercial pier alive with ghostly activity.

I had followed the morgue carriage on foot, and now I watched from the shadows of a freight warehouse as the youthful apprentice reined his horses to a halt at the end of a line of three identical vehicles. Like black-curtained taxis, the hearses waited on the pier, and in steady succession took charge of their hideous cargo.

From a longboat moored at the pier, white-sheeted human forms were passed up to bored, overcoated stevedores who loaded the bodies into the rear of the carriages under the hearse drivers' supervision.

Attentively standing guard were uniformed New York constables, nervously slapping ferocious-looking clubs into the open palms of their hands as they squinted into the surrounding darkness for signs of intruders.

The entire process was lit by two torches which had been lashed to the dock uprights and provided a thin corridor of light that ran from the longboat to the wagons. In contrast to the black-coated longshoremen and blue-uniformed constables, the sheets that covered the corpses assumed an unnatural glow in the torchlight, pulling the eye involuntarily to these rectangles of white as they were shunted about by unsympathetic, businesslike hands.

Though I knew I was merely witnessing the city-financed transferral of the dead to the municipal morgue, I was seized for an instant by the impression that I was eavesdropping on some unspeakable ritual carried out under cover of nightfall by members of a persecuted, pagan religion.

Once a hearse had taken on its quota of bodies, the driver presented the leader of the detachment of stevedores with a pen and a series of papers requiring his signature. As the bureaucratic regulations were attended to, the driver and his co-workers engaged in friendly chatter. Their business was conducted with an ease and informality common to merchants who have been dealing with one another for years; it was as though the parties involved were unaware of the morbid nature of the commodity with which they dealt.

Several hundred yards out in the bay, its facade nearly invisible behind an obscuring curtain of unusually thick Atlantic fog, was anchored one of New York City's "lazarettos"—floating quarantine hospitals. Because of the high incidence of cholera among immigrants, the city maintained these hospitals on Staten Island and on various specially fitted ships anchored well out in the harbor. When immigration or medical personnel detected the disease on board ships waiting to dock in New York, the infected victims were transferred to these facilities to await treatment—or death. I recalled what the young mortician's apprentice had told me of the lazarettos—nightmarish, makeshift prisons that even the bravest of doctors feared to visit.

Judging by the number of bodies now being brought to shore, it was conceivable that an epidemic was running more or less unchecked just a few yards from the tip of Manhattan. It was no surprise that the Department of Health had seen fit to post security guards at the docks. The threat of cholera is a certain inducement to panic, especially in a city such as New York which had as recently as 1832 endured a crippling epidemic of the dreaded disease.

And unless my suspicions proved totally unfounded, Mario de la Costa had taken refuge out there in that floating hell, relying on man's natural fear of cholera to render his hiding place all but impregnable. He could wait there without fear of capture for as long as necessary, until he could find a way to board one of the ships that regularly passed by.

I was anxious to question these hardworking stevedores as to whether they had seen any suspicious persons answering to de la Costa's description, but that seemed impossible given the presence of the constables.

As I was considering what course of action to take, my attention was aroused by noises that seemed to be coming from behind the warehouse that concealed me. Curious, I crept along the side of the building away from the activity on the pier, and rounded the back corner. Ahead of me stretched a narrow catwalk flanked on one side by the rear of the warehouse and on the other by water. I listened attentively for a minute, hoping the unexplained noise would be repeated. When it was not, I began a cautious passage along the shadowy catwalk, coming to a sudden stop as a door opened somewhere inside.

I pressed myself flat against the wooden wall beneath a window, relying on a meager collection of packing crates and the darkness to conceal me. From within the building there came the sounds of a closet opening and closing, of clothes rustling—as though a man were getting dressed. I raised my head and risked a look into the meagerly lit interior. What I had assumed to be a storage warehouse was in reality a dressing room of some kind. Against the far wall stood a series of wooden lockers which faced out on several scarred benches. Evidently the longshoremen changed here from their street attire into work clothes before reporting for duty.

There came the sound of water running, it stopped abruptly and from the recesses of the changing room walked another stevedore in work clothes. He came slowly, almost hesitantly, towards me, as though he were not comfortable in his surroundings. Because the interior of the building was lit, he passed within three feet of the window, unable to see my inquisitive face pressed against the glass. In the instant before he bent over to blow out the lantern, I recognized de la Costa!

I fell again behind the packing crates as the bandit flung open the door and emerged onto the catwalk, pulling his woolen cap low over his eyes.

Should I act now? What could I do without creating a disturbance, without alarming the constables and precipitating our arrest? Before I could reach a decision, de la Costa hurried away with a determined stride and disappeared around the corner to join the other stevedores.

Realizing that the bandit intended to infiltrate the ranks of the longshoremen and thus gain admittance to the hospital ship, I decided that if the ruse could work for him, it could work for me. In five minutes I had succeeded in disguising myself quite effectively, and clad in gloves, heavy black overcoat and overboots, I walked onto the pier where the last of the hearses was taking on its load.

I approached a group of four longshoremen who were sharing a cigarette and conversing quietly as they watched their chief and the driver complete the necessary paperwork. Before I could begin to fabricate an excuse for my presence, one of them, a spindly Irishman with a rasping, metallic voice, addressed me. As we spoke, the uniformed security guards eyed us reproachfully, as though they were hoping my presence could not be justified and they would be free to deal with me as they saw fit.

"Well, well, when it rains, it pours, by God. You're the second new one they've sent out tonight."

"Some sort of mix-up back at the office, I guess," I replied, happy to play along with the Irishman's misreading of the situation.

"Well, we're done with this load, but there'll be another. Hop into the longboat there—we'll cast off in a minute or two. We've got to dash this job off in the next hour—they want to set sail when the wind comes up 'round midnight."

"Set sail? I've never heard of a hospital ship setting sail! Are they moving her further out in the harbor?"

"Don't they tell you nothin' back there? This ain't no hospital ship at all. She arrived from France three days ago—half the crew and passengers already dead. Immigration won't let her in any closer! We filled up her larder for her last night, courtesy of the taxpayers, and after we off-load the dead, them that's still alive's gonna sail 'er back. God bless 'em is all I can say! Now get in the damned longboat and save yer wind!"

In that instant de la Costa's plans became obvious. He had somehow learned of the authorities' intention to send this ship back to Europe. All that was required of the cunning Corsican now was to disappear on board for two hours—once the cholera-infested ship set sail, no one would dare approach it. Whether de la Costa would survive a transatlantic crossing in the company of a highly communicable disease and its intended victims was another matter entirely.

I descended the five steps that led down from the pier to the longboat in the company of five other stevedores and a single guard and climbed aboard, taking a seat near the prow. I will never forget the look of total shock and disorientation that Mario de la Costa gave me as I reached across his lap to take my oar!

Beneath the bill of his woolen cap, the Corsican's eyes were sunk in shadow; black pits at the bottom of which burned a bonfire of unrelenting hatred. He hissed at me, yet owing to our circumstances he was powerless to attack, to curse or even to question me. The harbor silence was suddenly broken by the groan of wood against wood as the boatmen unshipped their oars. Under the direction of the Irishman, we began to row steadily out to the quarantined ship, carrying a second longboat in tow.

Into a cocoon of mist and darkness we rowed, and I returned de la Costa's fixated glare with an ironic, playfully victorious smile. He rowed with an ardor double that of the others, transferring his fury and frustration to the oars.

As the minutes passed and the ship came into view, a full-rigged, three-masted cargo vessel, I contemplated enlisting the stevedores and the constable in an attempt to overpower de la Costa. But I eventually abandoned this plan. The gunfire that would be unleashed could prove deadly, as he and the constable fired wildly at each other in the confines of the boat, their respective targets nearly invisible in the gloom.

Yet I had nothing else in mind. Once we were aboard the ship, I would be at a complete loss as to how to proceed. What could I, an unarmed man, hope to accomplish on my own?

My ruminations were interrupted by a shouted exchange between the Irish stevedore and someone aboard the quarantined ship. As we pulled alongside, the great curving hull loomed out of the water like a sheer wooden cliff. Though the waters were comparatively calm, our boat was tossed against the ship with surprising force, and I grew frightened that our little craft would be dashed to splinters. The others were completely at their ease, however, as they skillfully maneuvered the longboat next to a steep ladder affixed to the hull and, with the aid of two sailors, tied us off.

We shipped our oars and the stevedores reached into their pockets, and extracted masks of surgical gauze which they wrapped tightly about their faces until only their eyes were visible. De la Costa and I exchanged worried looks as we fumbled about in our own pockets for the protective masks we prayed would be there. Thankfully, the men whose clothes we wore that night proved to be prepared, and de la Costa and I breathed deep sighs of relief as we bandaged ourselves as well.

One by one we disembarked and climbed up the iron ladder onto the deck of the ship, which we identified from its life preservers as the *Montpelier*.

The scene before us was one of Dantean proportions: The decks were covered with sheeted bodies awaiting transport to the morgues on land, while white-masked sailors shuttled routinely between the prone figures on various errands, exercising only the most minimal care to avoid trampling upon the dead.

From the yards and rigging above us, shouted orders reverberated through the night, as other sailors worked to lower the sails in time for a midnight departure. Every thirty seconds or so, a hatch door would fly open as a lantern-bearing, bandaged crew member came up from below decks. In that instant when the door hung open, a faint choir of agony emanated from the holds below: the feverish groans of those victims too ill to work, yet not ready to join the dead.

Though the *Montpelier* was primarily a cargo vessel, she was also equipped to carry small numbers of passengers, and I reflected briefly on the tragedy of those passengers who had endured a six-week voyage plagued by illness and death, only to be turned back the day they reached their destination. I could vividly imagine the terrors the voyage had seen: The first victim falls, dehydrated, seized by muscular cramps, vomiting and diarrhea, his tongue dry and withered. The other passengers grow pale and weakened by fear—the disease is among them, yet, surrounded by ocean, escape is impossible. Confined as they are to the same three decks, they are forced to breathe the same air and drink the same contaminated water, wine and food. They are faced with the choice of either starving, dying of thirst, or risking infection. They hold out for several days, but in the end they succumb to thirst, allowing the disease to begin its slow, inexorable spread, cruelly striking some while leaving others completely unscathed.

It was those who were untouched by the disease who now scurried about the ship with apparent immunity, sailor and passenger alike, so concentrated upon their efforts to prepare the *Montpelier* for sailing that they appeared not even to register the fields of dead through which they moved.

Hovering above it all, like an immovable cloud of industrial smoke that is impervious to both wind and rain, was the bloated stench of death, so potent it easily penetrated our protective masks and burned its way into our nostrils.

As the stevedores began the grisly task of transporting the corpses across the deck, down the tiny iron ladder and into the longboat, de la Costa pressed his pistol into my back and led me quietly away from the center of activity into the shadows.

"You two," called the Irishman, noticing our apparent defection. "You're here to work, not palaver."

"We've been told there are some fresh ones below. My friend and I here thought it best to go down and investigate," replied the ever-inventive de la Costa.

"You can have it!" came the answer, as the Irishman waved us away. "I've been below once, and once was two times too many. Get some of these sailors to help you bring the rest up."

"Yes, sir," said de la Costa, as he watched the chief stevedore turn his attention elsewhere.

The bandit then motioned me towards the nearest hatch leading below decks. We slowly drew back the solid oaken door, and peered tentatively down the staircase. It seemed to lead into nothingness—its boundaries and destination obscured by a thick, lamp-lit mixture of shadow and haze. As we slowly descended into the hold, our sense of displacement was heightened by the same agonized choir we had heard up on deck, now louder, more demanding, more terrifying. Then, as the hatch was slammed shut behind us by a conscientious sailor, it was as though we were suddenly enveloped in the folds of Hell itself!

By the time we reached the bottom of the stairs, our eyes were fully accustomed to the darkness. We were surrounded by a scene of abomination more outlandish than anything our first unsettling encounters with the disease had prepared us for.

Stretching into the poorly lit depths of the cavernous hold were row upon row of beds, each occupied by an emaciated cholera victim. As we moved with trepidation down the narrow aisles between the bunks, desperate arms reached out to us for succor from between fetid, lice-infected sheets. The faces into which we stared with pity and morbid fascination—men, women and children alike—were sunken and withered, their eyes vacant and their cheeks collapsed. Their lips were blue, their faces chilled and clammy, and their tongues dry.

No medical personnel tendered comfort here, no nurses or orderlies patrolled this arena of misery offering consolation and medicine. Instead, those who had not totally wasted away cradled the frightened faces of those who had, making them sip from warm, contaminated water. So overwhelming was the magnitude of this suffering that de la Costa and I were numbed to silence, our personal vendetta seeming for the moment entirely insignificant.

"Why do you sacrifice yourself needlessly?" I asked, as we retreated to the foot of the stairs. "Three weeks aboard this vessel and you are certain to die."

"Cholera is never a certainty, Monsieur Poe, as the healthy sailors above decks are testimony to. Even if I were to become infected, the survival rate if untreated is 40 percent. And that is 40 percent higher than my chances here in New York. I must say that, given my desperate situation, the odds are not at all unattractive."

The hatch was suddenly thrown open and the voice of the Irish foreman called down to us.

"We've almost got a boatload ready to go. Are you makin' any progress down there? Do you need one of the boys to come down and lend a hand?"

"We're fine, there's not too many," de la Costa cried back. "You go on back with that load and we'll manage the rest in the other boat."

After a moment's hesitation, the foreman agreed.

"Suit yerself. My men are glad enough to be away from here. Just thought you might like a dollop of sea air to clear your head."

"No, thanks. I'd just as soon have done with it down here, if you don't mind." The Irishman seemed to accept this explanation, and after a moment, he slammed the hatch shut and we heard his boot steps retreat across the deck above us.

Then the steady parade of footfalls across the decks stopped, indicating the last of the bodies had been moved to the longboat. There came the sounds of oars and oarlocks making contact, and I knew the stevedores had cast off for shore. Their small part in our drama was finished, and with it all possibility that I could somehow enlist their aid. To whom could I now turn? A handful of disinterested sailors whose only objective was to survive the return voyage to Europe? A boatload of hopeless invalids?

"Please, Monsieur Poe"—de la Costa broke the silence between us—"your determination is almost Corsican. But I implore you to

Black Plume   297

abandon this madness. There is still one boat. Why do you not take it and return to shore, to your mother and your ailing wife? I'm sure it has been a long night for them as well, and they would welcome your return."

I peered deeper into the hold, as though I thought a way out of my dilemma lay hidden there.

The long, dedicated pursuit, the risk to life and limb, home and family, the months of struggling to unlock the secrets of the "affaire L'Espanaye" had all led to this final confrontation between us.

My gaze continued to sweep the bunks that had become hospital beds and the languishing, broken beings who occupied them.

They were desperate, but I was equally so!

"This man is a doctor," I shouted suddenly, as de la Costa turned white and incredulous before my eyes. "He has come to help you! *Il est médecin. Il est venu pour vous aider!*"

It was as though a sudden hurricane had risen from tranquil waters and seized the ship in its destructive grasp. The cries of pain became cries for help, the dull chorus of moans a piercing collection of shrieks and shouts—tormented but suddenly hopeful.

"What are you doing? *Mon Dieu!* You have gone mad!"

De la Costa, his eyes blazing, drew his pistol, but I dashed into the shadows behind the staircase before he could take aim. From behind the steps I watched as a scene of unearthly terror unfolded.

Like participants in a mass resurrection, two score or more ghostly figures fought to sit upright, their pitiful arms extended towards de la Costa in supplication.

"I'm not a doctor," he screamed. "I'm not a doctor. *Je ne suis pas médecin!*"

But the seed had been planted, and the sick and delirious would accept no denials—they had gone deaf at the word "doctor."

Those who succeeded in reaching their feet began to stagger towards de la Costa, lining up in single file to receive his imaginary curatives.

Faces and arms emerged from the dim background of the hold and began slowly to assume shapes vaguely human, their diseased skin appearing in the dim light as if tinted gray, blue, yellow and ash white.

De la Costa recoiled against the stairs in revulsion, brandishing his pistol wildly.

"I'm not a doctor, I can't help you," he insisted. "Please listen to me! Listen to me!"

His shouted protests were to no avail. Like an unstoppable army of the dead, the white-robed cholera victims advanced on de la Costa, some thrusting shriveled, squealing infants in front of them for him to examine. Some came forward in dignity, others in uncontrollable panic, still others in rude, jostling succession, as though they were worried de la Costa would not have enough time to minister to all of them.

The bandit was powerless, and terrified. The forty or more people who confronted him, their voices joined together in a coughing litany of "Help us, please help us," were a mob—decaying and gaunt, but a mob nonetheless. In their despair, they possessed an awesome, collective strength.

De la Costa fired into the air. The sick drew back, but only for the slightest instant. Bony hands grasped at him, hungrily seeking his flesh, tearing his clothing.

"Get back, please, get away from me," the Corsican howled.

"Why won't you help us? Why won't you help us?" came the droning, distraught reply.

De la Costa began slowly to retreat up the stairs as hands tightened their grip on his wrists, attempting to pull him back down among them. I quickly slipped out from my hiding place and began to fight my way through the tightly congested bodies.

De la Costa, unable to endure his situation any longer, hurled his pistol down into the darkness of the hold, and scampered up the stairs. With a shattering jolt, he threw the weight of his body against the hatch and it flew open. As I battled my way through the clammy, crying invalids, I kept my eyes on the hatch, and watched in dismay as it was slammed shut before I could attain the top of the stairs.

My boots threatened to snap the sagging wooden steps in two as I bounded up them furiously, praying that I could escape from the hold before de la Costa disappeared again—or the crowd began to transfer their maniacal pleadings to me.

To my good fortune, the hatch proved to be unlocked.

A second later I had burst through the narrow opening and out onto the invigorating openness of the deck. A pungent, salty breeze slapped against my face and the crisp night air filled my lungs. The contrast to the stultifying, deplorable conditions below was overwhelming.

The sounds of a far-off splashing were suddenly borne to me across the nearly deserted deck by a soft offshore wind. I ran to the windward side of the vessel, past two masked, unconcerned sailors who were occupied in unraveling a stubbornly knotted length of rope. I squinted into the coal black waters, now dappled with occasional whitecaps in response to the steadily rising wind, to see Mario de la Costa swimming swiftly and skillfully towards shore.

I ran halfway down the length of the ship and vaulted over the gunwale, landing on the top step of the wrought-iron ladder that led down to the second of the longboats still securely moored below.

I descended the narrow steps in a mad tumble, and hastily un-lashed the line that moored the tiny craft, not bothering to coil it and throw it aboard. As the boat began to drift away from me, I jumped aboard, and taking a seat in the center, clumsily unshipped a set of oars. As I began the strenuous task of propelling the long-boat towards shore, I glanced over the stern towards the deck of the *Montpelier*. Several of the strongest invalids from below had managed to battle their way up on deck, and were now gazing longingly at the lights that burned on shore: comforting and hos-pitable, so frustratingly near, yet so impossibly distant.

After no more than a moment's freedom, these white-sheeted wraiths were snatched away from the gunwale by sailors, angered and threatened by their presence, and forcibly dragged across the decks to be requarantined in the hellish confines of the hold. Then, as I gradually fell into the tedious rhythm of rowing, the *Montpelier* and its doomed cargo were swallowed whole by the mist.

Twenty-three

Though I worked at the oars with a strength and precision that, quite frankly, surprised me, I proved no match for the robust, sustained strokes of de la Costa. He had wisely realized that an amateur oarsman in a heavy, cumbersome longboat is no match for an experienced swimmer. The small, crisp splashes generated by his arms as they pounded the water grew fainter by the second. I knew the fleeing Corsican was directly in front of me but, owing to the darkness and mist, I could see nothing.

Yet I kept at it; pushing out with my arms as the oars were lifted from the water and brought skimming towards me, then pulling back as their broad, salt-slicked paddles cut deep beneath the surface, again and again with numbing repetition.

All the while I strained my ears, hoping somehow to detect the presence of my quarry. As I drew near shore I adjusted my course to the pier where the bodies were unloaded, its presence marked by two flickering torches.

At that moment, I heard to my right a groan of exertion followed immediately by the clumsy thump of boot heels on wood. De la Costa was climbing onto the neighboring pier!

In less than three oar strokes I had reached the pilings. I stood and swayed dizzily on the unstable bottom of the boat for a moment, before I was able to throw my balance towards the pier. I leapt onto a ladder as my craft floated uselessly away from me and climbed quickly to the top, until my head was level with the floor of the dock. Here I paused, and cautiously surveyed the scene before me.

I had heard no hastily retreating footfalls, so I judged that the bandit was still in the immediate vicinity—perhaps lying in wait for me. Though he had not intentionally attempted it up to this point, I knew that now, Mario de la Costa had no choice but to kill me!

Even though he had lost his pistol on the ship, the dock offered plenty of opportunity for him to find a weapon and stage an ambush: mountains of packing crates, boxed goods, freight containers, steamer trunks and baggage of various sizes blanketed the pier, turning it into a network of narrow alleyways and canyons—any of which could have hidden my adversary.

Rusty pieces of machinery and odds and ends of metal piping lay scattered on the ground—all potentially lethal weapons. There was nothing for me to do but begin a circumspect investigation of the area. I pulled myself up onto the pier and entered a thin passageway between two meticulously stacked rows of water barrels. My eyes roved from side to side, behind me and above me, seeking out a retreating shadow, or the pale blotch of a face—but I saw nothing.

Where was de la Costa? Why did he not show himself? Why did he not spring an attack? As the anxious minutes dragged by and my efforts continued to prove futile, I began to crave a confrontation—a final, lightning-quick climax to the drudgery of the chase. But none was forthcoming. I judged that more than half an hour had elapsed, and as I slipped away from the shadows of an empty service shed, and found myself back at the point where I had first stepped onto the dock, I gave up my search.

De la Costa had again dissolved into the night as though he possessed the formula for invisibility.

But as I plodded along the wharf towards the street, I grew conscious of an indefinable change in my environment. Something was suddenly different, different than it had been twenty paces behind me. Was it a sound, a sight, a sensation? The effects of depression, or exhaustion?

I retraced my steps to the ladder and stood stock still. It had changed again. What in God's name was it? I looked down at my feet and in the cracks between the planking I could see the waters of the bay quietly caressing the pilings.

And I could hear it! I could hear the water!

I rushed to the street end of the pier and stopped. There I heard nothing. I dropped to my knees and squinted between the boards into the darkness below the dock. The tide did not come in this far; it was perfectly dry down there.

An ideal hiding place!

To my left a wooden staircase descended sharply to the murkiness beneath the wharf. I walked down it one cautious step at a time, leaning against the ceiling formed by the pier to examine the foreboding region I proposed to enter. The scores of thick pilings which supported the pier stretched into the indiscernible distance, calling to mind a vast, primeval rain forest. The dampness that pervaded the air down here was more than palpable; it coated everything. The pilings themselves were nearly soft to the touch, and the dock above my head glistened with moisture, as though it were sweating.

I descended the last of the steps to the ground—it was spongy, indicating that a permanent water table lay not far below the surface.

With redoubled caution, I began to explore. As my eyes accustomed themselves to the darkness, I saw that potential hiding places were limited. The shipping operators, evidently deciding the moisture would prove destructive to cargo awaiting shipment, had only stored two or three large, impermeable containers down here. Back towards the water line, which was gradually becoming visible as I moved away from the street end of the pier, was a mammoth stack of reserve pilings. If de la Costa had taken refuge back there, he would feel cornered and desperate. Like a wild animal threatened by a territorial invader, he would be doubly dangerous!

I moved towards this potential place of concealment with sluggish hesitance: ears cocked for a telltale human breath or sigh; eyes peeled for movement, no matter how small.

I grew acutely conscious of the slightest noise: the creaking of an upright, the gentle, regular lapping of the waves on the sandy beach, the sudden clatter of hoofbeats as a lone freight wagon rumbled along the street above me. But there was something else down here that worked subtly on my nerves—a feeling that the entire dank, deserted region lived and breathed—that I was surrounded by hostile, alien figures. The closer I came to the water line, the stronger this feeling grew. I felt naked and exposed—like an intruder who is shortly to be punished.

Twenty feet from the mountainous stack of pilings I stopped. If I were to approach closer and peer behind them, I risked attack and perhaps death. But if I were to remain where I stood, and de la Costa were actually concealed there, what would happen? Minutes would drag by, perhaps an hour, but not more. De la Costa could not afford to remain down here until it grew light. He would grow impatient, frustrated—and would rush out, weapon at the ready. I had to act. Trembling, I emerged from the concealment of a piling and crept slowly forward.

"Poe!" came a maniacal shout from somewhere behind me.

I whirled around and from the shadows saw an outline whip from the right to the left side of my vision. I ducked instinctively. I saw de la Costa waving his right arm wildly in a circle, his body knotting into a tightly wound coil. Like a dervish, his arm continued to spin, until with a great gasp of exertion, his wrist snapped, sending a deadly, spiked object hurtling towards me!

I threw myself to the ground, choking on a mouthful of damp sand and rock, as a cruelly barbed marlinespike, fastened to a length of stout rope, imbedded itself in a piling less than a foot away! For a second, the razor-sharp, maliciously curved piece of iron vibrated in the wood with a low-pitched shudder—then once again, all was silent.

I raised my head as high as I dared and saw de la Costa circling to my left, evidently intending to surprise me by way of the two gigantic freight containers which lay behind me. Silhouetted against the gray background of the water, he was a fearsome sight: his clothes tattered and dripping with seawater, his face contorted with desperation, his hand clutching another of the lethal weapons that had nearly claimed me.

I jumped to my feet and attempted to pull the marlinespike from the upright. I quickly abandoned the struggle as hopeless; it had been thrown with such force that it would require several minutes to extract it. I broke cover and dashed across the slippery ground to my right, taking refuge behind a pillar facing the water.

I began to close in on the shipping crates—so massive they formed a veritable wall separating me from my adversary. He had disappeared somewhere behind them; but whether he stood just beyond, ready to spring an ambush, or whether he had merely used them to mask his escape, I could not determine.

I stealthily inched my way along the containers, their wooden facades marked by a myriad of hand-scrawled, exotic destinations. I hoped for a space between the closely stacked crates that would permit me a glimpse of the other side, but I found none. Reaching the corner, I paused to summon my nerve.

Seconds crawled by, but I did not move. I listened, praying for the Corsican to betray his position. At first, I heard nothing. But then, as I grew attuned to the steady lapping of the waves, I detected above the sound of them a slight, abrasive shuffling—as though feet were shifting their position in sand. This continued for several seconds, until it was replaced by soft, straining groans.

Was I imagining it, or had my ears suddenly become so sensitive that I could now detect the villain's heartbeat? Yes, there it was— a subdued, regular drumming that grew quickly in intensity . . . and speed.

He was back there, I was sure of it . . . panicked and plotting some final, deadly maneuver in what he thought was complete silence!

But it was not a noise which at that moment prompted me to turn around. I've relived the scene innumerable times, and to this day I cannot determine what it was that caused me to suddenly look over my shoulder. Yet look I did, and there, not fifteen paces distant, whirling the marlinespike in a circle around his head, was Mario de la Costa!

I did not scream, succumb to panic, or run.

I remained rooted to the spot, my eyes riveted on the barbed executioner and its dizzying orbit.

Then, from no recognizable source, from a throat not even remotely human, there came a series of wild, uncanny, blood-boiling shrieks. High toned and shuddering, they filled the night, bubbling out of some nameless Underworld.

De la Costa froze and let his weapon fall harmlessly to the ground, as he looked wildly about him. Though I, too, stood immobile with dread, my thoughts continued to race—if de la Costa had not been concealed behind those packing crates, then who . . . or what was?

A gigantic shadow rushed from the darkness and threw itself on de la Costa, blotting him entirely from my view. I stood by helplessly, as a ferocious, shadowy struggle ensued, laced with epithet-choked, decidedly human screams of terror.

"Poe, save me! For God's sake, save me!" came de la Costa's strangled appeal.

I attempted to reach for the marlinespike, but the furiously intertwined combatants rolled onto it. Sand and rock, spewed up by frantically kicking arms and legs, stung my face as I labored in vain to pull the weapon free.

But my efforts would have been belated at best; for in a matter of moments it was over. De la Costa's screams gave way to the uncontrollable, coughing gurgles of a dying man.

The great shadow that knelt over its victim then stood to the full extent of its height and turned to confront me. I stared into the quizzical, almost repentant face of the East Indian orangutan who had escaped from the carnival!

He remained erect, breathing heavily as exhausted, whistling whines escaped his throat. His reddish hair, now clumped together by seawater and sprayed blood, stood out from his body in bristling arousal, and for a moment, I feared he would attack me.

But he seemed more concerned with cleaning his blood-flecked hands than with the intruder who had discovered his ghastly crime. He withdrew several feet, rubbing his hands together, licking and shaking his fingers, throwing me an occasional sidelong glance.

De la Costa lay on his back, eyes open in laughing horror. Droplets of water fell onto his face from the dock above, mingling with the blood that eddied from a wide, crudely inflicted throat wound. His shirt was ripped open, exposing a chest of matted, blood-soaked hair and deep, randomly patterned lacerations. His pants, too, were torn, and his legs clawed almost beyond recognition. Several of his fingers had been gnawed down to the bone and his left thumb had been bitten off entirely!

Though I had become almost an expert on brutally murdered bodies, that of Mario de la Costa was undeniably the most gruesome. It was as if he had been deliberately tossed into some malignant, man-eating machine, had been chewed, carved and chopped in its awful interior, then spat out half-digested.

Keeping a careful eye on the great ape, I bent down and retrieved my identification papers from the folds of de la Costa's shredded shirt. The beast continued to ignore me, emitting a periodic grunt of satisfaction as he examined his brutal handiwork. I then slowly retreated through the forest of pillars, not turning my back on him until I reached the steps leading to the street. I took them two at a time, without so much as a single glance back at the orangutan and his dark, damp, now silent domain.

I was filled with a wonderful hollowness.

The death of one man was largely responsible.

To my readers in sunnier climes and more comfortable circumstances, whose flirtations with the darker forces of the soul have been transient at most—the results of schoolyard dares or tavern-inspired betting—this simple fact may seem incomprehensible.

Yet the death of Mario de la Costa severed the final link in the chain that had so long enslaved me. The consequent hollowness I experienced was, I knew, the absence of evil—an evil personified by temptresses and killers. I had succumbed to its lure, had confronted it headlong—and had emerged intact!

With the closing of the "affaire L'Espanaye" I prayed would come a permanent closing of my soul to evil.

I arrived home at dawn. The guilty exhilaration and horror I felt at the death of Mario de la Costa had combined to banish my exhaustion. I hurried through the foyer and bounded up the stairs and into Virginia's room.

There I found mother, Dr. Moloney and three assistants, huddled in anxious conference around my unconscious wife. They met my disruptive arrival with glares of indignation.

"What is it? Has she gotten worse?" I cried, bursting through their tightly knit ranks and kneeling at Virginia's bedside. She did seem to have deteriorated considerably. The breast that once rose and fell regularly, mirroring the healthy flow of air in and out of her troubled lungs, now fluttered only occasionally; her face, though perspiring profusely, was ice cold; what remained of her breathing was wheezy and irregular; and bubbles of blood formed and burst in steady succession on her lips.

I appealed to the four red-cheeked, mutton-chopped gentlemen, who absorbed my grief with stern, studious detachment.

"Please, tell me what is the matter! Can you do nothing? How will your silence save her?"

To a man, they wordlessly deferred to mother.

"Mother, please!" I begged from my kneeling position.

"They do not anticipate that she will live past noon. Her relapse during the hours you were away was total."

I scowled at the doctors, my impatience with their presence growing into fury at their helplessness.

"But you said there was no immediate danger, Dr. Moloney," I protested, recalling his visit the previous night.

"I did not anticipate that there would be. Please, Mr. Poe, please accept my profound condolences. Her relapse was totally beyond my expectations. Consumption is a fickle, headstrong disease, and we are not always a match for it."

"Leave us alone," I shouted, suddenly rising to my feet. "Leave my house at once."

"But, Mr. Poe," replied Dr. Moloney, "she may regain consciousness, and when she does she may be in great pain. There must be someone here to minister to her, to see that her final hours are at least as painless as possible."

"*I* shall minister to her," I declared. "*I* shall make those final hours painless. I want you all out of here at once, do you hear me? Mother, show the gentlemen to the door, and make sure that none of them remain behind to skulk about in charitable impotence."

"But, Eddie, listen to yourself. Do you have any idea what you're doing . . . ?"

"Show the men to the door," I growled, raising my hand as though to strike her. "I demand to be left alone with my wife!"

Moloney and his assistants backed away from me fearfully, whispering to one another in worried tones.

"If it's the bill that you're worried about, mother will settle with you. Now out, out, out!" I waved my arms about wildly, driving the doctors away as though they were a hungry band of alley cats howling outside my kitchen door.

After the doctors had gone I sat on the edge of our bed and lifted Virginia into my arms. With one hand supporting the small of her back, I ran the other around the graceful oval that was her perspiring, yet somehow placid face. Her skin seemed to twitch in response to my caress, yet she did not awaken. I took a handkerchief from my breast pocket and dabbed at her lips, removing the blood-tinted spittle that had collected there.

Virginia seemed to be wasting away by the minute—to actually be losing physical weight. How could I reverse this awful attritional process? And why was it happening now? Why was the very thing I had risked my life and soul to protect being snatched away from me on the eve of my victory? Was this the price Virginia was to pay for my artfully concealed nether life of drunkenness, debauchery and wickedness—not a loss of innocence, but a loss of life?

No, it could not be so!

I would not permit her to be taken from me! Not after all that had come before! My very existence had been tied up in the preservation of this creature. Were she to die now, we would both have lived our lives in vain.

I drew her tightly to my breast—as though life could pass from my body into hers; as though the comforting warmth of the blood pumping though my veins would stir her own blood as well; as though my breath, hearty and regular, could somehow have a resuscitating effect on her enfeebled lungs.

She was as limp and sweaty as a rain-soaked leaf; her neck fell back and her head lolled from side to side. The perspiration-drenched nightgown clung to her, outlining the rounded suppleness of a child-woman's body as it deteriorated into that of an elderly invalid. In the deceptive light of the candles which stood on either side of the bed, Virginia's unconscious form took on a silvery luminescence that seemed to radiate from her skin and clothing.

I returned her to a prone position on the sheets and gently kissed her blood-flecked lips. She stirred minutely, and this involuntary response, perceptible only as a slight relaxation in her tightly drawn skin, was more tempting and invigorating than a thousand passionate kisses she had bestowed on me throughout our marriage. I kissed her again, deeper, and was treated to the same, fluttering bodily reply. My hand glided from her rounded face, along the inswept lines of her vein-etched neck, to the folds of silk bunched around her breast.

There came an almost internal moan, and her tongue emerged from her lips to meet mine, then recoiled quickly. In her dreams, or whatever one wishes to term that mysterious, unassailable place where Virginia's unconsciousness now dwelt, she was being flooded with sensations—she knew she was dying, yet at the same time, someone from the outer world was attempting to revive her with his love.

She began to move beneath me, slowly and painfully as though the exercising of a muscle was a nearly impossible task.

I would be damned if I would let the disease resist me; the "great white plague" would be defeated, drawn from its resting place in Virginia's unwilling body and driven from our house!

I increased the tempo of my caresses and the ardor of my kisses. As I nursed the dying girl with my passion, there came no familiar sense of fear or guilt—for the first time I sensed that Virginia and I could continue as true man and wife—that our lovemaking would be natural, and devoid of the corruptive influences of a life I swore was behind me.

If only she lived.

My lips brushed her eyelids and they suddenly flashed open! A pale, nearly wasted arm slowly lifted of its own accord, and executed a gentle, flawless arc, coming finally to rest on my back. Fingers flexed as though they were being used for the first time, and their tips began to float up to the hairs on the back of my neck.

Her eyes were not properly focused, and though they did not meet mine, I knew that Virginia saw me. Her lips opened, and words were formed but went unspoken. I bent my ear to her mouth, praying that her whispered supplications would thus be audible.

"Buddie."

"Yes, yes, what is it? I'm here, for God's sake. Can't you feel me? I'm here."

"The weight . . . the weight."

"Yes, yes, I know."

"It's lifting . . . leaving me."

"What? Good heavens, I'll fetch mother!"

"No, please." Her arms softly restrained me. "Please stay. It's leaving me."

"But what shall I do? Virginia, tell me what you want."

There was a dreadful pause as she struggled to catch her breath.

"Just continue. Stay and continue." The effort required to speak had exhausted her. In a subtle, sideways movement of her head, she told me there would be no further conversation.

The disease had apparently reached its crisis and was now gradually descending. There was no way of determining just how far the consumption would descend, or indeed, whether it would ever quit her body entirely. But for the moment, she appeared safe. She had traveled to the gates of death alone, abandoned by earthly physicians, and had been summarily turned back. From now on, barring some terrible, unforeseen circumstances, I would be the sole physician to attend her!

And so, accordingly, on that winter dawn in 1837, I tended my adoring wife with love. As the gray, sunless morning light began its tired march across the four walls of our tiny bedroom, Virginia began to respond to my caressing attentions with a sickly, delirious passion all her own!

Towards noon, mother, sick with anxiety, looked in on us and found Virginia asleep in my arms, her breathing normal and her color slightly restored. Wearing a smile that stretched from ear to ear, she threw her arms around her substantial waist, as though to congratulate herself on her daughter's sudden recovery.

"It's a miracle," she declared in an excited whisper. "Moloney and those other quacks be damned, it's a miracle. Why, I may even stop by the church this afternoon, and put in a word of thanks!"

"Your shadow hasn't darkened the threshold of a church in years, mother," I laughed, looking fondly down at Virginia's contentedly sleeping figure. "You must consider this a bona-fide demonstration of His mercy!"

"By the way," she replied, "I noticed you returned alone last night, and now Mr. de la Croix does not seem to be in his room."

For an anxious moment, I struggled to supply a believable excuse for de la Costa's permanent absence.

"You're right," I improvised. "It was a curious thing. Just as we had done unloading his belongings, several burly Immigration officials swept down on us and carried the unfortunate Frenchman off with them. It seems he had entered the country illegally. The officials informed me that he will be sent back to France on the next ship. It is a pity—I know how much you were counting on his rent money."

I fully expected mother to explode into oaths, but her reaction to this newest financial setback was surprisingly calm. She merely smiled mischievously, reached into the pocket of her apron and extracted an envelope, which she laid dramatically on the nightstand.

"Two miracles in one day. That *does* give one cause for thought!"

My curiosity piqued, I opened the mysterious envelope.

It was a check from the *American Monthly Magazine* for my recent story, "Von Jung the Mystic."

"And they are 'anxiously awaiting further demonstration of your unique, remarkable talent,' " mother recited, quoting word for word from the letter of acceptance.

"This explains all the bustling about of late," I said, recalling mother's recent flurry of activity.

"Well, yes, Eddie, you were proving so stubborn with your refusal to go out and do an honest day's labor, that I decided it was high time that at least your writing went to work for us."

"But why didn't you tell me you were bombarding the publishers of America with my work?"

"For one thing, you are such a perfectionist, I doubt whether you could have found even one page you deemed worthy of publication, let alone an entire story. But primarily, it was because I am far better equipped to deal with defeat than you are. I have a stack of rejection notices bundled neatly in my writing desk, if you'd care to view them later."

"I'm not sure I approve of your underhanded tactics," I said, holding the check up to the light. "But your results certainly speak for themselves. Thank you!"

Mother bent over and hugged me with suffocating zeal.

"One just has to know where to look," she said, snatching the check from my hands. "I presume you know that Philadelphia is rapidly becoming the publishing and literary capital of the United States?"

"Well, of course I know that! As a matter of fact . . ." I paused, aware that an embarrassed grimace had invaded my features. ". . . I was considering a move there eventually . . ."

Mother greeted this now-familiar declaration with a scowl of undisguised displeasure.

". . . as soon as Virginia is well enough to travel, of course!"

Mother planted her hands on her hips and shook her head from side to side. Then she turned and left the room, a smile of resignation fixed on her lips. A moment later, I heard her footsteps in the attic and the sounds of her steamer trunk being taken out of storage.

Epilogue

The following day's New York papers were filled with news of the solution to the brutal murders of Madame and Camille L'Espanaye. An escaped carnival orangutan had, it seemed, been recovered beneath a West Side pier operated by the Magellan Cargo Company, standing over the corpse of an unidentified, severely mutilated male victim.

The constables, while swearing to reporters that the capture of the orangutan only confirmed their long-standing suspicions that the killer of the two women could not have been human, ultimately admitted that the report of an "anonymous informant" had guided them to the docks the morning of this third brutal slaying.

The most recent victim, a well-proportioned male, was interred in potter's field at city expense, next to the graves of Madame and Camille L'Espanaye, the orangutan's other two "victims." The papers went on to report that inasmuch as the case was considered closed, the official investigation into New York's Corsican community had been terminated.

Renzo Gentinetta's funeral was a private affair, attended only by his closest comrades. I watched from afar, not wishing to intrude on their sorrow, content that my presence was represented by a simple wreath of roses. A durable people, I was certain that their struggle for survival in New York, once it had recovered from this tragic setback, would go on with renewed vigor and determination.

Of Eustace Haverlock, whose culinary skill had unwittingly led to de la Costa's downfall, I have little to say. He recovered from his stressful relationship with the bandit, and succeeded against heavy opposition in opening a respectable tavern in a somewhat more prosperous neighborhood.

Throughout the period of the memoir you have just read, I had intermittently considered the publication of a tale detailing the adventures of a fictional practitioner of the tenets of logic and deduction to which I subscribed. This "adventure of detection" would, I hoped, lay the foundations for a more rational and readable literature of the fantastic.

With the murders of the L'Espanayes, a crime privately deemed insoluble by the New York police, this consideration hardened into resolve. Thus, the inspiration for "The Murders in the Rue Morgue," a macabre, ratiocinative tale featuring that worthy Parisian, Auguste Dupin, was founded firmly in fact. Indeed, my devoted readers will no doubt be shocked to learn that I was a direct participant in many of the awful events described therein. Certain liberties (which the conscientious reader will clearly recognize) were taken, and certain facts of the case added or deleted.

Following a four-year incubation period in which I derived a meager but steady income from various publishing and editorial ventures, "The Murders in the Rue Morgue" appeared in *The Gentleman's Magazine* in April 1841, under the guidance of George Rexe Graham, that publication's recent purchaser.

A reputation of sorts was assured me, though the groundbreaking qualities of the tale were not as widely recognized by the general public as I had hoped.

A rising salary and an increasing demand for my stories and

poems did not, however, prove to be a permanent antidote to tragedy.

Though I had succeeded in hiding the dissolute nature of my double life from Virginia that morning back in 1837, the consumption that was held temporarily in abeyance continued to plague the dear girl throughout the next decade. Health and prosperity seemed to be mutually exclusive, and I resumed my battle with alcohol—a battle my good fortune and Virginia's sudden, but short-lived recovery had led me to presume I had won.

Such was not the case.

On the night of January 30, 1847, Virginia Poe was taken forever from me, and all hope of my own recovery, both spiritual and physical, vanished forever.

And now, riddled with delirium tremens, my mind clouded by the oceans of brandy I have consumed throughout a mottled, inconsistent literary career, it is only the unselfish, sympathetic dedication of mother that sustains me—pushing me onward to this tale's ignoble conclusion.

But perhaps it is not ignoble to slide piece by piece into a hell if it is of one's own making. Or perhaps it is a thousand times more unforgivable. I do not now, nor shall I ever know.

Virginia left this world innocent of my failures, and of the curious pact I had made with evil—a pact broken and renewed countless times during my life. Should this not be satisfaction enough for a man who has tailored his life to protect the person he loves most? To forever change the face of literature, to leave one's mark so that it is not trampled into obscurity by succeeding generations—Are these truly glorious goals, or merely the products of an insufferably arrogant imagination?

Is it not enough to have preserved the innocence and integrity of one perfect person?

The right to judge I reserve only for the readers of this painful memoir.

Dec. 10, 1852

Dear Mrs. Clemm,

Please forgive my delay in responding to your letter of October 6. The appearance of your manuscript occasioned such excitement here that I felt bound to reserve judgment until every member of our editorial staff had perused it to his satisfaction.

Although the authenticity of the manuscript appears to be beyond question, regrettably it is not a project consistent with our current publishing plans. The prose, while compelling, is often devoid of the refinement and polish that characterized Edgar Allan Poe's best and most popular writing.

In addition, the nature of much of the confessional material is sufficiently sordid as to render the possibility of a public outcry a distinct factor to be reckoned with. I'm sure, as a woman not unacquainted with the world of affairs, you must understand that we, the publishers of much of Mr. Poe's work, cannot risk the threat of a censure the appearance of the manuscript might engender. In sum, it is our conclusion that certain facts are best left undisturbed, spared the cruel and unforgiving scrutiny of history.

Please find enclosed with the manuscript my personal check in an amount which I hope will aid you somewhat in your current fiscal dilemma.

Once again, thank you for the submission.

Very truly yours,
George P. Putnam